Bursting with Action and Drama

THE CAPTAIN—

Captain Bell had spent his life wedded to the passions of the sea—until the passion of a mysterious woman threatened his fidelity.

THE CREW—

Drawn from all nationalities and races, they were tough, hardbitten men of the sea—some savage, others kind; some wise, others foolhardy; some good, others cynically corrupt.

THE PASSENGERS—

A decayed Englishman with a harem of sensual native women, a washed-out missionary, a pair of Russian exiles, an alcoholic circus owner, and a beautiful widow with a bizarre secret—the passengers of the *Cannibal* were lost, wandering people, each with a past, each with hidden passions.

D1108889

Are there paperbound books you want but cannot find in your retail stores?

You can get any title in print in POCKET BOOK editions. Simply send retail price, local sales tax, if any, plus 35¢ per book to cover mailing and handling costs, to:

MAIL SERVICE DEPARTMENT
 POCKET BOOKS • A Division of Simon & Schuster, Inc.
 1230 Avenue of the Americas • New York, New York 10020

Please send check or money order. We cannot be responsible for cash.   *Catalogue sent free on request.*

Titles in this series are also available at discounts in quantity lots for industrial or sales-promotional use. For details write our Special Products Department: Department AR, POCKET BOOKS, 1230 Avenue of the Americas, New York, New York 10020.

TWILIGHT FOR THE GODS

Ernest K. Gann

A KANGAROO BOOK
PUBLISHED BY POCKET BOOKS NEW YORK

POCKET BOOKS, a Simon & Schuster division of
GULF & WESTERN CORPORATION
1230 Avenue of the Americas, New York, N.Y. 10020

Copyright © 1956 by Ernest Gann

Published by arrangement with William Morrow & Company, Inc.
Library of Congress Catalog Card Number: 56-10744

All rights reserved, including the right to reproduce
this book or portions thereof in any form whatsoever.
For information address William Morrow & Company, Inc.,
105 Madison Avenue, New York, N.Y. 10016

ISBN: 0-671-81199-1

First Pocket Books printing January, 1978

Trademarks registered in the United States and other countries.

Printed in the U.S.A.

To the young men of the California Maritime Academy, and their officers, who lead them down to the sea . . .

Acknowledgment

The names of ships used throughout this book are, with very few exceptions, the names of real ships. So are the names of many of the minor characters, and places of business . . . now long since gone. My gratitude to those salty gentlemen who so willingly assisted in the lengthy research required for this work.

To Captain Fred Klebingat, to Director Karl Kortum of the San Francisco Maritime Museum, to Captain P. A. McDonald, to John Lyman, Max Lembke, Captain Ed Kennell and to Captain Bill Holcomb, Glenn Berger, Albert Bigelow, Sterling Hayden, Jack Dickerhoff, and all the other old salts along both American seaboards who have helped in spirit if not in actual labor . . . this book is respectfully dedicated.

Additional appreciation is extended to the Directors of the Marine Museums in Mystic, Connecticut, New York, Paris, Barcelona, and Rotterdam, and to the Shiplovers Society of Victoria, Australia, for their careful preservation of invaluable material.

I hope they will all say,—This is the way it was.

E.G.

Notations found on the inner face of
Captain Bell's Journal

. . . . and so, by God, I wish I could meet myself, and be introduced, as a perfect stranger might—for then I could maybe judge my being, my soul, if that thing exists . . . . and my opinions.

Who in the world would not treasure, and at the same time fear, such a meeting? Stupid as I am, it seems to me it would be the greatest adventure of all, for aren't we, if honest . . . . vastly concerned with ourselves? And when you start doubting, like me now, during these times . . . . how can you tell right from wrong? What kind of a man could have the nerve to judge his fellow human beings? Who has the nerve to set himself up as God?

I find the exploration of others a discouraging job, and in seeking myself, an even greater confusion of parts. Now, it seems to me that no person is of one dimension, neither white nor black, evil or good. It seems to me they are like a ship, of depth and beam and frequently unpredictable behavior . . . . but who really knows?

Barquentine Cannibal *14 days out of Papeete—at anchorage—Suva.*

October 12, 1927.

Begins calm. Middle part the same.
Last of copra loaded today. Battened down and ready to sail. Took water and stores aboard. Water sour.
Port fees one pound three shillings.
Continues through the day very hot.

One

A VAST, OPPRESSIVE calm held over the mid-Pacific. For almost a week no one was able to explain the desertion of the trade winds. People who lived on the land looked up at the palms in wonder and tried to remember the sound of the fronds clicking together. It was a sound they knew since birth and the absence of it left an appalling void in their spirits. The land people were lethargic. They lay about and stared at the sky. The sea people were distraught, for their whole existence depended upon the trades. They worried, which was not in their nature.

And so they all said,—What is wrong with the world? The people on the beach said this, and the sea people, and the Chinese traders, and even those who had just never cared what was wrong with the world before the trades ceased to be.

Bell of the *Cannibal* accused the trades of conspiracy. He was convinced they were joining with many small disasters so that, in all, they would be big enough to overwhelm him. And so he fretted and massaged the scar which creased his face with a zigzag line of purple lightning from beneath his left eye to the under side of his chin. He rarely spoke to the small black dog at his feet, which left the animal confused and unhappy. Instead

1

he stalked back and forth on the *Cannibal's* quarterdeck and spit frequently to the east, where the sky was darkest and held some promise, and he said in a way that was partly exasperation and partly an appeal, —Jesus!

When he saw the representative from Morris Hedstrom and Company approaching in a shore boat, Bell walked quickly to the waist of his ship and waited impatiently until the boat was close alongside. He moved with a boyish smoothness and certainty that was surprising in a man so heavily built, and yet the only youth about his face was in his eyes. And even these were slits behind a mass of crinkled and crenulated skin which appeared to have been aged in vinegar and acid. Those who first saw Bell and had no time to consider the resonant gusto in his voice, often swore that he must be much older than his forty years. And in some ways, as time seasons all men differently, they were right.

Now he continued to ignore the small black dog which pressed hopefully against his leg and he called down as quietly as he could manage to the man in the boat, —Where the hell are my passengers?

—Ashore. Where else?

The representative stood up in his clean white suit and mopped his face thoroughly. He was a half-caste and so both his mannerisms and speech were studied and overpolite, as if he would constantly reassure the world that his worth was unimpaired by racial division.

Bell said, —How many?

—Fifty-two deck for Rotuma. Four cabin to Manzanillo.

Then taking his good time, the representative, who was more sleek than fat, climbed the Jacob's ladder and eased himself to the deck. Standing before Bell's blocklike figure he said, —That is not bad, considering.

Bell calculated quickly, pressing his fingers on the caprail to aid his addition, and some of the anxiety left his face. No. Fifty-two deck passengers at two pounds each was not bad. The Ford truck lashed on deck behind him was another twenty-five pounds, the mail and general cargo. . . . about forty pounds additional. The deck passengers, since they brought their own food, would be pure gravy if there would only be some wind. But if the wind stayed in hiding, the passage to Rotuma would be much longer than the normal three days, and the *Cannibal*

2

must feed them according to law. And no human beings could eat like the islanders! Bell glanced at the pigs grunting in their foredeck pen and hoped he would not have to slaughter one. The pigs were for later, during the long passage to Mexico.

—What's holding them ashore?

—Mostly asleep, Captain. It's only two o'clock.

—I said to have them aboard by noon.

The representative smiled and looked all around the harbor of Suva, slowly, as if he were a visitor and had not been looking at the harbor for most of his life. And he continued to smile even though he knew it tried Bell's patience, and because to smile at impatience was the way of the islands.

Finally he said, —They sleep in the shade of the trees. They say you cannot possibly sail without wind and they don't fancy lying about on a hot deck. Their headman said that to do anything else would be unintelligent.

—There will be wind.

—When it comes. . . . they will come. It is for certain. Here are the manifests for Rotuma.

Bell took the papers and stuffed them in his hip pocket without looking at them. He thought, as he had many times before, that if he could only collect a ton of cargo for the blizzard of papers which accompanied every sailing, his troubles with the *Cannibal* would very soon be solved.

—You tell them passengers to be aboard in an hour or I sail without them. Tell that to the headman.

Bell recognized the absence of firmness in his voice. He would not sail without the passengers if they chose to idle on shore for a month. The *Cannibal's* holds were full of copra, but God only knew what kind of a price he would get for it in Mexico. The passenger fares could make the difference between profit and loss on the whole voyage.

The representative made a rosette of his lips and spread his hands outward. He looked dubiously at the sky.

—You sail? With what, Captain?

—There will be a land breeze later. I'll be ready for it.

—I hope you are right, Captain.

The representative looked at him as he might regard a child born blind. Then he added, —I sincerely trust the wind will come for you. We are not thieves and wish you the best available under God.

3

—The only thing I can prove you steal is time. Who are the cabin passengers?

—Mr. and Mrs. Morris, for example. They are Russians . . . . *old* Russians.

—How do you mean, old Russians?

—They are old, that is all. Let us say they have better than sixty years.

Bell said Jesus again, but so softly his voice was inaudible. —Do they know what they're getting into?

—Conditions were carefully explained. They said no matter what your ship was like they had seen worse.

—Are they in good health? Do they know about the food and that the only excuse for a doctor aboard will be me?

—All was described. Even your dog.

—Why didn't you put them on a steamer? People that old. . . .

The representative shrugged his shoulders. —For the usual reason. . . . money.

—Who are the others?

—Reverend Butterfield and a lady.

—Is the Reverend leaving of his own accord or was he kicked out?

—He is taking the leave which is permitted him every five years. He has a small mission on Thithia.

—Is the woman his?

—No, indeed. She is the widow of a planter from Kandavu.

—This is going to be an old folks' home. Well, we can all fall to pieces together. Bell glanced up at the masts, his eyes running quickly over the rigging. —Including my poor *Cannibal*.

—Mrs. King will not fall to pieces for a while yet. The contrary . . . .

—They all do out here. It's too hot for women.

—You will see. She gave us some trouble. She desired a guarantee that you would not proceed via Honolulu.

—I guarantee nothing.

—Of course, Captain.

The representative turned away and slipped down the Jacob's ladder to the boat. Looking up at Bell, he smiled once more and then said, —I almost forgot.

He bent quickly and took a package from beneath the stern sheets. He handed the package up to Bell.

—Compliments of Morris Hedstrom and Company.

—Mints?

—Yes. See you next year, Captain.

The representative shoved off as Bell tore open the package. In a moment he threw the outer wrapping to the water and his fingers skillfully extracted a packet of mints. He popped one into his mouth and savored its sting while he stared at the water. Then, as an afterthought, he handed one to the dog.

The *Cannibal* was a three-masted barquentine. She was built near the California coast by Mathew Turner in 1871, and now she was fifty-six years old. Which accounted for many things, but not all of them. Turner had also built the *Galilee* and the *Tropic Bird* as he did many other fine ships, but when he came to the *Mendocino,* which was the *Cannibal's* original name, some said he was short of money, or maybe good timber. The solid, rather dowdy Turner lines were still apparent, but the *Cannibal* had been blessed with a lovely clipper bow and her long jib boom pointed snobbishly at the sky. There was, furthermore, a matchless grace to her stern and a pleasing amount of tumble home along her waist. Except for the peeling paint around her transom scrollwork and the telltale splotches of rust seeping down along her chain plates, she still managed a dashing look when viewed from either end. This illusion was most easily held from a considerable distance.

She had in addition a remarkable figurehead. And this was of a savage woman carved in line with the flow of her hull. She was full breasted, and somehow, through the pout of her lips or the way she raised her head, or the way her arms were swept behind her, the artist had captured a moment of secret pride in his model. So that the figure was at the same time both defiant and humble. . . . a contrast which created a great deal of comment wherever the ship ventured. Some said she was beautiful, some thought she was atrocious, and a great many people who were not of the ways of the sea said she was obscene.

Yet even distance could not disguise the *Cannibal*'s profile. The fault was subtle and of meaning only to seafaring people who invariably shook their heads and, thoroughly embarrassed, lowered their eyes, as no one, whether of land or sea, likes to recognize beauty in the process of decay. For any seafarer could see at a glance that her sheer line running from bow to stern was no longer a harmonious complement to her three smartly raking masts.

"She is hogged," the seafarers said, and even the people of the land murmured that she seemed dejected, which was as much as saying the same thing.

And the seafarers in San Francisco and Portland and Seattle and Honolulu, and Papeete, and Suva, and Manzanillo in Mexico, where the *Cannibal* most frequently called, were fond of saying that you cannot neglect a ship any more than you can neglect a woman. The more demonstrative spit on the dock or the beach, depending upon where they were standing, and added that since both were expensive and all binding, neglect was not always an easy thing to avoid. So usually the seafarers lifted their shoulders and turned their backs and were glad they were not sailing in the *Cannibal*, and so did the land people although they did not know exactly why.

There were accommodations for eight cabin passengers in the *Cannibal*. There was first the forecastle head, which was raised and eased gracefully aft from the bowsprit, and then a deckhouse containing a galley just abaft the foremast. Then there was the waist of the ship, which was mainly given over to cargo hatches. Various owners had left their mark upon the *Cannibal*, and each, it seemed, had followed his own idea of design, until now she presented many features which departed from Pacific tradition.

One misguided owner had even sacrificed cargo space and provided passenger accommodations below deck. At a place approximately three quarters of her length, the waist was broken. There were three steps up and then a rather cramped quarterdeck. A pleasing taffrail surrounded a low after deckhouse which contained the master's cabin, the mate's, and a room so small no one ever knew what to do with it except use it as a charthouse. Below decks, the saloon extended from beneath the quarterdeck to the main mast. It consisted of a narrow general room with a table set athwartship for dining, and then four cabins, each furnished with two narrow wooden bunks and a washbasin. The single toilet forward of the deckhouse functioned through a hand pump and did not always work.

In cabin number four, which was the most forward on the port side, Harry Hutton lay outstretched in the lower bunk. He was a very fat man and he was naked. He watched the rivulets of perspiration meet on his belly and form tributaries and then miniature rivers which slid over the contours of his body and eventually disappeared from his line of vision. When he became bored with watching the collections of moisture, he would raise his head so that he could see his toes and wiggle them experimentally until he lost interest. Then he stared at the wooden bottom of the bunk above him and watched the flies land upside down. It was no use going ashore in Suva to relieve his boredom. There had been enough trouble back in Papeete, he reasoned. The best thing to do was just stay aboard and wait. Suva was only a way station anyway. Once out of the South Pacific everything would be all right for Harry Hutton. The first leg of the long voyage was over, Suva. . . . Manzanillo, Mexico. . . . and then a train to New York. In four months, say six at the most, all would be well again.

He closed his eyes as if in pain and sought new reasons why things had gone so wrong back in Papeete. Long practice made the causes of failures come easily, but this time the causes had a familiar smell to them and it was distinctly unwholesome. The crust had looked fine, but when he dipped into the pie there was nothing inside except air.

Visualizing a pie, he licked his lips and thought, I am the deceived, not the deceiver. Everything was right with the idea except what you were told in San Francisco about the level of prosperity in the Pacific islands. Oh sure! Certainement! The French and the natives in the region of Papeete and the surrounding islands were starving for entertainment. A fortune to be made! They would spend their last cocoanut to hear a good Chautauqua and if they had anything left they would throw it away on the Penny Arcade. The tour would take a year and have a triumphal windup in Australia. Then possibly on to London and the Continent. Ho! Ho!

Hutton massaged his nose, which was decorated with purple veins and speckled with fine cavities as if it had once been a target in his own shooting gallery. He blew out his breath in several vast exhalations, finding the action helpful as always in the delicate separation of fact from fancy. I have been euchred, he thought, and it only proves what I have always said and that is, sir, that successful enterprise is an impossibility without sufficient capital. Next time, and there would be a next time of

7

course, because a man wasn't necessarily through at fifty. . . . next time I will be more selective about both capital and talent. A man could carry just so much of the world on his own shoulders. Well, good riddance to the whole shebang!

Now the jugglers were back in Japan. The magician, who was never once sober enough in Papeete to make any of his rotten tricks work, was finally in a French jail where he belonged. The Penny Arcade and the shooting gallery brought all the way from San Francisco were sold for just enough to pay passage on this floating bake oven. Passage for two. You and Ethel Peacock.

He turned in the bunk and raised himself on one elbow. He wiped the sweat from his bald head and listened. She was doing it again. . . . Ethel was singing. And he thought that her voice was becoming more and more like the wail of a persecuted child. He could hear her in the next cabin and she was singing "Don't Crush My Violets," and the sound of it made him groan.

Ten years before, when she fed the Yanks doughnuts from a Salvation Army wagon, Ethel was a different girl. She sang along with the doughnuts and the voice was good. . . . or so it seemed then. And when the war was finished she sang "Pack Up Your Troubles" and she was willing to become a star. Ethel Peacock. . . . Carnegie Hall. . . . under management of Harry Hutton. No matter. It never happened. The closest Ethel Peacock ever came to Carnegie Hall was singing at a Democratic clambake near Jersey City. She didn't seem to care. She used to say what she really wanted was to be just Mrs. Hutton and it didn't do any good to explain that the mixed smell of Bible leather and flowers put you in a suicidal mood. "Just marry me, Harry," she said a million times. . . . until finally one day something seemed to snap and she never said it again. Her voice changed and for no reason at all she dyed her hair bright red. She didn't make sense a lot of the time now, but she wouldn't go away. Not Ethel.

She is like a spaniel, Hutton thought. If I shoo her away she just creeps in a corner and looks at me with those big brown eyes until I notice her again. And you can't hurt a spaniel. . . . which is probably why I will be looking after Ethel Peacock the rest of my life.

He sat up in the bunk and lit a cigarette. Things would be

better once you got to Mexico. A smart man could make a fortune there. Things would be much better. They would have to be.

Lott, who was an Estonian and who was known as "Bonehead" among the *Cannibal*'s six foremast hands, squatted in a patch of shade beside the galley house and slowly peeled a mango. He tossed the bits of skin carelessly over the bulwark and listened with childlike excitement for the faint plop as they struck the water. Yancy, who was known as "The Artist" because of his skill with a tattoo needle, sat opposite Lott with his legs spread wide on the deck and his back against the bulwark. The mango peelings sailed directly over his head. He said to Lott, —Cut it out!

—I no hit you.

—Cut it out, I said. Throw them peelings somewheres else.

Lott grunted and shifted his great weight from one buttock to the other, and Yancy thought he was exactly like a bear he had once seen on a chain in Vladivostok. His arms and his chest and even his neck were covered with a thick pelt of black hair, but his head was shaven and so shaped like an enormous egg, it seemed as if he had borrowed it from another body. Only the bear was smarter, Yancy decided. And he said plainly to Lott, —You oughta be on a chain.

—What for?

—Because you ain't really human, that's why. There ain't nothin' in that bullet head of yours but air. No, I'm wrong. There ain't room for air when something is solid bone.

—You funny, Lott said.

There was no indication either in his pale eyes or about his heavy face that he was offended, or even that his feelings might be hurt, and Yancy wondered if that was perhaps the reason he loved him so. And for a moment he marveled at the peculiar love one man could hold for another when they had been shipmates a long time. It had something to do with shared misery, he thought, when you didn't get any sleep for nights on end and knew what it was like to flop in a sopping wet bunk which was never still, and envy all men who had dry beds. It had something to do with shared danger when you swung on the royalyard footropes together a hundred and fifty feet above deck in the middle of the night. It had something to do with fisting

9

heavy canvas in a freezing, whipping rain, which was the world's hardest labor and where no man could quit until the work was done. It had something to do with getting drunk in port and swearing together you would never go to sea again no matter what. . . . and it had something to do with fine nights when you sat on a hatch with other men who were crazy enough to be sailors and even the dumbest of them would find something worthwhile to say.

He watched Lott tear off another piece of mango skin with his fingers, which looked almost as large as bananas, and saw him lay the peeling carefully on the deck. Yes. Bonehead would do that. He would do exactly what anyone told him to do. . . . no more and no less. Unless it was sailor's work and then he was always a mountain of strength.

—Now yer litterin' up the deck. Why you want to eat them things anyways?

—I hungry.

—Yer all the time hungry. All the damn time like some kid. You still growin', for Christ's sake? Didn't they never feed you enough in Estonia? They run you out of the country because ya ate up all the chow in the whole country?

—I go to sea.

Lott said it very simply as he said everything.

—Don't ya know you can never have a woman if ya eat them mangoes all the time. . . . all the time chomp, chomp, chomp, like a human thrashin' machine?

Yancy waited to see if his warning would have the slightest effect on his friend. But he only continued to peel the mango.

—It's a fack. All the island people will tell ya about what mangoes do to ya.

—Then why they eat mangoes?

—They don't. That's just it. They only eat mangoes at special times.

Yancy discovered pleasure in his new-found theory. It was a lie, of course, but telling a lie was always more interesting than telling the truth. . . . especially to a man like Lott who might believe anything. Lying to Lott was always a sort of an experiment. It was like beating on a gong with a feather.

—They only eat mangoes when they know they will be away from women for a long time. . . . like when a headman sends his people to some deserted island or they have to go to war or something like that. Understand me, Bonehead? That's when they do it. Times like that. Mangoes do somethin' to a man's insides.

—What?

—Nobody knows except the witch doctors. Sometimes it takes years and years for a man to get over eating just one mango.

Lott peered at him from beneath his heavy brows and a little smile crossed his face. Yancy saw that it was his intelligent look, the one which preceded a thought which every once in a blue moon was worth listening to. Lott solemnly held out a piece of the fruit and said, —Then you eat some.

—Not me. I got a lot of unfinished business in Manzanillo.

—Maybe it be years before you get to Manzanillo. Maybe you never get there in this scow.

Yancy held out his hand and returned his smile. He was suddenly proud of his friend. There was, after all, more than bone to his head.

—Yer right. Give me a chunk.

—I tell truth. I say her'n frames is lousy dry rot. And she be hogged. And her'n planks is buckled worse'n washboard. I say her'n chain plates pull right out her'n sides. . . . bolts and all. And whole guddum riggin' come down on our heads to kill us. And her'n sails won't stand up to a easy fart without blowin' to pieces. And her cook would poison a goat.

—Long as the feed is accordin' to that there official card in the fo'c's'le there ain't nothin' you can do about it. You should've sailed with Hungry Olsen.

—When was you with him?

—In the *Crescent*.

—You lie. Her'n burned at sea.

—This was before. In nineteen fifteen. And don't call me no liar because I never forgot the way Olsen used to stare a man down with that glass eye of his. Once we told his highness that it was Labor Day and so how about we take things easy? Know what Olsen says?

—How can I know what he says when I not there? I dunno where I was in 'fifteen.

—Labor Day? he says all surprised. So, he says, we labor today.

—We get to Honolulu I jump this scow quick.

11

—We ain't goin' to Honolulu.

—Ya? We see. By and by.

—The skipper ain't puttin' in nowheres until we get to Mexico. Cook heard him tell one of the passengers.

—Skipper should sink her'n right here. Not so long swim to shore.

—Bell ain't goin' to sink her. She's all he's got besides his dog. You don't understan' the situation. Bell is like bein' married to some old whore. He don't stand no chance to get away from her an' he knows it. It ain't like he had a choice.

—Why he no get a new ship? Like steamer. He could get steamer and sail easy way.

—No, he coon't. Bell can't get no job nowheres even as a loblolly boy. He coon't get a job even as third mate on a steamer. The companies woon't let him near a steamer because they got him on their books. And alongside his name they got written down. . . . bum.

—He's a good sailor.

—He's a bum. That's why he chews on them mints all the time. . . . to keep hisself from swiggin' away on some bottle. The companies got to have reliable men and they can't have stew bums like Bell staggerin' around the bridge and runnin' their expensive machinery on the bricks like he done before. He sails the *Cannibal* or he rots on the beach.

—I never see him drink. Even ashore in Papeete I see him sober.

—Sure you didn't. He ain't that kind. He's a sneak drinker. . . . the kind which when he gets goin' is drunk all the time. All he needs is one sniff and he's gone. The only thing that keeps him from it is them mints. When he gets the yearnin' he swallows a mint and then he forgets about it for a while. Sometimes for weeks. . . . like he's been since we left Frisco. When the yearnin' comes back he takes another mint and that's the way it works, see? But when his mints run out he just can't stand it no longer and that's what the companies know, see?

Lott looked aft along the deck and for some time he studied the distant figure of the man on the quarterdeck. He saw the black dog watching his every move as he paced back and forth from rail to rail and finally he said to Yancy, —You ever seen him drunk?

—No. And I don't want to. You think he ain't very big?

Maybe he ain't, but kindly notice how he is built like a coal barge. Some wise guys spilled beer on his dog once for a laugh. It was in Seattle and it was snowin' outside the joint. He worked the place over and drug four carcasses outside and when they come to he made them lay there until they damn near froze to death.

—Drunk or sober I like him to Ramsay.

Yancy thought of the *Cannibal*'s only mate and he remembered with considerable pleasure how Ramsay had looked on the first day he threw his gear aboard in San Francisco. He was a fancy one then for sure, with a regular suit with a vest and a heavy gold watch chain to twist around his thumbs. You would have thought the *Cannibal* was a battleship the way he strutted her decks. No underwear and suspenders for fancy Ramsay. The crew knew he was a Downeaster the moment he hove in sight, just from his manners and all and his way of giving an order which to a Pacific man was almost past understanding. No chewing tobacco for Ramsay! He even set the crew to holystoning the *Cannibal*'s withered fir decks. A shipshape and Bristol-fashion mate if there ever was one, and at first the men were so amazed they did his bidding without a yelp. Oh, he knew his business. . . . it didn't take long to find that was so. If a sailing man's reputation didn't precede his actual arrival, it wasn't very long before his whole career was known. A boy in the *Gov. Robie,* and finally her second mate. Then finally mate in the *Erskine M. Phelps.* . . . Cape Horn square-riggers and much smarter than the *Cannibal.* But they were Downeaster ships and so his whole way of looking at things was bound to be different.

Thinking of Ramsay, Yancy turned back to his friend and said,—If Bell gets drunk, Ramsay is the one you'll like. All you got to do is understand the difference between a real gentuman and one which somebody tried to make.

Bell stopped his pacing and leaned against the railing to port. He looked down at the clear water which was so like a mirror. For a long time he studied his face reflected in the unruffled surface and finally he said to Anchor, the dog, —Yeah, I am slowly falling to pieces just like our poor *Cannibal.*

In the water he saw a nose which listed considerably to starboard and he saw the marked droop in his left eyelid where the scar terminated and somehow gave his whole face a look of perpetual unhappiness. The mate of the *Mary E. Russ* was responsible for that droop. . . . among other things he cut the nerve muscle so that the eye always appeared half-closed.

Resolving to smile more often, Bell continued to look at the water and tried to remember the mate's name. He failed, and this surprised him because he could easily recall most things about the *Mary Russ*. She was a four-masted schooner and she carried lumber from the various Mendocino dog-holes down the Pacific Coast to San Francisco or Los Angeles. She was sharp-bowed and had a centerboard and it was a hazardous business easing back into the little coves without any kind of power, maneuvering under the lumber wire, and hoping the weather held until the loading was finished. Still, the old *Mary Russ* was his first home at sea, and looking back it seemed a very pleasant one, even if being in her had marked him forever. And there were marks inside from Mrs. Weatherbee, the female cook. She dressed young David Bell's wounds when the mate decided you had too fine a nose and too many teeth to ever make a sailor. Now Bell smiled when he thought of the mate, and his grin broadened and he forgot his impatience with the passengers and the trades, as he remembered Mrs. Weatherbee.

He saw himself again on a drizzling afternoon, helping the mate splice a hawser. He was holding the standing part of the splice while the mate made the tucks, beating each one with a heavy fid. And the mate said, "Pull harder, you little runt!" And David Bell yanked with all his young strength, harder than either he or the mate believed possible. The mate's hand was pulled directly beneath the descending fid. Bell heard again the awful smack as the fid struck the mate's knuckles. He remembered how fast he had run for the main shrouds, but the mate caught him as his feet left the first ratlines. He hauled young Davey back to deck and began, in his own way, to make a sailor.

It was all over in a moment. Ordinary Seaman David Bell, age fifteen, was stretched out unconscious and bleeding on the deck while the mate went to work with his sea boots. . . . kicking you all over. Mrs. Weatherbee was the only person aboard the *Mary Russ* who dared to stop him. They told you about it later. She charged the mate with a meat cleaver, swearing at the top of her Irish lungs that she would kill him. She chased him to the end of the jib boom where she kept him stewing in fear of his life for hours.

In the water Bell saw his face crinkle and he wondered that he could remember such a day with actual pleasure. And suddenly he laughed aloud and he found it was good because it was a long time since he had known the urge to laugh at anything. Yes. . . . the marks left inside by Mrs. Weatherebee were far more important than what the mate had left on the outside. Now he could almost hear the peculiar lilt of her brogue and her profane way of putting words together which somehow never sounded like profanity.

"Dammit, Davey," she would always begin. "Dammit, Davey. . . . people are just as beautiful as you see them. Now a cannibal. . . . he thinks a woman with thick lips, a ring in her nose, and a big fat rump is beautiful. A Eskimo. . . . he fancies a tattoo here and there. . . . and a Frenchie likes a plump stomach goin' ahead of his lady. So you or nobody else can just rare back and say a person has to look so and so to be beautiful. It depends on who is doin' the lookin'. In your case no sensible soul would likely to be thinkin' of beauty. Your head is too small for your shoulders and your face is covered with a rash o' pimples. And your hair most of the time is matted with salt and your hands stink with Stockholm tar. Your damn ears stick out like stuns'ls. . . . and your arms hang down like a ape. . . . and that peach fuzz on your jaw, which maybe some day will be a beard, is the color o' dead seaweed And sometimes when you're thinkin' your mouth hangs open like a idiot. But you'll improve with age and a pretty man has got trouble from the time he is born."

In the water, Bell saw that his mouth was slightly open. He closed it firmly, amused at his sense of guilt, and he wished that he could listen to Mrs. Weatherbee again.

"But dammit, Davey. . . . to this tired female you are a handsome lad and I'm goin' to make it my business you grow to a handsome man. I got the call like they say, and I'll do it if I have to raid every Salvation Army library on the Pacific Coast. You're not goin' to wind up any punch-drunk A. B. with one foot in a saloon and the other in Mount Olivet Cemetery. You already been kicked around too much. For one kid you've had enough. . . . so this old girl is goin' to hang a oil-bag from the weather cathead and see you amount to something. Now, it

15

may seem like reaching for a kingdom to you, but some day you'll be master of your own ship."

Bell rubbed his left knee where one of the mate's kicks had broken the cap. It still ached in a certain way when the weather was about to turn and he considered it more reliable than any barometer. What the hell was that mate's name? Almost every sailor in the West Coast ships had a nickname and he could remember so many on the schooners. . . . "Hurry Up" Jack Bostrum. . . . "Hoodlum Bob" Walvig. . . . "Whispering" Winkle and "Nosey" Higgins. A nickname frequently became so much a part of a sailing man his original identity was lost entirely. And he thought that if Mrs. Weatherbee hadn't been so sea-wise his own nickname might have been "Mother's Boy" Bell, or "Cry Baby" Bell, or something equally embarrassing to live with. Which was probably the only reason she didn't actually kill the mate. How she dreamed, that Irish woman! And how she worked to teach an orphan boy who left school at twelve, to read and write.

Bell straightened and turned away from the water. For suddenly his image disgusted him. He tried not to think of Mrs. Weatherbee again. She wouldn't be happy if she were alive to see David Bell. She sure wouldn't, Anchor.

After counting twenty turns across the deck he saw movement along the shore. He went at once to the companionway hatch and called down sharply.

—Ramsay!

—Hello!

—Turn to the hands. The passengers have finally got a move on!

He heard the slam of Ramsay's door. In a moment Ramsay appeared in the companionway and Bell saw that he was clean shaven as always and his heavy black hair was combed as always and his shirt was clean, and he tried very hard not to resent his confident smile. He thought again, as he had so many times before, that he could not have chosen, from all the seas, a mate more in contrast to himself. For Ramsay was, as Mrs. Weatherbee would have said, a pretty man.

—Any wind?

—No. But shake out the foresail and lower topsail. Have the rest ready for hoisting. Then heave short and let me know. We'll slide out of here in an hour.

—I ought to pump first.

—There's no need of it.

—There was fifteen inches when I sounded the bilge this morning.

—If I thought we should pump, I'd ask for it. Now get forward.

Ramsay patted his hair and glanced at the box of mints on the cabintop. Their eyes met and Ramsay said, —Yes sir. The "sir" was mocking as usual, Bell noticed. Ramsay only employed it when he wished it clearly understood that he was carrying out an order against his better judgment.

As he turned his back and walked away, Bell heard the Peacock woman singing in her cabin. And the sound of her voice so scraped his nerves he forgot the heat and even the patronizing tone of Ramsay's Downeast drawl.

Begins hot and airless. Forenoon engaged in securing all about deck for wind and sea if they ever come. Middle part very hot with some land breeze. Tacked ship several times to little avail. A dismal beginning. Ends very light airs. Suva still in sight. Sky obscured. Six miles this day.

Two

EVEN THE GREAT triangle was finally dead. For sailing ships this vast design covered much of the world's oceans and kept them floating long past their time. It was Britain to Australia with general cargo. . . . whiskey and machinery, then Australia to San Francisco with coal, and then back again around the Horn to Britain with California grain. Now, even the rusty lime-juicers, who were the last to sail the triangle, had surrendered to steam, and a sail on the horizon was as rare as an albatross in the doldrums. Only the remnants of a once-glorious fleet remained.

There was still the big *Pamir,* the *Passat* and the *Herzogin Cecilie* running grain from Australia around to England. Less than a half-dozen of the "Flying P" nitrate barks still doubled Cape Horn. The Alaska Packers were still transporting fishermen to the salmon with their *Star of Lapland* and *Star of Asia.* Some said a man named Jack Dickerhoff was trying to fit out the *Lottie Bennet* against all sound financial advice, and the big *Monongahela* was still working the Pacific under Captain Asmussen although she was much rigged down. There were a few others—the *Argosy Lamar*, the *Centennial*, the *Benjamin Packard*, and the *Arago*—but they wandered almost alone on the oceans, fighting for their very lives, desperately striving through wit and restlessness to escape the ship-breakers.

In the Atlantic there were the French barquentines out of St. Malo, and a few schooners sailed very occasionally between New Bedford and the Azores with immigrants. A handful of coastal schooners carried logwood, coal, and codfish from the American seaboard to the West Indies. The Grand Banks fishing fleet and the Portuguese in Davis Strait were almost entirely dependent on power and their sails rotted on their booms. And to a sailing man they failed to qualify as true deep-water windjammers because they weren't in trade anyway. There were sails to be seen on the Baltic and there were still many small schooners working through the Mediterranean, but to blue-water men, that was a dishpan of a sea.

And there were the primitive fleets. . . . the junks of the China Coast, the lateen rigs in the Red Sea and the Persian Gulf, and the innumerable, dubious hulks wallowing about the Indian Ocean. These survived only because their economics were as frugal as their rigs, and the civilizations which they served were not yet ready for steam.

And so the little *Cannibal* drifting toward Kandavu Pass, which is to the south of Viti Levu in the Fijis, was one of the last sailing ships in the world. Touched only occasionally by a zephyr of wind, she rolled abominably on the long glassy swells and her sails slatted and her gear banged and there was a constant symphony of squeaks and mewings and the little cries and complaints of wood against wood to speak of her helpless suffering. Thirty-eight of her fifty-two native deck passengers were so sick from the unaccustomed motion they expressed in various ways a unanimous desire to die.

Bell sat at the desk in his cabin, bracing his body expertly against each roll of the ship. When he had completed his account book he left the discouraging figures and occupied himself in a more pleasant duty. He made an entry in his personal journal which he kept separately from the ship's log. He wrote slowly and with many flourishes as a man determined to make his script permanent and beautiful.

. . . When she boarded in Suva, Mrs. King took particular

pains to inquire about my routing. She first inquired to the agents for this voyage—Morris Hedstrom & Co. They thought it unusual that the routing should concern a passenger, but told her that in addition to our copra, we would take general cargo, mail, and deck passengers to Rotuma and then proceed directly to Manzanillo, Mexico. This was the truth and she was apparently satisfied, yet she again made inquiry of me just before sailing. Flattered at her interest, I explained very carefully that with the winds at this time of the year we would be lucky to weather the Gilberts, and in any event our course would most certainly set far to the west of the Hawaiian Islands. I also showed her on the chart how we would make as much Northing as we could until we brought up with the westerlies in the vicinity of forty degrees north, and would, with good chance, then have fair wind straight for the California Coast. I told her quite frankly that the present American import tax on copra made it impossible for me to deliver at any stateside port, and that I would therefore proceed directly to Manzanillo, railhead for Mexico City.

Bell paused and watched the oil lamp over his desk swinging in its gimbals. And he thought that he could easily touch all of the things in his cabin even if the lamp was not burning. For this was his home. And again the legacy of Mrs. Weatherbee was much in evidence since the main furnishing he had done consisted of books. There were a great many and all of them were dog-eared and sagging with use. He moved them about frequently as his curiosity compelled him and he often slept with several crowding his bunk. Just now his complete volume of Shakespeare stood beneath the after porthole together with his dictionary, a Lloyd's Register for 1925, a well-thumbed collection of Dickens, and a Bible which he had opened three years before to perform a burial at sea.

Mrs. Weatherbee would have been pleased, for despite the fact that she could barely read herself, she firmly believed the only hope for the poor man to improve his lot was in books. She treasured them and yet they frightened her, as if they were living creatures possessed of magical powers. She had enormous respect for any man who could read a whole book. And so she prodded young David Bell until she was certain he could survive the ordeal.

Those were the times, Bell remembered, when he read in his bunk off watch, and sometimes on watch when he could escape the eye of his mates. It was education come the hard way and yet they were happy years spent mostly in sugar barks between San Francisco and the Hawaiian Islands. There was the *R. P. Rithet* with Ordinary Seaman Bell trying to discover the mysteries of English grammar in a book that was sticky with salt and nearly memorized by the time the two voyages were done. He was still easy with grammar when he could set it down on paper, but he knew he slipped occasionally in the haste of speaking. There was the *Amy Turner* and the *Gerard C. Tobey* and more books. . . . mostly addition and subtraction, and finally multiplication. And eventually it was Able Seaman Bell, who slept with books beneath his head on the *Santiago* and the old iron clipper, *Roderick Dhu*. And always there was Mrs. Weatherbee waiting on the wharf in San Francisco, smelling of steam beer, and alternately crying and blowing her red nose as she yelled, "Welcome home, Davey!" And his homecoming present would be a stack of books, some of them obviously brand-new. It was much later that Bell discovered a good many of them were stolen. While Mrs. Weatherbee was otherwise scrupulously honest, she considered bookstores fair game.

Those in a way, he thought, were the best years of all. But Mrs. Weatherbee was sea-wise enough to know that books alone were not enough. She insisted on one last voyage before the mast because she said no man could command who had not been forced to obey long after he was capable of command.

"Before ye start hangin' diplomas in your cabin, there's one ye've got to hang in yer heart, Davey. No man can call himself a worth-a-damn sailor until he's worked a ship around the Horn." So she arranged a berth on the British ship, *Blackbraes,* and it took one hundred and thirty-seven days to reach Liverpool. The westward passage on the German bark, *Wandsbek,* was almost as long, and it was over a year before Mrs. Weatherbee stood waiting on the wharf again.

Bell looked at his hands and saw the dark splotches still showing beneath his skin where the sea boils came. Dampness, chafe, and poor diet forever marked the hands of many sailing men. More marks. . . . and just as important as the grades in

Captain Taylor's Nautical School on San Francisco's Battery Street. Mrs. Weatherbee paid for that too, out of the money she made slinging hash in a Channel Creek café.

Then one day Mrs. Weatherbee was gone. The first doctor said it was liver. The second doctor said it was her much abused kidneys, but it didn't make any difference because when Mrs. Weatherbee died in her room over a noisy seamen's saloon on East Street, the whole San Francisco water front mourned. Men who had been drunk for years stayed practically sober for days saying they just didn't feel right in any way, and men who seldom raised a glass to their mouths were found unconscious in the gutters. And when the first shock of loss was over, the men turned to young Davey Bell, who was in a sense the uncompleted creation of Ma Weatherbee. And they swore that he would be completed, because they were also mostly unfortunates and they knew it was too late to complete themselves.

Nineteen of them staggered down to the wharf for boisterous farewells when Davey Bell left as second mate of the five-masted schooner, *Inca.* They sacrificed drinks to buy him a sextant for his very own and they knew he would use it because by now he was a true deep-water man. So David Bell sailed away with knowledge bought by the only woman he had ever known, wearing clothes bought by men he barely knew.

There were very few of those men left along the water front when Bell became chief mate of the *Samar,* and none left to finally satisfy their dreams when the Alaska Trading Company chose him as master of the steamer, *Bear.*

Fortunately, Bell thought. They wouldn't have thought any more of you than the Board of Inquiry who expressed their final opinion in words you coud never forget. . . . "The total loss of this vessel on Montague Reef and the consequent drowning of thirty-seven persons is found to be entirely the responsibility of the master. Consideration has been given to the fact that this was his first voyage of command, that the chief mate was inexperienced in Alaska waters, and that the hazard of fog had been present for three days. None of these circumstances mitigate the gross negligence of the master who, at the time said vessel struck the reef, was found asleep in his cabin. We commend Captain Bell for his conduct after the grounding and his personal heroism in supervising the rescue operations, and the suppression of panic which twice threatened those surviving. However, we find no excuse for leniency. . . ."

Bell swung quickly around in his chair and closed his eyes. He wondered how many times his mind would trick him and repeat those words like a litany at moments when there was no reason for them to be remembered. The words came sometimes at high noon when the sun burned in his sextant, and they came sometimes in the dawn or the evening when the mirrors brought a star to the horizon. They came creeping through his mind and sank down through his whole body when he was alone, and they came sometimes when he hopefully surrounded himself with other people. There was never any warning and all of the preventatives against those words were used up long ago.

Three days and nights without sleep before the *Bear* struck Montague were not an excuse. A good captain would have rationed his energies, knowing there was always the danger of exhaustion. A good captain would not have been so confident of his position and so he would not have killed a ship and thirty-seven people. A good captain would know it was impossible to think straight after peering through fog for seventy-two hours. He would have stopped his ship dead in the water, waited a week if necessary, and forgotten about setting a record. He wouldn't have been so proud, and he wouldn't have spent the last ten years paying off a Chinaman who was the only owner in the world who would take a mortgage and trust David Bell with a ship. The Chinaman never expected to get his money, but he finally did. That was one thing anyway. Such as she was, the *Cannibal* was at last free and clear. What she was worth, with the world steaming by, was another matter. These days windjammers could be bought for promises.

When he opened his eyes Bell knew exactly what he would see. He would be looking at the piano, which was moored against the forward bulkhead of his cabin. There would be a basket on top of it. In the basket was a bottle of whiskey and on the label there was a marking—August 8, 1927. Almost three months ago. . . . the last time he had opened the bottle.

The bottle was there for a purpose. . . . in the open where he could stare at it every day and defy it. And there were many more in the locker beneath his bunk. . . . just in case. In case of what, Davey Bell? In case you wanted to get drunk again and forget the words. In case you want to feel sorry for yourself and say that no orphan boy who spends most of his life at sea ever has a real chance.

He pushed himself suddenly from his chair and approached the piano. He stared at the bottle. This was a good night for it. No wind. Let Ramsay watch the passengers feed the fishes. Let Ramsay stand two watches. . . . he is eager. Just like you used to be. Eager, and a certified gentleman. He was concerned about the leak. He looked down at Anchor, who wagged his tail.

—How about it, Anchor? Only one little leak in the poor old *Cannibal* when by rights there could be a hundred.

Let Ramsay worry about it and pump all he wanted. . . .

Pump the whole Pacific through her and coddle the cabin passengers while you and me, Anchor, just settle down and enjoy a little refreshment? No need to kill the whole bottle between us. Too hot. Just one glass, possibly two at the most and take our time. Your tongue's hanging out and so is mine.

He reached out for the bottle and then instantly jerked his hand away as if it had been bitten. He turned his back on the piano and went back to his desk. He sat down and looked at his journal for a long time before he picked up his pen. Then his hand, which had been shaking, became steady again and he began to write.

. . . Mrs. King is an American citizen. Rather attractive. More so in spirit than looks. Her passport gives her age as 31, although she appears younger. But then I have never been much at telling a woman's age . . .

He reached for the packet of mints on his desk and placed one on his tongue.

Morris Hedstrom and Company told me I would pick up another passenger at Rotuma. A male. I have been obliged to put Mrs. King in the same cabin with Ethel Peacock. I hope she can bear with that singing all the way to Manzanillo!

The night was heavy and dark and the few visible stars lost all of their brilliance in the haze which hung upon the sea. There was still the smell of land in the air and the porpoises who came to play beneath the *Cannibal*'s bows did so without enthusiasm, as if they, too, were drugged with the calm. No division separated the sea and the sky, there was no line of horizon as there might have been with even the lightest of winds. Instead there was only the slopping and eccentric wallowing of the *Cannibal* shoved into action by invisible forces far beneath the surface of the sea. It was a night of gasping death and so even a few insects dared the passage from land to the *Cannibal*. This invasion was so unusual some of the deck passengers captured the insects and held them to the lantern they had placed on the forehatch. And they said that never in living memory had such tiny creatures been seen so far at sea.

There was so little wind Ramsay could easily hear the ship's clock in the charthouse chiming off the divisions of sea time. And because he was bored almost to the limit of his endurance, he sought little ways to amuse his mind while he smoked one cigarette after another. As he waited through each half-hour for the clock to chime he thought of the centuries since the tradition of bells was born. He was not certain just when the custom began. Thinking of the faces of Lott and Yancy, who were sprawled asleep on top the deckhouse, and of Uala the Hawaiian, who was also on his watch, he thought that bell-time was created for their ancestors who lounged just as Uala did in the slit of light from a binnacle and probably cared even less about the passage of time. In the way of sailors. In the way of high-pooped galleons, long gone. Then a small boy would be standing near men with faces perhaps as sad and swarthy as Uala's. The boy would be watching a sandglass which measured the passing of thirty minutes. And when the last grain slipped through the neck, the boy would reverse the glass and strike smartly upon a metal triangle according to the running of the sand. One time. . . . one strike. . . . two times. . . . two strikes . . . . and three times. . . . three strikes until a total of eight half-hours were announced. Then the boy would sing out a falsetto prayer and the watch would change. So it was almost the same even now, only the boy was gone, and the prayers, and the sandglass, and the triangle. There only remained the same weathered faces and a clock with chimes.

Ramsay walked to the mizzen shrouds on the starboard side and then turned aft again. He paused opposite the small skylight over the master's room. Because he was well over six feet tall, he could just see down through it and observe a portion of the cabin. Master, indeed! The word was appropriately chosen so long ago, for certainly no man ever had the unique power of a ship's captain. Even a broken fool like Bell, he thought, could command obedience to his most ridiculous order and get away with it.

Ramsay thought of the splendid men he had sailed under. . . . the hard, capable men from Searsport and Thomaston who took Downeast full-riggers around the Horn. Then he looked down at Bell and the corners of his mouth descended. Idiot! He could see him standing before the piano and he knew the reason for it and he waited with anticipation to see him reach for the bottle. He was disappointed when Bell suddenly pulled his hand away and disappeared from beneath the skylight. Well, it would happen sooner or later, and one of these days it would happen permanently. In the meantime, patience. Bell was in so much trouble he would never be able to hang on to the *Cannibal*. She was officially his, perhaps, but sooner or later he would have to mortgage her to the scuppers. There would be a broom lashed to the *Cannibal*'s main truck some day soon, and when that happened, Elliot Ramsay of Boothbay, Maine, might be able to buy his first ship for a song. Not to keep her, of course. Buy cheap, sail cheap for a year or so, then junk her. Pocket the difference and invest in a small steamer.

In fact, Bell had already smoothed the way. By some persuasion plus a case of whiskey he had somehow managed to reduce the *Cannibal*'s tonnage from her honest two hundred and fifty-four to just under two hundred gross. And so she could sail with only two certified officers. All right. It might be rough just now with four hours on and four off, heel and toe in the British style, but the saving of a third mate's salary would be pleasant when David Bell finally fell flat on his face.

Ramsay saw the glow of a cigarette on the opposite side of the quarterdeck. The damn deck passengers had a nerve! They had no business aft the mizzen. He moved quickly and silently in his bare feet around the cabin trunk, passed Uala at the wheel, and in a moment he was standing beside the glowing cigarette. Yet before he arrived, he knew he had made a mistake. Not deck. . . . cabin. It was the woman, Mrs. King. . . . and she was alone. He had seen her only once from a distance, when she boarded, and he very much wanted to see her again. Just to be sure he was wrong.

—Good evening.

—Hello.

—I'm Elliot Ramsay. . . . the mate.

—Hello again.

She nodded her head and was silent looking at the sea. Ramsay lit a cigarette hoping the light would flare on her face, but she turned her head away.

—We've met before. . . . I think.

—Is that so? Where?

—I can't remember.

—That's hardly a compliment.

—I apologize. Could it have been Seattle?

—I've never been to Seattle.

Her voice was flat and completely without invitation. Ramsay waited, searching his mind, for he was not yet sure. He said,
—You're up late.

—I couldn't sleep. It's so hot and stuffy in that little cabin.

—You're in with Miss Peacock?

—Yes. She snores.

—She sure does. We've had her all the way from Papeete. Wait 'til she starts singing.

—I'll try not to be impatient.

In the dark, Ramsay tried to analyze her voice. It was low and remarkably soft, he thought. The voice of a well-bred woman. The accent was vaguely British and failed entirely to match the notion in his memory.

—You aren't from Boston, are you? Your accent reminds me. . . .

—I've never been in Boston.

—Oh. Then you lived in Suva a long time?

—A year.

—We spent so little time ashore I don't believe I could have seen you there.

—No. Because I actually didn't live there. My husband's plantation was on Kandavu and we seldom crossed over to Suva. I am five feet seven inches tall. I weight one hundred and twenty-five pounds. My hair is brown with a few blond wisps. My eyes are said to turn green at times. Now, Mr. Ramsay. . . . is there anything else you want to know?

—Do your eyes turn green when you're mad?

—Yes. I'm sorry you can't see them now.

—I didn't mean to pry.

27

—Then why don't you mind your own business?

She turned her back to him and for a moment Ramsay thought that it was perhaps best to leave her. But he hesitated, prodding his memory. What was there about her voice? Or was it her accent? It had a fake, experimental quality about it, as if she were not quite sure of herself. It contradicted the impression he had seen her before. He moved a step around her until he could see a part of her face in the glow from Bell's skylight. There was a sort of aristocratic line to her profile and that was also all wrong, but still the notion persisted. You might expect to see a profile like that on the first-class promenade of a steamer, but not on a broken-down barquentine.

—I didn't mean to offend you, madam. . . . believe me. I'm only a seafaring man and on nights like this with no wind, the watch hours pass slowly. I just wanted to talk to someone and had no idea I might be intruding. Will you forgive me?

—Why not?

—Perhaps you'll understand my curiosity. This is a very small ship. We'll be together on her for a long time, through good weather and bad. I should only like to help Captain Bell make the passage as pleasant as I can for every passenger.

—Just make it as fast as you can.

—You'll like Mexico.

She shrugged her shoulders, but made no other reply. Ramsay ventured another step around her and now he could see her eyes. And though they were entirely disinterested he smiled as the notion became strong again. He moved further ahead of her until the glow from the skylight fell on his own face and then he said, —I don't even know your name.

—Mrs. King.

—Your husband must already be a very lonely man. To send a young wife on a sailing ship. . . .

—My husband is dead.

—Oh. I'm very sorry.

She looked straight into his eyes. There was no change of expression on her face. Ramsay almost shivered in spite of the heat. This was a very good-looking woman, he thought, but she is solid ice inside.

—Are you really sorry?

—I. . . . I simply. . . . it's the customary thing to say.

—Do you always say what is customary, Mr. Ramsay?

—Before long you'll be calling me Elliot. You might as well start now.

—All right, Elliot. Now is the next thing you're thinking of saying. . . . time will ease my sorrow? Or are you going to be honest and say that my widow's weeds seem to hang lightly and it would be a shame to waste my most precious years grieving? When are you going to say I should better occupy my time letting you show me the stars, and later your cabin? Why don't you say that I look like an opportunity and what can you lose by trying?

—You mistake me. I only want to be. . . .

—I don't think so. You're too tall and too handsome. Your hair is too pretty and that smile came from a lot of practice in front of a mirror. I came up here because I wanted to be alone. Now run along like a good little boy and sail your ship. The sooner we get to Mexico the better.

Ramsay placed one hand on his belt and bowed slightly. And he continued to smile because now he was certain. Somewhere, and not so long ago, he had seen this Mrs. King before. Given time, he would remember. . . . and there was plenty of time. Touching his forehead in a mock salute, he said, —Good night.

He walked slowly aft to join Uala near the wheel, and he heard the clock in the charthouse strike seven bells. In half an hour Bell would relieve him. And if things were right, he might try again to place that lovely face.

Ida Morris lay in her bunk and looked at her husband sitting near her feet in his nightshirt. From time to time he would reach out and caress her hand and say in Russian that he was very sorry for her. The lamp above the washbasin was turned far down to minimize the rolling sensation of their cabin and he had propped her up as comfortably as he could, saying without conviction that seasickness was a passing thing, but still she was miserable.

When she retched, he held her head tenderly over a basin and afterward wiped her brow with a towel he had hung out the porthole to cool.

There were moments when she tried to smile. Then she told him to climb in the upper bunk and sleep, but he could not leave her. When her eyes were closed he would look at the light and think without bitterness of the years which had brought them to this hot little cabin with its strong smell of copra and the two cockroaches he had already killed. Ten years of wandering, he thought, and Ida still looked like a very young woman. A little girl with a stomach ache now, but that would pass. Ida Morevsky, who wanted to change their name to Morris because she thought the name was easier for English-speaking people to pronounce and remember.

He looked at her again, now that she seemed to be sleeping, and it struck him suddenly that he was a liar of liars. A fahvel. Ida was old and she was fat, and it was not the fat of well-being. There were crevasses around her eyes and two drooping pouches beneath her chin. Her hair, which she still wore Black-Sea style with two buns on each side of her head, was nearly white. And the hair on her upper lip, which was almost a mustache, was unfortunately not white. He reminded himself that these were the things he should not see after nearly fifty years of marriage, and he wished she would open her eyes so that they would disappear. For Ida's eyes, even in misery, were remarkable. They were small and bright blue, and they shone with a mysterious radiance he could never quite define. They twinkled and were never dull. Even during the long trek across Siberia. . . . even in Harbin for two terrible Manchurian winters. . . . even in the summer heat of Shanghai. . . . even when she was angry or despaired of ever finding a home, her eyes twinkled.

Finally she opened her eyes again and he was grateful. Yes, even in the dim light they were full of life. He pressed her hand and patted the worn gold band on her finger.

—How do you feel?

—Better. You must go to sleep, Feodor.

—You sleep. So I don't want to.

—I was thinking now. It helps my stomach to think. I was thinking that we make a terrible mistake to live in the past. I was thinking of the house in Sevastopol and I was thinking of the shop and the customers, and I was thinking of you going down to the shop in the morning in your black hat and white tie with the pin and your beard which you spent so much time every morning making just right, and I was thinking like it was only a little time ago. But it wasn't, Feodor.

—No? So it wasn't? So who gives a care?

—I knew there was something wrong with my thinking when I couldn't remember the bad things. . . .

They were silent for a moment and, with an effort, Feodor remembered the bad things. Two sons lost to the Germans somewhere in Poland—they never did find out where—and finally a crazy government which didn't thank them for the sons at all, but instead said that jewelers, even small jewelers, were utterly useless people and therefore must cease to exist. As if a jeweler could not produce happiness as well as farmers. He looked at the two cockroaches squashed in the corner and was sorry for them.

—Do you want some water?

—No, Feodor. I was thinking that too long we have been living in the past. We must live in the future.

—Not so easy. We are not young.

—We must borrow youth then. Like you go to a bank.

—Who is the lender? Be sick but don't be crazy.

—Ourselves. And so we are rich. . . . and young at the same time.

—Very easy to say. But I am tired. So are you.

—Now you are thinking in Russian, Feodor.

He shrugged his shoulders and tried to smile.

—I am a Russian.

—No. We will be citizens of Mexico so soon as we can. We must not even think in Russian. We must not speak it. It is no good to live in one country and carry another in our hearts.

—Yes. . . . that is important. Soon I will have a shop in Mexico. It will not be so large as the one in Sevastopol.

She held up her finger.

—Do not think of Sevastopol. . . . or even the word. Just think of borrowing from *us*. Think how they will welcome us if we are young.

—I hope.

—Do you want to say the lessons or do you want to sleep?

—I want to say the lessons, but what about your stomach?

—It will help me forget my stomach to think of our new home. Now say to me in Spanish, What is the population of Mexico?

Slowly, as if repeating a catechism, he gave her the answer in halting Spanish. And to her questions he repeated the length and breadth of Mexico, the location and altitude of the capital,

31

and the nature of the governing body. They continued to question each other until their minds were exhausted and neither of them could remember the principal product of the State of Chihuahua. Then Feodor kissed his wife twice on her cheeks, turned down the lamp, and gathering his nightshirt, climbed into the upper bunk. Just before he slept his voice came down through the darkness.

—Ida. . . . ?

—I am just here. I could not move.

—I love you.

She did not reply, knowing it was needless. She smiled in the dark and her contentment was so great she temporarily forgot the *Cannibal*'s motion.

The clock in the charthouse was still striking eight bells when Anchor bounded to the deck followed by his master. Eight figures moved about the *Cannibal* in the faint starlight, passing each other more at a stumble than a walk and with only an occasional grunt of recognition. For the men relieved in Ramsay's watch had been counting the minutes and they were almost as sleepy as those just roused from their bunks. Old Brown, who was sixty-four, and Sweeney, who was just twenty, and Keim, who was the bos'n, were the sailors in Bell's watch. When the others vanished forward, they yawned and stretched and shivered and rubbed their puffy eyes and urinated over the taffrail. They looked up at the night and sniffed for wind and, finding so very little, they knew they were in for a session of constant work with the sails. For it was much harder to sail a ship with little wind than with a great deal. Now they would have to brace around to take advantage of every puff.

They were also sure of some back-breaking time at the pump. And so they wished aloud that they had become farmers. Did a farmer go to sleep at four o'clock in the morning, just when the world was starting? He did not. Did a farmer have a choice of sleeping half an hour extra and missing breakfast, or having breakfast and missing sleep? He did not. A farmer had his life arranged so that he enjoyed both sleep and breakfast. He got up with the sun like a human being and ate his ham and eggs and kissed his wife and went out to his field for a go at driving around in his fancy tractor. If something went wrong with his tractor he just walked over to the shade of a tree and had a lemonade for himself while he waited for some-one to come and fix the tractor. Anyone who was a farmer was smart. Anyone who was a sailor was not in his right mind. Gradually, as the night air refreshed and awakened them, the sailors speculated wistfully on the life of a farmer and it made no difference that not one of them had even been near a farm.

Because he knew sailors, Bell allowed them to preach at each other and grumble for a full half-hour before he called Keim to his side.

Keim was a German. Every man on board including Bell treated him with marked respect, despite the fact his nationality catalogued him as a squarehead. While most seamen were violently prejudiced on many small things, their constant movement about the world gave even the most unintelligent a diplomat's understanding and interest in other nations. A seaman was a seaman, be he Pole, Swede, Kanaka, Jap, or Finn, and his race was of no importance. His social position in the forecastle depended almost entirely on his ability to hand, reef, and steer, and his skill with marlin spike, palm, and needle. As for Keim, they were always aware of his stature in a vanishing priesthood. He was a perfect example of the old-time able-bodied seaman. Some said his mother was the ocean and his umbilical cord was a halyard. His big hands were marvelously clever at fancy rope work. It was considered a tragedy that he traded his sea-chest shackles, sennits, plaits, and mats for cheap liquor the moment he was ashore. He claimed he could not remember when he first went to sea and Bell would not have traded him for three other sailors. Therefore when he spoke to Keim, he did so quietly, as one professional to another, and there was always more said silently between them than could be found in their words.

—Did you sound the well, Keim?

—Aye.

—How much?

—Sixteen inches. . . . a little more.

—Any new ideas?

—No. She's a bucket. An old bucket. It could be. . . . lots of reasons. It vill be vorse in the vesterlies.

—Turn to on the pump then.

—Aye.

Keim nodded his head and sighed. He beckoned to Old

Brown and Sweeney and led them forward to the waist while Bell took the wheel. The bilge pump was set just forward of the mainmast and they found it necessary to shove the bodies of several deck passengers aside before they could take their positions in reasonable comfort. The pump was of an old and primitive design, and though the men had already developed a special hatred for it, they were forced to admit its reliability. A long metal arm, set athwartships at almost the height of a man's belt, worked up and down to activate two suction pumps in opposition. The arm was supported by a cast-iron fulcrum set permanently in the deck, and the assembly could be operated by two, three, or four men depending on their strength and disposition.

They braced themselves, Sweeney and Old Brown on one arm, Keim balancing his strength against the both of them on the other. Swearing quietly, they began to pump. After a few moments the water was sucked upward to splash on the deck. The nearest passengers gathered their few belongings and straw mats and huddled out of the deluge wherever they could find a piece of dry deck. The seamen mixed their sweat with the cool water sloshing at their bare feet and pumped doggedly for nearly two hours.

There was so little wind, Bell was constantly obliged to spin the wheel as he felt for every puff and tried hopefully to keep the *Cannibal* on some semblance of a course. Anchor settled down on the grating beneath the wheel and when Bell thought about it he would reach out a toe and scratch him between the ears. But mostly he was thinking about the leak, which had plagued the *Cannibal* all the way from San Francisco.

During the first weeks and through the Marquesas it was not in the least alarming, considering the *Cannibal*'s age and the fact that she had not been dry-docked for almost three years. Now there was a jungle of grass and barnacles on her bottom and though this slowed her speed, it had nothing to do with the leak. Bound west from the Marquesas to Tahiti, the leak became much worse and he thought it might be her old lumber ports, which were no longer used. But he had inspected the ports, taking Keim along for advice, and found them surprisingly tight. The same applied to her stern, where they found only a colony of cockroaches. . . . all quite dry. A little water seeped through the rudder-post housing, but that was natural and not nearly enough to match the amount she made each day. He had inspected her planking down to both water lines twice, the first time in Papeete and then on arrival in Suva. Eight seams were found in need of calking and this was done thoroughly by Keim and Old Brown. She still leaked.

The leak was steady and so must be beneath the water line. Bell was sure of that now. It could be along her garboard strake, or maybe it was her keel which peculiarly had been scarfed in two pieces. It might be parting slowly. This could be serious since any separation between the two partners was bound to increase as the *Cannibal* worked her way through the seas. Or perhaps her hogging had something to do with it. . . . the planks just separating in their weariness. It wasn't this little passage to Rotuma. . . . nothing to worry about here. . . . but later, long after Rotuma, north of forty degrees in the westerlies, where sometimes the weather made it tough to keep body and soul lashings together. . . . well, what the hell? If a man wanted an easy life, he stayed away from the sea, and especially from sailing ships. The *Cannibal* would make it even if she did require a bit of nursing from time to time.

Listening to the monotonous pumping, he looked down at Anchor. He twisted his mouth slightly in the way he always did when he shared a secret with him and said, —Maybe we should have doubled our order for new pump leathers in San Francisco.

He reached out with his toe and was scratching Anchor again when he saw that he was no longer alone on the quarterdeck. Harry Hutton moved into the faint light of the binnacle. It so shone on his bald head, Bell thought he looked like an offended Buddha. He held an oversize bathrobe tightly about his middle and nervously massaged the frizz of hair along his ears.

—Captain. I demand to know how long this infernal pumping will continue?

—Until the bilges are dry.

—I can't sleep. How can anyone sleep?

—Nobody else is complaining.

—They should. This is ridiculous and. . . . dangerous. I believe this ship is sinking and has been all the way from Papeete.

—My feet are dry. So are yours.

—I demand that you put into the nearest port and fix this ship so it doesn't leak.

—Relax, Mr. Hutton. All ships leak a little. There's nothing to worry about. The nearest port is still in sight back there and you can damn near swim for it. If we don't get some wind tomorrow you might try it because it will still be there. Go to bed and count your blessings.

—Why haven't you got a wireless on this ship? We could all drown and no one would know it.

—Why haven't you got an opera star in your troupe? Same reason. Money.

Hutton massaged his nose for a moment and looked back through the darkness toward Suva. He blew out air and in doing so seemed to sag all over, as if a sharp instrument had punctured his fat body.

—I will let your remark pass, Captain, since I am well aware that a man suffering financial embarrassment himself is the first to wish others in his own stew. However, for your future guidance I suggest you remember that Miss Peacock is in great demand all over the world. Going to Papeete was a little frivolity of hers which I indulged in only because as a truly great artist she is a hopeless romantic and had visions of carrying culture to palm-lined beaches. I considered that a tour among more or less primitive surroundings might relieve the terrible strain of our recent metropolitan engagements. . . . and I booked passage on your ship because I believed the restful nature of sail might do much to recoup her strength. I had no idea it was going to be like this.

By the time he completed his speech, Hutton's body had re-erected itself upon invisible supports. He spread his feet wide apart and waved a loose bathrobe arm dramatically in the general direction of the mainmast.

—Junk! If I were the vengeful type. . . . if money meant anything to me. . . . I'd sue.

—You booked on the *Cannibal* for the same reason as everybody else. The fare is less than half a steamer's. We do the best we can, but you always get what you pay for.

—Nonsense. Both Miss Peacock and myself are accustomed to the best. On the train between Mexico City and New York I shall arrange for us to travel in a private car. It makes things much easier when handling the press, you understand. I'm telling you this only because I am anxious for you to realize that we wish to be good sports and are willing to view this voyage as. . . . let us say, an amusing adventure. We are basically very simple people. We enjoy contact with others less fortunate, and Miss Peacock particularly resents any suggestion that she might be treated better than anyone else. Do you follow me, Captain?

Bell extended his foot to scratch Anchor. He reached in his shirt pocket and pulled out his short pipe. Then without looking at Hutton he began to fill it methodically. He said, —I'm right behind you.

Hutton maneuvered the bathrobe arms to the vicinity of his hips and took a deep breath.

—Now. . . . you are not a youngster, Captain. I assume that you are a man of the sea and I respect you for it. We all have our niche in life. But there are certain things which I have observed besides the fact that this ship is sinking, and which make me extremely uneasy. What about those lifeboats?

He waved his bathrobe arm in the direction of the gallows frame spanning the forward deckhouse, where two boats were lashed bottom up.

—What about them?

—There are only two. There are, unless I have miscounted, fifteen hapless souls on board besides the deck passengers, and I understand you're picking up another passenger in Rotuma.

—Word sure gets around in a hurry.

—Those boats are not big enough to accommodate us all in an emergency.

—Would you like to have one for each person?

—Furthermore they are in poor condition. It looks to me like they haven't been moved in years. I doubt if they would float five minutes.

—You're worse than a marine surveyor.

—I'm just wondering if you realize your responsibility, Captain. A lot of lives are in your hands. It may be all right for you to eventually find a watery grave, but. . . .

Bell snapped his pipe out of his mouth. His words came so forcefully, Hutton retreated a step.

—Now you listen to me a minute, Mr. Hutton! Those boats are all right. What's more, the *Cannibal* is all right and she'll be sailing long after you and me are dead! I'm in business. If there's a little paint peeling off here and there it's because business isn't good and I have to make do with what I can. Just like you. Nobody shanghaied you on board. You can go ashore on Rotuma and stay there if you want, but I wouldn't recommend it. Don't worry about the *Cannibal* and don't worry about me. We'll get you to Mexico.

Then more gently, he said, —Why don't you go back to bed?

—But I can't sleep with that noise!

—Pretend it's your private car rolling along the rails. Or it could be applause for Miss Peacock. Anything you want, Mr. Hutton.

Again the punctured look came to Hutton. He lowered his head like a small boy caught thieving. He exhaled with the sound of a dying steam engine and his voice was a plea when he spoke again.

—You don't believe me, do you, Captain? You believe I'm making things up. You think I'm. . . . a failure.

—I meet all kinds of people, Mr. Hutton.

—Yes. . . . I suppose you do.

—Tough luck gets to be a habit if you let it. I know.

Hutton turned away suddenly and padded in his bare feet toward the saloon hatch. His shoulders were slumped and he did not look back at Bell. His bald head shone for an instant as he turned into the hatchway and then he was gone.

After a time, Bell said very quietly, —Anchor . . . I shouldn't have been so hard on that man. He wasn't trying to sell us anything. He was just trying to sell himself. . . . just lonesome. We ought to understand that better than anybody, I guess.

He looked forward and saw the length of the *Cannibal* to the tip of her jib boom, and because the starlight was kind to her, he saw only her secret beauty. Mrs. Weatherbee would understand how this could be done. And she would have understood Hutton just now and humored him. She would have been happy to believe in the private car. She would have understood Hutton just like she would understand why you named this little ship the *Cannibal* when the Chinaman let you buy in. Cannibals had their idea of beauty and so did everybody else and what was beautiful depended on who was doing the looking. No other living person would have thought the old *Cannibal* beautiful except David Bell just at that time, and no one would think so now. . . . except David Bell. Any more than anybody would think Miss Peacock could sing. . . . but Harry Hutton. Because he was lonesome and needed a love. And that was not an easy thing to find.

He leaned on the wheel, drawing on his pipe, and for a time he forgot the sound of pumping and the lack of wind and the impossibility of making a good course. He watched the mastheads scraping across the stars and he saw the *Cannibal* beating up Rosario Strait and the Gulf of Georgia. . . . bound for lumber on a cold and foggy morning. As she used to be. He saw her skating before a southeaster with a bone in her teeth off Tatoosh. . . . fighting for her life against the current from the Canadian shore. He saw her slipping quietly into the great lagoon at Rangiroa on the last of an evening wind. Finally, he smiled.

For he saw her now, alone on the night sea, and he was deeply satisfied.

As if to consummate his pleasure a light breeze began to cool the back of his neck. It held steadily from the east and then increased as the *Cannibal* abandoned her sluggishness and began to move through the water. The sails filled, the rolling eased. There was pressure on the rudder as Bell spun the wheel, and looking back at the *Cannibal*'s phosphorescent wake, he knew the trades had at last returned.

. . . continues moderate trades. Inner jib sheet carried away during night. Begins fine with Rotuma in sight on starboard bow. . . .

Bilges show sixteen inches of water again.

Three

THE REVEREND BUTTERFIELD made the sign of the cross over the King of France, and then exiting from the throne room to the sound of trumpets, he passed through a series of corridors in the Palace of Versailles. From the several doorways which led off the last corridor he heard the sound of feminine laughter, and popping alternately into one doorway after the other he found himself in various rooms surrounded by delightful young creatures who touched his robe and hung on his every word. They were powdered and wigged and in various stages of undress and the most full-bosomed chased him with screams of delight from room to room. One little vixen tickled his nose with a peacock fan and he brushed it away several times without success. Then he opened his eyes and saw that the palace was his bunk and the fan was a large black fly. He struck at it with all his might. Misjudging, he hit his nose instead of the fly and spent several moments trying to soothe the pain.

When he rose finally, he struck his head against the base of the bunk above his own and at once assumed a horizontal posture again. Rubbing his nose, he listened to the hissing

40

sound of the sea outside his porthole and found little comfort in it. The morning had started off very badly and he wanted to return to the Palace of Versailles. Mix with the vixens. He liked the sound of the phrase in his mind and he tried it audibly several times while he rubbed the bump on his head. Mix with the vixens. . . . mix with vixens. It was some time before he began to be ashamed of himself and turned his thoughts to Mexico.

Five years at a stretch on a Pacific island were enough for any man, no matter how devout. And the Catholic Church with its iron-bound bastions of faith might do something to restore his own, Butterfield thought. In Mexico he would begin by writing a treatise on the life of Junipero Serra and perhaps the labor of a year on such a man would prove everlastingly that the persuasions of the Devil were merely more logical and God's dictates should be accepted on faith alone. Who knows, he thought, I might even wind up a Catholic! And what would my own church have to say about *that?*

There were so many dangers in the Pacific. How could you carry the word day after day to people who listened with the utmost politeness and then secretly did as they pleased? To have order and worship you must have rules, and the differences between good and sin must be set by the rules. To make the rules obeyed, some sort of punishment had to exist for those who violated them, and the distant prospect of Hell and damnation meant almost nothing to the islanders. Viewed now, from the neutral territory of his bunk, it seemed they were perversely fascinated with fire and brimstone, and the idea of a mighty conflagration in which they might play a leading role if they should do wrong. The prospect of being so much the center of attention, whether it was the Devil's or anyone else's, almost made them court sin deliberately. Or so things went on the island of Thithia, which was just about the smallest parish the Society could find in the Fijis.

If the people who sent their pennies out from England could only see the trials and temptations which beset their appointed representatives! How could you explain God and be forced to use the word *Aitu,* which in actuality meant a malignant spirit or devil? How could Hell seem threatening when from six ancient states beneath the sea there arose the very real Atua, who would return to the land, capture the souls of friends they had known before their own death, and spirit them away to a mysterious submarine region known as Oroi? And eat them!

The route to Oroi? Much more clearly defined than the route to Hell! Via places known as Lulu and Chopunga. . . . and thence beneath the sea!

Butterfield sighed and sat up in his bunk very carefully so that he would not strike his head again. The danger in the Pacific was within oneself! There was a tendency to start believing in Oroi and its weird inhabitants. . . . so easy to understand against the complexities of Christianity.

And, he decided, I have been tried and found wanting. And he said aloud to the porthole, —Forgive me.

He went to the porthole, moving uncertainly on his spindle legs against the heel of the ship. He stood scratching his back and watching the dawn on the sea for several minutes; then he turned to the washstand and poured less than a glassful into the basin. He moistened his fingertips, tossed a few droplets of water into his eyes, spluttered unhappily, and groped for the towel beside the basin. He rubbed around his face twice, rehung the towel, and reached for his glasses. They were brass rimmed, almost opaque with fingerprints and moisture, and they were precariously held together with bits of wire.

He squinted through the glasses at the mirror and decided he could certainly go another day without shaving. He ran his fingers through his hair and saw that it was beginning to thin as well as turn gray, and the vision saddened him. He found that he could not look away from the mirror, for now, at last away from his flock for the first time in so long, the ravages of those years were startling to behold. His cheeks were sunken and the skin stretched drum-tight across the bones beneath his eyes. His teeth were a deep yellow and many were missing. His nose could no longer fit the description given on graduation by his classmates at the seminary in Sussex. . . . "The classical Greek profile of neophyte Butterfield should do much to assist his messages from the pulpit." No, now the nose seemed to droop and there were hairs on the end of it, and the profile was that of a gargoyle. And the eyes, dim and weak behind the soiled glasses, were afraid.

He turned quickly to his bunk and pulled his Bible from beneath the pillow. And to chastise himself he spent ten minutes resolutely engaged in reading First Corinthians.

Just after sunrise on this third morning, the *Cannibal* swept around the western end of Rotuma with her yards braced up hard against the strong trades. In an hour she had rounded the split island of Vea, come about on the port tack, and slipped easily into the bight which held the village of Motusa. With foresail brailed up, she held straight for shore, in Bell's way. She passed close under the stern of the Morris Hedstrom schooner, *Speedwell*, and came up into the wind opposite the Residency. When her square sails were taken aback, Bell tipped over his hand with his thumb pointed down, and Keim on the foredeck struck the anchor trip with a top maul he had ready in hand. There was a splash as the *Cannibal* began to slide backwards. In a moment she was straining at her cable.

It was a beautifully precise series of maneuvers, accomplished without commotion, for if there was one thing Bell hated it was shouting officers and the sight of sailors running on a vessel's deck. Commotion always betrayed the inexpert and he raised his voice just enough to be heard clearly when he ordered the jibs doused, tops'ls and t'gallants clewed up, and main and halyards let go. The spanker he left standing. Keim took three men aloft with him to furl the canvas on the foremast. Ramsay led Sweeney and Old Brown to the midship hatch, where they unlashed the Ford truck while the deck passengers laughed and shouted all around them and waved excitedly at the shore.

The *Cannibal*'s hook had barely touched bottom before a flotilla set out from the land. There were canoes and powered launches and several copra lighters lashed together for the truck, and there was a small scow overflowing with fresh cocoanuts and in the light chop of the anchorage many of the cocoanuts rolled overboard and joined the heads of the swimmers, until it was difficult to tell which was which. So, with her decks still wet in the early sun the *Cannibal* arrived in Rotuma, where no one ever drank water, where a ship was called an "Ahoy," a dog was called a "Comehere," and where elephantiasis was the curse of the people.

Bell sat down on the after curve of the taffrail, lit his pipe, and watched the approaching horde of visitors. There would be rejoicing all day long as relatives met relatives and the Rotumans found old friends among the native deck passengers, and in a way he woud be sorry to see them leave. But they would be lost souls in Mexico.

He looked at the shore, with more interest than he ever had before, and wondered how soon he would see Rotuma or any of the other islands again. Rotuma, like all the islands, was linked to the world with the meat of cocoanuts and unless some miracle changed the copra prices, he knew it would be a long time before the *Cannibal* could sail the Pacific again. Without looking down at Anchor, he reached out to stroke his head. And he said to him, —It's only a question of time. . . . but by God, we'll sure be the last!

The cabin passengers were lined along the starboard quarterdeck and some were not fully awake. They chattered amiably with each other, for now with land so close their interests found a common stimulus and much of the reserve which had held them apart during the first strange days at sea dissolved. As the first visitors clambered over the bulwarks, Ida and Feodor Morris attempted to describe the happy confusion in a mixture of basic English and even more elementary Spanish. Ethel Peacock, her bright red hair still done up in curlers, clasped and unclasped her hands and exclaimed that she thought the island with its long white beaches and wooded mountains was more beautiful than Moorea. When Harry Hutton told her she could not possibly know what she was talking about since she had only seen Moorea from a distance and a considerable distance at that, she merely laughed and said that he was always trying to show that he knew everything and she didn't know a single solitary thing about anything. The Reverend Butterfield pointed to the cathedral which faced the anchorage and said it belonged to the Marist Fathers, and explained how he had once considered joining them. It was some time before Bell noticed that Mrs. King had not appeared on deck.

There was a shouting from one of the shore boats and, hearing his name, Reverend Butterfield moved his glasses farther down his nose to peer over them.

—Butterfield! Butterfield!. . . . you old wowser!

Knowing only too well that a wowser and a religious crank were synonymous to any Australian, Butterfield frowned at the launch as he tried to identify the man lolling in the stern sheets. But even if his vision had been superb, he could not have been

44

certain, for the man's face was hidden beneath an enormous woven hat which he wore carelessly tipped over one eye. A pink shirt hung loose and unbuttoned over his shoulders, and his bare feet were propped high on the gunwale. He wore dungarees faded to a pale blue. His voice came from beneath the hat again.

—Spare me days if it isn't old Chisel-face!

Only the words reassured Butterfield he was being addressed by a white man. As the boat drew nearer he made out the figures of four young girls. They were very brown and they clung tenaciously to the man beneath the hat. They were alternately laughing and weeping as the boat drew alongside the *Cannibal*. The man beneath the hat kissed each girl, swatted them affectionately on the bottom, and then climbed clumsily over the bulwark. He was tall and very thin and far from sober. He carried himself with a pronounced stoop and weaved back and forth as if the *Cannibal* were already at sea. He carried a small bundle wrapped in matting which he carefully placed on the deck while he turned to blow a series of kisses at the girls. Then gaily, with the assurance of a boulevardier, he picked up the bundle and approached Reverend Butterfield. He pounded him so hard on the shoulder he almost fell down.

—What a hell of a voyage this is going to be! Spare me days if I haven't landed right in the lap of the Lord! You look awful, Butterfield. Dreadful! What's the matter. . . . they finally run you out of the whole archipelago?

Peering over his glasses, Butterfield saw the face beneath the hat and though he became even paler for a moment, he grinned mischievously.

—Wiggins! You scalawag! I should have known!

—Where's the captain? I want to register a complaint.

He stepped quickly to the rail and blew more kisses down at the boat. Butterfield joined him for a better look and smiled benignly down at the girls.

—Stop squinting, you old lecher! They don't want your psalm singing. They want life with Wiggins!

He turned away from the rail, pushed back his hat, and rubbed imaginary tears from his eyes. Then he said mournfully,
—Only they can't have it.

—Don't tell me you're going to Mexico?

—Why not? I always wanted to be a conquistador. It will no

45

longer be Wiggins of Rotuma. I fancy Wiggins of Mayheeko! Where's that captain? I want to be certain there will be no psalm singing after midnight and none of your rummy platitudes at any time.

—I am the captain.

Wiggins turned to see Bell standing beside him. He looked at him, trying to focus his eyes and control his weaving. Finally he smiled.

—What time does the bar open?

—It doesn't. There isn't any.

Wiggins was appalled. He smacked his lips and shook his head and leaned involuntarily toward the shore.

—I am dead and en route to purgatory.

—Are you the Rotuma passenger?

Bowing slightly, Wiggins said, —Oliver Spencer Wiggins.

—My name is Bell. Got your passport?

Wiggins pulled a black book from the bundle. He handed it to Bell.

—So? A Limey. . . .

—An Englishman, if you please, sir.

—This passport has expired.

—What hasn't on Rotuma? So have I in a way.

—The Mexicans will throw you in jail.

—How enchanting. Durance vile with castanets.

—You may not find it exactly comfortable. What you been doing on Rotuma?

Wiggins looked down at the girls who were chanting his name. He beamed at them and in spite of his dissatisfaction with the passport, Bell also smiled.

—Living. As you see, sir. But after three years. . . . even a caliph gets tired. There is something to be said for monogamy.

Butterfield giggled, then suddenly hid his reaction in the sleeve of his frock. When his face emerged again he winked solemnly at Bell.

—I've known Mr. Wiggins ever since he came to the islands, Captain, and I've no doubt the authorities will be delighted to get rid of him. His influence by behavior has never been exactly inspiring.

Bell glanced at the girls again and stuffed the passport in his hip pocket.

—It don't look that way to me, Reverend. That's quite a farewell committee.

Wiggins waved his arm proudly and said,—That one on the left is Cleopatra. Next to her is Circe. The one standing is Messalina. She has the most seniority. The one with the very white teeth and the tears on her cheeks is Madame de Pompadour. I named them all.

—The Mexicans may not even let you land in jail. If they fine the ship you'll have to work it out. It's up to you, Wiggins.

—I must see real green grass again and Mexico will be my first leg back to England. Here's my passage money.

He fished in his shirt pocket and brought out a fifty-pound note. Bell eyed it dubiously and then took it.

—All right. Get your baggage aboard.

—It's aboard, sir.

Bell looked down at the small bundle under his arm.

—You travel light and you'll freeze when we get north. But that's your problem. You'll be in cabin four with Mr. Hutton. Meals are at eight, twelve, and six. We sail as soon as that truck is unloaded.

Bell turned away and walked to the companionway which led to the saloon. He descended the short companionway ladder slowly, his mind already five thousand miles away. He was wondering if he had made a mistake in accepting Wiggins as a passenger. The damn Mexicans were sticky about papers. If they noticed Wiggins' passport had expired they would certainly yell for a fine on the *Cannibal*, and every penny of his fifty pounds would be needed if there was ever to be another voyage. As for working it out, the man didn't look like he could successfully hoist anything heavier than a bottle. But there was something about him worth liking. Bell chuckled. Maybe Wiggins had just left all his strength on Rotuma.

—What's so funny, Captain?

It was a moment before Bell could accustom his eyes to the subdued light in the saloon. Then he saw Mrs. King sitting at the end of the long table. There was a coffee cup before her and she was smoking a cigarette. He said good morning and then hesitated uncertainly.

—Why aren't you on deck with the others? Don't you want to see Rotuma?

—Why should I? It's just another island.

47

Meeting her eyes, Bell was suddenly uncomfortable. While he took a moment to seek the reason he passed the palm of his hand across the stubble of beard and found only that his thoughts were a mixture of the need for shaving, which was partially the reason he had started for his cabin in the first place, and a need to guard his words.

He had not spoken to her since before sailing from Suva when he explained the *Cannibal*'s routing, and the same uneasiness he had known then returned to him now. He had deliberately avoided eating with the passengers so far; standing heel-and-toe watches left little desire for anything except sleep, but he knew now that a part of his reluctance to assign permanent places at the table was due to Charlotte King. Like all the others, her passport was in his possession for the duration of the voyage, but there was nothing of interest in it save her age, the date she arrived in the British-controlled Fijis, and a very uncomplimentary photo. He had wondered, in fact, how the photo ever passed the immigration inspector since it resembled her so little. Her hair was longer and rather frowsy whenever the photo was taken, there was almost a snarl on her mouth, and her eyes stared vacantly into space. She looked like she might have just been awakened from a deep sleep, and he thought at the time that such a face might appear more at home at midnight in a waterfront bar. But this was no bar girl.

This Mrs. King was a lady. He was sure of it; and as such she might just as well have descended from another planet. She sat there at the end of the table, perfectly composed, while he squirmed inwardly and could only think of how Mrs. Weatherbee had once said his arms hung down like an ape's. He straightened imperceptibly. What the hell did you say to a real lady?

—A lot of people would pay good money to see Rotuma, Mrs. King. We won't be here long.

He mumbled the words, pushing them out before he really knew what he wanted to say, not moving, but standing rooted to where he had landed at the foot of the companionway.

—Good.

There was not the slightest change of expression on her face when she spoke the single word, yet Bell was certain she was laughing at him. Anchor pressed against his leg as if urging him on to his cabin. And when Bell ignored him, he left the leg and took a few experimental paces toward Charlotte King. She lowered her hand and Anchor went to it, sniffing suspiciously.

—What kind of a dog is this, Captain?

—A male.

She looked up at him. A smile played around her mouth and he decided she was no longer laughing at him. He wiped the perspiration which had unaccountably come to his brow and pushed his cap back on his head. Then he wished he had not done so. Pulled well down, the cap did much to conceal the scar and his drooping eyelid. For a moment he tried to tell himself that he didn't care what this woman thought. Mrs. Weatherbee had forgotten one thing. . . . how to behave around ladies. . . . if she ever knew.

—What *kind* of a dog is he, Captain?

—That's the only way to describe him. He's just. . . . a dog.

Now her hand, which Bell saw was so delicate it must be less than half the size of his own, was caressing Anchor between the ears. Bell saw that her fingernails were not painted and he thought that here was another sign of a true lady. There was a simple gold wedding band on one finger and above it was a ring set with diamonds. Her husband must certainly have been a more than usually successful planter, but if so, what was she doing on the *Cannibal?*

—What's his name?

—Anchor.

—I think he has a touch of schnauzer in him.

—He has a touch of a lot of things. Sort of like his master.

—Where did you get him?

—He came on board about four years ago in Honolulu and I never could get him to leave. I guess he just wanted to get out of Honolulu.

Her hand paused suddenly, then after a moment, resumed the caressing.

—He's very intelligent.

—I don't know what I'd do without him. He understands just about everything on the *Cannibal* except the navigation and sometimes I'm not so sure he doesn't check my figures.

—Does he understand you, Captain?

Bell was instantly ill at ease again, because when she asked the question she looked directly at him as if she could somehow penetrate any thought he might want to keep from her. And yet

49

her own face revealed nothing. She could be joking, which made the most sense, or she could be serious, and if so what kind of an answer could a man give without sounding like a damn fool? She was asking a question out of a different world, a place where ladies and college graduates spoke of such things and bothered to find an answer. But to ask a sailor with more calluses on his hands than his brain and black lines under his fingernails if his dog understood him. . . . well, there was just no way to say the right thing. So he murmured lamely,—I guess he does.

—Are you married, Captain?

Now Bell wished that he had just said good morning and continued straight on to his cabin. The questions ladies asked were worse than Chinese lanyard knots and as easy to fumble.

—Hell, yes!

The strength of his reply surprised him. What did such a silly question have to do with Anchor or what kind of a bitch he came from? Some sailors could find the time and the mood for marriage, but not the kind who had to make the long crawl from hawsepipe to bridge, or nowadays, try to make a living in sail. It was a crazy question. She might as well have asked him if his kidneys functioned properly and he would not have been any more uncomfortable.

He started for the door which led to his cabin, wishing he had not used the word "hell." It was certainly no way to answer a lady. . . . especially when her question probably seemed perfectly natural to her. Some people talked that way. But it was no world for Davey Bell. As he passed through the door with Anchor trotting after him, he heard her laugh as she said,—I don't think you're telling me the truth, Captain.

He grunted and closed the door behind him. How could you tell a lady you were married to a ship? She would think you were drunk, or an idiot with your mouth open like Mrs. Weatherbee always said. And she would have a good right to think so.

He entered his cabin and slammed the door behind him. He went directly to his desk, took a mint from the open packet next to the barometer and threw it in his mouth. He clamped down hard with his teeth, enjoying the crunching sound. Then he looked down at Anchor and grunted again. He pulled a blank sheet of paper toward him and quickly drew a rough diagram of the seats in the dining saloon. He scribbled a name by each seat except the one at the end of the table which Dak Sue, the cook, would know was his own. Clamping down hard on the last of the mint, he wrote "Mrs. King" by the seat which would be on his right.

Old Brown had seen it all. Every last disgusting bit of it. And now whenever he observed a warning wisp of smoke on the horizon, he looked the other way, or if near a port, where two or three steamers might encroach upon his vision, he would repair to the forecastle and sulk until they were gone. He called all steamers "rust buckets," and sometimes when he was in port himself and drunk enough, he would stagger down to the wharves and yell and shake his fist at the offending masses of metal. He would challenge their towering structures to personal combat and call them names dredged from his awful salt vocabulary, and if he spied a sailor on their decks, be he officer or crewman, he sometimes, when he was drunk enough, heaved his bottle at the man with deadly accuracy. This attitude sometimes landed him in jail, which he smugly considered a sort of decoration in his private war against all ships which had the gall to sail without a stitch of canvas. In some ports he was known as Don Brown Quixote.

He had seen it all for fifty years and no argument however violent could convince him the battle was over. He had seen the freight rates drop between New York and San Francisco from forty dollars a ton to fifteen dollars a ton. Less devoted men said the Panama Canal alone was enough to spell the death of the windjammers. The damn rust buckets just eased through in a hurry. Old Brown had seen all kinds of last-ditch skirmishes between sail and steam and he would admit the loss of none of them. He had seen the last of the packets, *Galilee*, *The Tropic Bird* and the *City of Papeete*. How could they vanish? Why for Christ's sake, man, *Galilee*'s *average* passage between Tahiti and Frisco was only twenty-eight days and twelve hours. . . . weren't it?

And what happened to the four-masted barquentines. . . . the *Charlie Crocker*, the *Lahaima*, the *Arago*, and the *Chehalis*? They weren't *Northern Lights*, perhaps, a name which he mentioned reverently, but they were sail. He was fond of quoting from the logbook of the *Northern Lights* though he was a child when they were written. He spoke the exact words written by Seth Doane, the chief mate, and he pronounced them as a high priest might recite tribal laws engraved on stone. "So ends this passage of seventy-six days and five hours from San Francisco to Boston!"

Then Old Brown would want to know what the hell everybody thought of that and especially since the record was set against the handicap of rounding Cape Horn.

At the slightest provocation Old Brown would quote innumerable other passages, as if they had only occurred within the past few weeks. "The *Messenger* . . . Frisco to Philadelphia in eighty-two days! . . . the *Hurricane* . . . Master Sam Very . . . Frisco to Rio in fifty-eight days! . . . the *Gallego* . . . Frisco to Singapore in forty-three days . . . and a bark at that!"

Economics were nothing to Old Brown, which was not surprising since he had never been to school and signed every ship's articles with an X. He could not understand why the Russian American Ice Company had ceased sending ice from Alaska to California in sailing vessels. Christ. . . . the Nobs still drank champagne, didn't they, even if there was prohibition? Who the hell was moving all the wheat and the barley, the hides, tallow, wool, lumber, and the case oil? Who the hell was taking the oats to Peru, and the quicksilver to China? The rust buckets? If they were, it was a government trick. . . . a goddamned plot, that's what it was. What happened to the sealing schooners like the *Sophia Sutherland* and the *Ella Johnson?* Where were the fur traders like the *Czarina,* the *Kodak,* and the *Nome?* Where was the *S. N. Castle,* the brig, *Consuelo,* and the pretty little *Lurline?* Where *was* everybody? Just where in the hell were they?

Old Brown spit tobacco juice directly into the eye of the strong trade without getting so much as a drop on himself or the *Cannibal.* He gazed at the utterly vacant space where the sky met the sea. He wanted to see a sail, any sail in addition to those above his head, although at the moment if he had a choice, he would have preferred a four-masted barque. Something with a skys'l yard to peek over the horizon first, and then come down with the wind all for-screaming, with royals pulling hard over double t'gallants. Or maybe something like the Hall brothers' pretty little *Albert* with studding sails stretching out from her yards and sweeping along the seas like the arms of an angel.

There would be men on her, by God! They would be on board because Johnny Felem collected maybe a hundred and twenty dollars per man, which proved he was the smartest boardinghouse crimp in San Francisco. He'd get them some clothes from Cohen on Stuart Street and personally heave their carcasses aboard whether they wanted to go or not. Maybe he would take them down to the "Bowhead" at the foot of Clay Street and get them drunk first, and maybe he wouldn't. It just depended on how his fight was going with Kate Johnson the Finn, who ran the rival boardinghouse on Howard Street.

There was a glint of sun on a distant wavetop and it flashed in such a way that for a moment Old Brown almost convinced himself that he had seen a sail. But the flash subsided and once more there was only emptiness.

He turned away sadly and looked at Bell, who stood half-submerged in the after companionway hatch with his arms spread out on the deckhouse top. And Old Brown thought that he didn't care what people along the water front said about Davey Bell. Maybe he did make a mistake. Maybe he did hit the bottle too hard and maybe he didn't replace gear like he should when it was ready to kill a man. Maybe he did pinch pennies and the chow was horrible, and he wouldn't go near a dockyard to spend a penny on the poor old *Cannibal*'s bottom, but he was still under sail, weren't he? He stood there in the hatch looking aft at the wake, like a skipper should, smoking his pipe and sometimes not saying a word to nobody for hours. God knows what he was thinking about most of the time, but when he did open his mouth you knew you were listening to a man. . . . and one who knew what he was talking about. He didn't kowtow to the men forward, and he didn't kick them around neither. Of course if the Union knew what went on aboard the *Cannibal* they'd keelhaul Bell, but they never could say he spared himself. And he didn't get palsy with his mate either. Davey Bell was more like the old-timers. Even when he kept his mouth shut, which was most of the time, you waited around sort of interested to see if he was going to say anything. And of course everybody knew he come up through the hawsepipe the hard way. People who said they should have left the rat guards on was wrong.

Old Brown looked at young Sweeney, who stood at the wheel. He was concentrating on his course now, because Bell was facing him and would know from the wake if he got off so much as a quarter of a point, but he still had a lot to learn. Who didn't, compared to Old Brown? And so because of his age and recognized knowledge, he ventured to speak out his thoughts and risk a frown from Bell.

—Hey, Sweeney. You a dancer?

Puzzled, Sweeney glanced up from the binnacle.

—How you mean?

—I mean do ye dance with wimmin and the like?

—Who else is there to dance with?

—I'll betcha there's a dance you never hear of.

—Yeah?

—Yer young and you think yer pretty smart, but this here dance I'm talkin' about took a real expert. It had class.

Warming to his subject, Old Brown placed one bare foot on the taffrail and made certain that Bell was listening with approval.

—I'll bet *you* never even hear of it, Cap.

—Could be.

—This here dance was performed by sailing men. . . . before anybody on this ship was born except me. I done it myself when I was Sweeney's age.

This was a lie, but Old Brown considered he might as well make the claim. He learned the directions from a British seaman when he was in a nitrate ship and the seaman learned it from his grandfather who was in the *Lightning*. It was that old.

—You want to hear how it goes?

Sweeney said,—Why not? You talk all the damn time anyway.

Seeing he had stirred their interest because even Keim moved in closer, Old Brown reached happily into his memory. He caught Keim's attention with an "Achtung! Squarehead," then took his foot off the taffrail and with the wind ruffling his white hair, struck a pose with his arms outstretched to greet an invisible woman. As he began to recite he smiled upon the air space between his arms and executed the first steps of a quadrille.

—Heave ahead and pass your adversary yardarm to yardarm. . . . regain your berth on the other tack in the same order

.... take your station in line with your pardner.... back and fill
.... face on your heel and bring up wi' your pardner....

Old Brown quickly reversed his position and faced forward.
Transferring his tobacco until it made less of a mound beneath
his cheek, he held his fingers delicately from his sides as if
clutching a wide skirt. He bowed demurely at his audience and
began to move again with mincing steps.

—Now.... she then maneuvers ahead and heaves all aback
.... she fills and shoots ahead again and pays off alongside....

Once more he reversed his pattern and swung gaily around.
He held one hand high above his shoulder with the tips of his
fingers touching.

—You then make sail in company until stern on with the
other line.... make a stern board and cast her off to shift for
herself.... regain your berth by the best means possible....
and let go your anchor!

He bowed low to his invisible partner and returned to his
place on the taffrail. The tobacco once again became a prom-
inent lump in his cheek.

—There now! What the hell do ye think of that?

Sweeney said,—If you were only a couple of years younger
I'd ask you to marry me.

David Bell said nothing. Keim emitted only a single grunt of
approval. But their guarded smiles were enough for Old Brown.
He looked away to the sea again and was content.

For a long time afterward Old Brown was lost beyond the
horizon. There was nothing to disturb his peace. The men on
the quarterdeck were silent and when Keim relieved Sweeney
at the wheel not a sound passed between them. The strength of
the trades increased as the sun rose higher and the *Cannibal*
seemed to make an almost visible effort to regain her youth. She
heeled far over in the gusts and shuddered from stem to stern
when an errant wave exploded against her starboard beam. Her
sheets and braces were bar taut as all her canvas pulled. The
taffrail log spun faster than it had since the *Cannibal* sailed
from San Francisco, and since the log registered distance made
and therefore progress, only Dak Sue, the cook, could find complaint. He leaned out of his galley house just beneath the
foremast and swore at the wind and the sea. Then he looked
back to swear more guardedly at Bell for carrying so much sail
when he should know that breakfast was in the making. But his

maledictions were carried away on a wind which blew unhindered to the coast of his native China.

From time to time the men on the quarterdeck would glance aloft at the sails and rigging, and they all knew, including Bell, that they were asking a great deal of the old *Cannibal*. Yet they were secretly proud of her response, betraying their admiration in quick little smiles. For a time they forgot about how her pump strained their backs and they ignored the condition of her gear in their game with the wind. Once a shower of spray carried all the way aft to the quarterdeck. The water sparkled on Keim's face, and Sweeney's and Old Brown's, and they only laughed. Even Bell shuddered good-humoredly as the droplets found a way down the back of his neck.

Bell was not sure why he left the relative comfort of the companionway hatch. Moving around the cabin trunk slowly, he thought, This is the kind of morning when a windjammer gets her reward. Why now, with the wind so, the *Cannibal* could show her stern to many a steamer! She is alive. . . . and I am a part of her!

Sensing her spirit as a musician might appreciate a symphony, Bell moved forward a few steps at a time. He descended from the quarterdeck and stood in the waist for a time, watching the rhythmic rise and fall of the *Cannibal*'s bow and studying the sea as it slipped swiftly along the hull. Yeah. Dragging grass, barnacles, and all, she was doing a good nine knots. . . . maybe a little better. Very satisfying, but who else could care in the same way? Only Old Brown perhaps, and Keim. Looking at the sea and the clouds still yellow in the early sun, Bell supposed that a man went to work for two reasons, pleasure and money. It was too bad about those who worked for money alone. They were cheating themselves of a morning like this when the result of work was a great deal more than money.

Then he continued forward and when he reached the foredeck, he leaned over the weather bulwark and looked down at the cutwater. And for some time he became lost in watching the *Cannibal* split the seas and send them away from her sides, foaming and sparkling in the sunlight. He watched the savage figurehead as she dipped her feet occasionally into the wavetops and without looking at Anchor he muttered, —I never thought of it before, but maybe from now on we'll call that girl Mrs. Weatherbee.

Smiling at the idea, he turned around and rested his elbows on the caprail. Anticipating more pleasure, he raised his eyes slowly. And above him he saw the great forecourse ballooned far out and pulling mightily. The sun betrayed a few holes, but just now they were unimportant. For there was the power of God and the sea. And above it the topsails, and then the t'gallants pulling. . . .

He caught his breath. For an instant his body became rigid as he stared aloft at the fore-topmast. He blinked in disbelief and a hollow feeling came to his stomach which he had not known for a long time. With every movement of the *Cannibal* the whole fore-topmast, which began some fifty feet above the deck, was bending like a giant whip! Tons of equipment depended on that spar. If it carried away. . . . as it must do any moment. . . . !

He stepped aft quickly, seeking the cause, and saw that the fore-topmast shrouds seemed slack, but that couldn't be the whole reason. Jesus! In spite of himself he watched the mast in fascination. It whipped viciously and bent as much as five feet each side of the vertical! It was going to break, it *must* break. . . . in a matter of minutes.

Half-expecting to hear a sickening crunch from aloft, he ran to the fo'c's'le hatch and yelled into the darkness.

—All hands! Smartly! Douse t'gallants and tops'ls!

The tone of his voice was such that it echoed in the darkness below and he knew that it would wake the dead. Yet there was even more power and urgency in his voice when he cupped his hands and shouted at the quarterdeck.

—Helm! Ease her off! Put her before the wind! Brown! Take the helm! Keim. . . . Sweeney. . . . slack braces! Then come forward.

As Lott, Yancy, and Uala came stumbling out of the fo'c's'le Bell saw them glance aloft and set immediately to work with halyards, buntlines, and clew lines. Good. When really needed they knew their trade.

The *Cannibal* swung slowly around until she was running down with the waves. The pressure of the wind eased as Old Brown nursed her around on the new course. And with the upper sails furled, Bell knew that some of the strain would be taken from the topmast. As the men worked in desperate silence he resisted the temptation to look aloft. Instead he concentrated on fashioning two strops of heavy rope. He was finished by the time Keim and Sweeney came forward and, looking at the ropes which were now great rings, he wondered how he could order any of the men to go aloft. Now, they were staring silently up at the fore-topmast, mouths open, and afraid. As they had every right to be, he thought. Though running before the wind eased some of the pressure aloft, it also caused the *Cannibal* to roll heavily. And with each roll the fore-topmast whipped so violently its recoil could be felt clear through to the deck.

The men knew what the rope strops were for; they must be doubled around the mast above the crosstrees and passed through their own part so that they would form two eyes. Tackles would then be hooked in the eyes and set up to form strong backstays. Only then could anyone feel reasonably sure of the *Cannibal*'s fore-topmast.

But to accomplish this task two men would have to go aloft and work against the tremendous force of the whipping mast. It would take strong men or they would be snapped off their perch as quickly as a finger could flick away a gnat. Fingering the rope strops, studying the faces of his crew, Bell knew that he could not order any of them up the mast. It would be useless anyway because a man who was thoroughly frightened would consume all his strength just hanging on.

Knowing he must go himself, he was about to ask for volunteer help when Keim stepped forward and took one of the rope strops from his hand. A look of understanding passed between them as Bell relinquished the strop. Without a word they both turned to mount the foreshrouds.

—Yancy. In the forepeak. Two tackles. . . . rig one block to the futtock shrouds each side. . . . send two blocks up to us. . . . and stand by to take the heaving end aft.

As Bell and Keim swung in to the lower ratlines, they paused a moment and looked up at the fore-topmast.

—You vatch it, Skipper. It's my fault and I don't want you be hurt.

And it might be Keim's fault in a way, Bell thought, because as bos'n it is his business to check constantly such rigging as the topmast shrouds, but then it is also my fault for asking too much of old gear.

—You watch yourself, Keim. I'd hate to lose a good bos'n.

—Vy you do this, Skipper? This is sailor's work!

—I am a sailor!

Keim shook his head and pressed his lips together as a father might scold himself for neglect. Then in silence, they began the long climb aloft.

They paused briefly when they reached the platform known as the foretop, and found that the iron cap band which held the base of the upper mast rigid had fractured on one side. For a moment Bell considered ordering Keim to remain on the relative security of the foretop. It was not his fault the iron had broken. The *Cannibal* had failed in a most vital spot, and he was the *Cannibal*. Yet before he could say anything, Keim was already continuing his climb.

On the quarterdeck, Old Brown found he could not watch them as their figures rapidly became smaller and they passed the level of the upper tops'l yard. When they fought their way into the crosstrees and he saw them shaken until they almost became a blur, he said to Sweeney, who had run aft for a length of rope,—Let me know when it's over. I swept too many good men off the deck.

Then looking at the binnacle, he concentrated on his course.

Bell and Keim had left the sound of the sea far beneath them. Here, so high in the rigging, there was only the vibrant moan of wind through a giant harp of wire and rope. They had heard it aloft in other vessels, sometimes at night when the moaning became a scream and every move a man made became the result of long thought and tremendous physical effort. It seemed ridiculous that on such a fine, sunlit morning even greater exertions were required. Once they passed the foretop they moved only inches at a time, progressing when the mast was relatively still. It was like climbing the side of a steep cliff during a violent earthquake. When they reached the crosstrees they were both bruised and nearly exhausted. They hung on to the whipping mast and gasped to regain their breath.

Far below them, the passengers gathered in the waist. They stood with their heads tilted far back, watching the diminutive figures swinging back and forth across the sky. With the tackles ready Yancy and Lott climbed to the foretop and set them so the strain would be on the futtock shrouds. Only then did Ramsay appear on deck. After he made certain there was nothing he could do for the moment, he moved around the passengers until he stood beside Charlotte King. Looking aloft, he said bitterly,—He's a fool. He'll kill himself and Keim, too.

—Why aren't you up there?

—No one bothered to call me out.

—How convenient.

—I resent that, Mrs. King. I also suggest you go aft to the quarterdeck. That mast may carry away any minute.

—I'll stay here.

When a momentary lull came in the mast's violent shaking, Bell nodded to Keim and they quickly passed the rope strops around the mast. Then, hanging on with all the strength of their legs, they each employed one arm in hauling up the heavy tackle blocks. They chanted boisterously as they heaved, gaining both strength and encouragement from the sound of their combined voices. They hooked one block into the port strop and then began all over again to heave on the other. They were forced to wait a long time for a chance to secure the second hook, but finally with the very last of their ebbing strength, they shoved it home. Below them they saw the men strain their backs on the heaving ends, and gradually the mast became rigid.

Then they rested, each with his cheek pressed against the mast, unable to speak of their relief. Bell listened to Anchor's continuous barking from below and wondered at the fear which overcame him now that the mast was relatively stable. At last he moved stiffly out of the crosstrees. The mast was safe enough for the time being. Heavier tackles could be rove later if needed. Looking at Keim's stolid face, Bell wished he could do the same rigging job on his own nerves.

—You hungry, Keim?

—Ya, Skipper.

—Let's get some breakfast then.

They descended the ratlines slowly. As he swung off the sheer pole and hit the deck, Bell almost landed on Charlotte King. He smiled wearily and said,—Pardon. I wasn't looking where I was going.

—I shouldn't have been in your way. Does that sort of thing go on very often?

—Not if we can help it.

Ramsay said,—Why didn't you wake me?

—There wasn't time.

—I'll take the rest of your watch. We may not make the same speed, but I'll try to keep things in one piece.

He turned away and as he walked aft, Bell looked at the tar and grease on his hands. And knowing Charlotte King was also looking at them he was suddenly embarrassed.

—I better go wash.

Then he saw that she was deliberately blocking his way.

—Why did you go up there, Captain? I can't help wanting to know why you didn't send one of the sailors.

—One of them was with me.

—Do you enjoy risking your neck?

—No. But once in a while it's necessary.

—If I were your wife, I don't think I'd like your being up there.

He looked at her and smiled.—You aren't my wife.

Still smiling, he moved around her carefully and walked aft.

Begins fine with strong trades. . . . starboard lower t'gallant sheet parted. Repaired.

Middle part ditto. (158) miles this day noon to noon. Latter part trades diminishing and wind backing to south.

Water in bilges 13 inches. Pumped 1 hour during dogwatch. Convinced it is bad for passengers to observe so discontinued until tonight.

Four

WITH THE EASING of the trades, the lighter clouds joined together as if exhausted from their hurried journey toward the west. They appeared to pause with the end of day and formed gigantic battlements obscuring the sun. Their bases were low and occasional rain squalls stabbed diagonally toward the water. There were crenelations in the battlements and through these the sun sent down brass shafts which seemed to penetrate the waves and instantly dyed the *Cannibal*'s sails a metallic yellow. The sea, with so much to reflect at this time of day, seemed confused, changing each moment with the sun until large areas were daubed with bronze and jet black.

All of this evening spectacle was lost upon Oliver Wiggins and the Reverend Butterfield as they paced back and forth in the *Cannibal*'s waist. For they were men who gathered excitement from their minds rather than their eyes and as a consequence they saw only the galley house, which provided one terminal for their pacing, and the break of the quarterdeck, which compelled them to turn about at the other end.

They walked together, heads bent and hands clasped behind

them, and if a rainbow had arced through the rigging they would not have seen it. Wiggins said to the Reverend Butterfield,—You, my dear sir, are bleeding from self-inflicted wounds.

Butterfield caught at his worn frock, which so flapped in the wind it almost tripped him in the *Cannibal*'s scuppers. When he recovered he said,—I'm not exactly certain what you mean by that. In fact I think I resent it. I detect irony in your voice and even more insincerity than usual.

—You are only partially a hypocrite. You have an octagonal brain which signals your bewilderment like so many heliographs. You are the one who is lost. Not me. You are forever reaching on high for a spiritual strap and obviously never finding it.

—Nonsense. My faith cannot be shaken. It only strengthens when I walk in the shadow of the Devil.

—Save the high-blown talk for your unsuspecting flock, Butterfield, or you go dry this evening.

—You promised me.

—I promised you a drink from my precious supply only if you would stick to facts and make sense. I defy you to name me one thing you have done within the past year to justify your existence. I am speaking of an action I can understand as a realist, not the vague mouthings you inflict upon the innocents who tolerate your preaching. Go ahead. Name me one single thing and you shall have your night's dollop. Otherwise I shall take the utmost pleasure in stepping on your tongue.

—Apparently you haven't heard that on Thithia the bastards are now baptized on Sunday right along with legitimate children. I was personally responsible for that, much against the advice of my superiors. I risked my career to bring that about.

—Your career! Now, Butterfield, I always thought a servant of God was supposed to be sans ambition. It never occurred to me that a churchman would buck for promotion just like any other corporate employee. I should have thought of it.

—My church is not a corporation and your suggestion is insulting.

—Is it, though? Then why be so concerned about your career when you honored the bastards? Can't the office boy save as many souls as the vice-president?

—If this voyage is long enough, Wiggins, I may be able to

extract your cynicism entirely. It is like a bad tooth in an otherwise well-formed head.

—Flattery will not guarantee your drink. Leave my teeth be.

—I will throw your unbelieving thoughts overboard like so
much garbage.

They halted in the shelter of the galley house while Wiggins
lit a cigarette. Butterfield tore a thread from his soiled frock and
made a figure-eight design with it across two fingers. Then he
peered around the corner of the galley house at the sun and
said,—I thought you promised when the sun was below the
yardarm. Well, it is.

—Patience, Saint Butterfield. Why can't you be like a Buddhist priest and learn patience?

—Because I am not a priest, Buddhist or otherwise. Or a
saint. Supper is almost ready and we won't have time. I can
smell it.

—I can smell it, too, and wish I couldn't. But I give you the
grim reminder, old boy, that I have only one jug. That's all the
girls could smuggle aboard in spite of their love for me. We
must ration ourselves severely.

He set off walking again and Butterfield fell in step with him.
They paced in silence to the break of the quarterdeck and as
they turned about Wiggins saw that Butterfield had made a
complicated design with the thread across his fingers. Now he
was fussing with it anxiously, studying it through his clouded
glasses, and holding it up to the wind to see if it would make
any sound. Wiggins smiled and said,—You are really in a bad
way, aren't you?

Turning the thread design one way and the other in the
wind, Butterfield said,—I am being patient.

—Keep your mind off things for another five minutes and we
shall have a session with the jug. Shall I tell you about the girls?

—No. I don't want to hear any more about your girls.

—You are drooling, Reverend. Why don't you ever polish
your glasses?

—I never think of them.

—Well, you should, and maybe you'd see what the world
looks like. Furthermore I could be sure your eyes light up like I
think they do when I mention the girls.

—I have utterly no interest in them. Fornication is a
dalliance of the weak.

—I should say it is an indulgence of the strong. You know, old boy, I like the way you roll out the word "fornication." It is positively frightening, like the voice of doom.

—It is, and always has been, a primary sin.

—Then why are you so interested? Why have you stopped fiddling with that thread?

—Sin is interesting.

—Bravo. That's the first sensible thing you ever said. I shall quote you.

—Your Rotuma girls were no better than harlots.

—I forgave them.

—*You* forgave them!

—Yes. In the absence of any higher authority, I forgave their tendency to enjoy life. But I could find no one to forgive me for envying them.

Butterfield looked up at the sky and said,—Give me strength!

He led off this time, as they resumed their pacing.

—Tell me, Butterfield, is there such a thing as a secondary sin?

—All sin is recognized in the commandments. I suggest you reread them.

—How about desire? Is that covered?

—Thou shall not covet. . . .

—I don't mean that. I am thinking of the desire for gain. I cannot seem to experience it and if there's a spare sin around I should hate to think I was missing anything.

—Look at that sun.

—Nervous, Pastor?

—Stop calling me pastor. I just asked you to look at the sun.

—You mean with regard to its position?

—Yes. Possession is making you a tyrant.

Wiggins looked solemnly at the sun.

—Tyrants are created by slaves, but come along. I'll quench your thirst.

—To your cabin?

—No. I don't trust that chap Hutton who shares my cabin. I have temporarily cached it behind the pig pen.

—It would be safer in my cabin. I'm alone in there, you know.

Wiggins looked at him with a tolerant smile and placed a hand on his thin shoulder.

—Thanks so much. I trust those pigs.

Dak Sue rang the supper bell promptly at six o'clock and for the first time since the sailing from Suva all of the passengers appeared in the dining saloon. They were affable and elaborately polite to each other as Bell stood at the head of the table and pointed out the seats they would occupy for the remainder of the passage. He wore a freshly laundered blue shirt for the occasion and tried in every way he knew to appear the genial host. Yet with all the passengers watching him expectantly, he was miserably uncomfortable as he said,—You might as well get used to your seats because that's where you'll take nourishment for the next two months. If you like something special for breakfast, ask Dak Sue. If he has it, you'll get it at your place. We share and share alike the other meals. Arrive on time and you'll always eat. . . . otherwise maybe not.

Since the seats were bolted to the deck, he could not pull out the one on his left for Ida Morris. He would have liked to do so because in a way, he thought, she was rather like a frail Mrs. Weatherbee. But he placed his hand on the back of the chair and she recognized his gesture with a little bow. He seated Feodor Morris next to her and indicated that Oliver Wiggins, who had even combed his hair for the occasion and had buttoned his pink shirt all the way to his neck, should take the next chair.

—That there chair at the other end. . . . will you sit there, Mr. Hutton?

He wanted to be as far as possible from Harry Hutton. Two months could be a long time and if the winds became contrary, it could be much longer. Hutton himself seemed pleased. He sat down abruptly as if fearing the Reverend Butterfield, who waited next to him, might usurp his place. Ethel Peacock, resplendent in an orange dress which clashed explosively with her hair, sat down in the chair next to Hutton without waiting for an invitation. She looked pleadingly at Bell until he said,— That's fine, Miss Peacock. I intended you should sit there. Reverend, will you occupy the next seat?

Butterfield sat down beside Ethel Peacock, and suddenly they all fell silent as they stared at the remaining chair on Bell's right. Then moving through the silence, Charlotte King approached the chair.

—I take it. . . . this one is for me?

—If you will, Mrs. King.

Bell reddened as he placed his hand on the arm of the chair and she slipped into it. Oliver Wiggins twisted his mouth into a thoughtful smile and murmured,—Jolly good planning.

—There will be times when I can't eat with you. In that case Mr. Ramsay will occupy my seat unless for some reason we are both required on deck. In any event, don't ever wait for us.

He sat down and picked up his napkin, which was already slightly soiled. He unrolled it, taking all the time he could to cover his embarrassment, and he was greatly relieved when Butterfield broke the stillness.

—I hesitate to interfere with the routine of your ship, Captain, but wouldn't it be appropriate if grace were said at least once a day?

Wiggins said,—Oh bother!

—Why, yeah. Why not? Will you do the honors, Reverend?

So, emitting exhalations of cocoanut brew which reached the length of the table, Butterfield peered above his spectacles for a moment, then closed his eyes and said grace. When he finished and they all joined in a mumbled amen, Wiggins reached for a piece of johnnycake and said,—Now having paid our respects—and next time cut it shorter, Butterfield—let us all return to our naturally barbaric state.

The stew which Dak Sue served out of a large metal pot was still flavored with fresh produce of the land and so it had not yet acquired the hopeless monotony of true seafare. There was also more than enough of it and this so pleased them all, they sighed and became mellow as they refilled their plates. Even Oliver Wiggins joined in the general feeling of well-being and told of his life in a German prison camp after being taken at Ypres.

—After that, all I wanted was freedom. . . . and as you must have observed by now, that is practically all I have. I am convinced that freedom is a personal state of mind rather than a political condition. Since the Germans seem quite incapable of acting or thinking individually, I doubt if they will ever achieve it.

Then both Ida and Feodor Morris found pleasure in comparing certain aspects of the German language with Hebrew. Much to Bell's surprise, Harry Hutton paused in his absorption with his plate and spoke so familiarly of German operas that he was obviously an authority on the subject. As tea was poured, Ethel Peacock insisted on singing a folksong in German and since it was very short, she finished amid genuine applause.

Bell found it easier to remain silent throughout the meal. He would have liked the conversation to flow along lines which were more familiar to him; then he might be less aware of Charlotte King at his side. But as always, he hesitated to interrupt people who seemed to have a formal education. Wiggins now, he must certainly have gone to a university of some kind in his native England, and Butterfield, of course, and maybe Harry Hutton. The conversation became heavily mixed with German phrases and he was desperately trying to follow it when he heard Charlotte King ask him a question. But her voice was so low he could not hear her above the others.

—I asked if you've been at sea all your life, Captain.

—Since I was thirteen.

—Isn't that rather young to begin?

He found suddenly that he wanted to tell her about dragging his father out of every bar in the Potrero. . . . and how he finally disappeared and was never seen again. Otherwise how would she understand why a thirteen-year-old wound up at sea? And looking at her now, he very much wanted her to understand.

—I really sort of fell into the sea. I drove a butcher wagon in South San Francisco and my boss had an interest in a bay scow schooner. They used to deliver hay and lumber and a lot of other stuff down to San Francisco from the Sacramento Valley. I don't know exactly how it happened but after a while them scow schooners looked as pretty to me as the *Dashing Wave*.

—The *Dashing Wave* was a ship?

—Yeah. A full clipper back in the 'fifties and she was fast right up to the end of her time in the coal trade. I saw her one day, just before she was cut down to a barge, and she did something to me. So I talked myself into the job as ship's boy on the *Hermine Blum*. . . . she was a bay scow. . . . and I never been ashore more than two months at a time since. Later on I worked on the coast schooners and finally went deep-water. Sounds like a pretty dull life, doesn't it?

He knew she was deliberately drawing him out, and he thought, What difference does it make? I can't sit here like a dummy all through supper and she don't have to listen.

—It sounds extremely interesting. . . . but it must be very hard on your wife. She must never see you.

He saw now that she was completely ignoring the others. And there was a mischievous smile about her eyes, half-mocking, as if she knew exactly what he was going to say. And suddenly the photo in her passport flashed across his mind and he wondered if what he had thought was sadness in the photo was really wisdom. He took his pipe out of his shirt pocket and filled it while he waited through a temporary lull in the conversation at the other end of the table. Finally he spoke softly so the others would not hear.

—Well, that wife of mine sort of goes along with me, Mrs. King. She happens to be the *Cannibal*.

—I thought so.

—What did you do? Ask one of the crew?

—I didn't have to. You give yourself away, Captain. I could see it in your manner and your eyes. I played an unforgivable feminine trick on you when I first asked if you were married. It's useless on a man who really has a wife. If he lies and says no, he's always unconvincing because he goes out of his way to explain why he could never be bothered with a wife and why he can do just as he pleases. He has been waiting for the question, anyway, and he is ready with his special set of answers which aren't so special because they all boil down to the same thing. But the question knocks a single man off balance and while he fumbles for words, he's wide-open for a moment. That's when a clever woman can see inside the man.

—You scare me. I got enough troubles.

—See, now you're embarrassed. A man with a wife would not be. But you're in love, Captain. That's also very plain indeed.

—If you mean the *Cannibal*, you're wrong. She's a floating headache.

—The more you deny it, the more you convince me. You also need a haircut.

—You can sure change subjects in a hurry, Mrs. King. I have trouble keeping up with you.

—Why don't you get one? Can't you relax your dignity long enough to let one of your men play barber?

—It's not a matter of dignity. It's more separation. The more a ship's master keeps his personal life to himself the easier it is to have his orders obeyed. The men understand that and they prefer things that way.

—Meaning you can't be a human being?

—It makes my job easier if nobody on board knows it.

He tried to laugh, but he found it difficult. He could not remember when he had ever sounded like such a dunce. It had been a great mistake to seat this Mrs. King so close. Talking to her was like trying to find a spar buoy in a fog. She should be down by Oliver Wiggins, whose way with words was more her style. But the only alternate was Ethel Peacock, God forbid!

As he toyed nervously with his pipe, she watched him a moment and said,—I like you, Captain Bell. I like you very much.

She made no attempt to lower her voice and he was certain everyone at the table must have heard her. But now a heated discussion of Germanic literature was in progress, and Feodor Morris had some definite opinions on Schiller which appeared to be exactly the opposite of Butterfield's. If they would talk about Dickens I might join them, Bell thought, but he had never heard of a writer named Schiller. Mrs. Weatherbee must have slipped up somehow. Charlotte King said,—Do you have a pair of scissors in your cabin?

—Yeah.

—Then could I invade your sanctum and cut your hair? I'll promise to do a good job. . . . at least it will look better than it does now.

Bell was astonished. For the ten years he had sailed the *Cannibal,* there had never been a woman in his cabin. . . . or any passenger, male or female. The crew would not have thought to enter it and even Ramsay seldom ventured inside unless it was absolutely necessary. There had been a few customs inspectors who needed persuasion, and a surveyor when the tonnage was changed. Before the mortgage was paid off the Chinaman would spend some time in the cabin looking over the account books when the *Cannibal* made Manzanillo, but now he would have no right or interest. Bell thought of the bottle on top of the piano and his work clothes thrown over the rumpled bunk, and for a fleeting moment he wondered what Ramsay would think if he knew there was a woman in his cabin. He looked down the table at the other passengers, still arguing endlessly, and made a sudden decision. He swung around in his chair and stood up.

70

—I can't guarantee Anchor won't take a bite out of you. He's not used to company.

Their departure from the table went almost unheeded except for Oliver Wiggins who raised one blond eyebrow and said,— Bless me. . . . Samson and Delilah in the old curiosity shop! But the others were so involved in the Treaty of Versailles and its consequences, they failed to hear him.

Bell preceded her through the passageway and opened the door to his cabin. Anchor growled ominously as he saw Charlotte King, but she knelt to soothe him and in a moment he was perfectly quiet. Bell turned up the lamp over his desk and fumbled with the wick a long time, mainly, he realized, because he couldn't think of anything else to do. How did you begin? How did you start finding things out about a woman like Mrs. King who seemed to say exactly what she pleased?

—Don't be so shy, Captain. The operation will be a success.

Bell was suddenly aware that the cabin smelled strongly of pipe smoke. He opened the after porthole and hastily put away the shirt and pants which lay across his bunk. He began an extensive search for his shears although he knew very well they were in the second drawer of his desk. He said uncertainly,—Please sit down.

He lit the large lamp which hung from the cabin center beam and he thought the noise of the match sounded like a ship scraping along a wharf. She was so quiet he turned to look at her and found that the lamps shone on her in such a way she appeared almost unreal. The shade of the larger lamp created a division of brilliance which placed her body in light and left her face in shadow. But the smaller desk lamp reflected as two points of fire in her eyes and he could not look away from them.

She said,—No. You sit down. The barber stands.

Waiting motionless in the light, she seemed to create a spell. He watched her lips part in a smile as he continued his half-hearted search for the scissors. She knows damn well I can put my hands on those scissors in ten seconds, he thought. But she'll stand there and let me pretend to look for them as long as I want, and laugh inside. The realization so annoyed him, he went directly to the second drawer in the desk and took out the shears. He held them toward her and said,—I guess I better put a towel around my neck.

—I'll fix it.

She went to the washbasin, took down a towel, and made a pass like a matador. She said,—Sit down and relax.

Bell eased unhappily into his desk chair. She moved behind him, and glancing at the after porthole he could see the men by the wheel, Ramsey, Lott, and Yancy. There was still just enough light in the sky to illuminate their features and he wondered which man would have nerve enough to mention his new haircut first. By God, he'd do double time at the pump!

—This will have to be quick. I relieve Ramsay at eight bells.

—It won't take long. I suppose you know about your bald spot.

—I sure do.

—Does it bother you?

—I never gave it much thought.

—It's rather distinguished.

He grunted as the shears began to snip along the back of his neck. She passed her fingers through his hair and they seemed to linger. . . . or did they? It was a most pleasant sensation, but he said,—Kindly hurry it up, Mrs. King.

—Yessir.

—Aye, sir.

—Very well. Aye, sir.

There was a long silence while she worked diligently. Her movements became so soothing he had difficulty keeping his eyes open. Finally she laid down the shears and began to massage the back of his neck.

—No extra charge for this.

—I'll have to admit it feels good.

—How far are we from the Hawiian Islands?

—Two thousand miles. . . . roughly.

—Are we near any land?

—Well, the Phoenix Islands are to the northeast. . . . tomorrow the Ellice group will be to the westward and all next week the Gilberts will be to the westward.

—Will we see any land?

—I doubt it. We might pick up Nui Atoll or Arorae in a day or so. If we do, I'll let you know. Oh, I almost forgot. . . . you don't care about islands, do you?

—I want to see Mexico.

—You will. God willing.

—Are you a very religious man, Captain?

—Maybe not in the way of most people. . . . but any seaman is, whether he admits it or not. All you got to do is get good and scared a couple of times, or maybe even once, and you start looking around for somebody to hear your prayers. You get awful sincere in a hurry.

—It's hard to picture you as being scared.

—You should see me in a blow with a lee shore licking its chops.

—I think I would like to. . . . once, anyway. But I wonder if you know what it's really like to be terrified.

Bell closed his eyes as Montague Reef came swirling across his mind. He saw the people in the water again, and he heard their ghostlike screaming through the fog. He stiffened and tried to forget her question.

—Relax, Captain. Something the matter?

—No, nothing. . . . I was just thinking it's almost eight bells.

—So we won't see any land all the way to Mexico?

—Not likely. If the trades back around we might possibly make French Frigate Shoal or Necker Island in the Hawaiian group. . . . hardly a chance, though.

—Good.

Her hands fell away from his neck and she patted his shoulders just as the saloon clock struck eight bells. Bell rose quickly from the chair.

—Thanks. I'm late. One thing I won't stand for is a man late relieving his watch. So I can't do it myself. . . . even this one, which is the easiest.

He went quickly to the head of his bunk and took down his cap. He smashed it on his head and started for the door. He opened the door and stepped into the passageway. Just before he turned away he said,—Stay here awhile if you like. There's some books. Read any one you want.

—Captain. Come back here.

He hesitated uncertainly. Damn the woman. He was already late. Ramsay would give him that superior look.

—With that towel still around your neck, you'll have trouble with your dignity.

He looked down and saw that in his haste he had forgotten the towel. He yanked it from his collar and threw it across the cabin. Then, smiling sheepishly, he turned away.

73

Ramsay was waiting beside the binnacle when Bell hoisted Anchor up through the after hatch. He said,—Good evening.

—Good evening, Ramsay.

Bell was damned if he would call him Mr. Ramsay. The *Cannibal* was a little barquentine, not a full-rigged ship, and if Ramsay wanted to be called Mr., he could join the Navy. He stepped on deck, saw the already retreating figures of Lott, Yancy, and Uala, and said,—Sorry about being late.

—It's breezing up again. More to the easterly. I doused the outer jib because it's starting to rip at the clew. Seems we have chronic jib trouble.

—Set Keim or Brown to work on it in the morning. Anything else?

—No.

—You're relieved then.

But Ramsay did not descend the hatch. Instead he waited while Bell checked the course Old Brown held at the wheel. When Bell turned to face forward, Ramsay was still standing by the hatch. Something was wrong when a man hung about after he was relieved.

—What's on your mind, Ramsay? Why don't you sleep while you can?

—I was wondering about our leak. So far we only pumped an hour today.

—Did you sound the well?

—No. I rather gathered the idea you preferred doing so yourself.

—I have no objections to your doing it. You are in command of this vessel when I'm off watch.

—I appreciate that.

Ramsay was silent for a moment. He glanced at the horizon, which was now clearly defined against the light of a rising moon. Before he spoke again he looked at Old Brown at the wheel, and then at Sweeney and Keim, who were huddled forward in the lee of the galley house. Keeping his voice low, he chose his words carefully.

—I am accustomed to a sound ship.

—So am I.

Bell took a step nearer to him and belligerently jammed his fists down in his pockets. He had a very good idea of what Ramsay would say. He had been waiting for it, and he thought. . . . My fists are better off in my pockets.

—I suppose it would be heresy to point out that the *Cannibal* has seen better days.

—Haven't we all?

—I'd like to make a suggestion if it isn't too much out of order.

—My mates have always been free to speak their minds. Why don't you stop backing and filling and let me know what's on yours?

—I was thinking it might be a good idea to put in to Honolulu.

—Why?

—If we hit heavy weather in the westerlies, the leak can become a lot worse. I hardly consider our spars or sails in condition to haul a half-submerged vessel. I'm simply trying to look ahead. We're shorthanded and if the men are at the pump all the time, they can't manage sail. They're grumbling already.

—You ever know a sailor who couldn't find something to grumble about?

—If we put in to Honolulu we can send a diver down or haul out and make sure it isn't something serious. All hands would be a lot easier. . . . to say nothing of the passengers.

—What do the passengers know about it?

—They're not stupid. They can make it very rough for you if anything happens.

Bell took his time. He turned his back on Ramsay, walked aft to glance at the binnacle, and then with his fists still jammed in his pockets, returned to the hatchway. He looked at Ramsay a moment in silence, cocking his head from side to side, and examined his handsome face as if he had never seen it before. By God! What kind of sailor was this Downeaster? Didn't he know there were times at sea when you *had* to take a *little* gamble?

Sure, Downeasters were fine seamen. None better. But the days when everything about a sailing ship could be perfect were gone. Ramsey's grandfather might have been able to go over his ship with white gloves and not discover a speck of dirt. . . . and there were Downeasters who had been known to do just that, but those men were long ashore now. . . . sitting in their rocking chairs. . . . dreaming of new white canvas against the sky instead of the patchwork rags which were all the *Cannibal* could afford.

—Ramsay. . . . dammit. . . .

He should relax and admit that he was a sorry substitute for his ancestors. Maybe it wasn't all his fault, because you couldn't go to a fancy-dress ball in dungarees, but, Jesus, was there any reason to be ashamed of dungarees if they were the only thing you had to wear?

These days you had to believe in your ship and especially yourself if you even hoped to win. And just because a man had served in larger ships than the *Cannibal* didn't give him the answers to everything.

Bell suddenly wanted to go down to his cabin and get a mint, but Mrs. King would still be there and for the moment he wanted to forget about her. Why didn't this proper son-of-a-bitch go get drunk himself and maybe it would do something for him? Right now. I would be glad to take his watch, he thought. . . . take two or three of his watches in a row, just to see him without a shave, or his face cut up from busting into furniture, or his eyes all bleary and sorry! Then for once maybe. . . . at least while a hangover was stirring his soup he'd grow up and stop thinking the world was the way it used to be.

Bell debated whether he should say anything at all and then decided he would make one more attempt to teach Ramsay the facts of life. He tried very hard to keep a patient tone in his voice.

—Look here, maybe your steel Downeasters were dry as a bone, but I've sailed in a lot of craft that leaked worse than the *Cannibal*. If I thought we were going to the bottom, I'd have put back into Suva and careened her. You know as well as I do it's a good fourteen days easterly bent to Honolulu from here. And it could be a lot more. But maybe there's something you don't know. . . . or haven't fully considered. Unless I can make this a profitable trip I'll have to stand by for scrap offers. Divers cost money. So does hauling out. But not much compared to Honolulu Port charges, a tug, wharfage. . . . food for crew and passengers. . . . agent charges, reprovisioning, and God knows what other charge if we have to go to a shipyard. We're not a rich tea-clipper and this isn't eighteen fifty. We're a tired little barquentine and it's nineteen twenty-seven. There's such a thing as steamships, and they're still hungry. That leaves us with two choices. . . . give up and hit the beach forever or keep on sailing in spite of everything. I intend to keep sailing as long as I can hold on to a spar and a piece of canvas. If you can't stand living by your wits, I suggest you go into steam and be damned to you. Now. Any more questions?

—You're a very stubborn man, Captain.

Although he was smiling, Bell was certain he intended no praise.

—I have to be.

—Perhaps. But you're pushing your luck. . . . and mine.

—You asked for work when you came aboard.

—I did. But I've never cared for swimming, so I might as well tell you now that I'll pay off when we make Manzanillo. . . . if we ever do.

—Fair enough.

Bell was about to tell him that it would almost be worth putting into Honolulu if he would promise to jump ship, when they both heard the sound of a piano. There were only a few chords, followed by a hint of melody, and then silence again. Ramsay looked down at Bell's cabin, then slowly turned back and smiled knowingly.

—Very attractive woman, Captain.

Bell jammed his fists down even harder in his pockets. What the hell did Charlotte King mean by playing his piano? The whole ship would hear it. He resolved that he would not invite her to his cabin again under any circumstances.

—What about it?

—Nothing. I don't know for sure, but I'd swear I've seen her before.

—So?

—It isn't easy to forget such a person. Is she an American citizen?

—Yeah.

—I thought so. Her accent is peculiar. . . . almost British.

—She was married to a New Zealander.

—Where was her passport issued?

—I haven't looked because I wasn't interested. And I don't see how it's any of your business.

—You will look. Good night, Captain.

Ramsay turned and decended through the companionway hatch. At the bottom of the steps, he paused thoughtfully, then entered his cabin and left the door open. His cabin was directly opposite Bell's and less than half the size although it held two bunks. These were set against the bulkhead fore and aft. The forward bunk remained from the more bountiful days when the *Cannibal* carried a second mate. Now Ramsay used it to store his scrimshaw. There was a figurine carved from driftwood which he had been working on ever since he came to the Pacific, the face of a South Sea god carved in ivory, and an intricate rolling-ball contrivance which was carved from a single piece of Burma teak and could be used as a level. All of the carvings had sharply opposing angles, and the surface planes were blocked out to balance precisely, as if their creator was more concerned with geometry than art.

There was a photo of Ramsay's mother on the after bulkhead, his mate's certificate, and two smaller photos of his father and brother at one side of the small washstand. His toilet articles were neatly arranged in a carved box of his own workmanship and it was hung on two brass hooks just beside the basin. His bunk was made military fashion with the top sheet turned down exactly six inches. There was a calendar on the forward bulkhead with the dates crossed off, each cross being of exactly the same size. A single book, Bowditch's *American Practical Navigator,* leaned at an angle in the porthole scupper and spoiled the otherwise antiseptic appearance of the cabin. As soon as he had lit the lamp over the washstand, Ramsay straightened the book. He was pleased. After months of association with Pacific seamen, he had managed to maintain his Downeast ways. He would never, he thought, use the sea as an excuse to live like a pig.

He took off his cap and hung it carefully on a brass hook above the washstand mirror. Then he washed his hands, scrubbing at them until they were immaculate. And while he scrubbed and studied his face in the mirror, he hummed softly, trying to repeat the melody he had heard on the piano. There was something to that melody. . . . more than a few ordinary bars of music. It was jazz and yet not so. . . . perhaps stolen from a classic. Trying unsuccessfully to recapture the tune, Ramsay was certain of only one thing. Somewhere, and it couldn't have been so long ago, he had heard the melody before.

That tune and Mrs. King? He tried to relate them, and when

he failed, it annoyed him because all of the Ramsays were noted for their well-ordered minds. He glanced at the photo of his mother and remembered that she had never once neglected to send a greeting card on the most distant Ramsay cousin's birthday. His father was of like mind, a man of conviction, and if he looked severe in the photo it was because he thought fathers should look severe and people who smiled for photographers were grinning idiots. He had not been master of a Sewall ship for nothing, and he had retired a fairly wealthy man. Ramsay thought of Bell in a Sewall ship and smiled. He would not have lasted ten minutes before he was sent packing forward, where he belonged. Looking at his father's portrait, Ramsay said aloud,—I apologize, sir, for serving under such a miserable clown. But I doubt if it will continue for very long.

Brother Marshall was a true Ramsay also. In Boothbay, Maine, where he now had a respectable dental practice, he was known as a man who kept his appointments to the minute. There were no magazines in his office because there was no need for them. There was never any waiting. There was a saying in the family, and Ramsay thought it was probably still being quoted in the neat house where they still lived on Elm Street, "Intelligence should never be handicapped by disorder. Details are important. They make the whole." Ramsay did not know how or where the saying had originated, but he considered it a very good one.

He was still trying to reconstruct the tune when he heard the door across the passageway open and close. He turned quickly away from the mirror and pretended to shut his own door.

—Good evening, Mrs. King.

—Hello.

She held a book under her arm. Ramsay tried to read the title, then decided he didn't care. It would only be some of Bell's tripe anyway. A detail, but not an important detail save for the mental notation that Bell was being about as clever as an ox if he thought a few books could make him attractive to any woman. Didn't the man know he looked like a sea lion who had lost a fight to a shark? She started forward along the passageway.

—I wish you had played more, Mrs. King.

—You wouldn't feel that way if I had.

—It was such an agreeable tune. What's the name of it?

She looked at him steadily for a moment, and he thought he saw a flash of anger in her eyes. They were green again. Good. It was a detail worth remembering.

—I don't know. I wasn't aware I had even tried a tune.

She turned down the passageway and Ramsay watched her balance against the *Cannibal*'s heel until she passed into the light of the saloon. He studied her walk and found it extremely satisfying. It was an easy, almost animal-like walk, and yet somehow it lacked confidence. Closing his door slowly, Ramsay thought about her walk and wondered how much it would change if he could see her on a street wearing high heels.

	Water in Bilges	Hours pumped
Oct. 16	12 inches	One
Oct. 17	14 inches	Two
Oct. 18	14 inches	Two
Oct. 19	17 inches	Three

Fortunately salt water does not damage copra.
David Bell—Master.

Five

BELL WENT FORWARD to look at the pigs. Their pens were built of Bursu wood and he had often wondered if there was not some especially succulent flavor to the Hawaiian saplings since the pigs were forever gnawing at them. The inevitable result was a loose pig or a drowned pig, depending on the weather.

He found the pigs asleep. Studying them in the moonlight, he almost envied them, for it seemed that true sleep had become only a memory. If it wasn't a leak, or breaking gear, it was the freight price of copra to keep a man's mind a regular battlefield. Noah may have had his troubles with the Ark, he probably carried pigs. . . . but did he have cockroaches? And now Ramsay looked like trouble. As long as he kept his complaints to himself it was of no matter, but he probably wouldn't. A word here and there to the crew, so easily done when he had the watch, could start a lot of grumbling. . . . the kind that was hard to handle. Yancy, for example, was a first-class sea lawyer, and Ramsay would only have to drop a hint for him to start talking. He could persuade the men into almost anything short of mutiny and the only reason he wouldn't attempt that was because Yancy and the men were too smart.

Bell thought of his own days in the forecastle and knew how easily a sailor could defy an order without risking charges. A sailor could sprain his back. No pulley-hauley then. A sailor could say that he was sorry as hell but he had too much sun and going aloft made him dizzy. Then what? You kicked him up the ratlines knowing damn well he wouldn't fall, but he would scream like a petrel that he was being persecuted, and if he was a good enough actor the others would start believing him. Sailors were children. They believed in all manner of ancient superstitions and taboos and nothing would drive them out of their heads. A hat on a bunk was bad luck. . . . so was losing a bucket or a swab overboard. A serpent or a tattooed dragon brought good luck. A rooster tattooed on the right foot would keep a man from drowning. A parson on board was a guarantee of contrary winds. Never hand anything through a ladder. You did not sail from port on Friday or disaster was inevitable. You scratched the foremast for wind. If someone fell from the rigging and got himself killed his ghost stayed aboard. You did not kill a porpoise. Whistling for wind only brought bad weather. You did not attempt to hook an albatross or in any conceivable way annoy him unless you were in the doldrums. There, for some strange reason, it was permissible. Cape pigeons were the souls of lost seamen.

All of these things and half a hundred others Bell could think of influenced a sailor. He could make himself happy or unhappy according to his whim, or the signs and portents he saw in the sky. These were most easily played upon by men who also knew them. . . . perhaps. . . . perhaps men like Ramsay? No. He wouldn't go that far.

Bell left the pigs and went to the weather bulwark where he could escape their odor. He turned his back to the wind and lit his pipe. On a ship, more than anywhere, the time to stop trouble was before it began. A ship was a civilization within herself, and though the citizens changed every few months, for a time they were completely dependent on each other. It was more so in the *Cannibal* with no machinery, barely enough men to sail her, and a certain call of all hands in even a minor emergency. Ramsay, of course, had a right to his opinion and at least some excuse to be concerned. All things being equal, the *Cannibal* might normally proceed to Honolulu and be hauled in a shipyard. But all things were not equal. This was a fight for survival.

Bell turned around and chuckled at the moon. Wait until Ramsay fried a few weeks on the beach in Manzanillo! The *Cannibal* would look like a luxury liner to him and he'd be begging for a job in some really rotten old schooner bound up the Gulf. And he just might sign on with a *really* stubborn skipper . . . . the kind who believed in the pilot book, which said that the only way to windward up the Gulf was to hug the Lower California side. Ramsay could then chew his fingers to bits while they tacked back and forth. . . . maybe forever. If he was lucky enough to land a berth as an officer he'd have crew troubles the like of which he'd never seen. His crew would be the scum from the gold fields and the jail, and they would be so full of tequila they wouldn't be able to stand up, let alone know which end of the ship went first. It would all serve him right. . . . but that wasn't solving the problems in the *Cannibal*. If Ramsay had any notions about persuading the crew he would have to be steered clear of them. To begin with there would have to be some explanation for this damn leak! The passengers might swallow any story, but Ramsay and the crew were going to need a logical reason to keep them in line.

Bell searched his memories of leaking ships. Only recently, Fred Klebingat in the *Fisherman* was driven almost crazy by a persistent leak. But that was caused by a sand hole in a seacock casting, and the Nova Scotians who built the *Fisherman* drilled the defect out and tapped it with a plug instead of condemning the whole shebang. Typical of some Nova Scotians. There were times when they slapped ships together up there with ten-year wood and it had done a lot of damage to their reputation. It happened on the Pacific Coast too when they were building in a hurry. But there were no sea cocks in the *Cannibal*.

The schooner *Melrose* damn near went to the bottom with a bad leak caused by some careless landsman. She lay to a wharf that was under repair. . . . Vancouver. Was it five or six years ago? No matter.

Instead of hauling the rotted piles ashore, the workmen simply dropped them in the water. . . . and of course one would have an iron pin sticking out of the top. It stuck in the mud and when the tide ebbed the *Melrose* settled down on the pile and the pin drove right through her hull. They had good steam-power pumps on the *Melrose*, which was a hell of a lot better than the *Cannibal*'s old contraption, and a good thing. . . . because they didn't find the true cause of the leak until they reached Australia.

Bell looked at the moon on the water and tried for a moment to forget about the leak. Dak Sue might lose his false teeth again. That would at least be a diversion because when Dak Sue lost his teeth everything stopped in the *Cannibal*. It had happened three times since sailing from San Francisco. . . . and as far as Dak Sue was concerned, no teeth. . . . no food. At night, Dak Sue might put them anywhere and since he could swear fluently in six different languages when he misplaced his teeth, all hands lay on the job to keep him quiet. The last time breakfast was held up two hours until Sweeney found the teeth in a soup tureen.

Bell sighed. It was better than thinking about the leak.

It couldn't be the scarfed keel. That didn't make sense. How about a planking butt somewhere beneath the water line? Or several of them. . . . each separating a little? All of the *Cannibal*'s planks were fastened with spikes, but in addition they were held to the frames by so-called tree nails. These were long plugs, fashioned of black locust because that wood did not weep. They were driven through holes which penetrated clear through planking, frames, and ceiling. They were wedged vertically both inside and outside the hull and cut off flush. They became part of the wooden hull itself and had a certain amount of elasticity as the *Cannibal* worked with the seas. Maybe? In 1921 the plugs cost fifteen cents apiece before they were driven. After the war some shipbuilders were not too particular, and when they could get away with it they drove dummy tree nails, which were only a small piece on the outside and inside. Old Mathew Turner would never stand for such workmanship, but maybe when the Chinaman first owned the *Cannibal* he was bilked by some shipyard, or was just trying to economize. He had never said anything about it, but why should he? It would have happened long before Davey Bell stepped foot on her deck. Or it could have been the former owner. . . . the one who placed the piano on board. The piano!

In his preoccupation with the leak, Bell found that he had temporarily forgotten about Charlotte King. He wondered if she had left his cabin and gone to her own. He looked aft to see if she had come up on deck, but a cloud passed over the moon and he could not identify the figures on the quarterdeck. It occurred to him that he knew almost nothing of Charlotte King and, he thought, I would like to know. For a change I would like to think about something besides the *Cannibal*. He rubbed the back of his head where the hair had been cut and walked thoughtfully aft toward the quaterdeck. She had spirit, that woman. She might have talent for making me feel uncomfortable, but it's beginning to be a pleasure.

Half-hoping she might still be in his cabin, he mounted the steps to the quarterdeck and saw that he must pass two figures sitting on top the after-cabin trunk. It was Hutton and Ethel Peacock.

He hesitated at the top of the steps as he heard Hutton say,—I think you're wrong, Ethel.

—Good evening.

—Good evening, Captain. Nice moon.

—Yeah. It is.

Bell passed them and continued aft toward the wheel. Didn't Hutton and Ethel Peacock ever go to sleep? It was almost time to start pumping again and it would be just as well if they weren't sitting there looking at the moon while the men cussed their hearts out.

Harry Hutton looked after Bell's retreating figure and then turned back to the woman who sat beside him.

—I can't see any reason why she shouldn't go to his cabin, Ethel. . . . and anyway what could they have in common? Bell is only a sailor and I'm not sure he's a very good one at that. Mrs. King is a cultured woman. . . . not like you, of course, but the idea of her going for Bell is ridiculous.

—She played the piano.

—How do you know it wasn't him playing?

—We would have heard it before. I never even knew he had a piano in there. After all, I share a cabin with your fine lady. I wouldn't put anything past her.

—Now, Ethel. . . . sometimes you're too hard on people. You can't expect every woman to match your standards. You're not possibly a little jealous, are you?

—Jealous! Of a strumpet?

—Now please! . . . . Ethel! You're not making sense again.

Remember you asked me to warn you when you weren't making sense. . . . and well, I'm doing it. Just take everything as quietly as you can on this trip and then when we get back to the States we'll have a long talk with the right doctors and you won't be so nervous. You're just going through change of life and you've got to realize it. Give that beautiful imagination of yours a rest and a year from now you can share it with your audiences.

—You're talking me into an insane asylum.

—Please don't say things like that, Ethel.

—You think there's something wrong with me.

—I only think you need a rest.

—Well, you keep hinting it.

—Hinting at what?

—That maybe I'm not. . . . just right. Oh Harry. . . . I know I'm ugly. I know my nose is too long and my eyes are too close together and I wish I could do something about my hips, but I'm not. . . .

—I think you're lovely. I've always told you so, and I mean it. When we get back to some kind of civilization everything will be all right. . . . you'll see.

—You won't send me away? Promise me that, Harry. I don't know what I'd do without you. The whole world hates me so I just couldn't face it without you.

—I won't send you away and the world doesn't hate you.

—When people look at me, they look away. I can see it. Even on this ship I can see it. When I sing they laugh. . . . just as they did in Papeete. Goodness gracious, I'm only trying to make people a little happier.

—You just imagine things like that. Please try not to. You sang very well at dinner. Everyone was delighted.

Hutton looked up at the moon which had just emerged from a cloud and blew out his cheeks. He let the air escape in a long dying whistle.

There was only the sound of the sea for a moment and then she said quietly,—Well, I'm not imagining Mrs. King.

—What do you mean by that?

—She, fine lady. . . . wants me to call her Charlotte. I refuse to do it.

—Why? What's wrong with calling her by her first name? This isn't the *Berengaria* and you're roommates.

—I don't want any closer association with a woman like that than I can help. You should see her underthings, and the way she lies around smoking one cigarette after another just staring at the ceiling. When she's in one of those moods she won't even talk to me.

—I didn't know she smoked.

—Of course you didn't. Oh, she's a smart one. She lies up there in her bunk without any clothes on smoking and staring at the ceiling and not saying anything for hours. She has the upper bunk and I'm not tall enough to see up into it, but I know very well she's lying there thinking about the captain.

—How do you know?

—I can sense it.

—Ethel. . . . what am I going to do with you. . . . if you won't help yourself?

—See? You won't believe anything I say. Oh. . . . !

She turned to him and her lower lip began to tremble. Suddenly she moved her head down to his lap. She clutched at his leg and shook with sobbing and she pressed against him with all her strength. —Oh Harry. . . . it's such a terrible thing to be a failure. . . . things would be so much better . . . if I'd never tried. Please help me! . . . . please keep me from losing my mind! . . . .

And in the moonlight he held her tightly and whispered, —Easy, little girl. . . . it will be all right. Everything will be all right. Now you just leave things to old Harry. . . .

He held her so, until she was quiet.

Bell slowly descended the after companionway steps. As he left the quarterdeck he noticed the horizon was unusually clear-cut, and he smiled inwardly when he thought that it provided a perfect excuse. He would go down to his cabin and fetch his sextant and shoot the lower limb of the moon for a longitude line. He had always considered a moon sight so unreliable as to be hardly worth the bother, certainly not after twilight, but now it could provide a reason for returning to his cabin. And if Charlotte King was still there he could explain that it was not on account of her he had returned, but rather a navigational necessity. He would have something to do with his hands and she might even be persuaded to help him. She could hold his watch after he had set it with the chronometer and call out the time of the sight. The process might even interest her, and later she might like to see how the line was plotted on the chart.

He paused outside his door and hitched up his pants. She must still be inside because there was a thread of light beneath the door and he was certain he heard her moving about. He looked down the passageway to see if there was anyone in the saloon. The area about the doorway, at least, was deserted. He opened the door to his cabin and entered.

The smile left his face as he saw Ramsay standing by the desk.

—What the hell are you doing in here?

Ramsay gave no sign of being surprised. Instead, he seemed preoccupied and his eyes were sleepy. He appeared to take Bell's entrance as a matter of course. He leaned toward the desk which held the chronometer beneath a plate of glass.

—Sorry. . . . I didn't think you'd mind.

—I mind a lot.

—I was just setting my watch against the chronometer. You're so particular about relieving on the minute. I wanted to be exact.

—Just so you don't try to tell me you're walking in your sleep. Set your watch and go.

Ramsay gave no indication he had heard the order. Instead he leaned over the chronometer and examined it thoughtfully.

—It seems the chronometer, like everything else on this ship, is defunct. Did you know it had stopped?

—If you're lying. . . .

—Have a look for yourself.

Ramsay shrugged his shoulders and stepped back while Bell approached the desk and bent over the glass plate.

—Of course you've had many. . . . interesting distractions. If you merely forgot to wind it?

—I wound it at noon.

Bell lifted the glass plate and took out the box which held the chronometer. The instrument was so important most ships carried two or even three against the remote possibility of one failing, but they were expensive and their maintenance could only be accomplished by the finest watchsmiths. If they lost or gained thirty seconds a month they were considered unworthy, for chronometers were any seaman's measure of the heavens. As an almost indispensable companion to his sextant, a chronometer enabled him to match the positions of the sun and the moon and the stars observed against those predicted for time, and so by comparison he could discover his exact location on the surface of the earth. Winding a chronometer was practically a religious rite to be performed at the same time each day, and their care was entrusted to the most reliable man on board. In smaller ships like the *Cannibal*, this man was almost invariably the master.

Incredulous, Bell looked at the face of the chronometer and saw that the sweep second hand had stopped and the time read four-twenty. He placed his ear to the box as a physician might listen for a heartbeat, but he could detect no sound.

Ramsay said,—From now on I presume our navigation will be by guess and by God.

—Shut up!

Bell took down the brass key from its special hook above his desk and inserted it in the chronometer. He turned the key experimentally. There was no resistance and the sweep second hand remained motionless. He gently shook the box. Nothing. He set the box down carefully.

—I suppose it would be out of place to ask when that ancient turnip was last rated? I couldn't see any date tag on it. Of course if we had wireless we could get a time check. . . .

—Why don't you go get some sleep!

—I'll try. But I can't say I'll sleep any better knowing we might pile up on a reef or an atoll. . . . tomorrow night or the next night, because we will have only the vaguest notion of our position.

—We've got the taffrail log. . . . we've got a fine compass and a good deviation card. We can take our noon sights for latitude. That's enough.

—Enough for what?

—To get us where we're bound! All we need is latitude.

Bell found his voice rising and he hated the sound of it. He deliberately forced it down, as Ramsay sauntered to the door.

—I must say I rather admire the way you dismiss the existence of longitude.

—Better men than I have done it.

Ramsay looked at him and then glanced thoughtfully at the bottle on the piano.

—Yes, Captain. They have.

Bell did not wait for him to close the door. He sat down before the chronometer and stared at it helplessly. No matter what gave way in the *Cannibal* he knew that somehow he could make repairs or find a substitute. Even if she was dismasted he could fashion a jury rig from odds and ends and eventually make port. But a chronometer was a delicate piece of machinery, and it certainly did not invite tinkering by unskilled hands. He closed the box and set it carefully back beneath the glass plate. The hell with it. Ships sailed the seas for centuries before chronometers were ever invented and there was no reason why the *Cannibal* could not do the same thing. But from now on he would send a man to the bow and make sure he kept a sharp lookout at night. The whole Gilbert Island group was just a little to the westerly, of course, and there were occasional isolated reefs all the way up to the westerlies. Without exact knowledge of her longitude, the *Cannibal* could easily punch one. And later, when the California coast was near, he would have to be careful. Damn careful. . . . even heave to, if there was fog. There must never be another Montague Reef.

He reached quickly for a mint and was about to go up on deck again when his thoughts returned to Ramsay. Just a minute! Since when did he get such a fire in the paint locker about the exact time? How long had he been in the cabin?

Bell looked about him. Nothing had been touched. Then he saw that his volume of Dickens was missing. Charlotte King, of course. She would have taken it to her own cabin. He wondered how many times Ramsay had entered his cabin when he was engaged on deck. Would he ever have snooped in his private journal? Not that there was anything special in it. . . . just random thoughts and remarks that never seemed proper for the ship's log. He reached for the journal and opened his desk drawer. He would keep it there from now on, because even Ramsay would hardly have the nerve to go through his desk. He was about to slip the journal in the drawer when he noticed the pile of passports which he had tossed inside. They were now neatly stacked in one corner and a maroon American passport lay on top of the pile. As he tried to remember when he might have so carefully stacked the passports, he pulled the one uppermost from the stack and flipped it open. And he saw the face of Charlotte King.

He studied the photo a moment and thought again how little

justice it did her. Perhaps she instinctively resented the photographer because there was a defiant look in her eyes, as if they held some deep anger. Absorbed, he turned back a page and saw that her name was not listed as Charlotte King. It was Inez Charlotte Liedstrom and her place of birth was given as Butte, Montana. The space for occupation was filled only by X's. Liedstrom? That must have been her maiden name and apparently she preferred Charlotte to Inez. Who could blame her? He quickly flipped over a page and found that the passport had been issued at Honolulu on October 20, 1925. She must have acquired it a year or so before she married King. Where would she be going? Why the mad-at-the-world look. . . . like she hated the photographer?

Suddenly he slapped the passport shut and threw it back in the drawer. Ramsay had been right. He remembered his words, "You will look."

As he left the cabin, he wondered why he was so disgusted with himself. People, he thought, should mind their own damn business. . . . and I haven't. My business is sailing the *Cannibal*. Nothing else.

He mounted the steps and emerged into the night. He breathed deeply of the wind and stood for some time looking at the moon. Anchor came to him and he automatically reached to scratch him between the ears. Old Brown was perched on the bulwark near the break in the quarterdeck and his frail figure was outlined against the moonlight. He was humming a chantey and he looked as old as Neptune and equally as wise. Old Brown would stand fast if there was trouble and so would Keim, who sometimes joined his humming with a froglike bass. For they were both so much of the sea they would do anything to save their world. And their world was now the *Cannibal*. Like mine, he thought.

Bell was reluctant to break their contentment, but he had postponed the fight long enough. He called out to Keim.

—Turn to on the pump!

And to Sweeney at the wheel, he said, —I'll take the helm.

Just as the pump started its rhythmic banging Ethel Peacock entered her cabin. The lamp was lit and Charlotte King lay in the upper bunk reading. Ethel kept her head bent because she

knew her eyes would still be red from weeping. She said,—
They've started that banging again.

—So I hear.

Ethel quickly slipped off her dress and began to unlace her
corset. She wanted to turn out the lamp, but then decided it
would be impolite. She sat down on her own bunk where she
could not be seen from above and took off her corset.

—Mr. Hutton says they shouldn't have to pump.

There was no answer from the upper bunk as Ethel pulled off
her stockings. She said,—Mr. Hutton doesn't think this ship is
safe. Do you?

—I don't know.

—Don't you care?

—No.

Ethel slipped a cotton nightgown over her head and began to
snap curlers in her hair. She wanted to stand before the mirror,
but then Mrs. King would see her. She wished she would go to
sleep.

—Am I disturbing your reading?

—Yes.

—I'll keep quiet then.

After a moment, she said,—What are you reading?

—Charles Dickens.

—Oh, I love Dickens. Which book are you reading?

—*David Copperfield.*

—I always adored it. David is our captain's first name.

—I know that.

—Mr. Hutton is not sure he's a very good captain.

—Mr. Hutton seems to be an authority on a lot of things.

—Have you ever read *David Copperfield* before?

—No.

—That's strange. Goodness gracious, I thought it was required in every school.

—Not where I went.

—Where was that?

Again there was only silence from the upper bunk. Ethel tied
the blue ribbon of her nightgown around her neck and began to
rub her face with cold cream. She applied it heavily and when
she was satisfied, she pulled off her eyelashes and carefully
placed them in one of her shoes. Then she took a linen cloth
from beneath her pillow, passed it under her chin and secured

the ends on top of her head with a safety pin. She massaged her breasts with exactly fifty circular movements, then breathed deeply twenty times. Finally she lay down and pulled the sheet up to her chin. She listened to the banging of the pump for as long as she could stand it. Then she said,—Where did you go to school?

—Here and there.

—Sometimes you seem to speak with sort of an English accent. I thought it might come from being in an Eastern school. . . . Vassar or some place like that. But it's not really English now that I think of it. I went to the Juilliard School of Music. I wish I was back there.

—So do I.

—That's not a very nice thing to say. I was only trying to be friendly. . . . Charlotte. We might as well talk. We can't sleep with that noise.

—I can read. . . . if you'll let me.

Before the tears actually came, Ethel Peacock knew she was going to cry again. She turned quickly on her stomach and pressed her face into the pillow. She could not control her voice as she murmured,—I'm sorry. . . . I play the piano, too. . . . I thought we could talk about it.

But this way, with her head in the pillow and the noise of the pump, she knew she would no longer disturb the woman above her.

In cabin number four Oliver Wiggins lay on his belly in the upper bunk and looked down upon Hutton, who was vigorously brushing his teeth. And he noticed that after a time Hutton's hand worked back and forth in rhythm with the clanging sound of the pump.

Hutton spewed water into the bowl and said,—You notice how they only work that pump at night?

—I hadn't thought of it.

—The captain doesn't want us to know how much water comes out. . . . that's the reason. He waits until we all go to bed.

—I'd just as leave not know.

—Well, I don't like the look of it. . . . not even a little bit. Booking on this ship was a mistake as far as I'm concerned.

—There doesn't seem to be much you can do about it now.

—Aren't you worried?

—I forgot how to worry on Rotuma. The natives don't even have a word for it. And I don't plan to take up the emotion again.

—You will. . . . when you get back to civilization.

—Where's that?

Hutton wiped his face and sat down on the lower bunk.

—Oh, New York. . . . or Chicago, say. . . . or San Francisco, say. . . .

—What about Reykjavik?

—Never heard of it.

—It's in Iceland.

—Well, certainly you wouldn't call that civilization. . . . with a lot of Eskimos around. No electricity, no. . . .

—There are no Eskimos in Iceland.

—Well, whatever they have. . . . seals and blubber and. . . .

—There are no seals either.

—I still say you couldn't call it civilization!

—They had a university five hundred years before New York or Chicago were even in existence. They still have.

—Doesn't do much good to have a university if nobody knows about it. Maybe what they need is a football team. Now when I was playing fullback for Notre Dame. . . .

—You played American football? That's a rough game.

—Sure. Almost made All-American. I could run in those days. Really kept myself in top condition. Of course if I wanted to train a bit and concentrate on it, I could probably give the boys a run for their money even today. Once an athlete, always an athlete, the old coach used to say.

Hutton quickly removed his pants and laid them out on the floor beneath his bunk.—Just in case. If we have to do any running for lifeboats I want my pants handy. A man can't really do anything without his pants.

—That depends. . . .

—What I mean is, you feel sort of naked even if you really aren't. That's why we took the belts off the Germans' pants when we captured them.

—You were in France?

—Sure! All over it.

—All over it? You must have been in the bloody thick of things.

—Humph! Couldn't help it. I was in the Flying Corps.

—A pilot?

—Yup. Eighteen victories. I don't usually tell people that. But since you were over there too, it's a little different. A fellow like you would understand what we went through.

Wiggins moved slightly in his bunk so that his head was over the edge and he could look down at Hutton. He wanted to see his face, but he could only see the top of his bald head. He was taking off his socks.

—By Jove, that's fascinating. What did you do with all your medals? Between football and flying you must have gathered a mess of them.

—Threw them in an old trunk. Haven't bothered to think about them in years. Medals don't mean a thing, really.

—Not to a man like you, of course. What kind of machines did you fly?

—DeHavillands.

Hutton lifted his feet off the floor and rolled into his bunk. He blew out his cheeks and sighed contentedly.

—Were they built in America?

—Sure. We built thousands of them.

Wiggins was sorry that he had disappeared from his line of sight. He wanted to see the man who had flown an airplane that never flew and he wanted to help him enjoy his victories. For he remembered his own days with the RFC, not as a pilot, but as a liaison officer. And one of his duties was to help the Americans get a single native-built airplane into combat. The attempt had been unsuccessful. He smiled thoughtfully when he said,— Good night.

—Good night.

Feodor Morris waited in his upper bunk while his wife braided her hair. It took a long time, yet he did not mind because the ceremony had marked the end of his day ever since he could remember. Usually it was a time he took for reflection and the sharing of his innermost thoughts with Ida.

It was while she was braiding her hair that he had first told her of the loss of their sons, and finally of his decision to leave Sevastopol and attempt a new life. And in Suva he had chosen this time to announce their departure for Mexico on the *Cannibal*. He supposed that all married people reserved some few minutes of every day solely for themselves and if anyone had ever bothered to ask him how he managed to seem so happy after fifty years with the same woman, he would have given Ida's time of braiding much credit. They had argued during this period, frequently with considerable spirit, but they had never fought; and always when she had finished, there was peace between them. And so now he said,—Ida, don't you want to do the lessons?

—I'm not caring about lessons tonight, Feodor.

—For why not?

She failed to answer him and for several minutes he occupied himself with listening to the pump. Finally he said, —I suppose they will stop that soon.

—Always they do.

—Why don't you want to do the lessons?

—Because I am too much thinking about the captain.

—What about the captain?

—A very nice man he is.

—So.

—And I think that very lonesome he is.

—Ida. Why borrow troubles? We have enough of our own. All sea captains are lonesome. Are you sure you don't want to do with the lessons?

—I do not mean he is lonesome for other persons. I consider more his spirit.

—Explain to me in Russian and maybe I know what you're talking about.

—No. I think in English and so soon as I can, it will be in Spanish. I say the captain is like a man who refuses to die. I cannot believe all Americans are like him. . . . but maybe they are.

—You are making riddles so late at night.

—Listen carefully, Feodor. This is important to us and we should remember it. How many people did we know commit suicide in the Revolution? And so they do it before any person ever touched them? So? I think the captain is like us because he has many troubles and will not just throw up his hands and say the world is coming to an end and so there is nothing I can do.

—How do you get the idea he had so many troubles?

—From his eyes. They are alive only when he talks of the sea or his ship. . . . then he fights the world with his eyes. The voice in his eyes is too loud for a man who is not deeply troubled. I think there are not enough men like the captain.

—I will look at him closer.

They were silent for a moment and then she said,—Or enough men like you, Feodor.

—Many thanks for the compliment.

—All people need men like you. The trouble is people don't give much in return.

—Perhaps nothing is expected or needed. . . . if what you say is true.

—Maybe. But I think that is why the captain is so lonely.

Ida finished braiding her hair. Then she blew out the lamp and stood for a moment in the shaft of moonlight formed by the porthole. Looking down at her. Feodor saw only a young woman. He reached out his arms as she moved toward him.

Reading his Bible, Reverend Butterfield waited patiently for the clanging pump to cease. He read without purpose or desire, and the process of balancing the book on his frail chest, the familiar feel of the leather binding, was more of a comfort to him than the actual words of gospel. For their impact upon his brain had diminished with the thousands of times he had studied the phrases and it occurred to him that his receptive powers had been worn quite as smooth as the leather. While his eyes automatically followed the words he listened to the pump and found himself thinking about Oliver Wiggins. If he was indeed a representative of the Devil, then he was at least a very pleasant one and in some ways it might be a shame to guide him along more virtuous paths. Was virtue animal, vegetable, or mineral? Delighted with the frivolous trend of his thoughts, Butterfield momentarily forgot the sound of the pump.

The formula for virtue was set down unmistakably in the book on his chest and there was, of course, no argument with the sacred document. Conforming to the formula was difficult, but the very hardship involved raised the man from a naturally spiteful and potentially dangerous animal to a creature with whom it was possible to live, and sometimes trust.

Butterfield caressed his long nose as if it was a pet animal resting on his face. How wonderful it was to be away from the mission and discover that it was still possible to think objectively! The formula for virtue was originally mixed to protect a society. Obviously, my dear Butterfield. What a clever theme for a sermon in Hell! The ancient ingredients were compounded not too long after men emerged from caves, although at the time they must have been completely mystifying to all concerned. The agent specified, among many other things, that it was no longer fashionable to abuse one's neighbor with a club. The catalyst rigidly limited the carnal pleasures.

Butterfield tried to chuckle, but the effort instantly became a dry cough and it was some time before he could think about anything except inflating his chest with air again.

Moses should have met Oliver Wiggins! Yes, even he might have called for an extra thunderbolt to capture his attention. Moses should have ventured among the South Pacific heathens and called particularly upon the island of Thithia! Perhaps he would have been more successful in convincing the inhabitants that they should accept a new formula and cast off their ancient taboos. . . . which were in themselves created to protect an existing society. Moses might not have come away a physical wreck, and it was conceivable that he would have been able to keep his own ideas on virtue. More so than the good Reverend Butterfield? The *good* Reverend!

He stopped massaging his nose and squeezed his lips until they became a thin mournful line. A sour taste came to his mouth and he wondered that emotion could so quickly destroy the physical memories of a good meal.

The good Reverend! How many times had you looked down on your flock, which in the beginning had gathered in the open beneath the cocoanut palms and sat about you like children awaiting a bedtime story. . . . how many times had you seen among them such temptation you had frequently to raise your eyes heavenward in the middle of a sermon and pray secretly for strength? The young girls of Thithia were supple and soft and round of body, and their skin was an almost golden brown without a sign of the lesions and eruptions which defaced so many islanders. They were equally as tempting as those who said farewell to Wiggins at Rotuma, and on any night they would have been happy to make an emperor's couch of your straw mat. It had never actually happened, but the thoughts and delightful visions which frequently occupied your mind for long periods would never have been approved by less of a libertine than Oliver Wiggins. Wasn't the harboring of such thoughts equally as sinful as the act? The formula was vague about this and hence, even for experts, it was easy to become confused.

Butterfield closed his Bible unhappily. I am confused, he thought. I am confused because I doubt when I should believe, and so I am close to disaster. Wiggins is the fortunate one because while his beliefs are wrong and evil, he does not bother to question them. Oh, Wiggins, you open-faced scoundrel. . . . you worshiper of false gods, you fornicator, you thief, you adulterer. . . . you animal without shame. . . . you usher to wickedness. . . . I will defeat you!

He looked downward at his frail body stretched on the bunk and saw the knobs and angles of bone ends which pressed upward against his worn frock. And he thought. . . . No, Wiggins! I am not a mere collection of calcium formations, gristle, and skin. I am more than a formula! I am faith!

He rose far enough to tip the lamp and blow it out. Then he fell back into the darkness, where he murmured over and over again. . . . I will believe. In time his repetition of the words followed the rhythm of the pump exactly, and long before it stopped he was asleep.

October 20

Suva toward Manzanillo

Begins fine. Middle part fine. Ends with trades diminishing and much cooler. Rain squalls throughout and particular during night watch. Seaman Lott had a bad boil on the back of his neck. I lanced it. Also killed and butchered one pig. Water in bilge eighteen inches at maximum. Pumped two hours. Made good one hundred and ten miles this day. Chronometer not operating.

Six

THE MOON HAD BEEN swallowed by a rain squall and Bell was still puffing when he entered the cubbyhole charthouse. After the first hour of pumping he had relieved Old Brown and sent him aft to easier work at the helm. Brown swore that his heart was pickled in brine and therefore he could take any amount of bending and heaving on the pump.

—You stick to yer charts, Cap, and leave us ignoramuses break our backs! Do the head thinking. You keep her off the bricks and us'll keep her afloat.

Bell gave him a good-natured shove away from the pump. He understood the furtive look of gratitude in Old Brown's eyes as he staggered aft. That pump, like all others ever invented, was murder.

Even the powerful Keim was too exhausted to make any comment when it finally sucked dry. Sweeney collapsed on the deck and in spite of the rain squall had not moved since. They were like dead men after only two hours of pumping. If the *Cannibal's* leak increased, the time of pumping must increase, and now with his own muscles aching, Bell wondered how long their reserve of strength could hold out.

He passed his heavy forearm across his face to wipe away the mixture of sweat and rain, then crouched over the chart table. It was a moment before his tired eyes could adjust themselves to the spatter of numerals and lines on the chart which told of ocean depths in fathoms, the variation, the latitude and longitude, and indicated by vague dots the location of countless islands and atolls which projected from the Pacific. Every indication of land was potentially dangerous to mariners unless the exact position of the vessel was known. But exact knowledge of position, Bell thought with a sigh, was a situation rarely to be enjoyed.

He took down a pair of brass dividers from a rack above the chart and slid them back and forth between his calloused fingers. He studied the chart and his own markings upon it which were already history. As always, he found deep satisfaction in his celestial navigation, which he had pursued far more diligently than most captains. The majority seldom bothered with the stars.

At dawn on the morning before, he had obtained a three-star fix which placed the *Cannibal* well to the west of the Phoenix Islands. The lines of position resulting from his sextant observations of the stars, Sirius, Capella, and Rigel, crossed to form a small triangle and indicated the *Cannibal* was then some eight miles to the north of his original dead-reckoning estimate. The Fijis and the Ellice group were well to the south. Apparently a current, unseen and unmarked on any chart, had given the old *Cannibal* a push. With the continuation of good star fixes, plus noon sights of the sun and an occasional morning sight of the same body for a running fix, only a very careless navigator need worry about atolls. He could set course to avoid them.

Yet now, with a useless chronometer, star sights must be abandoned. They would be totally unreliable without knowing the exact time of observation. There was always Polaris, the North Star, which required very little correction for time, but in these latitudes it was so close to the horizon and of such puny brilliance it was hardly worth considering. All right for Columbus, Bell thought, but then Columbus missed his true position so far it was only forgivable in view of his times. There was no room for such carefree navigation here, with the Gilbert atolls licking their chops just to the west of the *Cannibal*'s course. From now on, the only reliable aid from the heavens would be a noon sight of the sun. Fortunately, a noon sight did not require a knowledge of time. But it would only give latitude, and with islands to the west and the east, longitude was the more important factor.

Bell yawned. Christ, he was tired! The *Cannibal* needed sea room, hundreds of miles of open ocean where a man could run down a latitude line and reach a destination without worrying about the crunch of coral. Too many fine ships had been lost on just such a night as this when rain squalls concealed a low atoll, when there was no sense in posting a man forward as a lookout because he couldn't see the end of the jib boom anyway. Any shout of warning he might give would be after the fact. If he was smart he would just crawl in with the pigs to keep dry. So, until the *Cannibal* had more sea room it was risky to sail at night. Too risky. She must be hove to and move only between dawn and dusk for at least a week to come. If Davey Bell lost another ship and bothered to survive, he would be lucky to find a berth as an able seaman. There would certainly never be another command.

Balancing himself against the chart table, Bell pressed the palms of his hands hard against his eyes. He knew that in doing so he was hiding, if only for a moment, but in the quick darkness which followed he hoped he might be able to think more clearly. It was now, this night and not a week from now, that he must reach a decision on the *Cannibal*'s future because in any sailing ship, the future must be planned far in advance. The seacoasts of the world were littered with the bones of sailing ships, and nine times out of ten it had been the master who was at fault and not the elements. All too often the master failed to plan ahead and found himself close to shore and helplessly becalmed. Or some waited too long when driven hard before a full gale and found they were unable to wear ship for change of course lest they broach to and put the vessel on her beam ends. So they drove on hoping for a change in the weather. Finally there would be the shore and a desperate attempt to bring ship to wind and clew off. . . . which seldom worked. The sails would blow out of the bolt ropes and she would hit all-standing. It was of little purpose to explain later that the sky had been overcast and it had been several days since the master had been able to obtain any kind of fix. The ship was dead, a mass of crumpled wood, wire, rope and torn canvas. . . . and usually her people, including the master, were dead, too. It happened to steamers which could be maneuvered easily and even made to go astern at will. It happened many more times to sailing ships, which was why the normal hazards of the sea took almost as great a toll as the scrap yards. The proof was with the insurance companies. They carefully avoided any contracts with ships solely dependent on the wind.

No one had to tell Davey Bell that it took a determined man to master a sailing ship. And yet he knew there was real danger in blind determination.

It was like a water-front fight, he mused. A long one. If you were smart you never started a fight on any water front. There was always some guy who was a little bigger, and punching bigger people in the nose was never smart. Sometimes they got impatient and disgusted and broke your head. Like the sea. You didn't argue with the sea. It might be all smiles and soft one day, but it could get mad in a hurry and show a man how small he was.

He remembered only too well the beautiful *Tropic Bird* lost on the Mexican Coast, the *Carelmapu* on the wild coast of Vancouver Island, and the *Amaranth* and the *Benecia,* and he wondered if it was a week before their end, or only a few hours, before their masters yearned to talk with someone who might at least understand their problems.

Normally Ramsay, as chief mate, should at least be worth consulting. But no damn good. Ramsey's opinions would be so colored with his personal desires, they would be worthless. How about Keim? No good either. It would be like talking to a sea elephant. Keim would grunt and squirm uncomfortably at such attention and would soon be sure his captain had lost his mind. Old Brown, then? Could you go to Old Brown and wait for him to transfer his plug of tobacco from one cheek to the other while you said,—Listen, Old Brown, here are a few things to think about instead of mooning over days that are gone forever. You know and I know the leak isn't going to get any better. Maybe it's only a local leak that a caulker could set right in fifteen minutes. Anyway we can't get to it without hauling out. If we hit rough weather up north the leak will probably get worse. A man can pump just so long before he falls down on the deck and says the hell with it, if he has the breath left to say anything. Our rigging and sails aren't too much worry. We'll patch them up somehow and carry on to Manzanillo, but we better start thinking about food and water if there's going to be any long delay. And give me an opinion on next week. Should we carry on at night without a sure fix on our position and make speed so we don't have to worry about food and water, or should we heave to and begin cutting down some right now?

What about Honolulu? Maybe next week we better fall off on the other tack and start beating our brains out against the trades, trying to get to Honolulu before we go to the bottom? But when we arrive, if we ever do. . . . what do we use for money? There is more than one way to lose the *Cannibal* and she would sail poorly with padlocks on her doors and companionways and a sheriff's plaster on her mainmast. Or should we just carry on, taking our turns at the pump as they come, and try to remember that if we give the old girl a lot of nursing she'll get us to port somehow? Notice I haven't even mentioned the passengers, Old Brown, because you can hide in your forecastle and hardly know they're aboard, but I can't get away from their questions. If we don't progress at night, they'll raise hell. How about all that, Old Brown?

Bell smiled and shook his head. It would be almost worth talking things over with Old Brown just to hear his profane solutions. He would say,—Go down and get yourself a bottle, Davey, and git drunk and fergit about things. While yer below I'll heave the passengers overboard and the copra, too. Then with a light ship and a fine wind on our ass we'll sail off to Java or the Maldives where I'll look up my friend the Sultan of Minikoi and we'll die happy polishin' up the brass on his harem door. Nobody much would ever know the difference.

And maybe Old Brown would be right.

Bell interrupted his thinking to look down at Anchor, who was sniffing about his ankles. He smiled again and said,—I know. . . . I know, I stink. It's the damn rain, Anchor. Keep a man in salt air and water and he don't ever really stink no matter how hot it is or how hard he works. But douse him down with fresh water and stand back. I'll bathe up tomorrow, Anchor. In salt water, so you can give your snoot a rest. Maybe then you can listen while I ask *you* some questions.

Bell turned to leave the chartroom, then paused just inside the companionway hatch. For now he could see Old Brown at the helm. The light from the binnacle created an almost solid yellow shaft through the pouring rain and outlined his thin figure against the black sky. And though David Bell had seen men in just such a pose innumerable times, now, this night, the vision held him spellbound.

Old Brown had placed one bare foot against the binnacle. He was leaning back against the wheel casually, steering a spoke or two now and then with his shoulder blades. His hands, enormous on so thin a man, hung loosely at his sides and seldom deigned to touch the wheel. His pants had been worn so long they followed the contours of his leg muscles and were held about his waist by a plaited rope on which a small monkey's fist knot served as a buckle. His shirt was patched and frayed so thin Bell thought he could see his flesh through it. Now, both shirt and pants were sodden from the rain, and rivulets of water dripped from his extremities as if he were a leaking wicker basket. A sheath knife hung on his hip and Bell knew that it almost completed his worldly possessions. Being an old-timer, there would also be a pair of leather sea boots beneath Brown's forecastle bunk, at least one of which was certain to be badly holed. There would be a suit of oilskins, dirty and torn and reeking of tar and fish oil, and probably a cloth cap for cold nights. He would have varnished the cap many times to make it stiff and waterproof, but Bell doubted if the varnish ever lasted more than a single voyage. There would be a pair of socks and some shoes for going ashore. They would be at the bottom of his damp sea bag now and were probably covered with mildew. Aside from a few trinkets and possibly a suit of long underwear, these would be the accumulated rewards of a lifetime spent at hard and dangerous labor.

So it was, Bell thought, with all seamen before the mast. And so it was, very nearly, with himself.

But at seventy years of age, or whatever he was, Old Brown was not a poor man. Bell had only to watch his face to be sure of it. He had more strength and endurance than much younger men who spent their years acquiring a bank account and stomach trouble and breathing the foul air of cities until their faces looked like johnnycake dough before it was baked. Old

Brown had something they could never buy, and Bell thought it might be contentment.

Now watching his face in the light, he knew he would never forget it. Old Brown's jaw was thrust forward defiantly, and the stubble of his beard glistened with droplets of moisture. His cut of tobacco shone as a hump on the outside of his right cheek and a steady river of water spewed off the end of his broken nose. His white hair hung down about his ears and was pressed flat with the rain, and snakes of hair dripped more water down his forehead. Every portion of his body ignored the rain except his eyes which were crinkled tightly so that he might at least be able to see. From time to time he shot a challenging glance aloft. He shivered once and Bell knew that he must be very cold; yet even as he watched, Old Brown puckered his mouth experimentally and began to whistle. And then David Bell suddenly realized that in one old man, he was looking at both man and the sea.

He moved quickly out of the companionway hatch and yelled at Old Brown.

—What are you trying to do? Bring us bad luck?

Old Brown raised one eyelid just far enough to show a portion of his eye. A mischievous smile played around his tobacco-stained lips.

—You mean me whistlin', Cap? Them old wives' tales? Hell, I invented most of them long before yer time.

—Where's Keim and Sweeney?

—Sweeney's takin' a spell. Hidin' in the galley house to stay out of the wet. He is a smart lad. Keim's standin' lookout.

—I'll take the helm. Get the watch together. We've got work to do.

Old Brown moved reluctantly away from the wheel. He looked at Bell and the smile left his face. Turning his back to the rain he said,—Davey. . . . I got to talk to you. I guess I got to right now.

And because he said Davey instead of Cap or Captain, Bell knew that what Old Brown had to say would be worth hearing. His age and endless years at sea gave him the moral right, if nothing more, to address his captain by first name, but it was a privilege Old Brown would never abuse. Nor would he use the familiar at all unless he carefully chose the time.

—Davey. . . . I is older than you.

Waiting, half-knowing what Old Brown had on his mind, Bell deliberately focused his attention on the compass and seemed to ignore him. He knew that Old Brown would be even more ill at ease if he did otherwise.

—You're older than anybody, Brown.

—And I'm up past me bedtime.

—You're getting deaf, too. I said we've got work to do. Talk some other time.

Bell allowed a tone to carry his words which a seaman like Old Brown would be certain to recognize. The tone said. . . . for reasons we both understand, I cannot appear to be listening to you, but I *am* listening and although I have given you a definite order you may take your time about carrying it out. The bridge between us may never be crossed because that is not the way of things at sea, but if you will stand on the other end of the bridge and even so much as whisper I will hear you.

Old Brown spit to leeward because it was night and he could not be certain of his trajectory. Then he said,—I never give no man a Portuguese lift, Davey, and I won't begin with you. I never belayed myself to no officer before and I won't now. . . . and it ain't my habit to carry tales aft.

—Speak up, Brown. Blow and submerge.

Again Bell was careful to eliminate any severity in his voice. He allowed himself one glance at Old Brown and then looked back at the compass.

—You been hittin' the bottle, Davey?

Brown's voice was just loud enough to carry over the rattle of the rain on the sails and the deck. And they both knew it was a question no other sailor on the *Cannibal* would dare to ask, much less expect an answer.

—No.

—Them mints holdin' out pretty good then.

—You know too much. . . . even for an old man.

—What I'm gettin' around to say, Davey, is that I come to like you on this voyage mostly I guess because yer a good skipper without bein' no highfalutin solid-gold-spangled bastard I have to touch me cap to every time I pass him on deck. And I've sailed with plenty of that cut, Davey. You managed to squirm through the hawsepipe and make yer way aft where you could keep your hands clean most of the time, but you didn't git all the dirt off yer, thank God, and you ain't forgit entirely how to work with yer paws like t'other day with Keim on the fore-topm'st.

—Maybe I haven't had time.

—All of which is to say I woon't like to see you standin' into trouble.

—Like what?

—The men is tired, Davey. Yer shorthanded enough just with the regular workin' ship, but when it comes to breakin' their backs on that goddamned pump. . . .

—You sound like a union delegate. Maybe they would rather go to the bottom.

—They is awful tired, Davey, and sometimes tired men git unreasonable. They git ornery and mean. They already been wonderin' about yer behavior which is how I come to ask you about the bottle.

—Pass the word any way you like, Brown. . . . but let every man forward know I'll log him a month's pay if he gives an easy lift on the pump. Any man who refuses, I'll haul up on charges of mutiny. And by God, I'll make it stick.

There was no compromise in Bell's voice now. He had yelled back from the opposite end of the imaginary bridge and he wanted to make absolutely certain Old Brown would understand him.

—Oh, it ain't that bad, Davey. They know we got to stay afloat somehow or they'll be swimmin' themselves. For the kind of shipmates ye git these days they ain't at all bad. Hell, you know better'n anybody most of 'em won't even work cargo now, let alone go ten feet aloft without a bonus for every ratline. What's beginnin' to eat them is, they can't git it through their heads why you don't make for Honolulu, which ain't too far and where maybe the old hooker kin git patched up so's she'll stay afloat all by herself for a bit.

—Did they send you to ask me that?

—No. It wuz my own idea. I'm just lookin' ahead, that's all. I seen trouble on ships before and I don't so much care about seein' it again. You know how it is, accidents start to happen. People fall overboard who really shoon't. . . . and all manner of things like so. Everybody is sorry as hell afterwards and they is full of good sensible explanations which sound all right to anybody who gits curious, but they don't help somebody who is maybe unlucky and finds hisself all of a sudden some night swimmin' around in the ocean by his lonesome.

Bell waited a long time before he raised his eyes from the compass. He heard Old Brown spit through the rain again and he knew that he would be looking off into the night as if what he had said had never been said and he was merely standing by for an order. Old Brown knew his way about the tight little world of a ship. He should. But then so did Davey Bell. And they both knew that a master's authority remained supreme only as long as the crew wanted things that way, particularly on a sailing ship. The men forward could give more than a Portuguese lift, which was merely loafing on the job. Guided by a clever sea lawyer they could take command without ever really taking command, and when they reached port they could collect their full pay and walk ashore without a mark against their record.

Bell remembered an overeager young mate on the steamer *City of Portland* who had "fallen" down an open hatch. It was a twenty-foot drop 'tween decks and he hit flat on his back. He never walked again. No one saw it happen and no one could explain how an experienced seaman who must have known every inch of the vessel thoroughly could trip over a two-foot hatch combing. The young mate was sure he had been pushed, although he could remember no one near him at the time. To all appearances, he did not have an enemy on board and the crew sent a delegation with flowers and candy and games to the hospital. The police held a fruitless inquiry and were soon lost in a maze of contradictory stories. They were glad when the *City of Portland* signed on a new mate and sailed away.

From the way he turned his back, Bell knew that Old Brown had spoken his piece and it was doubtful if he would risk it again. He had his own welfare to think about and the chances of their ever being alone again were remote.

Bell held up his hand to shade his eyes from the binnacle light. He searched the deck forward. There was no sign of Keim or Sweeney. They might both be in the galley house. He waited until his eyes became accustomed to the darkness and then, still looking forward, he spoke in a low voice.

—Rouse out your watchmates, Brown. Douse jibs, clew up forecourse, tops'ls, and t'gallant. Leave the forestays'l set.

When you've finished, come aft and sheet the spanker in taut. We're heaving to until morning.

—Aye, sir.

—When you've secured, knock off and make a cup of coffee if you want. But one of you keep an eye out forward.

Old Brown looked at Bell questioningly, then started forward through the rain. Bell reached out a hand and pulled him back to the binnacle. Old Brown must be sure to see his face.

—And while you're yarning over your coffee you might find a chance to pass this along. I don't know where you heard it, but you did. This is my ship. She will sail where I want her to sail. I didn't serve before the mast for nothing and I know all the tricks. This ship is bound direct for Manzanillo and that's where she'll go if we all have to swim and tow her in with our teeth. But we won't have to. There's nothing wrong with the *Cannibal* but a slight leak. Now get forward.

Bell squeezed the old man's shoulder hard. The gesture was enough for Brown. It was a signal of understanding and for a moment the gap between them ceased to exist. Then Bell deliberately dropped his hand.

—Aye, sir.

Ramsay came on deck at exactly five minutes before midnight. His eyes were still puffed with sleep, but his hair was combed and his white shirt was neatly buttoned at the neck. The rain squall had passed, and while Lott, Yancy, and Uala shuffled silently about to relieve their opposite members in Bell's watch, Ramsay leaned against the deckhouse and looked up at the stars.

He waited until Bell walked stiffly toward the after companionway, and then in a voice loud enough for the others to hear, he said,—Fine night, Captain. Lots of stars. Beautiful. It's a pity we can't use them.

Bell grunted. —You may not find it so damn beautiful when the next squall comes along.

Ramsay looked at Bell's still wet shirt and smiled. He said, —I should think so much water would shrink your suspenders.

—I got another pair. You're hove to, Ramsay.

—So I see.

—Your watch is lucky, they can rest. Let them.

—Right.

—We'll make sail again at dawn. Leave things be until then.

Ramsay looked up at the stars again. He said more to the stars than to Bell,—This is unlike you.

—How do you mean?

—Such caution.

—Ramsay. . . .

Bell knew that if he paused any longer he would say a great deal more than he wanted to. Not yet. Ramsay was just waiting for a break in front of the men. Well, he wouldn't get it. . . . now.

Bell turned into the companionway and took a step down. Still smiling, Ramsay called after him.

—I assume we're in for some pumping.

—No. She don't need it.

When Bell disappeared, Ramsay sauntered aft to the binnacle. He glanced at the compass, then looked thoughtfully at the sea. He shook his head disapprovingly and while he checked the beckets which lashed the wheel, he said, —Hove to and drifting on a fine night like this. . . . drifting half a knot sideways. . . . well, I always wanted to see China.

He laughed dryly, then moved toward Yancy, who, true sailor-fashion, was making himself as inconspicuous as possible in the lee of the cabin trunk.

Yancy watched him with open suspicion. During a night watch, with the *Cannibal* nearly motionless in the water, there would ordinarily be little or no work required, but an officer like Ramsay wandering about the decks just might think of something. Yancy was pleasantly surprised when he saw Ramsay merely fold his arms and lean against the mizzen shrouds.

—How about you, Yancy? Ever been to China?

—Yessir. Three times. In the *Medway* . . . . the *William Dollar*. . . . and the *Eclipse*. I was bos'n in the *Medway*.

—So? How come you didn't stay with her?

—I swallowed the anchor. No man ever made nothin' of himself at sea. . . . not before the mast anyways. I jumped the *William Dollar* in Honolulu and settled down.

—In Honolulu? I've only been there once. . . . year before last. Honolulu is a place I'd like to know better.

—Mind if I have a smoke back here, sir?

—No. Go right ahead.

Yancy bent to roll a cigarette. If this fancy-pants mate

wanted to yarn through a watch it was a lot easier than working. He peered enviously at Lott, who was lying prone on the deck by the main hatch and was probably already asleep. Uala, too, had made himself comfortable as he possibly could alongside the wheel box. He was staring at the stars and Yancy thought he was young and foolish enough to be thinking about only one woman at a time.

—Yessir. I wisht I was back in Honolulu. I run the best tattoo parlor on the island.

—You might get back there, Yancy. Sooner than you think.

Yancy's fingers paused in their manipulations about the cigarette. Hello. When you chewed the fat with an officer and he let you smoke on the quarterdeck, you sometimes got more than scuttlebutt. You found out a lot of things which came along edgewise maybe, but which could be useful. The trick was to keep them talking. Yancy drew his fingers upward and neatly completed the cigarette. He placed it between his lips and lit it. If you say something is going to happen to an officer and he denies it, then you got your answer. If he don't deny it, then you also got your answer and it is going to happen.

—I guess I'll never see old Honolulu this voyage with the captain bound and determined to skip it.

—What makes you so sure?

Yancy considered his answer. This Ramsay was not so easily led on. . . . information would have to be squeezed out of him. . . . little by little. Shrugging his shoulders, he said, —I spend a good part of every day looking at the compass. I can't help but know. And then. . . . word gets around. You know how it is in a ship so small as we.

—Is that why they call you The Artist? Because you ran a tattoo parlor?

All right, Yancy thought. If he wants to veer away and go over on the other tack for a while, let him. I got nothing to do anyway but miss sleep.

—Yessir. I got some famous after a while. Made good money.

—Why did you leave then?

—The Navy closed me up.

—How could they do that?

—I had a little infection trouble. They got me on the sanitation code.

—Couldn't you clean things up?

—None of my customers ever got any real genuine blood poisonin' except a few sore arms now and then. . . . but you know how the Navy is always coddlin' their little boys. I dunno how they ever expect to make sailors out of them youngsters if they won't let them go adrift once in a while. My parlor put out the best work in the Pacific. I didn't bother with just plain stars, and snakes, and ships' names, and hearts with "Mother" in the middle. And I flat refused to do them cheap hootch-kootchy girls what wiggle when a customer worked his muscle. . . . or even flags that wave. I left that stuff to my competitors which is how I come to be known as The Artist. You ain't really interested in all this, are you, Mr. Ramsay?

—Certainly. I'm always interested in my shipmates.

Yancy took a long drag on his cigarette. *Shipmates?* Since when were Downeasters so cozy? And of a sudden. They usually looked right through a sailor unless he done something wrong. Well, gabble on if it'll keep his mind off work. See what happens and maybe wind up with some information. . . . like is the captain going to run the old *Cannibal* straight to the bottom or is he going to be reasonable and make for Honolulu.

—No, sir. I used my imagination and concentrated on designs which was unusual and what a man could be proud to wear around until he was dead. Most of them was my own designs like my number thirty-four which cost fifteen dollars. I put a water line across a man's shoulders and the rest was all underneath the ocean. I had fish, and rocks and sea fans in every color, and sharks attacking a diver, and wrecks along the bottom. A man could go as deep as he wanted except that below his navel I charged an extra five dollars. Number thirty-four was a house specialty, but my best design was my number one hundred. It cost a man fifty dollars.

—Your prices were not exactly cheap.

—A lot of work in number one hundred. It was my masterpiece. I called it the Fox Hunt.

Moving his hands across the stars, Yancy began to outline a design as he spoke.

—I had this whole lot of horsemen, see? They wore red coats and all, and they began by galloping across a man's chest and went over his left shoulder like it was a hill. Then the horsemen went on down his back full tilt after the fox. . . . but all you could see was the fox's tail disappearing up his butt. It was colorful.

Yancy thought the mate laughed a little too quickly. He watched Ramsay's face in the starlight and thought. . . . He was standing by to laugh no matter what I said. He's got something on his mind and it ain't out yet, but it will be. I got to keep him inarrested and feeling superior.

—Did you sell many fox hunts?

—Not to sailors. They didn't go for it. But two soldiers come in one day with their crap winnings and I put number one hundred on both of them. I like to think of those soldiers as sort of a permanent monument and I sure would like to see them again. When you put your whole heart in something like that you sort of want to stand back and admire it every once in a while. Understand, sir?

—Of course. But I don't understand why the Navy should put you out of business.

Yancy leaned forward to look at Uala and Lott. Thank God they were asleep or there would be a lot of explaining to do what with talking so long to an officer. Good. You had to be clever to get information out of a man like Ramsay who was educated. You had to give him a little bait.

—I was discriminated against. You see my parlor had sort of a side line. It was what you call a rendezvoos. That is, a sailor or a soldier could come in there and sort of arrange an appointment. After a while I just got too popular.

—An appointment with a girl?

—Naturally. What else can you rendezvoos with? But I didn't take no money from the girls. . . . and I didn't pay off nobody either, which was the trouble. So one day they just come in and lowered the boom and so here I am at the bottom of the heap again. But I'll make bos'n again. . . . someday.

One thing officers liked was a show of ambition. They thought every man who went to sea ought to want to be them. If you showed ambition you got out of more work than you got into. Sometimes they even let you tinker around with the charts, which used up time you might be doing a lot harder work. It made officers feel good to show how smart they were, while all the time you was the one who was being smart.

Yancy was seeking a delicate way to mention the *Cannibal*'s sad condition when he was suddenly caught off balance. Ramsay said,—Did you ever hear of a woman in Honolulu named Pimmle. . . . or Pinkney. . . . or something like that. . . ?

—Myra Pringle! Yessir, I knew that woman but I never had nothin' to do with her for sure! A regular vulture. Used to hang around them big hotels on the beach. She had them so-called moonlight girls.

Ramsay smiled. —That's the one! We were waiting to load our sugar and I read about her in the newspapers.

—Well, I hope you never got mixed up with Myra, sir. You're lucky to be alive if you did.

Now Yancy was confused. You never knew how things were going to turn out when you started yarning with an officer. Who would ever think this spit-and-polish, holy-stone-the-bejesus-out-of-everything mate, who should have been in the Navy where he could get saluted twenty times a day, would know Myra Pringle? Or did he really just read about her?

—I did *not* get mixed up with her, fortunately.

—Them poor tourists. Some of them used to get beat the hell up until they were lucky to make the hospital. It just showed what a good-looking woman and a little moonlight can do to a man. He don't stop to think. But I'll say this. Myra hired the best-lookers, even if they was all bums. Some of them you could hardly blame a man for thinkin' he was all set for a dandy amachur romance on the beach. They was trained to pick their customers, too. Just the ordinary guy got hisself nowheres.

—Didn't I read where one of the tourists died?

—Yessir. He did. But I never had nothin' to do with a shake-down like that. I run a nice honest place. How come you asked about Myra, Mr. Ramsay?

—Just curious. Until we got our sugar there wasn't much to do but read the papers.

—You said we might put in to Honolulu?

—I did not say anything of the kind.

—Well. . . . shoon't we?

—That's for the captain to decide.

Goddammit, Yancy thought, he is off the hook! Assuming the manner of a faithful underdog, he said,—I guess the captain knows we ain't so very happy about the general condition of the *Cannibal.* I guess he knows that, doesn't he, sir?

—Do you think it would matter what you thought? If you are discontented I suggest you do something about it.

—Like what, sir?

—You might begin by filing a formal protest. He would have to accept it and record it in the log. You would be quite within your rights and your records would be clear.

Who-ho! Yancy almost swatted his leg in triumph. Bottom at last!

It was no secret that Davey Bell and the *Cannibal's* mate were of a different cut and often disagreed, but for one officer to step over the line and side with the crew was so rare an occurrence Yancey was immediately lost in speculation. He saw endless possibilities, including a comfortable time on the beach in Honolulu, rather than pumping his heart out all the way to that hellhole of a Manzanillo. He said, slowly,—I'll see what the boys think.

—You're an intelligent man, Yancy. They'll think the way you do.

Yancy stared moodily at the black water beyond the bulwark. He was framing a question which might entirely relieve his curiosity, when he became aware that Ramsay had left his side. He watched him walk aft and stand near the binnacle, and he thought. . . . That is where the joker belongs. Turning back to the sea, he heard the slosh and snort of a porpoise. He flipped his cigarette at the sound. It would be interesting to know what Ramsay hoped to accomplish by suggesting a crew protest. Did he just want to lie on the beach in Honolulu, too, or was he honestly worried about the *Cannibal's* condition? If so, why didn't he record his own protest in the log? His would swing more weight. And the gaff about Myra Pringle? It didn't sound like Ramsay was just passing the time of day.

It was never, Yancy finally decided, never, never smart to trust a man who lived abaft the foremast. Certainly not a man like Ramsay. . . . or even a man who came up the hard way, like Davey Bell.

October 23

Suva toward Manzanillo

Begins fine with moderate easterlies. Middle part increasing to fresh in squalls, then diminishing rapidly to flat calm. During squall in the afternoon, and a mild one at that, the topgallant mast broke at the cap. Found the mast deadeye had parted so required to send down upper topgallant yard and fish a new three feet on the mast using capstan and chain.
Work continued until past darkness with Bos'n Keim in charge. Tiresome for all concerned.
Sounded the well during forenoon. Found twenty inches. This has been our maximum reading so far and is not encouraging. Pumped two hours until sucked dry—from one A.M. until three. No complaint today from passengers, but a fair round of grumbling from the men. I told them the way to heaven is never easy. Sixty-one miles noon to noon.

Seven

BECAUSE THE OFFICIAL log of the *Cannibal* simply recorded the weather and events according to the requirements of maritime law, Bell made his entries as brief as possible, and found little satisfaction in doing so. The log was kept in the cubbyhole chartroom and Ramsay's entries were as frequent as his own. In a sense the *Cannibal*'s official log, as on any ship, was public property. Any surveyor, passenger, or crewman might examine it on request. It was concerned with the technicalities and ship's business only, and served more to confirm uncertain memories than anything else.

117

Bell kept his private journal in his cabin. It contained notations which were of more personal use. In it he had written the names of agents in various ports, honest and dishonest ship chandlers, a record of past cargoes and possibilities for the future, and the names of various personalities stationed throughout the Pacific whom he might not see for long periods of time and who were more inclined to cooperate if Bell leaned over the taffrail and greeted them correctly. There were also some complicated rigging drawings, a carefully drawn plan for installing an auxiliary engine in the *Cannibal* if he could ever raise the money, and occasional random thoughts of his own which he felt worthy of committing to paper. It was a large, thick book and his peculiarly erect script rolled across the lined pages with considerable beauty.

Lately he had found that writing in his journal had become a little ceremony which he anticipated throughout the day. He thought it strange that in the past he had often forgotten the journal even existed, whereas now he took it out of his desk as soon as the evening meal was done and wrote diligently. He supposed that it had become some kind of an escape, a sort of sailor's scrimshaw which took his mind partially away from the *Cannibal*. At least it served to set his difficulties down on paper where he could review them at leisure.

Bell had known ship masters to take up all manner of hobbies in their spare time, although since the days of steam and consequent shorter passages, the custom had lost importance in the lives of sailing men. Captains were particularly addicted to hobbies and often brought whatever art they had chosen to a fine degree of perfection. Whether this was merely a result of their natural isolation at sea, or simply a means of remaining relatively sane, Bell was never quite sure. For it was true that unless a master was blessed with an extraordinary reliable mate, he was never off duty. Even in sleep he was besieged with problems.

There were captains who hung boxes of plants in the skylights of their cabins and nurtured them tenderly year after year as if contact with the foliage might at least keep a toe on the land. One captain even managed to raise a tree. On his retirement he took it ashore with him and transplanted it to his front yard. . . . exactly as he had sworn he would do fifteen years previously. There were captains who embellished Bibles, using a magnifying glass to guide their brush, and Bell remembered one of these as the most blasphemous man he had ever met. There was one old salt who fancied himself a chemist and pursued his hobby so extensively it was said his ship could be smelled long before her mast pricked the horizon. When he eventually blew out his skylight and simultaneously set fire to everything aft the mizzen, he was discharged on reaching port. Remorse was not in his makeup. He claimed that while he was somewhat disappointed in the success of his experiment he had at least found a valid excuse to finally leave the sea.

There were captains who painted pictures, usually of ships, and Bell thought little of their efforts. They were usually accurate to the extent of including every block and line, but Bell considered them hopelessly ugly. There was a captain who happily lost himself in making watches. His cabin was always strewn with cogs, spindles, and springs, and Bell wished he was aboard the *Cannibal* now so that he might repair the chronometer.

I am not so clever, he thought. I cannot do anything in particular with my hands except ordinary deck work, which it seems I have been doing ever since I was born and so there is no thought of accomplishment to it. Only my penmanship is better than most men's and I cannot account for it except that I take great pleasure in forming the letters. I like to watch the letters flow into words without really caring what the words are.

Now sitting at his desk with the journal open before him, he laughed silently. He thought that he might be just as content with a series of unrelated words. It was the neatness and legibility which pleased him, and he wondered if his pleasure had something to do with the fact that he was so sloppy about everything else. He liked the clean white paper and the very black ink as an amateur carpenter prizes good wood and a sharp saw.

Dipping his pen with a flourish, he made several circular motions before he finally brought it down to the journal. Still smiling at himself, he thought. . . . No matter how many fancy-pantsy swirls I make, it is still better than thinking about the bottle on the piano.

Beginning with the care he would give to the stitching of a sail, he wrote:

. . . . I went up on deck a little while ago for the sole purpose of placing a request. I looked up at the stars and asked Almighty God for some wind. Something is wrong with the universal machinery. We should be having strong trades still, but for two days there has not been enough wind to blow out a match, and I wanted to make this a fast passage! It appears we will never do so now.

. . . . Everyone's nerves are on edge and if we continue to slat and bang around in this ridiculous fashion, we will fall to pieces. Times like this persuade me that steam is the only answer. Poor, helpless, little *Cannibal!* Your day is almost done. We drift together upon a sea that does not seem to care what happens to us. Give you strength and give me patience!

. . . . Except for the sound of gear banging aloft, it is so quiet the noise of my pen scraping across this journal is enough to scare a man. I had Keim rig me a windsail over the skylight today for better ventilation, but now it is hanging limp. It sure doesn't send down any air. Instead I get conversation and much to my annoyance there are times when I can hear every word spoken on the quarterdeck. Fortunately, everyone is in a foul mood, so little is said anyway. Right now I can hear the goings-on of the whole ship, from the pigs grunting up forward to Miss Peacock humming "Don't Crush My Violets." And when she's through she'll say, Goodness Gracious, I will bet. I even heard the good Reverend muttering over his Bible a while ago. Oliver Wiggins and Hutton are playing rummy in the dining saloon. How their voices get back here I don't know. The sound must go up from the saloon skylight and hit the mainsail, then somehow come back and bounce off the spanker, and finally fall down my new windsail. Most of the time I can't make out what they say and don't care, but when they get excited I can hear plain.

. . . . A while ago I could hear Lott on the afterdeck telling Yancy about the whorehouses in Rotterdam and this set me to thinking about what kind of a life I have led. I have never been much interested in the seamy side of any port although wherever a sailing man goes he is bound to run into some phase of it. In Rotterdam there's the Schiedamse Dyk and in Antwerp it's Schelde Kade. In Copenhagen it's Nyhavn, and St. Pauli in Hamburg is the worst of all, with pimps coming aboard before the spring lines are fast to the wharf. I never had much to do with those places, being in need of money mostly when I was young and just mainly absorbed in learning my trade. In recent years when we make port I've been too busy trying to keep this poor ship from the auctioneer's hammer.... or maybe my blood has cooled considerable. Anyway I have no special regrets so far as whores go. They have their headaches and I sure have mine. If I was to get interested in a woman it would have to be some lady like Charlotte King, but then the kind like her wouldn't be likely to feel the same way.

.... I suppose any sailor just ought to make up his mind that he's married to the sea, like I sort of said to Charlotte King not so long ago. Right now with all this slapping and banging I hate this life, but then I notice that when the sea is in a good mood I'm the same way. Which I suppose also is something like being married. If I could stake out a piece of the sea and make it mine like a farmer does the land, I think I would do it. But the sea belongs to all men and always has....

Bell paused and nibbled at the end of his pen. It was pretty fancy thinking, but by God he was right. There were no areas of the earth known as "International Land" where the representatives of any nation could roam at will. There never had been, come to think of it. And there had been "International Waters" since the beginning of time.

He bent to his writing again.

.... So I guess I'm sort of a citizen of the sea and now looking back on things I can just about mark the time when I first came to realize it. When I was with Rasmussen in the *Inca* we ran across a derelict drifting in the Pacific. She was a lime-juicer and Rasmussen hove to and boarded her. The only thing he could find in her worth taking off was a sextant, and the second mate set me to work cleaning it up. I polished that old metal like it was a crown jewel. It was a Frodsham and Keen design of beautiful workmanship and gradually, as I worked, it became a symbol to me of the world to come. I had not the faintest idea how to use it, but I knew that sextant meant more to me than just something to reflect the sun and the moon and the stars. It was the companion of a real deep-water man. Those were the days when I was young enough to dream. And now, here I am, and it's sure a good thing we can't see too far ahead when we're young. Otherwise we might never have any ambition because when I dreamed of having my own ship some day I sure didn't picture myself having to listen to a woman like Ethel Peacock sing a song. Or spend a half-hour before supper nodding my head while she complained about the thousands of cockroaches which she says infest her cabin. I finally lost my patience and said I'd give her a bounty on every roach she caught beyond fifty. I may regret this. It may cost me money . . . .

Suddenly Bell turned completely about in his chair and faced the piano. Or whoever, when they were young, dreamed about a bottle?

Without taking his eyes from the bottle, he put down the pen and lit his pipe. He sat motionless for a long time listening to the murmur of the sea which came so cleary down the windsail. Then he rose from his chair and walked straight toward the bottle. He reached for it and, working his big fingers cautiously as if he were removing the percussion cap from a charge of dynamite, he unscrewed the cork. By God, it was about time! He brought the mouth of the bottle half-way to his lips when Anchor barked and he heard a knocking on the door.

He quickly replaced the cork and set the bottle in its place on the piano. Then stuffing his shirt in his pants, he crossed the room and angrily pulled open the door. Charlotte King stood in the companionway. She held out his volume of Dickens.

—I didn't mean to disturb you, Captain, but I hate people who never return books.

—Thanks. . . . Mrs. King.

He took the book and made a movement to close the door. There was the bottle.

—I thought that if I returned it promptly you'd let me borrow something else.

—Well. . . . sure. Come on in.

She moved past him before he had the door completely open. He hesitated, then closed the door after her.

—My cabin is a mess as usual. Excuse it.

She stood in the center of the room and as he drew the curtains over his unmade bunk and folded the towel over his washstand, he knew she was watching him.

—Don't bother, Captain. A man who lives alone is not supposed to keep things spick and span.

—Why not?

—I would suspect him of being less of a man and more of an old maid.

—It looks like I'll never qualify for an old maid's home then.

She took a few steps toward his desk and looked down at the open journal. He moved quickly to close it and in doing so he was forced to stand very close to her. As he reached across the desk to place the pen in its stand, he caught the faint odor of her perfume and his movements slowed as he picked up the journal. He held it between his hands, fumbling with it uncertainly. She was standing against the drawer where he kept it.

—Writing a book?

—No. Just some jottings now and then. Sort of a hobby to pass the time.

—I'd bet it's more interesting than Dickens.

—Didn't you like *David Copperfield?*

—Let's say it was a new experience for me.

Now, holding the journal, he didn't know what to do with it. He didn't want to ask her to move so he could open the drawer and yet he could no longer hold it so foolishly. He slipped it on the desk beside her. She placed her hand on it and smiled.

—I don't suppose I could borrow this to read?

—No. . . . it's nothing would interest you. I just like to practice penmanship.

—I'm sure it would be very interesting.

—Why?

—Because you are an interesting man. There aren't very many left in the world. Every time I think I've met a man I find out that what I've really met is a boy and his mother. You don't seem that way.

—My mother didn't live long enough to have much to do with me.

—In your case I doubt if it would have made much difference if she had.

They watched each other in silence for a moment. She made no move to leave, although Bell moved back a pace so that the way to the door was free.

It's strange, Bell thought. She was sitting right beside me in the dining saloon only a little while ago and she looked entirely different. He remembered the photograph in her passport and he thought that now some of the defiance had returned to her eyes. Through the wind chute he heard Ethel Peacock singing "Don't Crush My Violets" again and for once he was glad to hear her. It gave him an excuse to smile and look away from this woman. Raising his eyes toward the skylight he said,—She don't sing so good, does she?

—You're afraid of me, Captain. Aren't you?

—No.

The *Cannibal* rolled heavily to starboard and he moved his feet to brace himself. Here she was in his cabin again when he had sworn she would never enter it. Well, by God, she wasn't going to play the piano this time. Not by a damn sight.

She leaned forward a little from the desk and said,—Tell me something. Haven't you any desire to put your arms around me?

—Yeah.

—Why don't you?

—Because I know better. Is that what you came in here for?

—Yes.

—Well, then maybe you'd better get out. I got enough troubles.

To his surprise she began to chuckle and this concerned him more than if she had become angry. The corners of her mouth turned upwards in honest amusement and it occured to him that for the first time he was comfortable with her. She continued to laugh and yet he knew she was not laughing at him.

—For once I was right, Captain. You are a man.

—Some might not think so. . . . being so long at sea and turning down such a chance. But I need a shave and I might scratch your hull if I passed too close.

Now he joined her laughter and the more they continued the funnier it seemed to be. They laughed and reached out to touch each other and gasped for air as they tried to break through their crazy merriment. Wiping the moisture from her eyes she said brokenly,—It's a fine state of affairs when I can't make a man lose his good sense. But I suppose it had to happen sometime. I'd like to think I'm not just your type. . . . make me feel better. Say I'm not your type, Captain. Say I'm not too old or beat up. Say something nice, Captain. . . . try it for size and let me hear it in that bullfrog voice of yours. . . .

Now Bell was not certain whether she was laughing or crying. A lock of hair had fallen over her eyes and he could not see them. Her shoulders shook convulsively as she fumbled with a handkerchief to wipe away the tears.

—Go on, Captain. . . . say something nice. . . . grumble like a bullfrog down in the bottom of a swamp because that's the way you always sound. . . . but say something a girl would like to hear. . . . you have a moon and everything! . . . .

—You're a pretty good girl.

Bell laughed again to cover his embarrassment.

—That's a matter of opinion.

Obeying a sudden impulse, Bell struck her shoulder lightly with the flat of his hand.

—How about a drink, Mrs. King?

—Sure. . . . sure.

He moved quickly to the piano and took down the bottle. He took two glasses from the washbasin and recrossed the cabin to set them on the desk. The cork squeaked as he jerked it from the bottle and in his haste he splashed whiskey on the journal. He did not bother to wipe it off, but thrust one glass toward Charlotte King and raised the other.

—Good to have you aboard, Mrs. King!

The glasses were more than half full of whiskey. Bell drained his without taking it from his lips, then slammed it down on the journal. She said thoughtfully,—You kind of like that stuff, don't you?

—It's been a long time.

He seized the neck of the bottle and was about to refill his glass when there was a sharp knock on the door. Bell sighed. He turned reluctantly away from Charlotte King and looked at the door. He tried without success to keep the annoyance from his voice.

—Well?

—Ramsay, Captain. Could we have a word?

—What's on your mind?

Bell glanced at Charlotte and then at the bottle and the glasses. As if he had given a spoken order she picked up the bottle and the glasses and placed them behind the desk where they could not be seen. Then she moved quickly to the piano and sat down on the stool. From behind the door, Ramsay called,—May I come in?

—Why not?

The door opened and Ramsay entered. He stopped immediately on seeing Charlotte there, then turned as if to retreat.

—Oh! Pardon me. I didn't know. . . .

—Come on in.

Bell thought. . . . He didn't know? The hell he didn't. He heard us laughing and he had to make sure. He watched Ramsay smile at Charlotte and saw him slowly remove his cap.

—Good evening, Mrs. King.

Bell was pleased to see that she only nodded her head, and then he wondered why he cared what she did. Ignoring Ramsay for a moment, he watched Charlotte and thought how foolish he had been to want her to leave. She thought fast, this woman, and she acted fast. She had nerve, for now she sat on the piano stool and lit a cigarette as coolly as if she were in a deck chair. And the defiance returned to her eyes as she looked at Ramsay. Why should that be? Ramsay was a dunce, but what did he ever do to her? She looked ready to spit in his eye. Well, bully for her if she did.

Bell sat down on the corner of the desk and reached instinctively for his pipe.

—Well, Ramsay? I assume you got a good reason for leaving the deck.

—The wind is picking up. There's a full moon and it's bright as day. I want permission to make sail.

—You're in a hurry, eh?

Ramsay continued to smile and he looked directly at Charlotte King again.

—So are the men. We lack. . . . certain amusements, to help us pass the time.

Bell bit into his pipe. He saw Charlotte stiffen and he wished he had never had the drink. He could not trust himself near Ramsay with the whiskey still burning in his stomach. So holding firmly to the edge of the desk, he said, —Ramsay, you have a very handsome face. I hope you always manage to keep it that way.

—Do I have your permission. . . . sir?

—Yeah. Put a good lookout on the foretop. And leave.

Ramsay's eyes searched the cabin quickly. The bastard is like a bird dog, Bell thought. He smells the whiskey. In silence he watched Ramsay turn to the door.

—One other thing. The wind is fair for Honolulu. It would be a shame not to take advantage of it.

—You keep her nor'east by east, and I will hold you responsible for any deviation. We are not going to Honolulu. Is that clear?

Ramsay looked at Charlotte again, then touched his cap.

—Yessir. Pleasant evening.

He closed the door and they waited until they heard him mount the companionway steps. Bell pried open the top of a tobacco can with his thumb and thoughtfully repacked his pipe. He said very quietly, —Do you want the rest of your drink?

—No. Thanks.

She rose suddenly and crossed the cabin. She took the match from his hand, struck it, and held it to his pipe. As he puffed, the flame blossomed and she watched his eyes above it.

—How about you, David Bell? Want me to pour you another?

—No. I guess I don't need it.

—Where did you get that scar?

—Somebody didn't like me.

—What was she wearing?

—It wasn't a she.

He took the pipe from his mouth and slowly put his arms around her. He was suddenly confident, more so than he had ever been with her. It could be the way she stood waiting now, or was it just the way she had treated Ramsay? I will be clumsy about this, he thought. And she will have a perfect right to laugh. But at least she'll know I'm not dead.

—I was right. You're trouble.

He bent his mouth toward hers and before he touched her lips he chuckled and said,—It's a pity to scratch such a pretty hull.

Later he wrote for a long time in his journal.

. . . . Things are quiet again with us heeling to this new wind. In spite of some risk I find it pleasant to be under way at night again. I suppose I should catch a nap before relieving Ramsay, but I know it wouldn't be any use to lie down. Too much fills my mind. So I might as well take further soundings and try to find out why I am more inclined to smile at my troubles than I have been in a long time. It seems reasonable to assume there must be some special cause for the way I feel and I wonder how much Charlotte King had to do with it. I put the bottle of whiskey back on the piano myself and didn't even want to pull the cork. So there has been a change, and I think it began when she entered my cabin.

. . . . There must be some value in looking back over past hours in this fashion because doing so now, I discover I actually found out very little about Charlotte. Then how can I feel that I know her so well?

. . . . Maybe Mrs. Weatherbee would have said that when a man and a woman meet and are mutually attracted, the less the causes are examined the better. Easy enough to say, but if I am making a fool of myself (and it is quite possible I am), I would at least like to find a good excuse. I did not fall in love with the *Cannibal* because I sat down on a dock one day and figured out with pencil and paper that she could hold so much cargo and make so much money. I did not calculate the crew I would need, their salaries, their keep, or the need for this and that about her sails, hull, and rigging. I should have done so maybe, but such considerations are for businessmen whose feet are solidly on the land and not for seamen, worse luck.

. . . . Most Captains I know fancy themselves very shrewd with a dollar, but they are in fact hopeless sentimentalists or they would never have gone to sea in the first place. Since the days of the tea-clippers and the whalers no man has ever become wealthy through his personal labors at sea.

. . . . I bought the *Cannibal* because I fell in love with her sheer line and a lot of other things I can't exactly figure. There was a saucy lift to her jib boom, and her transom caught my eye, the way it so beautifully met the rest of her hull. Her tumble home was unusually pronounced for a ship of her size and era, and maybe that was it. Anyway she sure captured my heart the first time I laid eyes on her, and I would have sold my soul to possess her. Perhaps I have, for now she is my world. Unless I force myself to think about them I don't see her faults, or what neglect and time have done to her. I don't see the checks in her masts or the grass and menagerie of marine life clinging to her hull. I don't smell or see the rot in her horn timbers and I try to ignore the splotches of rust around her chain plates. To me, the little *Cannibal* will always be beautiful and most of the time I see her only as I first laid eyes on her. If I got away and came back after a long time maybe it would be different and I would see what others see. I think the same must be true between a man and a woman. So maybe I better not try it.

How many times have I seen Charlotte King? Once. This night. If we should never see each other again, or spent the rest of our lives together, I am bound to hold that special impression. It is of no matter that I saw her before—I have seen the other passengers too, many times. But their faces are just faces to be remembered or more likely forgotten with passing time. I saw beyond Charlotte's face tonight. But it was only for a few moments, but I think I will never really see her face again. It seems to me that once the outer mask of someone is passed we uncover a different person entirely. It's the person that suits us. Like looking at a ship, we provide our own ideas and are never again capable of looking at that person cold and straight on. Even now, I must make an effort to recall Charlotte's mouth, or her eyes, or the fact she is somewhat shorter than me. If I was any kind of an artist I might try to paint her portrait, if only to prove that all portraits written or painted are not much good. How can they be if every person holds his own private idea about people they meet?

. . . . All this is mentally a hard beat to windward for me and the fact that I ever got mixed up in such thinking indicates change.

. . . . One thing I can't figure out. Is this the way a grown man falls in love with a woman? Sort of like sailing into a strange harbor without a chart? Maybe I better clew up and sail easy for a while, before I stand into danger. I lack experience at this sort of thing.

Yancy was perched on the lower topsail yard, some seventy feet above the *Cannibal*'s deck. He sat in the moonlight with his back against the foremast and one bare foot braced against the yard. He could see plainly to the horizon where the lighter sky merged with the black water. There were no signs ahead of breaking water which might indicate the presence of a reef, and in time he became hopelessly bored with his assignment as lookout. Passing his arm around a halyard lest he fall from his perch, he tried dozing for a while, only to find that his attempt to sleep was unsuccessful. Here aloft, the familiar and monotonously soothing sound of the sea was reduced to a mere whisper. It was replaced by an erratic symphony of creaks, scrapes, and groans which seemed timed by the devil to keep him awake.

When the wind fell light, the sails would deflate, and then as the *Cannibal* rolled to the swells, they would refill again. The result was an endless series of flutterings and muffled thunder. Gaff jaws grated for lack of grease, the foremast creaked as if it were in continuous agony, the sheet chains clinked with every roll, and somewhere a heavy wooden block thudded against a spar.

Angered, both at the sounds and his forced isolation, Yancy tried to amuse himself by watching the miniature world below him. He saw the long column of phosphorescent water which streamed from the *Cannibal*'s stern like a bridal veil and he watched it join with the path of the moon. He could see Ramsay pacing the quarterdeck, his white shirt seeming to reflect the moon, and he could see Uala lounging at the wheel. Beside him was the figure of Lott, and Yancy thought that even in the moonlight his head looked like an egg. He could see down into the saloon through the open skylight, and beneath it he could see Hutton's bald head and the long blond hair of Oliver Wiggins. He thought that if he had a telescope he might be able to identify the cards they held in their hands, and he spent some time forming an elaborate plan whereby he might engage one of the passengers in poker and post someone in the rigging to signal down his opponent's hand. He thought that it would not be very long before he was rich if he chose Lott as his lookout. . . . Lott, who was so willing and stupid, would not demand too much of a share.

He saw the King woman emerge through the saloon hatch and go to the weather rail where she stood for a long time looking at the moon. Finally he saw Ramsay approach her and he waited expectantly for some indication their meeting might be prearranged. He was disappointed. The King woman turned away from Ramsay almost immediately and descended the saloon hatch. They could not have exchanged more than a few words. Almost directly below, he saw Dak Sue come out of his galley and dump a pail of garbage overside. He streamed the pail aft to the full length of its lanyard and sloshed it about as a gesture to cleanliness. The *Cannibal* took an unusually heavy roll. The force of the sea jerked the pail from Dak Sue's hand and it vanished instantly. Even from his perch Yancy could hear his shrill profanity.

But activity viewed from such a distance soon palled on Yancy. He thought it was like being dead and gone to heaven and so it might be to the angels looking down on people who were still alive. He turned to scan the horizon again, almost hoping he would sight a reef; anything to relieve his aerial captivity. Then suddenly he became aware of a new sound, and it mystified him because it was very near and yet bore no relation to the others. He looked aloft at the topgallants and then down at the forecourse. They were all too far away to make this sound which he identified as metallic. It was a harsh and intermittent crackling sound, as if something were being tortured under enormous weight. As he listened Yancy decided that he had in fact heard the sound ever since he climbed aloft, but it was so buried beneath the other noises he had failed to notice it. Now, in his boredom, he was determined to find the cause of it and he swung down into the footropes where he could move back and forth along the yard.

He waited patiently for the sound and suffered long periods when it was not evident at all. He found its odd recurrence maddening, and he decided that it was a sick sound and he hated it and if he had to stay up on the yard all night he would discover the cause of it. After considerable experimentation he found that the farther he moved away from the mast, the more the sound diminished in volume. So he moved inboard again, searching all of the rigging and cocking his head like a hound waiting to pounce on a clever bird.

At last, watching a patch of moonlight on the rigging, he knew he had found it. He crept toward the blob of light cunningly, as if the sound came from a living thing and might fly away before he could reach it.

The sound originated in a part of the yard itself. Set at right

131

angles to the foremast, the yard weighed more than a ton and was fixed to the mast by a heavy metal bracket. The bracket extended forward and formed two bands which encircled the yard. A thick steel pin passed through the bracket fitting near the mast, allowing the yard to pivot and so be set efficiently to the prevailing wind. Now, in the patch of moonlight, Yancy saw that the metal forging had cracked in its upper part where the pin passed through it so that all of the strain was on half of it. The slight redistribution of weight caused the two parts to separate and scrape together each time the *Cannibal* rolled.

It was not anything to get excited about, Yancy thought. There was still the pin holding part of the bracket plate. It was probably strong enough to prevent the yard from breaking away. But any weakness aloft suggested possibilities.

Lying outstretched on the yard, Yancy studied the crack and tried to think how he could tell Ramsay about it without becoming involved in the work of repair. He had almost decided to let someone else discover the fault when he saw Lott, far below in the lee shrouds. Apparently the port running light had gone out, for he was tinkering with it and he saw Lott's face turn from amber to a brilliant red as he closed the lantern glass. Watching him swing around the shrouds and drop to the deck, Yancy suddenly remembered Ramsay's words,—They'll think the way you do. . . .

Now there was a smart mate! There were a hell of a lot of things wrong with the *Cannibal* and the rest of the crew being so ignorant and all they just went along with whatever Bell wanted.

Well, I'm not willing, Yancy thought. I got brains. I'm like they say, one of them natural-born leaders. I proved it before when I was bos'n like I really should be here, and I can prove it again. Ramsay knows it or he never would have spent so much time yarnin' with me. Knows class when he sees it. God helps them who help themselves and if you ever expect to put your feet on dry land again you better do something about it. You got brains. Start using them.

He called down to Lott and saw his face turn upward.

—Hey, Bonehead! Come bear me a hand!

He waited, knowing Lott would start up the ratlines, for at sea no call from aloft was ever ignored. Not, Yancy thought, by a genuine dumb seaman like Lott, who never avoided work. Men like Lott always needed a leader.

Lott came up fast, his big feet sure on the ratlines, and in barely half a minute he hoisted himself over the yard to face Yancy.

—What's the trouble? See somethin'?

—Yeah. Remember what I told you about them mangoes?

—So? Are you growin' mangoes up here?

—No, Bonehead. But I told you if ya ate one you'd be no good with a woman for a long time, didn't I? Well, how would you like to never see a woman again?

—I woon't.

—You may not unless somebody starts using their heads.

—Somebody who? What you call me up here for?

—Ya told me back in Suva this bucket weren't fit for sea, didn't ya?

Lott shrugged his powerful shoulders and looked down at the sea.

—She ain't so bad. I seen worse. Leaks a little.

—Leaks a little for Christ's sake? She's sinkin' right under our feet! It's a good thing you can't read, that's all I got to say.

Lott rubbed his bullet head and frowned at the moon.

—You call me all way up here just to say that?

—No, Bonehead. I called you up here because I'm concerned about your welfare. . . . you and me and all the rest of the crew. And this is a good place to talk things over without everybody and his brother interruptin' all the time. We got to do somethin'.

—Ramsay is lookin' up at us.

—Let him look. We got a right to talk. If you'd do some thinkin' while you're breakin' your back on that goddamned pump you'd understand why somethin' has got to be done. I took a peek at the logbook this morning and you know how much water is in our bilges?

—How can I know?

—Sure, how can you know? How can you know anything if Bell don't want you to? All you know is how much water comes out and the only way you got to measure it is by how much your back aches. I tell ya I seen it in the logbook!

Since reading the logbook was strictly a product of his imagination, Yancy decided he might as well not bother to exaggerate. It was enough that he was holding Lott's attention. A born leader had to know when to take things easy. Furthermore, there was always the chance that Lott would pass the word and someone else in the crew like Keim might actually read the log.

Edging along the yard so that he might be closer to Lott, he said,—There was thirty-four inches. Thirty-four inches, that's what!

—I no believe you.

—You sayin' I'm a liar? You think I didn't look at the log?

—I no say nothin'! But I sure we have not so much. We pump all night if so.

—Pretty soon you'll be pumpin' all night and all day, too, if Bell has his way.

—How you mean? He's the old man, ain't he? Who's tell him what to do?

—You are. . . . me and you and Uala and Keim and Sweeney and even Old Brown, if he's got any sense. We are goin' to tell him for the good of the ship and if he won't listen we'll make him listen. We ain't Ethiopian slaves, by God.

Yancy found that he was strangely exhilarated. Now he was not at all sure that he had not actually seen the logbook. The sound of his voice pleased him and his choice of words pleased him and the more he looked at Lott in the moonlight the more he became convinced that he had discovered a natural talent in himself. Who else, he thought, would be able to convince a bonehead like Lott that his life was in danger? Who else would have the brains to lead a bunch of dumb sailors and perhaps save the whole ship?

Bewildered and unhappy, Lott said,—I dunno what you talk about, but I no go for rough stuff with officers.

—Who said anything about rough stuff? That's mutiny and we don't want no part of it. Ya think I want to get three and a half years like them dumb monkeys in the *Manga Reva*? We sign a protest, that's all, and Bell has got to read the protest whether he wants to or not.

—What's protest?

Yancy sighed and forced himself to be patient.

—A protest is a piece of paper which says on it what you want to happen. This one would say that we think the old *Cannibal* ain't seaworthy and that we don't think she has any busi-

ness goin' up to forty north where the weather is tough. . . .
and that we think she ought to head straight for Honolulu
where she can be hauled out and repaired and all like that. And
we say that we have signed this paper out of regard to the
safety of the passengers and the crew and we list all the things
which has gone wrong and which we can show to any inspector
who is inarrested. Why, Bell wouldn't have a leg to stand on.
And maybe when we got to Honolulu me and you could get a
couple of women together and get our achin' backs straightened
out.

—I like Bell. I don't want him in no trouble. He's good sailor.

—Don'tcha *see*, Bonehead? There won't *be* no trouble! It's
all perfectly legal and we can count on Ramsay to back us up.
What we're really doin' is makin' things easy for Bell. He can
show our protest to the passengers and say what the hell he's
got to go to Honolulu. . . . follow me? Bell might even thank us.

—But there ain't much wrong except the leakin'.

As Lott scratched his head, Yancy knew the time had come
to clinch his argument. He moved backward on the yard and
pointed a finger accusingly at the patch of moonlight.

—Oh no? You think I just called you up here to pass the time
a day? Look at that crack! How about that? The metal is tired
and it's busted wide-open and if it weren't for the pin it woulda
been down on your thick head a while ago when you was fixin'
the runnin' light. . . . and besides killin' you it would probably
go right on through the deck and stove a hole in the bottom and
maybe shove you through the hole. What have you got to say
about that?

Lott stared at the crack in the metal and passed his banana
fingers along its length as if he were probing a child's wound.
He shook his head and murmured,—Jasus Chreest!

—And that ain't all. I'll bet there's a hundred places we
could find in her riggin' from her sheer poles to her tops that is
just waitin' to give way. I tell ya, Bonehead, it's gettin' so I'm
afraid to climb around up here. Look around for yerself in the
daylight tomorrow if you don't believe me. It ain't bad enough
we're sinkin', too. *Now* will you sign a protest an' quit worryin'
about the old man who don't give a damn what happens to you
or me or nobody else so long as he gets to Manzanillo and gets
rich?

Lott looked up at the fore-topmast and his face was as expressionless as the moon above it. He rubbed his jaw and said,—I think. . . . I think.

Then abruptly, without pausing to look at Yancy, he lowered himself off the yard and started down the ratlines.

Watching him, Yancy saw that his descent was much slower than usual. He stopped on many of the ratlines and carefully examined their lashings.

Yancy smiled. If there were not enough things wrong with the *Cannibal*'s rigging. . . . there always could be.

Eight

For more than a week the *Cannibal* slogged along in a general northerly direction. She sailed only during the day. After the one night of full moon the sky had been heavily overcast and almost continuous rain squalls cut visibility to a minimum. While only a hundred-odd miles north of the equator, she was struck by a violent squall. The flying jib blew away and the spanker split from foot to head. The same night her entire rigging was illuminated by St. Elmo's fire, causing the pigs to squeal in terror and Dak Sue to light a special good-luck joss in the galley which somehow permeated the food and gave everything a foul odor. The decks were never dry, nor was anything else in the *Cannibal*. The skylights leaked and a bucket was set in the center of the saloon table to catch the water. As the passengers fretted below deck, a fine green mold formed on their clothing, and the skin on the seamen's hands withered and crinkled and in places turned a baby pink from constant exposure to water. The sails were so stiff and heavy with rain a job of furling which normally took two men, required four. Every sheet and halyard, every buntline, downhaul, and clew line, was swollen with water until they became like iron wire.

137

Handling these ropes was exasperating and the men's voices sometimes reached a crazy falsetto as they swore at the kinks and tangles.

And always it was Bell who lent the extra hand. No one knew when he slept, for he seemed to appear everywhere, regardless of time. He was on the jib boom to hand and furl at nightfall, and he was on the yards when the sails were shaken out at dawn. He took Old Brown's place at the pump and he did most of the sewing on the torn spanker. Engulfed in wet canvas, he sat hunched on the after cabintop working with palm and needle until he could no longer see. Sensing his master's need for companionship, Anchor never left his side except when Bell went aloft. Even then, though he was always soggy and shivering, he would wait patiently at the foot of the shrouds until Bell descended.

Defying the trades, the squalls came from all directions and confused the sea until every heave and roll of the *Cannibal* came as a physical surprise. She would pitch for a time, and then yaw drunkenly to port or starboard as if the sea despaired of a plan for her. The galley was a shambles as Dak Sue struggled to start fires with wet wood. He cursed the pots and pans which were either spilling a part of their contents or capsizing entirely, and he screamed that he had never seen anything like it since he was cook on an Alaska packer. One evening Dak Sue lost his teeth in the noodles and for the whole next day no warm food came from the galley nor did anyone, including Bell, dare approach the galley house.

There was no easy change in the weather as the *Cannibal* maneuvered against every kind of wind to make northerly progress. The long-awaited change came within the space of two hours.

While she was in the latitude of twelve degrees north, a fresh trade made up from the east and gave the *Cannibal* wind again. The skies cleared and the rain ceased, but with the yards braced sharp up and every fore and after sail drawing well, the *Cannibal* dove into many seas and her decks were continuously lashed with salt spray. The wind was surprisingly cold for this latitude and it drove the spray down the men's necks and somehow found ways to penetrate to every part of their bodies. There were times when even to walk the length of the *Cannibal*'s heaving deck became a minor struggle.

There was no sense to the wind. It should have been a strong trade and yet occasionally it became very near a gale. The last two pigs were washed overboard, and even the high fiddles could not always hold plates on the saloon table. It would have been a magnificent wind for a smartly rigged clipper, but aboard the *Cannibal* every man watched the rigging aloft with growing anxiety. The mainsail began to split gradually across several cloths at the head. The clew on the inner jib carried away, the downhaul jammed, and the sail thundered for a wild twenty minutes before it was finally secured. The gaff topsail blew away entirely, leaving only threads whipping from the jackstay. A freak boarding sea stove in the saloon skylight and effectively put an end to violent argument between Hutton and Reverend Butterfield. Both were drenched to the skin and Hutton's bald head suffered numerous minor lacerations from the flying glass.

Bell wrote in his journal:

. . . Two things give me heart in spite of this most unusual and miserable weather for this latitude. The trades have given us such a push we are now in relatively clear water and I dare to sail at night. There is only Rional and Rene Reef to the north now, and nothing else is shown on the chart. Both were reported in 1923 and may not exist at all. Anyway, with clear skies I am able to obtain a good latitude sight each noon and I can avoid passing in their vicinity at night. So there is really nothing to worry about as far as navigation goes all the way up to forty north and once up there we will have a clear run for Mexico. If our present unusual weather is any example of what is in store for us further north, I'm guessing it's going to be awful cold. We may also be somewhat short of food due to the loss of our pigs. But we will make out on rice and salt horse. This may not please either crew or passengers, but at least they will find out what the food was like when I first went to sea. No one will starve anyway and during the rains we collected enough fresh water to last us indefinitely.

. . . . I am much encouraged about our leak. We have been making very heavy weather of it for over a week and certainly if a plank butt had started or something of that nature, the amount of water we take in every day should in-

crease. These seas, plus the strain on masts and standing rigging, would not be kind to any hull, and I have never heard the little *Cannibal* groan and complain so hard as she works. But there has been no noticeable increase in either our time of pumping or water in the bilges. We still make between fifteen and twenty inches of water per day and pump about two hours to get rid of it, but that is all. I cannot explain this.
. . .

As long as the wind held strong, Yancy had little opportunity to discuss the protest with his shipmates. It had now become an obsession with him and he had carefully rephrased it several times until he was certain every objection was covered. When he was off watch in the fo'c's'le, he read it aloud to Lott and Uala. Knowing they were more than weary, he tried everything he could to capture and hold their attention. He would stand in the center of the fo'c's'le beneath the smoking oil lantern, and assume the most dignified pose he could manage in the cramped little room where six men ate, slept, and tried to live. He spoke to them first as a tolerant father, and if their attention wandered he would become the desperately pleading and righteous leader.

—Listen to me, you dumb sonsabitches! You wanna drown? Don't you give a damn if we go to the bottom? Are you so beat with workin' this hell ship you never wanta see a woman again? Listen to me! . . . you can sleep when you're dead which is the way you will be if you don't sign this here protest! We ain't got all year. We're gettin' up north and once Bell picks up the westerlies he won't never stop, and he coon't anyway. . . . even if he wanted to, once we get to the easterly of Honolulu. You think it's cold now? It's balmy! Wait'll we get north a bit, if you don't fall out of our rotten riggin' and get yourselves killed in the meantime. . . .

They were like animals, Yancy thought. Dumb animals. Who but a sailor would live month after month in conditions no man ashore would tolerate for five minutes? Who but a sailor would catch what sleep he could lying in a wet bunk in wet clothes and be on call at all hours of the day and night? Who but a sailor would be content with coolie wages and a tin plate of bread and beans and rice three times a day? And some salt horse if he was lucky.

When straight persuasion failed to move them, Yancy became the philosopher. In a quiet and most reasonable tone, he said,—This here condition like we have is a thing of the past. Old-timers like Brown don't know no better and so they just go on until they die in the Sailor's Home, if they're lucky. I been on steamships and I know it ain't nothin' like this. You practically got a stateroom all your own and you get eight hours off between watches just to lie in your bunk and listen to the machinery run and count your money. You live like a human bein', what's more. . . . and eat like one. . . . at a table which is set with a white tablecloth and all. This here is straight insanity. If the *Cannibal* weren't under Mexican registry, Bell would never get away with it. There is unions now and they don't take it for granted a man is a idiot just because he is a sailor. Let me ask you somethin'? You. . . . any of you. . . . ever been in a jail anywhere in this world, even for one night in any jail which is so goddamned miserable and uncomfortable as this ship and didn't feed no better? Why, the investigating societies would have a fit if any prisoner had to live like this no matter what he done. . . .

Yancy had little opportunity to talk with members of the opposite watch except at mealtimes. He approached them differently, more as a man vexed by a problem, because he knew that Keim and Old Brown were held in deep respect by the others and both nursed a strange loyalty to sail. So to them, more than to Sweeney, he said,—Sure, I like windjammers. I been in them for a good part of my life and I got no use for a sailor who never done anything but float around in some rust bucket and maybe wave a paintbrush once in a while. Them ain't sailors, they are just plain ordinary workin' stiffs who are generally just tryin' to hide from their wives. But it seems to me. . . . and I may be wrong, mind you. . . . that we got to recognize that windjammers is finished. . . . not only this one, but all of them. Bell now, he can't admit it, because he goes broke and sits on the beach if he does. But I don't see no reason why the few of us should be pallbearers at the funeral, do you now? Especially not if maybe it turned out to be our own funerals just because we didn't have sense enough to stand up for our rights. What the hell. . . . every ship has got to make her last voyage sometime and it seems to me. . . . and I may be wrong again, mind you . . . but it seems to me the old *Cannibal* has tried to make just one voyage too many. . . .

He rubbed his calloused foot along the deck and shook his head mournfully. Then he said,—Yep. . . . in a way you might say she's a casket.

Looking at the sea, he shivered and said,—It's sure deep out there. I imagine at least two thousand fathoms. And the water ain't gettin' no warmer. . . . day by day.

The rains accustomed the passengers to a confined life below deck and now the cold wind gave them little encouragement to pass their time on deck. Oliver Wiggins, protected only by his thin pink shirt, never ventured on deck except at noon when the sun's warmth was greatest. The moment the sun disappeared behind a cloud even for a moment, he would swear softly and descend at once to the saloon. He would take up his place at the long table and lay out a pack of worn cards and pretend to play solitaire. But he had long before lost interest in the game. Now, much paler than when he had boarded the *Cannibal* at Rotuma, he would sit thoughtfully twirling the long hair about his ears into ringlets, and play the game which had come to interest him far more than any device of cards. He said quite openly that he was gambling for the Reverend Butterfield's soul, but his methods of approach were devious and seemingly without plan.

Since the saloon was the only common room aboard the *Cannibal*, the passengers were obliged to choose between it, the deck, or remaining in their cramped rooms. As a result, Wiggins was almost never without an audience and escape for the Reverend Butterfield was nearly impossible. And in time Butterfield discovered that being the center of attention, or at least the subject of discussion, was a delicious sensation and he grew restive if Wiggins ignored him. The others were secretly grateful, for they found that with so much fire their close association was more easily borne.

Now, for close to a month the *Cannibal*'s passengers had faced each other along the table at least three times a day. Their personal habits and mannerisms, largely unnoticed at first, became targets of ridicule, until finally they generated little explosions of pure hatred. Ethel Peacock had a genius for finding hairs in her food. The fact that the hairs were bright red and matched her own exactly was of no consequence to her.

She invariably accused one or several of her fellow passengers of scheming to spoil her appetite. It was true that upon occasion Oliver Wiggins supplied her with tangible evidence. He mischievously placed a blond strand from his head in her plate of tapioca. He was bitterly disappointed when she failed to recognize the hair and, for once, blamed herself.

Like a family too long together, the smaller conflicts magnified until there was often open warfare. Wiggins' Continental method of using his knife and fork, which reversed the American style, almost drove Hutton out of his reason. Nor did he approve of the way Wiggins bobbed his head toward his plate for every bite, and he wanted to know if it didn't remind everyone at the table of diving in a tub for apples on Halloween. Or a pelican stabbing a fish, perhaps?

The Reverend Butterfield ate very slowly, picking at his food and munching endlessly on every mouthful. Dribbles of gravy would leak from the corners of his mouth during this long process of mastication. Unable to avert their eyes for long, the others would watch him with profound disapproval.

And if Butterfield ate too slowly, another man at the table seemed determined to balance the distribution of food. For Harry Hutton, eating was a business, and it was also a matter of urgent survival. His plate was full before the others had a chance to lift their spoons, and his pudgy hands darted so swiftly to the platter of johnnycake and back to his open mouth his table companions were never certain he had moved at all.

The Morrises ate silently, nibbling at their food as if they had no right to it, and in time their very shyness became annoying. Ramsay seldom ate with the passengers, although the exacting manner with which he arranged his food in little piles on the plate did nothing to enhance his popularity. Bell alone escaped open censure, perhaps because he sat at the end of the table and his appearances were as likely to occur at the end of a meal as the beginning. His hands were often creased with tar from the rigging, and his hair was rarely combed, but after his vigil through the rains and long absences from the table, the passengers easily forgave him.

And so, exposed to each other through most of their waking hours, the passengers were always relieved when the focus of attention fell upon Butterfield. Wiggins would arch one eyebrow, smile sourly, and signal the beginning of the game by pointing a fork across the table.

Now he said,—Regard our apostle. Hasn't said grace for at least two weeks. I would like to know, sir, the reason for this omission, although I cannot detect the slightest difference in the food, blessed or unblessed.

Butterfield was not in the least displeased as he sensed every eye upon him. He finished chewing a morsel of the salt beef and swallowed demurely. Staring at him in fascination, Wiggins said,—And what is that mechanical contrivance which rises and falls in your throat when you swallow? Is that large and vulgar bump your Adam's apple?

Envious of the attention which always seemed directed toward Butterfield, Ethel Peacock plucked a thought from the air and gave sound to it. She said,—I saw that rat outside my door again! It's the same one I saw before.

Feodor Morris said,—Perhaps there is only one.

—Well, I can't understand why there should only be one. Goodness gracious! There are probably hundreds of the beasts.

—Madame Peacock. . . . Wiggins said.—There is only one rat and I doubt if rats are capable of immaculate conception.

—Maybe they are like chickens.

—No, Madame. It takes two to tango.

Ethel Peacock appeared about to burst into tears. She pushed out her under lip and glared across the table at Wiggins.

She said,—I consider your remark uncalled for and ungentlemanly. You have shocked Mrs. Morris and I think you should apologize to us all.

—Your rude interruption of my conversation hardly qualifies you to set a code of manners. The rest of us are waiting to hear from Doctor Butterfield.

—He isn't a real doctor. . . . Ethel Peacock said desperately. —Are you now?

—I am a Doctor of Divinity, although my order does not approve public use of the title.

—Come now. . . . Wiggins said. —We are digressing from the remarkable size of Butterfield's Adam's apple. Miss Peacock, you might be useful when we get to Mexico, so will you kindly go some place and fill your head with pebbles? Shake the contents well and when you have learned to keep an even rhythm. . . . come back and we'll start a maraca band.

—Oh! said Ethel Peacock. —Harry! Make him stop.

Harry Hutton squeezed a chunk of johnnycake into his mouth and mumbled,—You watch your step, Wiggins. I won't have you talking to Ethel like that and hurting her feelings. You just better watch your step.

Wiggins' smile became sad.

—Are you threatening me with bodily harm, sir?

—I'm just telling you we all have to get along.

—Why should we get along? What possible things can we have in common except the unfortunate circumstances that we are all genteel poor or we most certainly would not be aboard this ship. I see no reason whatsoever for us to get along. It is far more amusing if we fail at every attempt.

—Bravo. . . . Charlotte King said quietly.

—If we learn to hate each other sufficiently we shall at least have some stimulus for our minds.

—Hatred is sinful. . . . Butterfield said. —It is an emotion created by the Devil.

—I don't care who creates it if it will keep us from turning into vegetables.

—I'd like to eat some real fresh vegetables. . . . Hutton said.

Wiggins slapped his hand on the table triumphantly.

—Observe, Butterfield! Our human garbage pail desires fresh vegetables! And desire is also an emotion created by your friend the Devil, right?

—Oliver Wiggins, you are a dreadful man. . . . Ethel Peacock said. —Harry. . . . do something! Make him stop.

—Aha! See, Butterfield? Hatred! Miss Peacock is just now possessed of the Devil. Observe her dilated eyes. . . . her quick breathing. . . . and her tightly pressed lips! A certain sign that her heart has been captured by your horned friend. Save her, Butterfield!

—Miss Peacock has a right to her opinions.

—But don't you see? They are *not* her opinions. How could so lovely and talented a lady, a woman whose face time forgot to mark. . . . how could such true beauty be transformed into a face that would frighten an eagle?

Ethel Peacock was undecided whether to smile at Wiggins to prove that his surprising recognition of her merits was correct, or cry. Her voice lost much of its venom as she said, —I'm going to speak to the captain about you, Oliver Wiggins. I'm not at all sure you should eat with the rest of us.

—And where else would he eat?. . . . Ida Morris asked sympathetically.

Charlotte King said,—I think the captain has other problems without worrying about who eats with who.

—You should know. . . . Ethel snapped.

—I should know what?

—What the captain has on his mind. You spend enough time with him.

—Jealous?

—What you do is your own affair.

—I can see that.

—Providing you don't take up too much of the captain's time when he is supposed to be resting. . . . in which case your conduct affects us all.

With a sly glance at Oliver Wiggins, Charlotte said, —I am driving the captain mad. He can't sleep.

—Well! What I mean is, he doesn't seem to be the type who would be . . . .

—Interested in a woman like me?

—I didn't say that!

—Why didn't you?

—*Delightful!* . . . . Wiggins said happily, rubbing his hands.

—Besides. . . . Ethel said lamely, —it's who eats with *whom* . . . . not the other way around.

—I stand corrected.

Looking at Ethel Peacock, Wiggins said, —Coward. See, Butterfield? The Devil has left her. Did you just pass a miracle?

Pleased that he might again become the center of attention, Butterfield swallowed hastily and said,—Your conception of the Devil belongs in the mind of a very small child.

—Then he doesn't have horns and a tail?

—I haven't the faintest idea what physical form the Devil might assume, but I shouldn't be too much surprised if he looked like you.

—I thought God created man in his own image.

—The Devil is clever at disguise.

—Apparently. When I was in the Army he seemed to resemble my colonel. When I was in prison camp he bore a remarkable resemblance to the Oberleutnant. On Rotuma I

146

rather fancied him as a mosquito. In every case he seemed to have abandoned the business of temptation and concentrated on making life miserable. If such pleasures as drink and women are also within the province of the Devil then he seems most inconsistent and hardly to be feared. You amaze me, Butterfield. You don't know what your villain looks like nor for that matter do you offer any information as to his whereabouts.

—It is enough to know that he exists.

—An intriguing chap, anyway, I should think. And most ingenious if he was really responsible for such a magnificent Adam's apple as your own.

Butterfield instinctively touched his neck and swallowed. Then, as if to cover his embarrassment, he wiped his mouth on the sleeve of his frock.

—You believe or you don't.

—Ha! But you are beginning to doubt. . . . for which mental progression, I salute you.

—You will never convince. . . .

Butterfield never finished his sentence. For suddenly every person at the table lost interest in him and looked at the ceiling. They sat rigidly, as if they could see what they heard. Hutton's knife tinked against his plate. A fearful little cry escaped Ida Morris.

The pump had started on deck. This was the first time it had ever been worked during the daylight hours and its rhythmic clanging seemed to hold a much greater urgency than ever before. At night, in their cabins, the passengers could press their heads into their pillows and try to ignore the pump and some of them even managed to sleep, but now with the sound directly overhead, the clanging and sucking dominated everything.

—I'm going on deck. . . . Hutton said solemnly.

One by one, the others rose from their places and followed him toward the saloon companionway.

The pump hardly clanged twenty strokes before Bell was on deck. He saw that there was a quick lashing on the wheel and then, rubbing the sleep from his eyes, he walked wearily forward to where Ramsay stood by the pump. He looked at Lott, Yancy, and Uala working the pump; then he turned to Ramsay.

—What's this?

—I've only just left the helm. She'll hold for a moment like this.

—How come you're pumping in the daytime? I gave plain orders. . . .

—I considered it necessary.

—Oh, you did?

—I became curious and took several well soundings. We've made three inches in the last hour. Something's finally given way below, I guess.

—You guess? I suppose if you considered it necessary, you would have put back for Suva?

—Honolulu would be closer, sir.

—We are not going to Honolulu!

Seeing the men could hardly pump for listening, Bell turned to them and said,—Belay that!

That pump clanged to a stop and the men leaned on the lift bars as they regained their breath. Now the passengers had gathered by the saloon skylights and Sweeney, Keim, and Old Brown had come from the forecastle. Even Dak Sue had left his galley and stood curiously watching Bell. In a few moments he was almost completely surrounded.

No one spoke as Bell studied the sky and the sea. And for a time he seemed to have forgotten the circle of people about him.

Now, he thought, the time has come. . . . at least the first time. And something will have to be done. Ramsay, he thought, had deliberately chosen a time when everyone aboard the *Cannibal* might be awake. He wanted an audience and he had one.

Bell studied the faces of the crew. Sweeney, confused. . . . and a little afraid because he was so young. . . . the same for Uala. . . . and Yancy, plainly excited about something. He kept looking from Ramsay to Bell as if he knew there would be an open argument. Well, he wouldn't get it. Lott and Keim stood together. . . . as wooden and strong as two masts. They only waited to be told. . . . anything. Old Brown, looking curiously naked without a plug of tobacco in his cheek, was worried. And kneeling to scratch Anchor's ear, Bell remembered their talk.

He took his time, tenderly caressing Anchor, as he watched the sky and the sea. There was very little wind and the sea was slight. The sun was almost directly overhead, but there would be no noon sight taken on this day. Finally he looked up at Ramsay and said very quietly,—Heave to.

Ramsay's smile faded. He motioned uncertainly to the men at the pump.

—Now?

—Now. And be quick about it. Keim, take your watchmates and douse all heads'ls. Bunt up the fores'l.

As Ramsay and the others moved to the halyards, clew lines, and downhauls, Bell continued to fondle Anchor. He yawned deliberately and smiled at the anxious passengers. He said,—Isn't he a wonderful dog? Real gentleman, this fellow. He gives. . . . all the time.

Hutton took a step forward.—Captain, there's a lot of things going on aboard this ship. . . .

—Mr. Hutton, I'm sorry if your meal was disturbed, but maybe it's just as well. Rumors have a way of floating around a ship, and if we could remember they are just rumors and let them go at that, sometimes life at sea would be a lot easier. But it's hard to do, I know. . . . and I wouldn't be a bit surprised to hear a rumor that the *Cannibal* was unfit to go to sea and would go to the bottom if we didn't keep pumping. . . . I'll tell you now, each one of you, that if you hear anything like that, it is not so. . . . and in a few minutes I'll prove it to you so everyone can eat and sleep in peace.

Bell sighed and stood up. With Anchor pressing against his leg he looked thoughtfully at the horizon, and his deep voice seemed as heavy as the sea itself when he spoke again.

—We are better than a thousand miles from the nearest land, but instead of letting it bother you, I recommend you learn to enjoy it. When you get ashore you'll have money troubles, or fight with your relatives, or get sick, and you'll wish you were here. For peace of mind, and I guess we can all use a little of that from time to time. . . . there's no place like being at sea. You're about as close to God as you can get, out here. . . . beggin' your pardon, Reverend. But you show me a church that has a dome like that cloud over there, or a stained window that has as many colors as the sea right this minute, or an organ that plays as pretty a tune as a fair wind in the riggin', or candles that can light up a man inside like the stars out here. . . . and you'll find me in the front row of that church all the time.

Bell slowly ran his finger along the scar and glanced at

Charlotte King. He looked down at the deck, embarrassed, because she deliberately raised her hand to her lips and then turned it toward him. There was no mistaking the gesture and he was thankful that none of the others appeared to have seen it.

—Now as to this ship. All ships have trouble of one kind or another. Mostly, on the bigger ships, the passengers never know about it. And you wouldn't here if we could help it. It don't make any difference if the ship is a steamer or what. . . . no voyage is completely without trouble. . . . sometimes serious, and sometimes not so serious. Now we have a leak. All ships leak a little. There never was a ship built that didn't have to be pumped sometime during a voyage, either by hand or by machinery. Our leak. . . . or leaks maybe, because there may be more than one, seems to be somewhat more than normal. I don't honestly know what the cause is, but I'm going to find out. Whatever it is, remember one thing, like the old saying. . . . we're all in the same boat and I'm no more eager to go to the bottom than you are. And there's a lot of things we can do to prevent such a thing happening. I think the more you understand, the better off everybody'll be. . . .

Bell walked to the starboard pinrail and took off a coil of line. He threw it on the deck and then, holding the end, he whipped a large circle of rope in front of the passengers.

—If we was to have a hole in us as big as that. . . . he said, pointing to the circle, —we still wouldn't go to the bottom. We'd do what we call Fothering. . . . the name came from a British apprentice who saved a ship right in these waters a long time ago. What it amounts to is taking an old sail and slipping it overside so it covers the hole. We lash the sail good and taut and the water presses against it, but damn little goes through. You'd be surprise how many ships have sailed for weeks with just such a rig. We'd have to pump a little more, and that's all. But we don't have a hole as big as that or anywhere near, or we'd have known it long ago. . . .

Bell pulled the loop of line toward him, passed it beneath his arms, and made a bight. As he talked, he formed a bowline at his chest and jerked it taut. Every movement he made was easy and certain. He kept his manner casual as if the gathering on deck was an everyday occurrence.

—I'm not much of a speechmaker maybe. . . . but while we're

waiting to heave to, maybe I can pass on some of the thinking I done since I was a little kid.

—What happens if a storm strikes us? . . . Ethel Peacock asked nervously.

—I'm glad you asked that, Miss Peacock, because if it does, it might help you to think this way. . . . not only while you're in the *Cannibal,* but in any other ship. . . .

Bell looked forward along the *Cannibal*'s deck and for a moment his eyes came to rest on Keim and Sweeney, who were heaving on the foresail buntlines. Then he glanced aloft, as if what he had to say would come more easily, and turned away from the faces around him.

—A ship is lots more than just some wood and rope and canvas put together. Men have been building ships and gone down to sea in them ever since they could find a tool to work with. They built houses too, and strong ones, but you can just imagine how long a house would last out here what with being twisted and bounced and hit and tossed around twenty-four hours a day. . . . and all kinds of heavy strain bein' put on it from every direction. . . . and sometimes bein' turned clear over on its side and then being tossed clear over on the other side. Even the best-built house wouldn't last very long, would it? But somehow ships get some of a workman's heart put into them, and with some care, the good ones last a long time. And it's a funny thing about sailing ships. After experimenting a couple of thousand years, the shipbuilders reached sort of a peak all of a sudden. . . . roughly about the time the *Cannibal* was born.

He lowered his eyes and smiled at Ethel Peacock.

—So if we hit rough weather I'd advise you to just snuggle down in your bunk and forget about it. The *Cannibal* can take the worst.

He looked at Charlotte King and saw that she was smiling in a peculiar way and he hoped that he hadn't made a damn fool of himself. That was a pretty damn fancy speech. The silence lasted so long when he had finished he was greatly relieved to see Ramsay walking toward him.

—Hove to, Captain. We're as dead in the water as we'll ever be today.

Bell went to the bulwark and placed his hands on the caprail. He looked down at the water, now almost smooth as the *Cannibal* drifted gently backward. For a long time he examined the sea both fore and aft of the ship and as far abeam as he could see clearly. There was no unusual movement below the surface except a few showers of algae glistening in the sun.

He turned to Keim, and pointing at the coil of line on the deck, said, —Pay me out easy. If I give two jerks, heave in smartly.

Keim nodded and picked up the coil. The others slowly closed in around Bell as he bent to pat Anchor on the head.

—Be smart, he whispered. —Stay here, mate, where it's warm.

To Ramsay he said, —Now we'll settle your worries, son. Bell kicked off the slippers he was wearing and quickly stepped up on the rail. He looked at the sea once more and took a deep breath. Then suddenly he was gone. Only the line slithering over the caprail marked his progress downward.

For a moment there was absolute silence on deck as both crew and passengers lined themselves along the bulwark. Old Brown looked at Keim and both of them shook their heads unhappily, for there was something about being in the water rather than on it which frightened every true sailor. Keim carefully payed out the line, allowing just enough slack for Bell to swim freely.

It was Anchor who broke the stillness. Sensing that his master was at the other end of the moving line, he whined for a moment and then broke into a spasm of barking. He ran excitedly back and forth on the deck, leaping at the line and barking continuously. He put his paws against the bulwark and tried to see over the caprail. He raced the length of the *Cannibal*'s waist and then scampered all the way aft to the poop. And though he barked continuously, no one noticed him. They were too absorbed in looking down at the water.

The fact that he could swim at all was unusual for a sailing man, yet Bell's powerful shoulders seemed designed for swift progress beneath the surface. As he glided along the *Cannibal*'s hull he thought that in a series of dives he could easily examine her entire underwater body if the water were not so cold. But already he felt the chill through to his bones. Time was precious. He decided to ignore the grass and sharp stubble of barnacles which coated her planking. Following the curve of the hull, he swam straight down for the *Cannibal*'s keel.

On deck they watched Keim pay out more and more line.

They remained silent. Lott and Sweeney stood behind Keim, waiting to give a heave if needed. Then Old Brown, who had been watching the water suspiciously, pointed to the top of a long green swell which rose halfway between the *Cannibal* and the horizon.

—We better heave in! There's the first one. They always come.

He was pointing at a small black triangle sliding stealthily along the top of the swell.

—Shark! . . . . Keim snorted his disgust and took a firm grip on the line. He looked up at Ramsay, who stood on the caprail.

Ramsay held out his hand.

—Wait! He'll keep his distance.

They watched tensely as the black triangle reversed its course and made a slow S pattern along the face of the swell. The swell moved on and the triangle was hidden.

The line became slack in Keim's hands. He hauled in rapidly and after a moment Bell's head appeared directly beneath him. He looked up and shouted.

—Give lots of slack! Stand by to port with a line! I got to go all the way under!

—Shark, sir! . . . Old Brown yelled. —Over there!

Bell looked over his shoulder. The triangle reversed course again and vanished.

—Keep an eye on him!

Bell took a deep gasp of air and submerged. Again the line payed swiftly through Keim's hands. Charlotte King seized Ramsay's arm. She made no attempt to hide her anger.

—How can you let him go!

Ramsay looked down at her and a half-smile crossed his mouth.

—He's trying to prove something. I told you he was a damn fool.

He turned quickly away.

—Sweeney! Uala! Main tops'l halyard! Make a bight and stand by to heave over the port bulwark! . . . . And somebody quiet that dog!

Ramsay jumped off the rail and crossed quickly to the opposite side of the *Cannibal*. All of the others moved with him except Keim, who still tended his line.

The sound of Bell's voice coming from the water caused Anchor to be seized by a paroxysm of barking. He ran wildly back and forth in the scuppers trying to locate his master. Keim continued to pay out line. He watched the black triangle and saw it swerve toward the *Cannibal*.

Bell swam downward through a world which changed rapidly from blue to a pale green. For this dive at least, he was not overly concerned about the arrival of a shark. In these waters he had expected at least one and there would certainly be more. Sharks had an unbelievable ocean telegraph system. Let a boat be launched or anything of possible interest thrown overboard from a slow-moving ship and they would appear. No one knew how or why. And they didn't need the sight or smell of blood. If the object was of enough interest, they would attack. But they took their time about it and there were always several minutes of grace while they circled and investigated. Bell hated sharks with the passion born in every seaman. He thought that when he was on deck again he would break out his rifle and try to shoot this one. It he was successful he would join in the happy sailors' butchery to follow and he would hang its tail from the jib boom for good luck as sailors had always done.

Now slowing his descent, he glided to a place along the keel he had seen on his first dive. Easing a little air from his lungs to gain time, he saw that the keel had once been scarfed, and where the two great timbers joined, a few fastenings had given way. He moved under the keel for a look at the opposite side. He had guessed right. The iron shoe had separated a little way from the keel, and the old fastenings were not strong enough to keep the heavy under timbers tightly together. He could just force his finger into the place of maximum separation. Also the wooden plug which served as a stopwater between the keel and the garboard strake was gone. So! Not good, yet not really bad. The pump could easily handle such a leak if the separation did not increase. But there was no way to make repairs. That was the most annoying thing. And at such a location even Fothering would be useless.

His air was going. He shoved himself away from the keel and struck out for the light above. It seemed a long way through the green to the blue again and he wondered that it should seem so much farther ascending on the opposite side of the ship.

He broke water and gasped for air. Immediately a bight of line fell about him. He secured it beneath his arms and signaled the waiting Sweeney to heave in. In a moment he clambered dripping over the bulwark. He shivered and said to the anxious faces around him, —I found it, all right. It isn't pretty, but it will have to get a lot worse before there is really anything to worry about. So just do your best to relax and let me do the worrying.

Harry Hutton said, —Are you telling us the whole truth, Captain?

—Yeah. It wouldn't be right to do anything else. Just remember life at sea don't go any smoother than it does on land.

As he began to take the line from around his chest, Keim gave a shout from the opposite side of the deck. He ran to the main shrouds, took down a boat hook and bent far over the bulwark. He swore violently and so loudly his voice easily carried across the deck. And something in his voice caused Bell to whip the line down past his legs. He quickly scanned the deck.

—Where's Anchor?

There was no need to wait for an answer. Keim was yelling savagely and prodding down at the water with the long boat hook. Bell ran across the deck. He threw himself against the bulwark and looked down. His heavy breathing stopped.

Anchor was in the water, paddling and barking frantically. A few yards away, beneath the black triangle, Bell could see a gray-green body undulating slowly.

Keim yelled, —He jumped from aft! After you!

The gray-green body turned easily and rose to ruffle the surface of the sea. Keim aimed the boat hook. Seeing his master's face above him, Anchor suddenly stopped barking. His black eyes begged as he fought to paddle along with the slowly drifting *Cannibal.*

Bell yanked the sheath knife from Keim's belt. He jumped to the caprail. He saw the gray-green body vanish momentarily in the depths and then return from another angle. It moved swiftly past Anchor and turned again.

Bell crouched and said, —Heave a line after me!

Ethel Peacock screamed as he leaned out with one hand on the shroud. Poised tensely, every muscle in his body taut, he waited until the gray-green mass turned to pass directly beneath him.

Bell let go the shroud, balancing himself on the caprail.

—You're crazy! Ramsay shouted.

155

As if Ramsay's words were a signal, Bell was suddenly hauled off the rail. Old Brown knocked the knife from his hand. Sweeney and Uala seized his arms. Bell twisted and threw them off. He started back for the rail only to meet Lott, Uala, and Keim, who stood like a barrier before him.

Lott said, —Better you stay here, Skipper!

—Get out of my way! My dog!

His voice was a broken shriek as he threw himself at the men. But now Old Brown, Sweeney and Uala were on their feet again. They closed in on the wildly struggling Bell. He twisted and dodged. He knocked young Sweeney halfway across the deck. His gasping for air became a pitiful sobbing. Yancy closed in and caught a fist across his ear for his efforts. He retreated immediately as Bell brought the powerful Lott to his knees with a vicious kick. He squirmed away from the others and would have made the rail again if Keim had not come up behind him with a belaying pin. Sighing unhappily, he brought the pin down on Bell's head. The stroke was short and so expertly laid, Keim was able to catch him as his legs buckled. Easing him to the deck, Keim said quietly, —Maybe better this way.

Only Ramsay saw the gray-green body turn. The corners of his mouth went down as he watched the tail whip around suddenly. Then with tremendous speed, the whole body darted straight for Anchor. The body revolved halfway and Ramsay saw the sickly sheen of its white belly. There was an explosion of water about Anchor. He vanished instantly. And where he had been, the water became still. There was, for a moment, no movement or change to be seen.

Ramsay turned away and looked down at Bell.

—Is he all right?

—I didn't hit so hard.

—Take him down to his bunk. Then get back to the pump.

Nine

BELL ROSE SLOWLY through the deep green water, and as he reached the blue it pressed in on his head and squeezed it with increasing force until he thought he would never reach the surface. Then he opened his eyes and saw the ceiling above his bunk and the telltale compass, and he felt something cool pass across his brow. And beyond the something there was a hand and an arm and finally a face which he recognized as Charlotte King's. She pulled away the cool towel and said, —All right?

—My head.

He groaned and tried to touch the place just behind his ear where it hurt the most. She took his hand and held it tightly.

—Take it easy, Captain.

—Where's Anchor?

She was silent. She took his other hand and pressed it against herself.

He glanced quickly around the cabin and saw no movement except his shirt and pants, which someone had hung over the back of his desk chair. They swayed slightly as the *Cannibal* heeled. He closed his eyes and said, —I lost my friend. You don't know. . . . there will never be anybody like him.

157

He pulled his hands from hers and jammed them against his eyes. Charlotte saw his jaw quiver and she knew that he was weeping, deep inside. With his eyes still covered he spoke slowly and his voice was almost a whisper.

—He was so goddamned brave. . . .

—Yes.

She waited until the movements of his body subsided.

—Would you like to be alone?

—Yeah.

She touched his cheek tenderly where the scar cut down to his chin, then she slipped off the edge of the bunk. She started toward the door.

—Ramsay said, when you woke up to tell you he'd stand your watch.

—I'll stand my own. How long have I been out of business?

—Almost an hour.

—I got plenty of time then.

—You have a new scar. . . . above your right eye.

—Right now I don't care much what happens.

—You will. You're that kind, David. And I'm glad.

She hung the towel on his washbasin and went to the door. He turned his head to look after her.

—You called me David. Nobody's called me that since I was a little kid. Funny. . . . because right now I feel like a kid.

—That's why I called you David. It helps to slip back sometimes. I'll look in later and see if you need anything.

She went out the door and closed it gently behind her. She started toward the saloon, then changed her mind and turned around to the companionway ladder. She mounted it slowly to the deck and breathed deeply as she emerged into the sunshine. She leaned against the cabin trunk and looking at the sea she knew that she was in love with David Bell. She was surprised how calm she could be about it, and how certain, and how the fact that it was probably too late didn't make any difference. The discovery was sudden, but the process wasn't. It was a long time back to Suva.

She saw Ramsay coming toward her, and she knew he was going to break into her thinking. She was almost grateful. The others had been more like Ramsay. Men like Bell were a different matter. They stayed with you a long time after you left them.

As Ramsay approached, she tried to light a cigarette. The match went out. Ramsay quickly cupped his hands for her as she struck a second match.

How is our would-be shark killer?

—He has a headache. . . . and a broken heart.

—Maybe Keim knocked some sense into him.

—You were a big help. Did you push Anchor over the side?

—That's unfair. I think if I were you. . . . I'd be nicer to me. You're a good-looking woman and that chip on your shoulder doesn't become you. It might even be a good idea if you distributed some of your sympathy around and didn't waste it all on Bell.

—What's your trouble, Junior?

I've been at sea a long time, too. And I'm a lot prettier than Bell.

She blew a cloud of smoke directly into his face and he backed away slightly.

—That isn't very polite. . . . or at least I've been holding the impression that ladies didn't blow smoke in people's eyes. And you're supposed to be a lady now, aren't you?

—What are you driving at?

—Your real first name is Inez, right?

—What if it was?

—And before your convenient marriage your name was Liedstrom. . . . right? Inez Liedstrom, from Butte, Montana. . . . Honolulu. . . . and way points in between. A lot of way points. . . . one of which you're very anxious to avoid seeing again. Could that possibly be Honolulu?

—You sound like a tour director.

—I just like to put two and two together. It's always been sort of a habit with me. Now is it my imagination or excellent memory that brings up another name? Myra Pringle. I don't suppose you've ever heard of her?

She looked at him without the slightest change of expression on her face. Then she said, —No. I have not.

—Of course not. Why should a lady like you know about Myra Pringle and her moonlight girls? Why should a lady know that one of Myra Pringle's girls got herself involved in a very nasty mess and had the thrill of seeing her picture on the front page of the Honolulu papers several times? Even though they were taken in court they were good pictures and she was a striking girl. . . . with the kind of a face it isn't easy to forget. Shall I tell you more or aren't you interested?

He waited, but she made no answer.

—You know, you don't talk enough. You're cold. Or is that part of the reserved and ladylike upbringing you had in Butte, Montana? I've always thought your accent had a peculiar charm. . . . sort of a mixture of British colonial and Montana copper miner. Go on. . . . say something.

—Go away. You bore me.

—Now is that ladylike? You should watch those little slips. They might give you away before we have a chance for an understanding.

She started to move away. As if he were making a friendly gesture he put his hand on her shoulder and pressed her back against the cabintop.

—Bell is a very unsophisticated man. . . . which makes him inclined to be stuffy. I'm sure you wouldn't want him to know about Myra Pringle.

—Take your hand off me.

—And you wouldn't want the crew to think Bell refused to put into Honolulu because he lost his head over you. They could make life very tough for him. He might lose more than his ship. So I suggest you be more friendly. You might begin by coming to my cabin tonight. I'm off watch from eight until twelve.

—You make me sick.

He released her and stood back smiling.

—Make it about nine, he said easily.

He turned his back on her and sauntered aft to look at the binnacle.

Charlotte finished her cigarette without moving from the cabin trunk. She needed time to think. She told herself that she should have known better. Dreaming like a school kid about David Bell when there would always be Myra Pringle? Dreaming about going to Mexico where no one ever heard of Myra? A laugh. The world was made up of Ramsays and it was hopeless trying to fight them.

Looking at the sea, she remembered the first talk she ever had with Myra Pringle, who was thin and smartly dressed instead of fat and blowsy like she should have been. "Look here, honey," Myra said. "You spent your last dime coming to

Honolulu because a man in a sailor suit said he'd marry you. Now you're broke, and you're going to get awful hungry because the sailor ran for his life. This happens to be the reason Myra can stay in the escort business."

Myra always spoke of herself in the third person as if she was referring to the career of a casual acquaintance.

"Ninety per cent of Myra's applicants come to her because some joker promised to honor and cherish and found a way out of it. They come to Myra because they like nice things and they like to eat and they would a lot rather sleep late in the morning. Most applicants are pretty sad when they can't qualify to be one of Myra's girls and some of them, I'm sorry to say, wind up down on Hotel Street sleeping with Chinamen or whoever else happens to have two dollars. Myra can't afford to have such girls associated with her. They're bums. Myra's escort service means just what the newspaper ads say. . . . selected clientele. Service, understand? A businessman comes to the islands and he's tired. He wants a rest, but he wants some fun, too. Most of them don't know their way around and even if they did it's no fun dancing or hitting the speak-easies alone. They want a girl, and Myra's clients won't settle for tramps, or the kind who can't pass as an old friend of the family if they happen to run into somebody they know. They want a girl like you who can carry on a conversation at least for a while. . . .

"Sure you'll have to fight for your honor. . . . they'll all make the pitch. But you don't have to sleep with them. Just kiss them good night and put them off until next time. Now, sweetie, old Myra has expenses. . . . telephone, advertising, Christmas presents to bellboys which don't come cheap, loans to girls who want a new dress, and certain other expenses. The introductory fee is twenty dollars. You get fifty per cent of that. Now Myra's not suggesting that a girl like you would bed down with a client, but if you should feel inclined that way, charge what the traffic will bear. And you keep it all. Myra wants no part of that sort of thing. But take Myra's advice and don't give it away for free. And never stay more than once with the same man or sooner or later you'll find yourself doing it. You've only got one thing to sell. *Sell* it, honey. All you have to do is follow certain instructions to make Myra happy. And who knows? You may wind up with a husband. Some of Myra's clients are very nice people. And some are very well loaded. I'll tell you about those special ones as they come along."

Nice people! They were. Nice lonely men who started out the evening smelling of cologne and wound up reeking of okalihow or bourbon if they could afford it. The pattern was always the same. The meeting in the hotel lobby. The uncertain bow. The envelope with the twenty dollars inside according to Myra's rules. The remark about the weather and the standard answer. The moment of embarrassed silence while the man jangled the loose change in his right-hand pants pocket. The compliment on the flower in her hair. The inquiry for a restaurant. The taxi. The steak and potatoes. The poorly hidden shock at the check. The shrug of the man's shoulders. Taxi again. Cigar. His business. Suggestion he might need someone to show him around the other islands. Speak-easy. Okalihow or bourbon. Sometimes it ended there with the man asleep at the table after he had talked endlessly about how much he loved his wife and what a fine family he had. Sometimes the first pawing began at the table. They were always shocked at the check. Some shrugged their shoulders again, too drunk to care. Some made a scene and that was when a Myra Pringle girl vanished. . . . according to instructions.

No wonder Myra was satisfied with fifty per cent of the introduction fee! It didn't take long to discover why. You steered the men to certain restaurants and the headwaiter always pretended he had never seen you before. Myra took a cut from the restaurant check. You steered him to the right speak-easies, where again you were treated as a total stranger although you knew the name of every waiter in the place. Myra took a cut of the check. She seldom cleared less than fifty dollars per man. Service. For nice people. After a while you began to feel sorry for a few of them, and submitted to their pawing, and finally went to their rooms. . . . and took your own cut. Just as Myra thought you would.

It wasn't so bad, even when sometimes the man actually believed he had made a conquest and you went away without a dime. Myra's girls never mentioned money. As a result, the average man left more than he should on the night table. It was smart. Myra knew her lonely men.

The so-called "specials" were another matter. You hated Myra when she broke the news that one had been spotted.

They were always new clients and sometimes Myra knew all about them long before they were persuaded to call her number. She might play along with them for a week before they were assigned a moonlight girl. And the girl had to know what she was doing. You kept the whole introductory fee with a "special."

When the usual round was finished, you suggested a walk along the beach. Myra showed you the exact section of the beach to take the "special." It was romantic and almost always deserted. You lay down on the sand and it was never very long before the man joined you. Sometimes he came very near satisfying himself before you felt his whole body become rigid.

There was no escaping the bright beam of the flashlight. The two policemen would be standing above you and one of them would shake his head sympathetically while the other helped the man to his feet. Disorderly conduct. Sorry, fella. Both you and the girl will have to come along. Embarrassed and frightened, blinking at the flashlight, the man was in no condition to think clearly. And when it was suggested he might pay the fine immediately and so avoid the humiliation of waiting in jail for morning court, he always paid. The fine was as much as the man had with him, or if he was short, the officers carried blank checks already made out to "cash." And they knew the man's right name.

The girl was required to go along with the officers. She did, weeping according to her acting ability, and the police who were not police at all but employees of Myra's in uniforms which only faintly resembled the Honolulu police, took her home. Myra was smart. She would never hear from the client again, but even if the man finally realized he had been taken for a fool, it was not the sort of thing he would be inclined to make a fuss about. Or even talk about. . . . Over a year of that and you were just about ready to tell Myra to go to hell when along came George Ewing Baker. Myra made one of her few errors. She misjudged him. He was a little man and he was almost bald-headed and he wore rimless glasses. He was quiet, almost shy, and he drank carefully. He owned a small factory. . . . something to do with air-brake equipment. When the police came to the beach something happened to George Ewing Baker. He put up a fight. He struck out at Myra's police like a crazy man. They couldn't run from a little man like George Ewing Baker. They worked him over and left him unconscious on the beach.

The next morning he was found dead. The coroner said overexertion brought on a heart attack. And the strain obviously came as he tried to defend himself against persons unknown. The newspapers demanded action. Such things were bad for the tourist business. In the headlines, George Ewing Baker became a business giant who was only trying to relax in the Hawaiian sun. Editorials demanded the police do something and they started by finding the hotel bellboy who recommended Myra's escort service. The rest was a field day for the newspapers. Eventually, four girls were given suspended sentences, and Myra was out of business. The two police finally caught five years each for manslaughter and extortion. And for Inez Liedstrom? If she ever came to trial it was a cinch for three years at Oahu women's prison. . . . aiding and abetting a felony.

Nice people. The bail for knowing them was set at five thousand dollars. But the court calendar was jammed and before the judge had a chance, a total stranger from a place called Kandavu, which was near a weird place called Suva, laid it on the line and you walked out of jail into the sunlight. He was a fine-looking man except for the pouches under his eyes, and he said he was a planter. He also said he needed a wife and the pictures in the paper looked like just what he had in mind. You were for sale on the bargain counter, and it looked too good to be true. It was.

You skipped bail on the arm of Bruce King and got all the way to Kandavu before you found out that what he had in mind was a punching bag. Bruce like to knock people around when he was drunk, which was most of the time. He preferred women. . . . and he should have stayed with them because one of his workers finally picked up a machete and killed him. Nice people.

Charlotte angrily flipped her cigarette at the sea and walked forward. She slowly descended the three steps which led from the break of the quarterdeck to the waist. She wanted to walk alone and think about Davey Bell. How strange it was to feel needed. . . . and wonderful. . . . even if it was hopeless. Forget about Ramsay. For just a little while there was no harm in trying to be happy.

She was alone for some time before Harry Hutton emerged from the saloon hatchway. He carefully adjusted his walk so they would meet alongside the galley beneath the starboard boat. His round face was grave and his little eyes darted nervously back and forth in their sockets as he touched her arm. He said, —I'd like to talk with you, Charlotte.

—Does it have to be now?

—Yes. You don't mind my calling you Charlotte, do you?

—It's my name.

—I can see you'd like to be alone and I can understand it and I know it's a rare thing to find any chance for being alone on this little ship. We all get in each other's hair a lot, I guess. Believe me. . . . just as soon as I've had my say, I'll leave you.

She wondered at the humility in his manner. It was something she had never seen in Harry Hutton. All the bluster was gone, and now he was just a fat man with one shirt tail flapping in the wind and a discouraged droop to his shoulders. He said, —It's about Miss Peacock.

—What about Miss Peacock?

—You don't like her, do you?

—Is it important?

—Yes. It is.

—Oh. . . .

—I know she wasn't very nice to you during lunch today. She said some things she shouldn't have said and you had every right to take offense. She really didn't mean it and if you're angry with her I want to fix things up. After she thinks things over I'm sure she'll find a way to apologize.

—I don't remember her saying anything that would bother me.

—I mean about the captain. She shouldn't have said what she did.

—Why not?

—What I'm trying to explain is that Ethel is not. . . . entirely well these days. She's going through a stage which comes over all women at a certain age. . . . I'm sure you know what I mean. . . . and her change is especially difficult because of other circumstances. You're young and attractive and you've been so fortunate in life it may be extremely difficult for you to understand a woman like Ethel, but I wish you'd at least give her some thought. Failure is a peculiar disease and I'm beginning to think that people who catch it never really recover. It is much worse when they realize it like Ethel does . . . much worse, Mrs. King. That's why I'm so worried about her. Even though you've lost your husband, you can at least begin to live in the future. Now I must presume on our short acquaintance because I am desperate. Nothing I can do seems to help Ethel.

She searched his face carefully. She pictured him at the saloon table, shoveling in his food, and she tried to remember him blowing up his cheeks before he started on one of his financial flights of fancy. Yet now she could see none of the usual Harry Hutton.

—What do you want me to do?

—Be a friend to Ethel. Right now she needs friends more than anything else in the world. In the end I think you'll find a friendship with her more than worth the effort. Ethel is a very rewarding woman.

—How long have you known her?

—Almost eleven years.

—And you've been traveling together all that time?

—More or less. You must not misunderstand. Our relations have always been professional. . . . artist and manager.

—That's all?

—A companionship, of course. We have naturally shared a great many things together.

—Have you ever tried sharing yourself? Right now, while you're in this mood, why don't you stop kidding yourself? Ethel is more than just a singer to you or you wouldn't worry about her. Ever think of marrying her?

Hutton quickly puffed out his cheeks and looked away. But after a moment his cheeks deflated and the sag returned to his shoulders. He passed his hand slowly across his bald head and then his fingers moved down to tug at the lobe of his ear. He looked at Charlotte unhappily and then gazed at the sea again. Finally, as if his thoughts were so foreign he hardly dared to recognize them, he said, —Mrs. King. . . . Charlotte. . . . I'm afraid you don't know much about me. I've formed a habit of living and I doubt if I could ever change it. When you live by your wits you forget how to be honest. After many years, lying ceases to be lying and becomes the truth. . . . as you see it. Even now when I will attempt to tell you the facts as they are exactly, I am sure lies will creep in. But I will try, if it will help Ethel.

He swallowed, tugged at his ear lobe again, and chose his words even more cautiously.

—I am not a rich man who took a sailing ship because I thought it might be unique. I didn't have enough money to take any other kind of a ship. I have never managed a successful show in my life. I even lost my penny arcade. I have talked millions with other men while my stomach was growling for want of food and I am an expert at temporarily removing the shine from a pair of tired pants. I can convince some people that my credit rating is magnificent when my landlord has locked me out in the street. I have a way with bill collectors which has a touch of genius. They depart empty-handed, yet happy. Credit managers are a challenge to me. I consider it a personal defeat when they refuse me and I brood about if for days afterward, wondering how I misused my technique. I have sold raincoats in a section of Peru where it never rains and straw hats to the Indians in Northern Minnesota. Perhaps I have convinced you I know something about opera. You would be wrong. The truth is I know very little about it, or anything else. The same goes for painting, sculpture, the drilling for oil, trout fishing, the culture of pearls, or trends of the stock market. I pick up a few odd facts and phrases, agree with the real experts heartily, and am soon regarded as a fellow authority. I have been invited to speak before men's luncheon clubs on international finance and accepted because the free lunch would be the only meal I would see that day. I was always roundly applauded. I wrote a series of newspaper articles on the military situation in Europe although I've never been there nor have I ever heard a shot fired. My byline was Major Hutton. I received countless letters of agreement on my views from genuine military experts and stopped writing only because I had read so many books I actually began to know what I was talking about. It was thus. . . . no longer interesting. I became morose because the gullibility of my fellow man always saddens me. I made quite sure I never really knew what I was talking about again. Does all this surprise you?

—The truth always does.

He peered at her intently for a moment and wet his lips. Then he laughed hollowly.

—I rather suspected I had failed to take you in. But my mind was not on my business. It was on Ethel and has been for some time. I am still telling the truth, Mrs. King. I will send up some easily recognizable signal when I can no longer stick with it.

—I'm beginning to like you, Harry.

—You asked me if I ever considered marrying Ethel. I have .... many times. But there I am defeated. The one thing I cannot bring myself to do is to look Ethel Peacock straight in the eyes and ask her to share my duplicity. I am an expert in failure and nothing else.

—I don't remember anything about money in the marriage ceremony.

—Money is not the basic reason. You see, Ethel believes in me. She is the only person in the world who always has. For her sake I must keep things that way.

—Are you sure you don't need Ethel more than she needs you.... or that maybe she doesn't care what you are?

—Frankly, I never considered the possibility.

—You may be a phoney, but you're not entirely selfish. You give it some thought.... and I'll try to be her friend.

The relieved watch stumbled into the forecastle and threw themselves on their bunks. Lott murmured Estonian curses, and Uala instantly fell asleep. Yancy, still breathing hard from his labors, prodded suspiciously at the region around his heart. He spoke from the darkness of his bunk and his voice cracked with self-pity.

—That goddamned pump! That goddamned pump will kill us before we have a chance to drown! And what does Bell say about the leak? Go ahead, Uala. Tell me what he says after we been breakin' our backs two extra hours tonight. Go ahead and tell me what Bell says when the ocean keeps comin' and comin' and we don't get nowheres hardly. I just like to lie here and listen to someone else repeat what Bell has to say because I can't believe my own ears!

His only answer was Uala's heavy breathing which soon became a deep and troubled snore.

—All right! Snore, goddamn you! Snore your bloody blood out through your nose because your heart don't need it no more! Lie there and not give a damn for all I care, but just tell me what Bell is goin' to say when we all drop dead on deck because we pump the whole Pacific Ocean through his ship. He is going to say now ain't that just too goddamned bad and Old Brown you just sew the boys up in some rotten canvas which is the only thing we got plenty of and weight 'em down with some rusty chain which we also got plenty of to spare, and I'll read from the Good Book while they slides over the side. Yessir. I can see it now with that cuckoo woman passenger singin' "Many Brave Hearts Asleep In the Deep". . . . and all like that. The way I feel now I'm lookin' forward to my own funeral. But before I die I want to hear just once more what Bell says when we point out that with all due respec' the water in the bilge ain't gettin' no lower no matter how long we pump. Go on, Bonehead, tell me! You was there.

From the upper bunk aft on the port side there came only a grunt of sullen anger and then the sound of a man breaking wind.

—Exactly! That amounts to just what Bell said! Here's a man tries to tell us he swum down and seen the leak and it don't amount to nothin' and there ain't a solitary thing in any way to get concerned about. It's only the shoe is fallin' plumb off the keel and she's opened up along the garboard strake and so she may leak a bit now and then, but it ain't nothin' serious! Jesus no! We could sail around the bloody world and think not a thing about it. Ventilation is all we got. . . . just a little ventilation to let the bloody ocean go in and out. I tell you somethin' right now. You got to sign the protest! We got to do somethin' right this here night and give it to that crazy Bell in the morning. We just can't afford to do nothin' else! We got to make Bell stop thinkin' about his dog and start thinkin' about our bloody lives!

Lott said, —You give me paper when sleep finished. I sign.

—Now you're makin' sense! Comes change of watch we'll get hold of Sweeney and Keim. Even if Old Brown is so dumb he won't sign, we'll hit Bell with that paper in the mornin'.

Ramsay stood in front of the small mirror which was screwed to the bulkhead above his washbasin and combed his hair. Now he took a special pleasure in the process and frequently tipped his head from side to side as he made certain every strand was in place. After thoughtfully admiring the very slight indications of gray which had just begun to touch his temples, he wet the ends of two fingers and smoothed his eyebrows. He wondered if he should grow a mustache, and then he decided against it.

There was, he thought, always something untidy about a mustache no matter how carefully groomed. He adjusted the collar of his clean white shirt until the points were exactly even, then stepped back to more fully appreciate his efforts. Like a trim ship, he thought. . . . a place for everything and everything in its place. A neat body and a neat mind. Things carefully planned bore fruit, he remembered, and made a determined effort to hold down the excitement which had grown within him ever since the charthouse clock chimed two bells. Nine o'clock. She would come.

She had to come, because the forces had been set in proper order by a man who knew what he was doing. It was not luck that would bring Charlotte King to his cabin. . . . it was an accumulation of detail, absorbed and skillfully pieced together until the whole puzzle resolved itself. It was a unique example of the curiosity and enterprise for which the Ramsay family had always been noted. Any male member of the family would undoubtedly approve.

He looked around the small cabin and smiled as he reviewed the sequence of his conclusions. Charlotte King's curiosity about the *Cannibal*'s course to Manzanillo invited the first interest. Then the walk. It lacked the stiffness and poise of a lady's walk, true confidence was missing. The accent was more difficult to catalogue, but listening was its own reward as Father Ramsay had often said, and in spite of Charlotte's economical speech, which had at first confused matters, she revealed herself little by little. A word, a phrase, even pronunciation could sometimes tell more than a whole conversation. *If* one listened, he reminded himself, and pointed an accusing finger at his image in the mirror. Regional influence or accent had to be ignored while one waited for the slips. And mannerisms must be watched. . . . they were important, no matter how insignificant. Charlotte could fool Bell, who wouldn't know a lady if he saw one. She had apparently deceived everyone aboard the *Cannibal* simply because they were not alert. Otherwise they might have added many things together and come up with the first answer. Mrs. King had a reason for acting the lady she was not. Why? What had she to gain or lose?

One began with elementals in solving any riddle. The passport and the photo proved invaluable. The Honolulu date mark jarred an almost forgotten trigger in his brain and the photo became haunting in its similarity to one seen long before. And Yancy? That might be called a stroke of luck. . . . but no, it was not. Logic led the way to Yancy, who was forever talking of Honolulu. It was only luck that Yancy could provide the correct name of the Pringle woman. The rest was logic which was the most potent force in the world and would even supply the needs of a man who had been too long at sea.

Ramsay searched the immaculate cabin for any detail he might have left unattended. His wood sculpture was neatly aligned in the forward bunk. He would show her these. There must be some pretense of conquest and she might even like them. The blanket on his own bunk was properly turned down. The pillow was fluffed and should be inviting. His oilskins were hung in the corner near the door and tucked snugly behind a short length of rope. His sea boots stood side by side just below. The brass lamp gleamed with polish, but he decided it was turned up too high.

He crossed the cabin to adjust the wick and as he did so, he heard the door open behind him.

He took a moment to compose himself before he turned around. He waited until he heard the door shut again, then still making a show of adjusting the lamp he looked over his shoulder and smiled.

—Welcome.

He saw that she was wearing a black satin dress which was new to him. Detail. He thought, She is anxious to please me.

She moved a few steps from the door and the lamp outlined her hips and breasts in a way that caused Ramsay to lose some of his assurance. She placed her arms behind her and looked straight into his eyes.

—Well, I'm here.

Ramsay coughed nervously. She was not behaving exactly as he had expected. She was not angry; rather more than casual, he thought, and it disconcerted him.

—Have you got anything to drink?

—I'm sorry. I never touch it. One drunkard aboard is enough.

—I could have guessed.

—You should wear that dress more often. It becomes you.

—Shall I take it off now?

Her tone was completely disinterested. As she reached for

the hooks at her side Ramsay was openly disappointed. Some fight would have made things more intriguing.

He pointed to the forward bunk.

—Would you be interested in seeing the work I do in wood? I've been told it's quite good.

—No.

—Perhaps. . . . we should talk a little. . . . first.

—Why?

—I'd like to know more about you.

—You know enough already.

Ramsay walked slowly to the door and snapped the lock. He was angry now. He seized her arms and spun her around.

—Listen, you little bitch. . . . be nice to me! I didn't ask you to come here like a cold fish!

—You didn't ask me to come. You told me. You keep your part of the bargain. I'm keeping mine.

She twisted away from him and continued to unhook her dress. In a moment she had pulled it over her head and kicked off her shoes. Ramsay tried his smile again as he said, —Do you have to be so hasty? You go about that. . . . as if you were a machine.

—I've had plenty of practice.

Ramsay turned to the lamp and lowered the wick until the cabin was nearly dark.

—I suppose I'm just another man to you.

—What the hell did you think you were?

As he watched her move toward his bunk in the halflight, he slowly, almost reluctantly, began to unbutton his shirt.

For a time there was only the sound of the sea sloshing past the cabin porthole. Then the charthouse clock struck three bells and Ramsay felt her move away from him. It seemed only a moment before she was fully clothed again and had gone to the mirror, where she stood wiping her lips with his towel. He watched her apply fresh lipstick and thought that under the circumstances things had not gone too badly.

—Would you come here again. . . . if next time, I asked you?

Turning to him with a smile that both surprised and pleased him, she said, —That depends. . . . on whether you would really want me to come.

She put the lipstick in the pocket of her skirt and walked to the door.

—Well, Mr. Ramsay. . . .

He saw with considerable satisfaction that she was still smiling as she clicked the lock off the door. He raised himself on one elbow and sighed happily. This woman, no matter what her history, appreciated a good man. Not very intelligent, perhaps, but quite capable of making a miserable voyage more pleasant. But now there was something different behind her smile and he became strangely uneasy.

—Any reason I shouldn't want you?

—Well, Mr. Ramsay. . . . I was about to say it's a shame there isn't a doctor on board.

—What do you mean by that?

—Just what you think. You're going to need one. I'm a whore. . . . remember? Pleasant dreams, Mr. Ramsay!

She slammed the door behind her and was still smiling as she walked along the narrow companionway toward the saloon. And she wanted to laugh aloud because of the sudden fear in Ramsay's eyes. Let him sweat! It would be weeks before he discovered he really had nothing to worry about.

November 3, 1927

Suva toward Manzanillo

This day begins cold and with fresh trades. During night, lower t'gallant sail split a seam and was sent down for repair. Wind increased with the sunrise and two lanyards of the forerigging parted. New ones rove of the last hemp rope aboard. At same time, lower t'gallant split a second seam and was unbent again and sent down for repair. Entire new cloth required for same which will use last of our new canvas. During forenoon trades increased still further and we are taking occasional slop of green water aboard. At approximately eleven A.M. eye of throat halyard band on main broke and down came gaff, block, and all dependent gear. Temporary repairs made with chain. At approximately ten minutes before change of forenoon watch, crew gathered on quarterdeck and presented the attached (see below). Witnessing signature of Chief Mate Ramsay also attached.

Being as how we believe the Barquentine *Cannibal* to be unseaworthy due to her leaky condition, us of the crew do not consider her fit to continue passage as is.

Therefore we respekfully request to put the ship on a course for Honolulu where she can be repaired good.

If this don't happen we say that there has been negligence. We hereby say so in this here legal protest.

| Yancy | — | A.B. | Uala | — | O.S. |
| Lott | — | A.B. | Sweeney | — | O.S. |

Ten

BELL WAS ENGAGED in taking a noon sight for latitude when he saw the men walking aft from the galley house. At first he thought it was merely the normal change of watch. Yet his sextant told him the sun was still considerably below the zenith and no crew, much less on the *Cannibal,* had ever been known to relieve a watch more than five minutes ahead of time. The relieving men were Ramsay's and Bell saw that they walked close together as if proximity would give them comfort. Their faces were solemn and their heads bent slightly. All three, Lott, Yancy, and Uala, were freshly shaven and this in itself was remarkable. Bell turned to took at the men of his own watch and saw that the usual stubble of beard was gone from their faces. Why hadn't he noticed it earlier in the morning? They must have slipped forward and shaved sometime during the watch.

He put the sextant to his right eye again and saw the amber ball of the sun outlined in the mirrors. With his legs spread wide he braced himself easily against the *Cannibal*'s heel. He slowly moved the sextant's vernier arm. Carefully, choosing the moment when the intervening waves would subside and leave a

175

clear-cut line, he brought the sun down to the horizon. He had taken three previous sights of the sun at intervals of approximately two minutes. Each measurement of its altitude had given a higher reading on the vernier arc in degrees and minutes. Thus it was still in ascent and his purpose was to capture the maximum altitude the sun would attain. The amber ball would "hang" a moment then, and appear motionless, as if time were suddenly suspended.

Rocking his sextant back and forth caused the ball of sun to skid along the horizon with a pendulum-like motion. He adjusted the vernier arm until the bottom of the sun just scraped along the distant water. Through long practice he would sense the proper moment to take the sextant from his eyes and study the vernier arc. Then by applying a simple formula to the reading on the arc, he would know the *Cannibal*'s latitude.

But Bell had lost interest in the sun. He was standing near the port taffrail with his back to the quarterdeck. Now, hunching his shoulders, he moved the arm which controlled the sextant mirrors so that he would see directly behind him. He saw the three men of Ramsay's watch join Sweeney, Keim, and Old Brown near the wheel. They looked at each other uncertainly and shuffled into a semblance of a line. They stood waiting, with their eyes on Bell's back.

He quickly realigned his sextant with the sun and brought it down to the horizon again. When he was satisfied, he took the sextant from his eyes and examined the vernier through the small magnifying glass attached to the arm. He turned halfway around for better light on the degree and minute marks, and as he placed his eye to the glass he heard Old Brown say, —Captain, sir, the men has got somethin' they want to say to you.

Bell did not bother to look up. Continuing to peer through the magnifying glass he said, —I'm busy. Can't you see that?

He turned his back again as if to take another sight on the sun. But he was already satisfied he had caught the last observation at local apparent noon and he had only to remember the degrees and minutes of altitude. He could apply the formula at his leisure. Once more he adjusted the arm so that the mirrors would reflect the men behind him. He studied their faces and saw that they were whispering together. He took a moment to observe each man, trying to discover their leader. By the time he turned around to face them, he was very sure it was Yancy.

—Now. What's on your minds?

Old Brown took a hesitant step forward. He hitched up his pants and said, —The men here has ast me to present this here paper.

Old Brown held out a rolled sheet of lined copy paper. Bell took it from his hand and read it through quickly. When he finished he looked down at the deck and moved his finger along the jagged line of his scar. He tapped the paper on his sextant.

—Who put you up to this?

He had not expected an answer and there was none. The men stood uncomfortably, shifting their weight from one foot to the other as they stared at the deck. Keim and Old Brown found it necessary to examine the calluses on their hands. Bell's voice became a tightly controlled basso-profundo when he said, —I suppose you know this constitutes mutiny?

Yancy said, —No sir. Beggin' your pardon, it don't. That there protest is only a statement of our opinions.

—You are refusing to sail this ship?

—No sir. You read it wrong. We are only saying the ship ain't fit to sail.

—You're quite a sea lawyer, aren't you, Yancy? I would do you all a favor by throwing this paper overboard.

—It should go in the log, sir.

—Keim. How come you didn't sign this?

Keim kept his eyes on the deck. He muttered uncomfortably, —I no believe she so bad.

—Lott. Do you know what this paper says?

—Ya.

—How can you know? You can't read.

—It read to me.

—Who read it to you?

Lott scratched his belly and looked unhappily at the others.

—Yancy read it to you. Right? And he read it to all the rest of you, right? Old Brown, your name isn't on here either. Why?

—I'm sorta neutral, sir.

—How would every damn one of you like to spend some time shackled to the foremast?

—You coon't do that, Captain. We ain't refusin' to work or

obey no orders. Put over for Honolulu like a sensible man and see.

—You'll obey orders no matter what course I choose, unless
. . . A sly smile played around Bell's mouth as he searched their faces. —Unless you want to take over the ship. Maybe you want that.

Yancy quickly raised his hand. —Oh no, sir. We ain't pirates!

—Pretty smart, Yancy. You should have a degree in admiralty law. But you forgot one thing. You all signed articles for Manzanillo. As long as I'm in command, that's where you're going. There is nothing seriously wrong with this vessel and any hindrance to her progress toward her stated destination will be dealt with according to Mexican maritime law. I warn you, it isn't an easy set of laws and I have yet to see a United States consul who went out of his way to help a sailor.

Bell strode to the companionway and called down the hatch. —Mr. Ramsay! On deck and lively about it!

He squinted at the sun and then looked down at his sextant. He seemed to have forgotten the men who were still clustered about the wheel. When Ramsay appeared in the hatchway, Bell maintained his air of careless confidence. It was not easy, he thought. . . . when you were bluffing. Yancy hadn't missed a trick and he knew it. With the protest officially recorded in the log, the men could justify almost anything short of murder and possibly even that. God alone knew what the Mexican maritime laws might be. They were in Spanish and he had never bothered to have them translated. It was unlikely the Mexican authorities would trouble themselves about the difficulties of a gringo skipper anyway. But he thought the mention of them had at least sounded well, and seemed to have impressed the men.

He handed the roll of paper to Ramsay. —File this meaningless paper in the log. Read it and witness with your signature, recording the time of receipt. Report to me immediately any crew disobedience of an order or loafing on the job.

The charthouse clock chimed eight times. Bell touched his scar thoughtfully and said, —Your ship.

Then without so much as a glance at the men, he turned and descended the companionway steps.

Ethel Peacock closed the toilet door and tiptoed along the deck. When she reached the companionway to the saloon, she looked about her cautiously and tried to gather her thoughts. It was difficult. It was always difficult lately and now her mind was spinning with excitement at what she had heard. She clucked her tongue against her teeth several times and gathered her bathrobe tightly about her. She must tell someone, but oh, it was so confusing these days. . . . even Harry was completely unpredictable.

It was almost, she thought, with a little titter, as if she was a small child hearing voices. Ever since yesterday Harry had been unbelievably nice to her and spoke of things in the future as if they might really happen. And now this! But would Harry believe her? It might spoil everything if she told him and he didn't believe. If he just smiled in that way of his and said now Ethel you're imagining things again, it would be terrible. Or he might mention the doctors again and that would be worse. No, it would be better not to tell Harry. He would change back again and that look would come to his eyes, and he would be distant again, and he would act as if the whole world was on his shoulders and you were the heaviest part. But someone must know. It could be important. It might even make a difference in how things went in the future between you and Harry. Now don't get too excited. Goodness gracious! Just go down into the saloon and keep a perfectly calm expression as if you hadn't heard a single solitary thing.

Dak Sue was setting out the lunch in the saloon. The Reverend Butterfield was already seated and Harry Hutton was tucking a napkin in his collar. He looked at Ethel and smiled and she was extremely happy because she had never seen him smile in just that way before. He said, —You better hurry, Ethel.

—I will! I will! I'll just be a minute.

Tell him? Oh no! He would never smile like that again. He would go right back to thinking she was crazy. With a quick apology, she moved past Ida and Feodor Morris, who had just come into the saloon. Half-running, she turned down the narrow passageway which led to her cabin and collided full on with Oliver Wiggins.

—I say. . . . you are in a panic. Why don't you blow your whistle?

—I'm just. . . . it's just. . . . well, it's *late!*

—What's late?

—. . . . er. . . . lunch! Don't you know it's lunchtime?

—Of course I know it's lunchtime.

He looked at her quizzically. He saw her hands flutter nervously upward and downward along her bosom as if pulled by invisible strings.

—Are you by any chance practicing the harp? What are you in such a swidget about?

—I'm not in a swidget about anything. I'm just in a hurry to get dressed for lunch.

Wiggins bowed and waved his hand along the passageway.

—By all means do then. It might improve my appetite. But next time you run over me please pause to sop up the blood. I have so little to spare.

She continued along the passageway until she came to her cabin. She opened the door and saw Charlotte King touching up her lips at the washstand. Of course. Why hadn't she thought of Charlotte? She too had changed. . . . the whole world had changed since yesterday. It would be all right to share her secret with Charlotte, who never said much of anything anyway. The whole thing was simply scandalous!

She made a deliberate and almost successful attempt to calm herself. Goodness gracious! It was so difficult sometimes to know how to say things!

—My dear, you wouldn't believe what I just heard!

—Oh?

Charlotte continued to look in the mirror.

—I've been to the toilet!

—You sure get around.

—I've just heard the most terrible thing. . . . at least I think it's terrible.

—What are you panting about? You sound like a steam engine.

—I've been running! Maybe you never noticed that ventilator in the toilet roof. Well, you can hear everything and. . . . well, something should be done!

—You're not making much sense, Ethel.

—Please don't look at me that way. I get all confused. You must believe me.

—All right. I believe you.

—Well. . . . I didn't hear the first part, but I know that all of the sailors were back by the wheel and they gave Captain Bell some kind of a paper and he was very angry about it. And they had an argument and the captain said he would tie them to the mast. . . . and gracious he was mad. I could tell by the tone of his voice.

For the first time Charlotte lost interest in the mirror. Ethel was delighted that at last she had captured her attention.

—Why should the paper make him mad?

—I don't know, but the captain said the Mexicans would put everyone in jail because they wouldn't obey orders. . . . and. . . . and I'm frightened. Those men are likely to do almost anything!

—I'm sure the captain can handle them. Now take it easy. If you want lunch you'd better hurry and put on your eyelashes. You know how it is in there. . . . if you're late, an empty plate.

Ethel's face fell as Charlotte started toward the door.

—You *don't* believe me, do you? . . . . she whimpered. —You think I'm making all this up.

—Now, Ethel. I said I believed you.

—And that isn't all. The captain called Mr. Ramsay and told him to read the paper and witness it and report any of the men who were bad. And well. . . . it just doesn't seem right! I don't know anything about ships, but I just know it isn't right. Not what Mr. Ramsay said after the captain left . . . and I feel so sorry for the captain. . . . he lost his dog . . . and it just seems like he can't trust anyone. . . .

Charlotte suddenly turned back from the door. She placed her hands on Ethel's shoulders. Looking intently into her eyes, she said, —*What* isn't right, Ethel? Stop wandering and try to remember. What did Mr. Ramsay say?

—Well. . . . the captain left. . . . I don't know where he went, of course . . down to his cabin maybe . . . and hasn't the captain got the strangest voice. . . . why, it's so deep sometimes it sounds exactly like Chaliapin. . . . you've heard of Chaliapin the great basso of course. . . . buy anyway the men were still there and they were grumbling and one of them said the paper didn't do them any good and now the captain would watch everything they did and they swore frightfully all the time and. . . .

—Ethel. What did Mr. Ramsay say after the captain left?

—Well, that's what so surprised me! He said they had done exactly the right thing and that now they could see what kind of a man the captain was and that he had probably gone down to his cabin to get drunk. . . .

—Is that all?

—No. He said that as far as he was concerned maybe the time had come for them to start getting rough and that whatever happened they could depend on him to be looking the other way.

—Ethel. Are you *sure* you're not making this up?

—How could I? Mr. Ramsay said that he wouldn't help them in any way, of course, but he felt it was his duty to tell them he had personally seen the captain drinking in his cabin and that he probably did it all the time and so the captain could hardly be expected to show good judgment where the safety of the ship was concerned. He told the sailors they had better start doing something pretty soon or it would be too late to turn for Honolulu. It. . . . it just doesn't seem right to me, Charlotte. . . . I. . . . why! I just don't know what to think!

—Ethel. Listen, I want you to make me a promise. Girl Scout's honor now, no matter how bad you want to. . . . promise me not to repeat what you have heard to anyone else. Not even your friend Harry.

—Oh, I wouldn't tell him! He might not believe me.

—He just might. . . . because I have a hunch he's very much in love with you. Concentrate on that and forget about everything else.

—If you were only right. . . . it would be so easy.

Now the Pacific began to repudiate its name. From somewhere off the coast of Japan a cold wind swirled down to the south and overwhelmed the trades. The sea lost its lush feminine colors and became a wrinkled and choleric old man. Spume flew off the wavetops. Each crest was followed by a trail of hoary foam which lay like a giant's spit on the water. As the wind veered to the northwest, the *Cannibal* was put over on the port tack and her sail was reduced to inner jib, stays'l, square tops'ls, and reefed main and spanker. Even so she plunged drunkenly into the seas and was sometimes swept from bow to stern by solid green water. The sound of the wind in her rigging changed gradually from a dismal moaning until it became a shriek in the stronger gusts, and the *Cannibal* trembled and cried out through all her parts like a small terrified animal faced with a monster. Two men were often required at the wheel to keep her from coming too much up in the wind or falling off too far before it. They were frequently assaulted by great sheets of spray which defied the laws of gravity and shot almost the full length of the *Cannibal* and rattled against their oilskins and stung their eyes until they were nearly blind.

There was no rain with the gale. The sky was a heavy, flat layer of cloud, so close to the surface of the sea, the *Cannibal*'s mastheads appeared to touch it. The cloud mass stretched to every horizon without variety or interruption and by its very weight seemed to press the little barquentine harder into the sea. Had she been a schooner, the *Cannibal* would have made even rougher weather of it because she would sail closer to the wind, but she would also have been able to make better progress northward.

Only a few years before there would also have been brigs like the *Siberia*, barks like the *Pacific Slope* and the *Golden Gate*, whalers like the *Charles W. Morgan*, great Yankee square-riggers like the *Moshulu*, the *St. Paul*, and the *Dunsyrel*. And there would have been little schooners like the *Anna*, the *Claus Spreckels*, and the *Bob o'Link*, whose masters ventured an occasional trading trip to the southerly islands.

Yet now the little *Cannibal* was forlorn and alone with the wind and the Pacific. Her solitude was complete. Surmounting every wave became a separate ordeal, and she progressed like a bewildered hag seeking to visit the grave of a last friend. Time and again she was turned about and allowed to run down wind while repairs were made. The order for execution of the maneuver became monotonous. —Stand by spanker sheet! . . . . Hard up helm! . . . Douse down fore-topm'st stays'l sheet! . . . Weather fore brace!

The bolt rope of the lower topsail parted along the leech.

A boarding sea broke through the skylight and flooded the saloon again.

The inner jib sheet parted and whipped the block into the sea.

The outer jib parted at the clew and nearly shook the jib boom from its fastenings before the sail was smothered.

Several reef lashings tore away on the mainsail and it split instantly from head to foot with a series of explosions like rifle fire. Repairs to such a large sail were impossible until the seas and the wind subsided.

Bell wrote in his journal:

. . . . In a lifetime at sea, I have never seen such peculiar weather! It has been blowing Force Eight to Nine and often Ten, for days. But it is not a storm. . . . at least as I have known storms. It's just a plain gale such as could be found more or less regularly down between the Horn and Cape of Good Hope, or between the Cape and Australia. Or it could be the North Atlantic. But even in those regions a wind of gale force veers sooner or later and at least adds spice to things. Not so, here. I doubt if the wind direction has varied half a point since it commenced. The Force has also remained almost constant, neither diminishing nor increasing with nightfall or dawn. I have read Bowditch until I'm bleary-eyed trying to find some reasonable explanation, but no luck. The seas are long and very regular, similar to those found in a typhoon, but there are absolutely no indications of any kind that a storm of such nature is anywhere about. The air is dry, even if we seldom are. It is very cold on deck and from the looks of the sea and everything else I wonder if we have skipped over the miles between and somehow plopped down into the Gulf of Alaska.

. . . . I would not be too much surprised considering the very vague idea I have of our position. There has been no chance to catch a sight of the sun for days although I have been on deck every noon and stood around rather stupidly waiting for a break which might at least be as long as a porgy hole. Thank God we are in clear waters. On the other hand it is a pity we didn't pick up this wind somewhat farther to the north, say a week or so from now. We should certainly have set the world's record for California and made the old runs of the *Galilee* look like the meanderings of a potato barge.

. . . . Here, where it may remain a secret, I confess that for the first time I am seriously concerned about our leak. We are now pumping as much as four hours out of every twenty-four and I suspect that this time will soon have to be increased. Surprisingly enough, the men have given me no trouble of any kind. Either they are too tired or too scared, but they have set to everything willingly enough since presenting their protest. Or perhaps they believed my nonsense about the Mexican maritime laws. Having served before the mast myself. . . . and that does seem a long time ago. . . . I cannot help but feel sorry for them and have ordered Dak

Sue to give them coffee whenever they ask for it, or soup if and when he has any left. He scalded himself today, poor fellow. A heavy sea rolled us over more than usual and his stewpot capsized. A part of the contents hit his bare arm and he got a bad burn out of it. I dosed him liberally with Dr. Gratiot's famous ointment and bandaged him to the best of my ability, but he is far from comfortable. Which brings me to mind of Ramsay.

. . . . I cannot account for his recent behavior. He does his duty, strictly according to the book as always, but he seems terribly worried about something. It can't be our leak because he has not mentioned it for days when he had every reason to, and anyway we long ago had it out about the leak. I can't believe that a man of his experience can be worried about the wind. . . . hell, it's just another gale and is even blowing in the direction which should please him if he's so bound and determined to go for Honolulu. He came to me in a most friendly fashion the other day and asked what I knew about various illnesses and what kind of stuff I had in the medicine locker. I told him the truth, that as a captain I had long ago made it my business to learn how to care for injuries and could bouse and belay a broken arm or leg with the best of them, but when it came to inner ailments I didn't know a whooping cough from cholera. I offered to look at his tongue, but he said there was nothing the matter with him, he had just run out of reading material and thought that if I had anything on the subject he might as well start learning because some day he hoped to have his own ship. I loaned him my copy of Adam's *General Practitioner* which I have never been able to make head or tail of any more than I have Bowditch. He's been hard at reading it ever since. If he's sick he sure don't look it. Maybe he just thinks he's sick. So am I, when I think of our puny day by day progress toward Manzanillo. . . . here it is almost noon of our twenty-seventh day out of Suva. . . .

Bell laid down his pen and sighed. After a moment he whirled around in his chair and stared at the bottle on the piano. Since the heavy weather he had lashed it as firmly in places as he would a valuable deck cargo. But the knots were seaman's knots and they could be slipped so easily.

185

He rose and walked to the piano where he stood before it uncertainly. Someday, he thought, I will get up the nerve to throw that bottle overboard and all the others with it. His right hand rose slowly toward the bottle and he watched its ascent with detachment, as if the hand was not his own and he had no means of controlling it. God! How he could stand a drink! If ever a man! . . . .

He suddenly withdrew his hand and forced it down toward the piano keys. It would be no good to take a drink now. He would start thinking about Anchor. Soon his fingers were poking aimlessly at the keys and he found that he was trying to duplicate the melody which Charlotte had played. He managed to connect a few notes so that they pleased his memory and as he continued to experiment, he thought of Charlotte and his desire for the bottle subsided. He had almost picked out the entire melody when he heard Uala calling down to him through the skylight.

—Captain! Mate says to tell you there's a break in the sky ahead! Says you can probably get a shot of the sun if you want! Says it's close enough to noon!

—Right!

Bell stopped his playing and returned to his desk. Even an approximate noon sight would help. He closed his journal and placed it in the lower drawer. He opened the wooden box which held his sextant, carefully lifted it out, and started for the door. Passing the piano he glanced at the bottle, halted, and returned to his desk again. He took a mint from the open packet beside his inkwell, tossed it in his mouth, and turned resolutely for the door. He smiled inwardly as he opened the door. Someday, and very soon, he would throw the damn mints overboard, too.

The *Cannibal*'s jib boom pointed directly at a patch of blue in the sky ahead. It contrasted brilliantly with the ceiling of heavy gray cloud, and the shaft of sunlight which poured through the hole made a lozenge-shaped pattern of yellow on the sea ahead. Bell studied the break, hoping it would remain open until the *Cannibal* passed beneath it. About as big as a Dutchman's pants, he thought, but good enough if it holds.

Instinctively, he walked forward for a better view beyond the sails. Even if he could sight the sun within a few minutes of noon, the observation would be interesting. Holding his sextant protectively so that his body would guard it against the occasional wisps of salt spray, he stood in the lee of the foremast and watched the hole almost close and then enlarge again. He waited impatiently, for it seemed that the hole was staging a race with noon and the *Cannibal* would always remain just a little ahead of both. Finally a second hole appeared, united with the first, and the *Cannibal* plunged into momentary sunshine.

Bell stepped away from the mast and brought the sextant to his eye. He was now so unaccustomed to the sun's brilliance he was obliged to use two shades across his reflecting mirror. Even so his eye watered as he quickly brought the sun's image down to the horizon. He had just captured the luminous orb to his satisfaction when the *Cannibal* passed into gloom again. Rubbing the moisture from his eye, Bell turned aft and started toward the quarterdeck. The appearance of another hole seemed doubtful so he would read the minutes and degrees in the shelter of the charthouse.

He took only a few steps before he heard a whirring sound and then a sharp chunk against the deck. He halted. Still wiping his eye, he stared unbelieving at the heavy steel marlin spike protruding from the planking. It was less than a yard ahead of his feet.

He looked up quickly and saw Lott descending the foremast shrouds. Despite his bulk, he slipped down quickly and in a moment he was running across the deck.

—Capt'n! I sorry!

Bell looked down at the spike and thought how easily it could have penetrated his skull.

Lott nervously clasped and unclasped his enormous hands.

—I dunno how it happen! I reach to swing around from yard und . . .

Bell bent down and yanked the spike from the deck. He fingered the sharp point and looked thoughtfully at Lott.

—You ever drop a spike before, Lott?

—No. Never. . . . yah. . . . vunce. . . . long time ago. In the *Kurt*. She be a bark und. . . .

—Did it kill anybody in particular?

—No! No, I never hurt no vun!

—Well, this almost killed me.

—Accident. I *sorry*, Capt'n!

Bell handed the spike to Lott and saw that he accepted it reluctantly. His whole great body drooped, and Bell thought that if he could only meet his eyes, he would be inclined to feel sorry for him.

—Yeah. Maybe you are.

Bell turned away and walked aft, but he had lost interest in his sextant. He told himself that a sailing ship was never a baby's crib and that marlin spikes had been dropped from aloft before. But things were usually dropped by fumbling fools who were new to ships and the sea. . . . not by an experienced sailor like Lott. And normally he wouldn't go aloft without a lanyard on his spike; a length of marlin would be rove through the hole in the thick end and passed around his wrist, just in case the tool should slip from his grasp. There was no lanyard on that spike. The hole was empty.

Bell mounted the quarterdeck and strolled slowly aft toward Ramsay.

—Did you get a sight, Captain?

—Yeah. So. . . . so.

—I think it's breaking some. We might have more sun tomorrow. And the wind is easing.

—Possible. By the way. . . . what was Lott doing in the forerigging?

—I sent him up there.

—Why?

—There were a few loose shackles about. I told him to take up on the pins. Just a precaution I thought it past time we did something about.

—Which shackles? Where was he working?

—On the lower tops'l yard. I noticed the lift shackles weren't moused and why take chances. I don't like to see anyone hurt.

—Is that all he went up there for?

—Yes. Why? Something wrong?

—No. I was just. . . . wondering. . . .

Bell looked at his sextant and for a moment he appeared to have become absorbed in it. He scratched his jaw and one finger moved slowly upward along the jagged line of his scar. The charthouse clock chimed eight times and he said without looking at Ramsay, —You're relieved.

Eleven

LATER, AS HE bent over his figures in the charthouse and plotted his sun sight, Bell tried to forget about the spike. He opened his dividers and measured off the distance between his last sight taken so many days before, and found that the *Cannibal* had averaged a bare seventy miles made good each day. He was both disappointed and surprised; not so much at the *Cannibal*'s miserable progress, but at his inability to forget the spike. You're getting old and you're getting jumpy, he thought. If this sort of thing keeps up, you'll start shortening sail when there's no need to shorten sail, and you'll hear foghorns a hundred miles at sea, and you will start taking soundings in mid-ocean. You'll be like so many old-timers who said that after a man got scared enough times he just plain stopped growing and the only place for such a man was on the beach. Every lump of sea would start looking like a rock. . . . every channel a trap, and every harbor cursed with disease and disaster. Damn Old Brown anyway! His sour warning made every little thing that happened seem deliberate.

Bell chuckled. Next time I slip on the deck I suppose I'll accuse somebody of putting a banana peel under me!

—What's so funny, Captain?

Bell turned around and saw that Charlotte King stood in the charthouse door. She was wearing the old pea jacket he had loaned her when the weather turned cold. Now she leaned against the door and lit a cigarette, and Bell thought that even in his old jacket, which hung on her like a windless mainsail, she looked attractive.

—I was just laughing at myself.

—Good for you. Not very many people can.

—I guess I'm getting old.

She smiled and Bell thought as he had so many times recently that if he had a woman like Charlotte King for his own it would be worth spending some time on the beach. She nodded at the chart and said, —How are we doing?

—Little by little. We sure won't set any records.

—Still direct to Manzanillo?

—Yeah. When we get there will you tell me why you're so all-fired anxious about the course this ship sails?

—Why shouldn't I be?

—It just isn't natural for a passenger. . . . especially a woman.

—Some people like to know where they're going. . . . even if they are women. Aren't you ever going to eat again? We haven't seen you in the saloon for days. It's been dull.

—I've had a lot on my mind so I have a bite in my cabin now and then. I had some thinking to do and thinking is hard for a bonehead like me.

—You're always running yourself down, Davey. You shouldn't.

—To tell the truth some of my thinking was about you.

—Was it pleasant?

—Yeah. . . .

He looked at the chart because now the time had come to tell her at least one of the things he had been thinking about and he knew the proper words would not come easily. He shifted his weight uneasily and jammed his hands down in his pockets. Then sternly, as if he was ordering himself aloft in a gale, he said, —I wish I'd met you somewhere ten years ago.

—So do I.

She left the door and moved into the charthouse. For a moment it appeared that her only interest was in the chart. Bell pointed at his sun line and said, —We're here. . . . along that line somewheres. Dead reckoning puts us about here. See? I got no secrets. If I said I know exactly where we are. . . . I'd be a liar.

He laughed, nervously, but his laugh faded as he looked into her face. —Davey. . . . you've got a lot of troubles and I don't like adding to them. But I've finally decided I should. I've spent since yesterday wondering if I might do more harm than good because it's your ship's business and none of mine. . . . and maybe it doesn't mean anything, anyway. I've always been afraid of gossip, having had some experience with it. . . . and maybe what I have to tell you is just that. You were the one who told us not to pay any attention to what we heard on a ship. . . . and I know that my source is not the most reliable in the world. But first, I want to ask you a question. Did you receive some kind of a paper from the sailors?

—Yeah. It's there in the logbook. Sailors always find something to beef about. Do all the passengers know about it?

—No, they don't. That's just it. How far do you trust. . . . Mr. Ramsay?

—About as far as I can throw him.

—Good. It seems he doesn't think too much of you.

—That's no surprise to me. He's able, but I never should have signed him on. We come from different schools.

—He's going to make trouble for you. . . . or try to. Ethel Peacock heard him talking to the men. You know how she is. You can take it for what it's worth. I. . . . I hate to see you so alone, Davey.

He took his pipe from his shirt pocket, considered its empty bowl for a moment, and then reached for the tobacco can on the chart table. He carefully stuffed the bowl with tobacco and said, —It looks like I'm *not* alone. Good feeling. . . .

As he tamped the tobacco down she struck a match and held it out to him. He took the match and puffed methodically until his pipe was well lit. Suddenly he reached for his sextant and handed it to her.

—Do you think you could carry this under that jacket so it wouldn't be noticed? Seems like there's plenty of room.

—Easy. There's enough room between me and this jacket to smuggle a Chinaman.

She buttoned the jacket around the sextant and placed one hand in the breast pocket to support it.

—Dont' drop it. You and me are going to take a little stroll on deck. . . . for fresh air. All right?

—I refuse to ask why.

—That's one of the things I like about you.

Bell set the pace. For a time they remained on the quarterdeck and she walked silently at his side. Sweeney was at the helm; Keim and Old Brown were huddled out of the wind on the lee side of the cabin trunk. One of them should have been on lookout, but Bell decided that for the moment they were better off where they were. They averted their eyes and their conversation stopped as Bell and Charlotte passed them. In a voice which was unnaturally loud, Bell said, —Let's go forward, Mrs. King. There's more room.

He took her arm as she descended the steps from the quarterdeck to the *Cannibal*'s waist. They strolled forward side by side. Oliver Wiggins' head popped out of the saloon companionway. He sniffed at the wind and then watched Bell and Charlotte with mild disapproval. He said to them as they passed, —Hardly a fit day for a constitutional.

Bell said, —Nope. It sure isn't.

—Then why do it? Why do some people insist on making themselves uncomfortable? Or do I detect a mutual attachment and a consequent desire to avoid your fellow men?

—Maybe tomorrow will be better.

Wiggins screwed his face into a pout and said to Bell, —Beastly weather. Since I'm not pretty enough to borrow your jacket, I wonder if there is any way you could recommend I might get drunk. If you could let me have even half a bottle I could buy the Reverend's soul.

—You can get drunk in Manzanillo.

—No fear, I will. And I venture to say. . . . so will the Reverend.

Wiggins sniffed the air once more and immediately ducked down the hatch.

They took three turns along the *Cannibal*'s waist, reversing their course each time at the quarterdeck break and beneath the boats over the galley house. Finally, Bell stopped. He looked at the sea and then casually surveyed the *Cannibal* from bow to stern. Now, Sweeney, Keim, and Old Brown were yarning by the wheel. Let them. There was no sign of life forward.

Except for himself and Charlotte, the *Cannibal*'s waist was deserted. Bell turned and faced forward.

—Now. Open the collar of your jacket and keep it open. Hand me the sextant.

As she worked with the neck button Bell moved his feet slightly until he stood directly over the gash left by the spike in the deck planking. Then he took the sextant from her hand and placed it to his eye. He moved the vernier arm until he had exactly aligned the double image of the lower tops'l yard in the mirrors. He aimed the sextant at the place where Lott would have been working on the shackles and quickly read the angle on the vernier arc. Nineteen degrees and thirty minutes. Repeating the figures in his mind, he returned the sextant to Charlotte.

—Put it back in your coat. I wouldn't want anyone to see me monkeying around with the sextant when there isn't any sun. They might think I was crazy.

She replaced the sextant and buttoned the coat over it. She murmured, —I still won't ask.

He laughed.

—Good. Maybe I'm crazy. But this is one sure way to find out.

—If you do. . . . will you let me know?

He took her arm and they started walking again. He said, —Sure, I'll let you know.

Oliver Wiggins shivered and closed the hatch tightly behind him as he descended into the saloon.

—Leave that open a little. . . . Harry Hutton said. —We could use some air in here.

Wiggins frowned at him and sought his most acid voice.

—My dear fellow. If you wish to be a fresh-air fiend and flex your muscles with the hardy types, I suggest you take your fat carcass to the deck. Where you may find more agreeable company.

Butterfield asked, —Who is on deck in this weather but the poor sailors?

Wiggins clasped his hands behind him and began to pace the length of the saloon. He mumbled and shook his head sadly as he staggered back and forth like a caged animal.

—Evil! . . . . he said. —Evil on every hand. It is terrifying!

Butterfield asked, —What is so terrifying?

—The solace two troubled people can find in each other.

Ethel Peacock said, —Stop your silly pacing. You'll drive us all mad.

Wiggins stopped in his tracks and fixed his pale eyes on her.

—I am taking my constitutional, Madame Peacock, and I shall take it where I please. As for driving you mad I should like to remind you that the distance between London and Yarmouth is very short and therefore the journey is bland, incredibly boring, and entirely devoid of challenge. As a consequence I never attempt it.

As he turned his back and charged off again, Harry Hutton pushed himself halfway up in his chair.

—Just what are you implying, Wiggins?

—That the distance between sanity and insanity is also very short.

Butterfield said, —I still can't seem to find out what was so frightening on deck.

He suddenly cupped his hand and swung it past a fly which was moving along the saloon table. He raised his fist proudly. —I caught it!

Wiggins said, —Release him. You of all people murdering one of God's creatures!

—But it's only a fly!

—You ought to be ashamed of yourself. Go somewhere and pray forgiveness. The poor beast is paralyzed with cold or you should never have come within a mile of him.

—Yes. Let him go. . . . Ethel Peacock said.

—Let him go. . . . Ida Morris said softly.

Feodor Morris patted his wife's hand and said, —Now, Ida. It's his fly and he can do what he wants with it.

—Certainly he can do what he wants with it. . . . Wiggins said. —Proceed, you psalm-singing Caligula. Pluck the wings from it. Torment the poor creature.

—I have no intention of tormenting him.

Butterfield shook his fist and his face lit up as he detected a faint buzzing sound. —I can hear him!

Wiggins sang, —Somewhere a voice is calling. . . .

Butterfield held out his fist triumphantly. —Listen!

—They could hear the Christians all over Rome when they were thrown to the lions.

—You are exaggerating the importance of this fly.

—No, you are. You have already made a monumental project of that poor chap. Mrs. Morris, I invite you to look at the Reverend Butterfield's face this very moment. Won't you agree that all of the cruelty of mankind may be seen there? Aren't his eyes like those you might have seen in the head of a Cossack or a commissar, depending upon which barricade sheltered you? Won't you agree that very suddenly the Reverend has lost all dignity and has himself become an animal? Look! He is already contemplating ways to destroy.

—Let the confounded fly go. . . . Harry Hutton said with a sigh. —And maybe Wiggins will shut up.

Butterfield looked up and down the length of the table. His eyebrows puckered unhappily and, withdrawing his arm, he stared at his fist again. The saloon was silent. The fly buzzed and they all leaned forward. Butterfield looked appealingly at Wiggins, whose only reply was a shake of his head.

Gradually, as if moving them with a great effort, Butterfield separated his fingers. The fly buzzed out of his palm, circled, and then vanished into a corner of the saloon.

—Ah! . . . . Wiggins said. —How does it feel to be victorious?

—But I didn't kill it.

—You killed the urge to kill it, which is much more difficult for the powerful. Now you can see how simple life is for us pagans. You all see it, don't you?

—I don't know what the hell you're talking about. . . . Harry Hutton said. —But that's nothing unusual.

—Nor do I. . . . Butterfield said, gazing despondently after the fly.

—Then you are quite hidebound in thought. You were like a panel of gods sitting in judgment on that fly. If you were the fly you would know how it was useless to protest. Either the hand would open to release you. . . . or it would close forever.

—But the fly did protest. . . . Feodor Morris said earnestly. —He buzzed.

—Exactly. To us his frantic buzzing was obviously a complete waste of energy. Project yourselves beyond this saloon. . . . look down upon us in this miserable excuse for a ship. See yourselves as the gods see us and appreciate the design. Butterfield, my addle-brained friend. . . . now what do you see?

—I refuse to participate in this childish game even to pass the time. It's downright sacrilegious. . . . that is, I think it is.

—Miss Peacock! You are a woman of imagination. Surely you can look down and see us in true proportion. Look down upon the bald pate of our companion Harry Hutton. Play a goddess for the moment. . . . Minerva would rather suit you. Can't you see our friend scurrying about his penny arcade as he tries to make a go of it? And can't you see that it would have been impossible? Can't you see him trying to convince himself that he is a shrewd businessman, and a much-sought-after impresario when in fact he is only a fat and frightened little man?

—Wiggins, I'm not going to stand many more of your insults!

—Can't you see him as really much more than he pretends to be. . . . a brave coward? And there is no braver mortal, Miss Peacock. Can't you see him as willing to combat a world he knows is antagonistic and will almost certainly defeat him? Look down and see that he is incapable of true anger. See how he is as honest with himself as he is dishonest with the world. Your friend Harry Hutton is a great man, Miss Peacock. . . . if you look at him from far enough away.

Ethel Peacock shook her head and said softly, —I like the view. I do.

—Mrs. Morris! Regard the Reverend from whatever lofty perch you may have chosen. Do you see a true apostle strewing a glorious path of rescued souls behind him? Of course not. You see a mortal named Butterfield who is actually much too intelligent for his job. You become aware that his tragedy is simply being accepted. . . . So much so that he must go halfway round the world to seek a real struggle. His tragedy is that there is almost no possibility of tragedy. It's a pity our friend Butterfield could not have dedicated himself two thousand years ago. As a martyr he would have behaved admirably.

—This is a lot of fuss for a fly. . . . Harry Hutton grumbled.

—Is it, though? You are an intrepid airman. Make an ascension and look down for yourself. See the Morrises, bless them, futilely wandering the face of the earth in search of safety when in fact their refuge is in each other. Take a look at Charlotte King if she does not affect you as she does me. . . . with a certain mental astigmatism. Look down on the captain. Look at Miss Peacock. . . . and even look down on me, if you can stomach it. Watch us all buzz.

—I thought you were a pagan and didn't bother with buzzing.

Wiggins smiled wistfully and patted Harry Hutton on the shoulder. —Unfortunately, I am also mortal. The only thing in my favor is that I realize buzzing is quite useless.

—You don't believe in hope then? . . . . Feodor Morris said.

—But I do. The gods may release me at any moment.

Feodor Morris was about to say that he would be very sorry for anyone who could not hope, when the pump suddenly started on deck. The sound of its sucking and clanging filled the saloon and they all raised their eyes to the ceiling. They were silent and continued to stare upward as if it were possible to see the pump. Finally Harry Hutton bent his head and took out his watch.

—That's the second time they've pumped in five hours.

Still looking uneasily at the ceiling, Wiggins said, —The distance between London and Yarmouth is becoming even shorter.

Bell put Old Brown on the wheel and pumped along with Sweeney and Keim for more than three hours. Yet when he measured the well, he found four inches of water remaining in the bilges. He looked aft toward the men and for a time the heart went out of him. They were sitting hunched over on the quarterdeck steps, with their heads in their hands, and they sighed great gasps of air as they sought to regain their strength. Bell leaned against the mainmast for a moment, and closed his eyes. Jesus, what a leak! It had suddenly become so much worse. Ramsay's watch would have to pump too, and they would barely be finished before it would be time to pump again. For the first time he looked up at the *Cannibal's* boats and wondered if it would ever be necessary to launch them. And he murmured, —No, I'll be damned if I'll even think about it!

The deck still swam and buckled before his eyes as he made his way to the quarterdeck. He passed Old Brown and saw him tighten his lips and shake his head forbiddingly, and as he went down into the charthouse he heard Old Brown say as if he were speaking to the wind, —I dunno what's drivin' you, Davey, but mebbe I'd ast myself if savin' the *Cannibal* was really worth it.

In the charthouse he fumbled a long time with a pencil before his stiff fingers were capable of recording the amount of water in the bilges and the time of pumping. He was still comparing the figures with those recorded in the past when the clock chimed eight times. Then Ramsay stuck his head in the door and said that he was ready to relieve him.

—Your watch will have to do some pumping, Ramsay. Maybe a couple of hours.

—Didn't I just hear you pumping. . . . or was I dreaming?

—You weren't dreaming.

—Why don't you be reasonable and make for Honolulu?

In spite of his efforts to control it, Bell's voice rose until he could hardly recognize it.

—Because this ship is bound for Manzanillo! And that's the last time we discuss the matter!

The corners of Ramsay's mouth went down and Bell thought that it was a gesture he was rapidly learning to despise.

—Very well. . . . sir.

Bell took up his sextant and half-stumbled down to his cabin. He found it necessary to hold on to the hand rails as he descended the companionway steps, and when he reached his cabin he fell into the chair before his desk and it was a long time before he would bring himself to make the slightest movement. Finally he reached for a sheet of paper and began to draw a triangle. He labeled the vertical line "foremast" and the horizontal line "deck." He studied his sextant again and then drew a line from a point he had marked "spike" at an angle of nineteen degrees and thirty minutes.

He forgot his weariness. The angled line which he had drawn represented the path of Lott's spike in its descent to the deck. The obvious result shocked him. He reached for a mint and chewed on it as he tried to discover where he might have been wrong. But there was no argument with such elementary geometry. He had very nearly been killed by the spike and it was obvious that it had not descended according to the normal forces of gravity. Such an angle, even allowing for a heavy roll, would be at least eighty degrees. He drew in the rigging, which he knew so well, on the remote chance that if Lott had merely dropped the spike it might have ricocheted off the mainstay, or possibly the forecourse yard lifts, and somehow bounced to the spot where he had been. No, there was only one answer. Unless a miracle had occurred, Lott had thrown the spike.

He stared at the paper a long time, trying to put down the anger that welled up within him. He heard the pump start again and he thought of Lott and what Charlotte had told him.

Lott was a child. He was a harmless child unless someone had spent a great deal of time persuading him to be otherwise.

He felt the blood in his face suddenly race along his scar. He threw down the pencil and doubled his fists tightly. They wanted to get rough? They thought Davey Bell was an easygoing drunk who didn't have it in him to get mad? All right!

He tipped back his head and bellowed at the skylight, —On deck!

—Aye!

It was Ramsay's voice.

—Come down here!

—I'm at the helm!

—Put somebody else on and come below! Smartly!

There was a moment's silence except for the sound of the pump and then he heard Ramsay descending the companionway. Bell stood up, jammed his fists down hard in his pockets, and faced the door. When Ramsay entered he told him to close the door.

—See that paper on my desk. Take a look at it.

Ramsay sauntered across the cabin. He picked up the paper, glanced at it, then tossed it back on the desk.

—It looks like some kind of a triangle.

—You're goddamned right it's a triangle! And it's proof enough to me that somebody is either trying to scare me to death or just plain kill me. You wouldn't know anything about that, would you?

Watching Ramsay, Bell was sure that he saw a suggestion of uncertainty in his eyes. But he quickly recovered himself and assumed a sympathetic air. Bell marveled at the sincerity in his voice as he said, —Captain. Are you. . . . all right?

—Yeah. But I got one trouble. I can't decide whether to throw you overboard or just beat the hell out of you.

Ramsay sighed as if he were summoning patience to hear out a small child.

—Simple men always solve their problems with their fists. But, Captain. . . . I doubt if I'd be much sport for you. I am more accustomed to sailing with masters who are gentlemen and so I've never had much practice. In spite of my feelings, which I frankly stated, I have done my best for this ship. So before you relieve whatever is gnawing at you, would you mind telling me what I've done now?

—You've set the men against me.

—That's preposterous.

—You were behind that protest and you offered to stand aside while the men took over the ship.

Ramsay picked up the pencil from the desk and casually tapped his fingernails.

—Of course you can prove all this.

—I can. Yesterday, just before noon you were heard advising the men that the time had come to get rough.

—Nonsense. Not even you would make such a stupid accusation. Who planted that little gem in your mind?

—That's none of your business. I'm going to break you, Ramsay. You'll stay in your cabin until I tell you to come out. Keim will take over as mate. If you give me any more trouble, I'll put you in irons.

—Then it is my business! I have a right to protect my career. . . . Suddenly Ramsay's manner changed. The tenseness left his body and he cocked his head to one side inquiringly. —Just a minute, Captain. By any chance, did this rumor come to you through one of our passengers? . . . . Say, Mrs. King?

—What difference would it make who it came from?

—It would make a lot of difference. And I would not be so surprised. Pardon me if I say that as well as being stubborn. . . . you are a very naïve man, Captain. You may be a fine seaman, but your experience with women has necessarily been rather limited. I don't suppose it's occurred to you that Mrs. King's interest in our destination is abnormal. . . . and is not founded on a passion for navigation? Have you ever asked yourself why she's so anxious to avoid calling at Honolulu? She is well aware that I have urged you to make for Honolulu and would do anything to discredit me or my opinions. She even came to my cabin one night and used her very obvious charm trying to persuade me. . . .

—You're lying, Ramsay.

—Am I? Ask her. Ask Mrs. King why she left Honolulu. . . . in haste. Ask her what she did for a living before she so conveniently became Mrs. King. You have a great deal to learn, Captain. Mrs. King doesn't care what happens to this ship, or you, or me, or anyone else, as long as we avoid Honolulu. If I may say so, your ordinary judgment has been . . . pleasantly clouded. I don't blame you. She is quite a woman but also a mite disappointing. I don't like knocking her off the pedestal you put her on. But I'm not going to stand by while you call your chief mate a liar and take the word of a proven whore!

Bell's fist shot out and Ramsay staggered back the width of the cabin. He bounced hard against the door and almost sank to his knees. A dribble of blood oozed from his lips. Bell grabbed his shirt and yanked him erect.

Ramsay did not even raise his arms as Bell struck him again. But as Bell poised himself for a finishing blow his arm stopped before the swing was completed and he allowed it to fall slowly to his side. For a moment there was only the sound of the pump and their heavy breathing. Then, gradually, Bell's anger subsided, for looking into Ramsay's frightened eyes, he knew he had told the truth.

As the tenseness left Bell and his shoulders sagged, Ramsay wiped his mouth. Finally he said very quietly, —I'm sorry, Captain. I. . . . I didn't realize you were in love with her. . . . or I would have waited until you figured things out for yourself. You've had enough hard luck lately.

Bell turned away from him and walked stiffly toward his desk. Jesus! Why couldn't a man hold on to himself? What woman was worth it! And what difference did it make what Charlotte King had ever been?

The silence in the cabin emphasized the sound of the pump. Bell did not turn around. He kept his head bent and he spoke to the cabin floor. —Get out of here. . . . with my apologies.

Ramsay had just opened the door when a sharp clang came from the deck. It was a brittle sound of metal against metal and the pumping ceased instantly. Now Bell turned his head to look questioningly at Ramsay. They waited. They heard a curse and the shuffle of feet. But there was no sound from the pump. Bell raised his head and shouted at the skylight.

—On deck! What's the matter there?

Silence again. Then Uala's excited voice came down through the skylight.

—The pump, sir! The main casting is busted! We can't pump her nohow now!

Bell and Ramsay exchanged a glance and moved quickly toward the deck.

Twelve

BELL STOOD with his back to the wind and contemplated the pump. And he fingered his scar for a long time seeking a solution. The problem before him wiped both Charlotte and Ramsay from his mind. Like all seamen he prided himself on his ability to fix anything; it had to be that way with sailors, for once land had dropped astern of their craft whether large or small, they were wholly dependent on themselves. And so sailors were both ingenious and resourceful far beyond the abilities of normal men. They could extract teeth and repair the ordinary wounds they suffered from the sea, and often months later, the shoreside doctors who might examine their makeshift splints, slings, and trusses were astounded at their practical excellence. It was taken for granted that a sailor could sew, but most of them could also rally around a stove and bake breads and cakes if the cook was taken ill.

The larger sailing ships always carried a professional carpenter, but in smaller craft the sailors themselves were obliged to take over his functions. And so to assure their self-reliance, the little ships carried spare materials and tools to meet almost any emergency and their sailors often accomplished the impossible with zest and confidence. When a jib boom snapped they would sometimes substitute a yard, and when every spare spar had been used they had been known to fashion a gaff or a yard or even a boom out of deck or bulwark planks cleverly glued and lashed together. Good sailors could work with wire of every dimension. They could splice an eye in wire or seize a heart in a backstay as neatly as a shipyard rigger who worked at nothing else. They were experts at tackles. Given a few blocks and enough line and they could lift incredible weights and set them where they wanted them. They were engineers enough to careen their own vessels on a handy beach for bottom cleaning, and they were artisans enough to fit a plank exactly though it might have both a twist and a curve beneath a vessel's transom. They knew the strengths and durability of rope and could do things with it no other men would ever attempt to do. They knew paint and how to mix it to proper consistency coat by coat, until often their vessels appeared far smarter after a month at sea than before they had sailed. And on the larger, better found ships, there was normally a man who could double as a blacksmith and who could hammer and forge anything from a link of chain to a mastband or a stewpot.

But in the *Cannibal* there was no such man, nor was there a forge or any collection of tools which might repair the heavy metal casting which had broken at the fulcrum. And so Bell stared at the fractured metal and knew a feeling of helplessness he had never known in his life, and he thought of all the various equipment in the Cannibal which might have broken down and somehow been repaired. But this pump, now so vital to her life, had failed in such a way both pumping arms were useless. And the men, he knew, were aware of his discouragement. They squatted around the pump still breathing hard from their exertions and they looked at the broken metal and at Bell almost defiantly, as if they were saying, Now what the hell are you going to do about that? There was no flood of suggestions as there might normally be with any broken piece of gear. There was not even any grumbling about a ship so old and in such a state of repair even her main pump came apart when most needed. They simply waited in silence, looking from the pump to Bell and back at the fulcrum again.

At last Yancy broke the stillness and said, —I'll be just plain goddamned, that's all!

Bell frowned at him because even Ida Morris had come to the deck and stood with everyone on board in a tight circle around the pump. Wiggins waited, shivering in the cold, and Ethel Peacock waited, and Harry Hutton, and Butterfield, and Feodor Morris, and Bell thought, without turning his head, that Charlotte must be standing behind him. Would she look as afraid as the rest of them? Finally he said, —How many buckets do we have aboard?

Ramsay answered quickly and said that he thought about five. And Bell noticed that he was careful to keep any resentment from his voice. Dak Sue said he had two buckets in his galley. There was silence again.

—Mr. Ramsay.

—Sir?

Now, Bell thought, we are really in trouble because I have called Ramsay Mr. and he is answering "sir" as if he meant it! Things were more comfortable the old way. He knows as well as I do that we'll have to bail by hand. And he also knows the bailing will have to be continuous in order to move anywhere near the same volume of water as the pump.

There was a narrow shaft just foward of the pump known as the trunk well. It was normally used for cleaning the sucking valves in the bilge and could barely accommodate one man.

—Open the trunk, Ramsay. Turn to with the buckets. . . . one man below. . . . and one on deck at the hatch combing to seize and spill. Let your third man spell through the chain in rotation every half-hour. That will give everybody a breather and I guess it'll be welcome.

—Aye, sir.

—Take the helm yourself. Every hour or so, sound the well. We'll have to watch it careful. If she gets down by the head, shovel some copra out of the forehatch, but don't waste none. Call out my watch if you need any sail work done.

—Right.

Bell turned to the passengers and saw the mixture of fear and disappointment in their faces. The poor devils. In a way, he thought, their stake in the *Cannibal* is almost as much as my own. He tried to smile.

—I haven't any choice now, so I'm setting course for Honolulu. But don't worry. I know you paid fare to Manzanillo and it wasn't easy. I don't know just how. . . . but I'll see you get there.

Then his eyes met Charlotte's for an instant and he could only think of her with Ramsay. And he thought that of all the passengers, she seemed the least afraid. The smile left his face and he walked away.

In the charthouse, Bell took up his parallel rules and drew a line between the X which he had marked on the chart as his assumed position, and Honolulu. He stepped the parallel rules down from the line until one edge intersected a compass rose. He noted the course in true degrees and added the local variation. The *Cannibal* was far enough north so that at least it would be a reach to Honolulu. . . . relatively easy sailing. That would make things easier, although how long the men could stand hoisting heavy buckets to the deck from twenty feet below was another matter. And as the water gained against their efforts, as it would unless they bailed like machines, the *Cannibal*'s pace would slacken no matter what the wind. She would probably start down by the head, a little more each hour or each day. . . . depending. The rudder would gradually become less effective and the greater draft forward would compound itself until the sea licked at the bowsprit. . . . and then there would only be the boats.

Separating his dividers, Bell pricked off the distance between his assumed position and Honolulu. At best twelve hundred miles! He sighed heavily. It was a long way to the cemetery.

He stepped out on deck and called to Ramsay.

—Mr. Ramsay!

—Aye, sir!

—Steer southeast by east!

—Sou'east by east it is, sir!

Ramsay called out the order for bracing around the yards and eased the *Cannibal* little by little on her new course. Bell watched his face and wondered if he had been entirely wrong. Was Ramsay no worse than a different kind of seaman who simply could not adjust himself to the easier ways of Pacific vessels? There was now, in his manner, not the slightest indication of superiority. Against his protests his captain had gambled and lost and yet he neither crowed nor seemed resentful. He was simply doing his duty and doing it well.

Bell turned down the companionway steps. He paused at the

bottom and tried to review his thinking. If he had indeed let a woman influence his decisions and the *Cannibal* went down at sea, then he was as much to blame as for Montague Reef. And suddenly he saw the passengers in the water again and he heard their screaming in the fog. He shuddered. The nightmare had not returned for a long time.

He opened his cabin door and slammed it behind him. He crossed the cabin rapidly until he came to the piano. He stood before it a moment and then resolutely reached for the bottle. His fingers moved about the knots with nervous haste until he had whipped off the lashings. He took a deep breath and raised the bottle to his lips. Then suddenly, deep within him, he heard the screaming again. He lowered the bottle slightly and then his arm snapped out. The bottle sailed across his cabin and shattered against the base of his bunk.

Charlotte heard the crash of glass. She was standing outside Bell's door trying to compose her thoughts. The time had come, she knew, and she was determined the things she had to say would make sense. How did a mature woman. . . . "mature," she thought, was a nice way of putting it. . . . how did she go about telling a man she loved him and yet make it sound as it was. . . . entirely on the level? It was not going to be easy.

She tapped on the door and there was no answer. There was only the sound of the exploding glass and then silence. She was about to knock again when she thought how little difference anything meant now. As long as he knew. She hesitated and then turned the knob on the door. She waited for Bell to turn around and when finally he looked at her she saw that all the color was gone from his face. His scar stood out in a deep purple line and his eyes were expressionless and strangely still, as if he was looking through and far beyond her.

—Looks like you had an accident.

—Just got rid of an old friend. What do you want?

—I had to come. Don't get rid of all your friends. I had to come because of the way you looked at me. . . . and because you seemed so alone.

—It's customary to knock. . . . and I don't need anything except a lot of wind and some luck.

—I did knock.

She knelt and began to pick up the pieces of broken glass. And avoiding his eyes, she said, —I knew a man once who had an accident like this every time he finished a bottle, which was usually once a day. Before I came along he used to cut himself badly because sometimes he would just fall down in the mess.

—Leave it alone. I'll get it later.

—I don't mind. I've done it before and it will keep me busy while I tell you about some other men.

—I don't want to hear about them.

—What difference does it make? You've already made up your mind about me.

—Don't waste your time trying to talk me out of going to Honolulu. We'll be lucky if we make it.

—Lucky?

—Dammit, woman. . . . belay that glass and get off your knees. It makes me feel wrong. . . . like I made a mistake.

She rose slowly and carried the glass to the wastebox beside the desk. —I would stay on my knees before you a long time if I thought it would do any good. I know it's never smart for a woman to say a thing like that, but so I feel.

—No matter what you do we're bound for Honolulu now. Working on me won't keep water out of this ship.

—It isn't that. And I wouldn't care if we didn't make it. . . . because I only go to prison if we do. Does that surprise you? Or was that one of the things Ramsay neglected to find out about me? I'm only sad because I enjoyed pretending a little while, Davey. . . . and now the pretending is over. I knew it would have to end sometime but that doesn't make me feel any better about it. . . . any more, I suppose, than an actress is glad when the curtain finally goes down. I wanted to dream that I was just like any other woman who had finally discovered she was complete and had found a man she could love. I know it was silly of me. . . . and childish, maybe. . . . wanting to spend time with a man who would be interested in something besides going to bed with me. Because you're the kind of man you are. . . . I picked on you. It wasn't fair.

—I just wish you weren't such a liar.

—I've never lied to you, Davey. There's a lot of things I neglected to tell you. . . . yes, deliberately. . . . but my dream wouldn't have lasted very long if I'd told you everything. Now I wonder if I would ever have had the nerve to smash it like you did the bottle.

—Did you go to Ramsay's cabin?

—Yes. I did. And I would have gone again if it would have saved my dream. You believe me now, don't you? I can tell by your eyes that you would believe me. . . . even if I should tell you that I was honestly in love with you.

—Did you lie about Ramsay and the men?

—No. That was the truth.

A silence fell between them and the lines in Bell's face softened. Finally he said, —Ramsay's case I'll handle in my own way. About you. . . . I want to do some thinking. . . .

—Don't bother, Davey. I'm not worth it.

—Probably not. But from time to time you might at least get my mind off this ship.

After three days the *Cannibal* sloshed through the seas like a stricken animal. She whimpered aloft and groaned below. There was three feet of water in her hold, and the dolphin striker which extended straight down from her bowsprit was often half-buried in the water. She rolled hideously with the Pacific swells and every recovery was delayed until it often seemed that she would remain heeled over to one side or the other and never again manage to right herself. The wind was free and of such ideal force she normally would have danced with life and speed; yet now she shoveled a great white bow wave before her and the figurehead of the savage woman was sometimes first submerged to her knees, and occasionally even to her thighs. The crew leaned over the forward bulwarks frequently to observe her. She became their sounding rod and they knew as well as Bell and Ramsay how certainly the life was going from their ship. In order to lighten the *Cannibal*'s head, some twenty tons of copra had been laboriously shoveled from the hold. Two whips, the simplest of tackles, had been rigged to raise buckets direct from the hold and so speed the bailing.

Bell carried every piece of canvas the *Cannibal* possessed. He even rigged crude stunsails from a pair of ancient jibs he discovered in the lazarette. They ripped soon after they were set and he sewed them and almost at once they ripped again. And though they added much less than a knot to the *Cannibal*'s speed he worked and improvised with the fragile canvas until they were flying again. Every hour counted.

As the *Cannibal*'s bow descended, the stern rose until half the rudder was exposed. The wake lost its foam and became merely slick water sliding slowly aft. The masts gradually lost their rake, passed the vertical, and began to take a forward cant in line with the horizon.

The two boats were turned over on their skids and made ready for sea. Each was provisioned with yam, salt horse, rice, and a barrel of water. Each contained a small spirit lamp, a thin spar to erect for a mast, rope, rags dipped in oil for smoke if a ship should be sighted, and Bell personally made certain there were spare oars and rowlocks. There were tin cans for bailing, a boat hook to discourage sharks, and under the thwart of the starboard boat which would be his own command, Bell had placed his Bible. Both boats were half-filled with water to soak up their seams, and for the first few days they leaked so badly it was like passing through a rain squall to walk beneath them.

The crew stumbled about their constant work. Their eyes were bleary and expressionless as if they slept even as they moved. Their curses ceased for it seemed that every breath was drawn from a fast diminishing reserve. Each bucket of water weighed almost thirty pounds and to lift even ten or twenty to the deck would normally have meant nothing to a sailing man. But now the buckets were hoisted twenty-four hours a day, a never-ending chain of hundreds upon hundreds of buckets, every one to be filled and lifted and returned to the bilges again.

Lott and Keim worked like automatons, silently, their great muscles bulging and glistening with sweat during the warmer periods of the day; yet in time, even they found it necessary to pause and wait for a return of their strength. The others, Sweeney and Old Brown, Yancy and Uala, labored in a continuous daze and sometimes fell down with the weight of the buckets and had to be helped to their feet again. They tried everything to inspire their energies. Old Brown led them in chanteys until his voice cracked and he could barely whisper such ancient reliables as "Strike the Bell," "Early Morning," and "Johnny Boker." In time he found he was singing alone and became as grimly silent as the others.

They tried gambling on the number of buckets raised between the periods of chiming on the charthouse clock. The wagers ran to millions of dollars, but the amusement soon palled and eventually their conversation consisted mainly of grunts and sighs of relief as another bucket was spilled. For three days they hoisted four hours, were relieved to eat and sleep another four, and then went back to hoisting again. And still the water level rose in the hold.

Bell and Ramsay appeared to sleep standing up. The two of them nursed the *Cannibal* like an ailing whale, bracing the yards and trimming the main and spanker sheets according to every slight variation of the wind, driving her sluggish body with every ounce of strength and skill they possessed. Alone they accomplished tasks which customarily required two men, and they found ways of working together so that the two of them, hauling desperately, could do the work of four. They invented sails no one had ever heard of before or would see again, employing such unlikely canvas as hatch covers to serve as skysails. And as they worked, often side by side high on a yard at night, they found new values in each other and the tension between them eased.

Ramsay no longer bothered to comb his hair and his shirt was filthy from bending over the yards. There were now great circles under his eyes and the stubble of his beard was as heavy as Bell's. And like Bell, he worked timelessly with every sail on the ship, paying off a sheet a few inches when the wind afforded, heaving it in again if a new setting would gain a scarcely perceptible increase in speed.

On the fourth night the wind blew hard from the northwest and the *Cannibal* rolled drunkenly before it. The outhaul on the main gaff topsail parted and the sail thundered free in the wind. It shook the topmast so violently it could only be a question of time before the spar snapped. As Bell ran to the downhaul which would collapse the sail, he could feel the angry trembling even on deck. He whipped the halyard off the pinrail, heaved with all his strength on the downhaul, and the hollow booming subsided aloft. He made fast and took a moment to find a safe niche for his pipe on the saloon hatch.

Sighing heavily, he walked to the main shrouds. Then, like an exhausted soul climbing out of purgatory, he slowly began to mount the ratlines.

As he moved upward he wondered if he would have the endurance to pass a gasket around the topsail and so save it from tearing itself to pieces. Working alone it would be like wrestling with an escaped balloon, but Ramsay needed sleep. Looking down now, he could see the bailers moving mechanically in the light of the hurricane lamp. They were already far gone and were certainly in no condition to work aloft. Bell knew exactly what he had to do and he dreaded it. Climbing out on the end of the gaff to reeve a new outhaul would be a bastard of a chore. The spar was thirty feet long and stood at a forty-five-degree angle. While it appeared deceivingly steady from the deck, it would actually whip back and forth viciously with the *Cannibal*'s crazy rolling, and a man clinging to the end of it always had a dangerous and extremely uncomfortable time under the best of conditions. Clinging like a fly on the end of a long weaving stick, he would have only seconds to work between bouts of just plain hanging on.

It was certainly no job for a tired man! It was more suited to a combination steeple jack, tightrope walker, and judo artist, who would probably quit instantly if any circus required such a wild performance. And Bell decided he was almost of the same mind. After the sail was secured he would let the rest wait until morning. The hell with it.

He reached 'he main gaff throat, fought his way past the still shivering sail, and looked out along the spar. And at the end he was astonished to recognize the dim figure of Ramsay scraping back and forth against the stars. He must have raced up the ratlines, Bell thought, while I ambled along like the ancient mariner. He saw Ramsay wait his opportunity, lean far out to make a quick pass at the outhaul block. In a moment he was slithering back along the spar, the end of a line held between his teeth. Bell reached out for the line and quickly bent it to the clew of the topsail.

—I thought you were asleep.

—I was.

—Well done. Looks like I gave you a Portugee lift.

Bell swung off the gaff jaw and returned to the shrouds. He expected Ramsay to follow him and he was about to descend when he saw that Ramsay had not moved. In the starlight he saw him squat on the gaff and pass one arm around the mast. The other arm moved toward him and for an instant Bell thought he was trying to knock him from the rigging. Then he felt Ramsay's hand descend gently to his shoulder and he knew that he was wrong. Ramsay said, —I've been doing a lot of thinking. And some of it hasn't been too comfortable. I certainly won't admit you've been right all along, but this is as good a time as any to tell you about the men. The King woman was right. I gave you the lift.

Bell looked up at Ramsay and wished there was more light to see his face. But the sound of his voice was enough.

—Forget it. I will.

—Down East we like a man who doesn't know how to quit.

Bell looked straight down at the miniature figures moving in the puny circle of light. Silhouetted against it, his own feet seemed enormous in comparison, like a pair of bottles. There was no sense now in telling Ramsay how the bottle on the piano almost proved him wrong. He said, —Let's get this sail on again. We need it.

Then he started down the ratlines.

On the fifth day Oliver Wiggins came to Bell while he stood at the wheel. He looked up at the strange assortment of sails thoughtfully and said, —Captain, would you take offense if I said your vessel is beginning to look like the monster child of a Dutch windmill bred to a Chinese junk?

Bell smiled. —Say what you like about her, Wiggins, we're still afloat.

—I occasionally used to steer an aircraft, Captain. . . . and if you'll bear with me a while I think I can hold your ship on course. If we're going to the bottom I'd like to have an active hand in it. Work of any kind bores me, but you deserve a rest. We've been talking about it in the saloon. You all do.

—We're getting along.

—Why not at least let me have a go at it?

Bell looked at Wiggins and saw that his usually contemptuous manner was gone. In his way, it seemed, he was trying to be sincere. Ever since the casting broke it had been in Bell's mind to impress the male passengers, for to do so was well within his rights. But considering them one by one, he had decided calling on them would create far more trouble on deck, and anxiety below, than they could possibly be worth.

—Steering this ship right now is a serious matter. If your attention wanders you can do a lot of damage.

—I shall be as reliable as Charon.

—Who would he be?

—The man who escorts one over the river Styx.

212

—Just what are you up to, Reverend?

Butterfield looked up from the hatch and even his yellow teeth failed to spoil his smile.

—I didn't think you'd mind, Captain. One can spend just so much time praying. And of course you've heard that the Lord favors those who help themselves.

Struggling ineptly, he maneuvered another bucket to the hatch combing, spilled it, and said, "Hail Mary!"

—Who's down below?

—Feodor Morris.

—But he's an old man!

Bell was shocked. He bent down over the hatch combing until he could see Feodor Morris in the deep shadows of the hold. He was standing above his knees in sloshing water and when the bucket came down he dipped it to fill quickly and sent it upward again.

—Mr. Morris! Come out of there! You'll get pneumonia!

Feodor Morris raised his head and even in the half-light Bell could recognize the peculiar innocence in his blue eyes. But now they held a new and defiant look, almost as if he was enjoying himself. His voice echoed with ghostly clarity through the hold as he called up to Bell.

—So I get the *gesundheits!* Captain! Don't be with a single worry! Ida will take care of me!

—Jesus. . . . Bell said softly. And then aware that Butterfield could not have avoided hearing him, he added, —Begging your pardon, Reverend.

He watched them work a moment and then decided he might as well leave them alone until their enthusiasm passed. After an hour or so with the buckets they would be much easier to handle.

He returned to the foredeck and stood for a long time with his fists jammed down in his pockets and his feet spread wide apart. He looked along the line of the *Cannibal's* bowsprit, which was now almost parallel with the surface of the sea, and though he yawned frequently and blinked in a constant effort to keep his eyes open, his mind was strangely alert.

Before him was the sea and he had no difficulty in seeing it as an enemy. Yet now, when by all rights he should fear it, he found it soothing and he remembered that it was also his friend. He supposed that some men felt the same way about mountains, or perhaps vast fields of grain. . . . or even the plains and jungles and deserts or even cities, God forbid, if in their youth they were exposed to them and later came to know them. But for Davey Bell the sea was enough. It was more than a restless friend. It was life, and there was no purpose in even trying to think about a way to escape it.

He looked down at the *Cannibal*'s withered foredeck and turned his back to the wind. He placed his hand on the caprail and caressed it affectionately, moving his fingers slowly over the dents and cuts formed by lines sliding along the wood through years of usefulness. As if she were a living thing, he touched gently at the spots where the paint was peeled away and the bare wood exposed to the sun, and he thought again of the craftsmen in Turner's yard on the shores of Carquinez Strait who had put much more than mere skill into the building of a ship. Most of the true shipwrights were long dead now, and their arts were lost forever. . . . because even they were not clever enough to compete with rivet guns. No younger men apprenticed themselves to the adze and saw. If they entered a shipyard they labored without pride and without love. And when a ship went down the ways and slid into the water, no part of them went with her. This, he thought without bitterness, was progress.

And now the *Cannibal* was dying. He could sense her slow convulsions beneath his feet and he knew that even if he could stretch her life as far as Honolulu, no combination of enterprise and skill would save her. The need for sailing ships had vanished almost as fast as the men who built them.

Then how long for Davey Bell? It was a strange sensation, this being a relic at forty, when most men were just reaching the climax of their careers instead of what seemed like the end. But you couldn't die with the *Cannibal!* A ship was only a ship, wasn't it. . . . and the sea was the sea? Just don't forget the *Cannibal* is only a decrepit old bucket which may yet get around to drowning you. What difference did it make if her kind was never seen again? Yeah. . . . a hag and a junkpile. If you insist on staying together you may possibly avoid drowning, but you will most certainly starve. Bury the old bitch and forget her!

Bell smiled at his thoughts, for he knew he was making clumsy work of deceiving himself. His smile faded when he turned to look aft and appreciate, as he always did, the gently flowing rise of the *Cannibal*'s decks. There was still symmetry and line to satisfy the eye of any sea-going man and she still managed to appear graceful in spite of her sickly wallowing. Now he saw, as he had seen so many times before, how the flow of the rail about her quarterdeck made a lovely and harmonious combination with hed bulwarks and he saw how pleasingly her trunk cabin was set into the deck until it became a part of her, rather than an eyesore perpetrated only for shelter and convenience.

As he wondered how he could ever look at any ship in the same way again, he saw Charlotte King come out of the galley house and walk purposely toward him. The sun was almost directly behind her and he thought it strange that she should move so carefully, until her body obscured the sun and he saw that she was carrying a steaming cup of tea. Then in silence she held it out to him as if she understood his mood, and after he had accepted it she started to turn away.

—Thanks.

—I thought you might need it.

She looked toward the sun and as Bell brought the cup to his lips he studied her face and tried to find some resemblance to the photo in her passport. God knows, he had spent enough time looking at it, trying to match the sullen hardness in the photo with the woman who stood before him now. A tramp, he had said to himself a hundred times. . . . you have been mooning like a lovesick apprentice over a conniving little tramp. But now he could find no resemblance to the photo. It must be the sun, he thought. Going down in the afternoon it picks up haze when there's plenty of wind, and the light is soft enough to cover all kinds of faults.

He quickly looked down into his cup when she turned to him and said, —Your wife is pretty sick, isn't she?

—Yeah.

—Will we make Honolulu? I'd appreciate the truth.

—I don't know. It's still a long ways.

—What happens to you if we do make it, Davey?

He shrugged his shoulders and sucked hungrily at the cup. The tea was good and it was very hot and instantly revived him. He was grateful, but he told himself he had learned a lesson. He would never again put any woman on a pedestal. Like ships, their appearance could be deceiving.

—I suppose you'll be off to sea again soon.

—That may not be so easy. Berths don't go begging these days. . . . especially for me.

—Why? I should think a man like you could always find a ship, even if the *Cannibal*. . . .

—I made a mistake and drowned a lot of people. I'm still paying for it.

He took a final draw at the cup and flipped the few remaining drops overboard. Then he wiped his mouth with the back of his hand and returned the cup to her. —If you see Mrs. Morris down in the saloon tell her to come get her husband. If he doesn't get pneumonia he's a cinch for rheumatism.

Holding the cup she passed the tips of her fingers along the rim where his lips had been. Finally, in a voice he could barely hear above the wind, she said, —I made a mistake too, Davey. Don't hold it against me forever.

Then she turned quickly and walked aft toward the saloon.

That night the wind eased and Bell wrote in his journal:

. . . . I should sleep, but I have lost the habit. And I feel compelled to write this now because I may never have a chance to make another entry. My main hope was the wind. If it would only hold we might stand a fair chance, but our speed is slowing every hour and as a result the distance to Honolulu increases as far as time is concerned. I think we should have taken to the boats by now if it were not for the amazing contributions of our passengers.

. . . . What a miserable judge of human nature I have been! Who would have thought Oliver Wiggins could spend six hours at the helm without complaint? I had to drag old man Morris out of the hold and even then he refused to leave until I lied outrageously and said we were getting away ahead of the water.

. . . . I actually carried the good Reverend Butterfield down to his bunk. He stayed in it only after I had made him a solemn promise he could resume bailing tomorrow. Tomorrow. He won't have to let his bucket down very far.

. . . . It took a direct order to get Harry Hutton below. He puffed and blew like a harpooned whale and he took time off to eat supper, but he went right back to the bailing. I think he must have lost twenty pounds this day.

. . . . Even the women wanted to bail. I lied again and said we were getting ahead of the water and they weren't needed. The only difference was, I am fairly sure they knew I was lying. But they did what they could. They were all the time bringing the men hot tea laced with plenty of sugar to give them energy, and after supper Ethel Peacock stood on the saloon hatch and got everybody to singing as they bailed. And no "Don't Crush My Violets" this time. She had them all bellowing "Workin' on the Railroad," "Pack Up Your Troubles," "It's a Long Way to Tipperary" and the like. Even Dak Sue joined in though he had the very hell of a time with the tunes, and when he finished cleaning up supper he laid on with a bucket himself. The Peacock woman has fight. . . . and she knows how to put fight in others. Old Brown says he is going to teach her some sea chanteys. I just hope she has time to learn "Miss Bailey's Ghost"!

. . . . If I should ever have crew trouble on a ship again, I think I will deliberately sneak down in the bilges and drill a hole in her. Since the pump broke down I have not heard one word of complaint from any of the men, Yancy included, nor have I seen any evidence of loafing on the job. They have all worked like coolies watch after watch. I have doubled their rations because our food will far outlast the time we can stay afloat anyway. I don't have to drive them. . . . they drive themselves, which convinces me that they are basically more seamen than agitators, and also plenty scared. For that matter, who is not?

. . . . My own fears, of course, can only be admitted here, and it is at least some relief to finally record them. While I can continue to hope, I must be very careful not to ignore the facts or we might be too late in taking to the boats. A vessel so out of trim as the *Cannibal* may be. . . . and I here record that she has already lost much of her natural stability. . . . will have a hard time of it if the wind blows too hard. She may sail herself right under by the head. Or if the seas make up too high, she can broach to and capsize in a matter of seconds. Or finally, if she is carrying too much water and she takes a wrong roll, or the wind swings around suddenly to starboard or port, she can just keep rolling over, and never come back. Also a matter of seconds. With the forehatch open she would go down in a hurry.

. . . . I have no desire to see such wonderful people hanging on to a spar or hatch cover, so far from land. I must look ahead and yet it is extremely important not to abandon ship any sooner than absolutely necessary. Once in the boats I propose to continue for the Hawaiian group. We could have at least a reasonable hope and there is always the chance a ship might come along before we had to sail the whole way.

. . . . So the dismal facts are these. We are now approximately one-eighth full of water, perhaps a little more, judging by the way she is down by the head. We have had a full day's bailing with help from the passengers and have not reduced the water level more than a few inches, if any. While the regular watch is bailing now, they are actually falling behind and will continue to do so until the passengers find strength to lend a hand again. Therefore, each day sees us lower in the water and, presuming the rate will continue, we must be very nearly decks awash in eight or nine days. Because of our broken chronometer I cannot be at all certain of our longitude, but my most optimistic figures make it a minimum of nine days to the Honolulu breakwater.

. . . . It depends on the wind. If it holds just right, neither increasing nor diminishing, and, God willing, our strength prevails, there is hope. Otherwise, the boats. I will go on deck now. Ramsay is walking about in his sleep.

November 10

Begins fine with wind diminishing somewhat during early part, then increasing with the sun and holding steady. Water in bilges estimated (not measured since above top mark on sounding rod), 4 feet forward and approx. 3 feet aft. Forepeak awash to height of man's waist. Approx 20 tons copra shoveled overboard in attempt lighten ship. Back-breaking work and does not seem to improve matters. Cannot spare men or time from bailing to jettison more. Stability dubious and helm tricky. More southerly course would possibly improve matters, but even with this unusually favorable wind we can barely lay a course for Honolulu. Smoke sighted on horizon during forenoon. We immediately lit the fire which we had prepared in an empty iron drum atop the galley house. Plenty of oil rags and plenty of smoke. No luck. Seaman Keim climbed to upper topgallant yard. He reported a steamer as hull down. She made no visible change of course in response to our signals. Did not dare change course ourselves since bearing to steamer would have put us directly on the wind. We have made a raft in case of a freak sea which might lay us on our beam ends and not give us time to launch the boats. All hands took part in its construction including the women passengers. We are quite proud of it considering it is made of spare spars cut up, hatch boards, and other odd bits and pieces. It is set on top of the after deckhouse, provisioned, and ready to go of its own weight. We are all of good heart and continue to bail. Eighty miles this day.

Thirteen

IN A WEEK the *Cannibal* had lost every quality of a trim bar-quentine. She dipped soggily into the seas and often scooped up solid green water from waves of little consequence. The savage figurehead was sometimes buried to her breasts and the great weight of water in the *Cannibal*'s hold, shifting slowly and massively through the solid grid of copra, caused her to hesitate interminably before each recovery. There were times when she could be persuaded back to an even keel only by putting the helm hard over and waiting for several minutes while she crept around on a new course. And then there followed the slow business of gingerly working her back again until she was headed in the proper direction. The maneuver took time. On the eighth day the *Cannibal* made fifty-six miles by the taffrail log. On the ninth day, she made forty miles. On the tenth day, plowing before a strong northwest wind, she barely made thirty-two miles.

Because of the unpredictable speed with which the water shifted in her hold, too much pressure aloft became increasingly dangerous. A combination of the water against one side of the hull and a hard gust in the higher fore and aft sails could easily overcome what little stability the *Cannibal* had remaining. The main topsail was doused first, and then the ringtail on the spanker. Finally even the topmasts were sent down to remove every possible bit of weight from aloft. They later formed a part of the raft.

The major portion of this strenuous labor was accomplished by Bell and Ramsay, working alone. Any sailing man would have said that under the conditions it could not be done. And so, sagging and bald-headed except for her foremast, the *Cannibal* slogged to the southeastward.

In the forecastle the men had normally slept with their feet pointed aft and their heads forward. Now, their bunks so slanted forward that they were forced to reverse their positions. On the eighth day, Sweeney became hysterical from lack of sleep. He cried and blubbered and swore that he would never hoist another bucket, and rocked his head back and forth in his bunk and moaned about how the blood was still running to his head no matter what position he took. He was left alone until he started to yell. Then reluctantly Old Brown put him to sleep—with his fist. When the opposite watch was below, Yancy said it was good for blood to run to their heads because it would fill the vacancies, but he soon changed his own bunk.

—There's just one thing I want to know before I drown like I told you we would all along. . . . Yancy went on. He was lying face down on his bunk listening to the water sloshing about in the forepeak only a few feet below him. He looked across the forecastle at Lott, who was spread out like a dead ox with one arm and leg hanging over the side of his bunk, and he said again, —There's just one thing I got to know.

—Shut up and leave me sleep. You talk too goddamned much. Like always.

—I got to know if you heaved that spike at Bell and when you done it how come you ever expected to get away with it? I told you we got to have a protest, not a murder. Jesus, what a dumb thing to do! Supposin' you killed him? Where would we be now?

—I no heave it. I drop it.

—Yer lyin'. Since when you go around droppin' spikes?

—Don't call me no liar. It be so.

Still not believing, Yancy sighed heavily. Then more to himself than to Lott, he said, —I'm glad you missed, Bonehead.

He sighed again and closed his eyes, and was instantly asleep.

The *Cannibal*'s saloon was no longer a battleground. The passengers gathered only at meals, and these were taken hurriedly as if absence from their self-imposed duties might be a disgrace. After consulting with Bell, the men had scheduled themselves so that they assisted with the bailing two hours out of every six. They frequently worked long beyond their time and in their activity many of their differences were forgotten. They talked of things they would never have dared to mention before, and they spoke of them almost gaily, as if they challenged each other to show fear.

Wiggins, who had become very proud of his exacting work at the helm, came down to supper on the ninth day and said, —The captain has just informed me that our time below is limited. Tomorrow, or certainly the day after, we will be eating and sleeping on deck. He doesn't want us caught below if she goes over in a hurry. A jolly prospect, I must say!

Ida Morris turned to her husband and said, —Then I make a tent for you, Feodor. So it rains and you are dry when you rest.

Feodor chuckled and beamed at the others. —So the Jew are used to sleeping in tents for ten thousand years! What difference does it make?

Ethel Peacock, her voice slightly hoarse from practicing boisterous chanteys, laughed and said, —I'll sing you a lullaby Mr. Morris. How about "By-By-Sleepyhead"?

—You mean "Potch-Potch Kichelach." As if I need anything to put me to sleep these days! Hola! If a man has nothing to worry about he sleeps anyway like a baby. But thanks kindly all the same.

—Don't tell me. . . . Wiggins said as he jauntily speared a yam,—that you're not worrying about becoming shark bait?

Chewing with a gusto he had never shown before, Wiggins did not wait for Feodor Morris' reply, but looked across the table at Butterfield and said,—Tell me, old boy. The death historical routine is dust to dust. Yet science claims we originated in the sea. In that case, if we drown. . . . will it be water to water?

—In your case. . . . Butterfield said plucking smugly at one of the many blisters on his hands,—the combination would undoubtedly be mud.

—Humph! . . . . Harry Hutton said happily to his plate.

—His name is mud. . . . or will be!

—Ouch! Where is that vaunted American sense of humor, Fatso? You constantly betray your country's reputation.

—You can't call him Fatso any more. . . . Charlotte King said.

Hutton patted his middle. He said that it could no longer be considered a belly and that the captain had told him he was digging his own grave with a bucket, and he didn't care.

Wiggins said, —I wonder if people who die together . . . stay together, God forbid!

—You would unquestionably go one way and the rest of us would proceed in the opposite direction. . . . Butterfield said. He was hoping to produce a laugh among the others. It was a talent he had only discovered within himself since the crisis of bailing, and he found it almost as satisfying as leading off a good sermon. But now he was disappointed. A sudden silence fell upon them and he saw that he had not even been heard. They were all looking at Ethel Peacock who had dropped her fork and covered her eyes with her hands. She shook her head trying to hold back the tears and murmured brokenly, —I wish you wouldn't all talk this way. . . . I'm so. . . . afraid. . . .

She rose abruptly, and still holding her napkin to her face, half-ran to the passage which led to the cabins. Charlotte King left her chair quickly and followed her.

Wiggins said, —I suppose we have been carrying things a bit far.

Charlotte reached the cabin just as Ethel Peacock tried to close the door. She took Ethel in her arms and, holding her tenderly, waited for the sobbing to pass.

—Now take it easy. . . .

—I. . . . I don't want to. . . . drown. . . .

—You won't. They were just joking.

—But. . . . Harry has been so different lately. I was beginning to hope we. . . . I'm so ashamed . . . . I'm the only one who's afraid.

—Don't kid yourself.

—I'm so sorry. . . . I don't want to be a trial to anyone.

—You've done a lot more than I have. I don't know what we would have done without your singing.

—You've been so kind to me. You're a wonderful woman.

—I wish I could convince someone else of that. Now, come on. You've got mascara all over your face. Fix it, and let's go back.

Charlotte patted her cheek gently and led her to the wash-stand. Ethel glanced apprehensively in the mirror and said, —I can't seem to stop shaking. But I feel better. I won't do this again. . . . I promise. No matter what happens.

Rubbing away the streaks of mascara, she tried to smile and said, —You're the only woman friend I've ever had, Charlotte. Why is it that when we are young girls we are so anxious to make friends, and yet when a woman grows older she often becomes suspicious and all wrapped up in herself. . . . just when she needs friends the most? I don't understand it. What happens to us?

Repairs completed, she studied her image in the mirror for a moment. Then she took a deep breath and said, —Oh! I don't want to become a waspish old hag!

—You won't. Not as long as you remember there's always the possibility. Mrs. Morris is pretty wonderful and she's a lot older than you are.

—Yes. But to some women being attractive comes easily. Like you. The rest of us have to work at it. And I'm right at the age when for some strange reason so many women seem to stop working.

—I have a hunch that feeling sorry for yourself is sort of a whistle to stop working.

—Charlotte. . . . I don't ever want to let you go. When we get to Mexico. . . . wouldn't you consider going to New York with Harry and me? Or goodness gracious. . . . maybe we can arrange to take a boat direct and not have to bother with Mexico.

—I would consider it. But I doubt if it would do any good.

—You mean you don't want to?

—No. I'd like to.

—At least we can be together in Honolulu for a while.

—Even that may be difficult.

—You have friends there?

—Yes. . . . a lot of them.

—You're lucky. I'd like to meet them.

—I'm not so sure. Come on. You look beautiful.

On the eleventh night Bell stared incredulously at what appeared to be a rock standing out of the darkness. The *Cannibal* was technically afloat, but now her decks were but a few feet above the surface of the sea and there was six inches of water in her main saloon. All of the passenger cabins were flooded to the same height. Bell's cabin and Ramsay's were still dry, although the water could be heard swishing constantly beneath the decking. As long as the seas were easy, Bell allowed Ida Morris to sleep in his bunk. Charlotte and Ethel Peacock temporarily occupied the two bunks in Ramsay's cabin. This arrangement lasted for only one night; then the wind came on and the seas with it, and Bell regretted that he had left them so far from immediate reach. For on that night the *Cannibal* took one heavy roll from which she failed to recover, in spite of a violent change of course. She lay sluggishly, almost on her beam ends, with the end of her spanker boom dragging in the water. She went over to starboard, and as she put the length of her bulwark under water Bell was convinced he had waited too long. There would never be time to launch the boats and the women below would be hopelessly trapped. He actually started down after them, expecting any moment to feel a rush of water on his back, when a second wave struck the *Cannibal* broadside, exploded over her entire length, and half-drowned everyone on deck. Later they spoke of it as a miracle. For as they wiped their eyes and choked out water, they saw that this cross-sea had swept the *Cannibal* back to an even keel. Moreover, she was very nearly on course again.

Now for two nights, everyone on board had been ordered to sleep on deck. The women slept on top of the trunk cabin, huddled together for warmth, and when the men were not actively engaged in bailing they slept wherever they could find a reasonably dry place to lie down. Bell and Ramsay dozed in turn, but they were seldom able to achieve more than a few hours' rest at a time. They rarely spoke and their minds were as irresolute as the *Cannibal*'s movements.

So when Bell saw the rock it was some time before he could convince himself that it actually existed and that its dark bulk looming against the sky was not just a product of his exhausted brain. According to his calculations the rock had no business being where it was. If it really stood there, then the chart must be wrong. But charts were rarely wrong. Not in these waters. Watching it, waiting for the rock to vanish suddenly, or sink beneath the sea and prove that it was only a monster of his imagination, Bell began to sweat about his face in spite of the cold, and there was a deep, hollow feeling in his belly which he knew came to a man when he first begins to doubt his position.

He was lost. . . . or was he? The chart indicated no rocks or even shoals within more than a hundred miles of the X he had carefully plotted at noon. The nearest projections from the sea were the Gardner Pinnacles, or French Frigate Shoal itself, and both, according to his navigation, were considerably farther to the east. Of course his longitude had been a matter of guesswork for weeks, ever since the chronometer broke, but if the *Cannibal* had managed to work her way so far east, then it was barely five hundred miles to Honolulu! Or if the rock was one of those about La Perouse Pinnacle, it could be even less.

Hardly daring to hope the rock would remain visible, Bell sent Old Brown forward to look out for others. Then he blinked and rubbed his eyes and chewed on his pipe and tried to visualize the shape of the rock in daylight. He searched his memory for some exact time during the past weeks when he might have made a major error in plotting his longitude.

Perhaps he should have made more allowance for leeway and for current? But he had always found the books and charts which described the invisible rivers of the sea extremely unreliable. They were as likely to lead a navigator astray one way as the other, advising of favorable currents when none existed, or warning of contrary sets, when in fact the vast undersea forces decided to work the other way around. Except for such obvious ocean rivers as the Gulf Stream and the Alaska and the Peru Current, no one could predict the exact behavior or location of any current. The charts were forced to generalize with indicative arrows and could not account for the vagaries which confronted every sailor. Currents changed with the seasons, with the state of weather, with the influence of storms a thousands miles over the horizon, and Bell thought that sometimes they changed just for the hell of it. Yet if this rock was genuine, then the current which had favored the *Cannibal* was a blessed one.

Bell saw a bird ghost through the stars and then he heard the high-pitched crying of a multitude upon the rock. He saw white foam licking along the base of the formation and then he heard the beginning hiss and dull booming as the surf smashed against it. His nose detected the musky mixture of guano and sea vegetation, and his legs told him that the *Cannibal* had taken on new movement. The sea was smoother.

Convinced at last, he turned immediately and went down to the charthouse. He turned up the lamp and bent over the chart. It was dirty now and marked everywhere with his figures and smudges left by his soiled hands and the stains of salt water. It was some time before he boldly drew a line for Honolulu. Then Ramsay came to stand beside him.

—You know about the rock?

—Yeah. We must have picked up one hell of a current somewhere.

—How much difference does it seem to make?

Bell threw down his dividers. He glared at the chart for a moment and growled as if it had given him a direct challenge. He fingered his scar and wondered how much he might allow himself to hope. How far could he trust Ramsay. . . . not to mention himself!

Finally he said, —Don't tell the men or the passengers. They might get ideas and we would be stuck with them. But if this rock is where *I* think it is. . . . it could make all the difference.

In the early morning, shortly after the sun had crested the mountains of Oahu and defined the wharves of Honolulu, the passengers on board the new fifteen-thousand-ton liner *Malolo* threw their flower leis into the water. Without exception they gathered on the port side of the ship for a last look at the island. They saw the clock tower slip away and the wharves; then the individual buildings of the city and the houses on the hills above them merged into indistinct groups. As the *Malolo* turned for Diamond Head, they saw the hotels and the green surf pounding on the beaches. Those who had any leis remaining finally dropped them into the water. Some of the passengers wept and some of them yelled at the island, which was not yet fully awake. Then most of them went below and sat down to an elaborate breakfast.

The decks on the starboard side of the *Malolo* were deserted, for they faced the open sea. But on the bridge the third officer deliberately walked to the starboard wing because he was heartily sick of looking at Honolulu. He was a very young man. Now he paused and looked to seaward, yawning in his boredom. For a moment, his mouth remained open and he appeared a ridiculous figure in his immaculate white uniform. He quickly brought his binoculars to his eyes and focused them on a small object in the distance. And he forgot his boredom. For standing in from the west he saw a sailing ship, and while he had never stepped aboard one in his life, he marveled at its power to intrigue him. He observed that she was barely moving in spite of a brisk wind and he was puzzled to see that her decks appeared to be so close to the water. That fellow had a load, or was it just a trick of distance? He could not make out her national flag, but raising his binoculars slightly to accommodate her upper rigging, he saw the yellow quarantine flag, and several others.

He studied the flags for a moment and then walked quickly to the pilothouse, where his captain sipped at a cup of coffee.

—Sailing ship on the starboard quarter, sir.

The captain frowned at him. —What kind?

—I. . . . I don't know, sir. She's making for the breakwater and flying F-M for I am sinking, and X-W for I want a tug. Do you think. . . . ?

The captain quickly put down his coffee and made for the wing of the bridge. He silently held out his hand and accepted the third officer's binoculars. He peered through them a long time and then turned aft to look back over the *Malolo*'s stern. He saw a tug and a fast launch emerge from the mouth of the breakwater and proceed at full speed toward the sailing ship. The third officer swallowed importantly and said, —Sir, ... do you think . . . ?

—No. She's been sighted. We'll proceed.

The third officer was surprised when he looked into his captain's eyes. They were moist as if he had been crying and his voice was strangely gentle when he finally spoke again. He held out the binoculars as if he were awarding a diploma.

—Take a good look, son. In some ways you aren't as lucky as I was. Take a good look and take your time. . . . you may never see anything like her again.

When Keim put his foot on the cathead to brace himself and knocked out the pin which held the *Cannibal*'s anchor, he did so with a flourish, for he could see that his movements were appreciated by a considerable audience. Then he joined the others in making up the headsails on the jib boom, moving surely in spite of his weariness, making certain that each sail was furled smartly, as if in doing so he might salvage some pride for the *Cannibal* and by a last gesture overcome the disgrace of being towed in from sea. Bell had no other choice, of course, but there was a professional matter involved. The diminutive figures who lined the wharves and the sailors who hung raptly over the rails of the steamers along the piers, putting out for the *Cannibal*, must know that she would have been sailed within hailing distance of the breakwater if everything was normal. The distant audience had to realize an emergency was involved. Otherwise, Keim's life might be miserable once he went ashore, for there were still enough sailing men along the water front to taunt him and boast of their own days when there were no tugs available.

Out of the corner of his eye he could see that some of the men on the steamers were aware of the *Cannibal's* misfortune, and he noticed that the crew of the tug, who would ordinarily have turned their backs and hastened back to their pier-side coffee, still hung about, staring and shaking their heads sympathetically, and sometimes making a hushed comment as if they stood in the corridor of a hospital. Occasionally, Keim heard a yell float across the quiet harbor and though he told himself the hollering sonsofbitches were surely dock wallopers and had never been to sea in their lives, their words infuriated him.

—Hey, Columbus! Since when you change to a Chinese junk?

—Halloo the bucket with the rags! Come to do some laundry?

—Whyn't ya get an engine?

—Git that obstruction to navigation to hell out of the harbor!

—Hey mate! What ya got for cargo. . . . ? Old beer baa—les?

—Hey mate! How much ya charge to see the museum?

There was a roar of laughter from the piers and Keim glanced across the jib boom at Old Brown, who worked opposite him. Their melancholy eyes met for a moment and they lowered their heads. Then immediately, they resumed their angry pounding and furling of the canvas.

The *Cannibal* lay just inside the breakwater and out of the fairway, according to the orders Bell had placed with the tug. There was no money for wharfage. . . . it was going to be hard enough to pay for the tug. The anchor chain had hardly finished rattling out of the hawsepipe before a small boat equipped with pumps was alongside and hoses were shoved down into the trunk well and the cargo hatch. Two gasoline engines began immediately to suck thousands of gallons per hour from the *Cannibal*'s bilges. More money, Bell thought as he watched other boats proceed toward the *Cannibal*. There was first the quarantine launch with the Health Department men. Then the Customs and Immigration. A small launch from the ship chandlery. A launch from the Harbor Police, one from the Coast Guard, and one from a shipyard. Lots of company, Bell mused grimly and turned away. He went down to his cabin where he could properly receive them.

The official formalities were brief, undoubtedly, Bell thought, because the *Cannibal* now had only tea instead of coffee to offer and none of the officials showed any tendency to prolong his stay aboard. They descended to Bell's cabin in groups of two and three. The Customs men barely glanced at his simple manifest. Sniffing unhappily, the Immigration officers accepted the bundle of passports and seamen's papers and said that they would complete their examination on deck. Bell could only admit that the smell of wet copra which permeated his cabin was hardly perfume.

After shoving thermometers into every mouth aboard, Health and Agriculture occupied themselves in a half-hearted search for rats. Bell said that if there were any they would most certainly have taken to the upper rigging long ago. The Coast Guard wanted a fuller report on the *Cannibal*'s difficulties and where were the fire extinguishers? Bell patiently explained that the *Cannibal* was not on fire, but was in some hazard of sinking. The Coast Guard said they must survey the fire-fighting system anyway. Bell directed them to the six wooden buckets set in a rack atop the galley house. He pointed out that they were painted red.

Two men from a shipyard found their way to Bell's cabin. They shook their heads sympathetically and said that they were in a position to accommodate the *Cannibal* in dry dock immediately. When they stated their price, Bell said he would call on them later. Before they were well out the door, the man from the ship chandlery pushed into the cabin. As a special favor he could make Bell a price on blocks, rope, canvas, oil, chain, paint, wire, nuts and bolts, sheaves and shackles, wax, marline, and needles. Bell told him to jump overboard.

The last man represented a ship's agent. It would be his pleasure to provide the *Cannibal* with all manner of foodstuffs, including the freshest of vegetables. The prices were outrageous and Bell was certain any of the items could be bought for half the price in a regular store ashore. But so it was, he thought, with all the pariahs who serviced ships. If their fresh eggs turned rotten, or their fresh vegetables spoiled a few days after sailing, they knew very well it was always too late to turn back.

He said to the agent, —Sell what's left of my copra and make yourself some money.

The agent was both shocked and disappointed.

—There's no market for copra here. It would have to be tran-shipped!

—I know that. But sell it.

—It's soggy.

—Salt water don't hurt it and you know it.

—You wouldn't be satisfied with the price.

—I'm sure of that. But sell it. I got some bills to pay. And don't make yourself more than two hundred per cent commission.

—I'll see what I can do.

After he left, Bell stood for a moment in the center of his cabin. By God, landsmen were busy people! How they hustled! How their faces were filled with worry and self-importance! It was strange that not one of them had asked about the long voyage of the *Cannibal* or seemed to have any conception of her difficulties. Of course. Why should they? Their worries were mainly of security or finance, which were both a drain on the spirit and unending. They rarely had a chance to know the sweetness of peace after danger. He snapped at his suspenders and laughed. The whole lot of them should run away to sea for a time. . . . long enough, anyway, to see themselves without looking in a mirror. But there I go judging, he thought. Yeah. . . . already the special diseases of the land had found their way aboard the *Cannibal*.

He went on deck and found an Immigration officer waiting for him. The man was obviously distressed and said, —What are you going to do about your passengers, Captain? I can give them clearance to land under your "force majeure" entry, but they can't stay indefinitely. When do you sail?

—Maybe never.

—You can't do that. The American citizens, of course, are all right, but your aliens. . . .

—Forget it. They'll be put up in a hotel until the next ship sails east. I'll guarantee their tickets and be responsible.

—We are detaining one of your passengers. The Leidstrom woman.

—I have no such. . . . Oh. Yeah.

Bell looked along the deck and saw Charlotte King standing in the shade beneath the starboard boat. He pushed his hands down in his pockets, and casually, as if interested only in the progress of the pump boat and the furling of the last sails aloft, he made his way along the deck until he stood beside her. And for a time they watched the shore in silence. Finally he said,

—Looks like we both sort of lost a gamble.

—Yes.

—Anything I can do to help you?

—I'm afraid not. Well. . . . you might drop me a postcard someday. . . . saying. . . . wish you were here. I'll promise not to say the same thing when I answer.

—How long?

—Three years. Two, maybe, if I'm a good girl.

—That's not so long. Meantime maybe I can come see you if they'll let me.

—No. . . . I'd rather you wouldn't. Just write. Good luck, Davey Bell. And take care of your wife.

—Yeah. I will.

—If you write. . . . it will be like hearing your voice.

He took her hand and held it a moment. And he thought again how small and fragile it seemed beneath his own. Finally he released her hand and walked away without looking back. He shoved his cap forward until his eyes were entirely in shadow.

He kept his cap in this position when he said good-bye to the Morrises and Oliver Wiggins, and to Harry Hutton and Ethel Peacock and the Reverend Butterfield.

Ida Morris said quietly, —Thank you, Captain. . . . and pressed his hand.

Feodor Morris had put on a tie and he fumbled with it nervously as he said, —I have the feeling in me to say. . . . God bless you.

Oliver Wiggins said, —I shall doubtless regret ever leaving Rotuma, but my first drink will be to you, sir.

Harry Hutton blew up his cheeks until his face seemed almost ready to explode. He took Bell's hand and shook it heartily. —If you ever get to New York, Captain. . . . look me up. I'll either be on Park Avenue. . . . or The Bowery.

Reverend Butterfield was at first too emotionally upset to say anything, but as he climbed down into the shore boat and gathered his frock about him he looked up at Bell and murmured, —When I return to Thithia I am going to ask God if he will arrange the passage with you. He seems definitely prejudiced in your behalf.

Bell smiled. He said, —Tell me, Reverend. Did Wiggins finally win? I was told he was gambling for your soul.

Butterfield placed one scrawny finger to his lips, then cocked his head quickly and tittered into the sleeve of his frock.

—Captain, I shall let you in on a professional secret. Those who begin by denying, often become the most devout.

He tittered again and descended to the boat. Ethel Peacock came to Bell and said, —Goodness gracious! Do get some sleep. You look so tired.

And then they were gone.

Nor could the crew see much of Bell's eyes when he paid them off just before noon and waved each one of them over the side.

By evening he was alone with the *Cannibal*. She was well up in the water and the pump boat would not return until morning. Seeing a chance for a quick and easy profit, the agent had acted with characteristic dispatch. He sold the *Cannibal*'s copra to his uncle and by noon the lighters were alongside. In four hours, her holds were empty of everything but the smell. For his enterprise, Bell received a check for five hundred dollars. It would be just enough, he reckoned, to pay his passengers' fare on a steamer to San Francisco. So that was that. The agent, who had never even seen the copra, let alone soil his hands, would make twice the amount for his morning's transaction. But that was the way of things and it was some satisfaction to know that his uncle would probably make much more. They were shrewd and more power to them, Bell thought, and at least they were not ghouls. He frowned and bit into his pipestem when he thought of the two men who had come aboard even before the stevedores had finished unloading the copra.

They were evil-looking and foul-smelling little men and Bell first saw them at a distance rowing toward the *Cannibal* in a dilapidated skiff. They both wore black derbies, which were ill-suited to Honolulu, but Bell finally decided that derbies could not have been more appropriate to their calling. He considered them as a cross between undertakers and gravediggers. They clambered over the bulwarks without bothering to ask permission and had been all over the ship before Bell realized they were aboard. Dodging around the sweating stevedores, they caught up with him as he went to the galley house to make himself a cup of tea. They handed him a card and announced themselves as salvage experts.

—Salvage experts! You look like shipbreakers to me!

—In a way you might say we are, Captain.

Bell crushed the card between his fingers. He said quietly, —Get off my ship.

—We wouldn't be so hasty, Captain.

—We are prepared to make you a very generous offer.

They spoke as twin mouths, each triggering the other, and Bell could not for the life of him separate the two, either in voice or manner.

—Of course she is very old.

—And sadly beyond repair.

—Impossible to get crews for her these days.

—A relic.

—But we like to gamble, as it certainly would be.

—Full repairs would cost a fortune.

—So obviously that would be unwise.

—Her gear, of course, is worthless. We wouldn't bother with that, if you cared to try selling it yourself.

—Fortunately, there is some need for firewood so we might possibly break even if worst came to worst.

—We really want her for a coal hulk, but the deal may not work out. That's the gamble. So we can go just so far and no further.

Bell looked at them in disgust. Shipbreakers aboard the *Cannibal!* They would reduce her to ruins in a matter of a few weeks, selling a part of her here, another part there, and leaving her remains to rot on the handiest beach. And they would have gathered all the necessary information, of course, before they ever ventured aboard. They would know that Davey Bell was broke.

Suddenly an idea flashed across his mind and he wondered if it would have come to him if he were not so weary. The more he considered it the more appealing it became, and eying the ship-breakers thoughtfully, he became convinced that it would be far more satisfying than just throwing them overboard.

—Just how much did you figure on paying?

The two men looked at each other quickly, a trifle bewildered at his sudden change of mood. They glanced up and down the decks, and then tilting their heads upward they spoke to the rigging as if Bell had suddenly risen into the air.

—We would have to make the deal right away.

—Right now.

—All in all, she is in a terrible state of decay.

—True. . . . true. Of course her ironwork has some value, although shipping it to the mainland for melting down should be almost too expensive to bother.

—Then there would be the cost of towing her in where we could go to work on her.

—Legal fees, too.

—And advertising for bids.

—And storage overhead, of course.

—Really we would be fools to make any offer at all.

—From the shore it appeared she was in much better shape. We really shouldn't have come.

They looked down from the sky and Bell said, —How much?

His manner was so friendly, they relaxed somewhat, and tried furtively to peer beneath the shadow of his cap. They bent their heads to confer in whispers and then one of them said, —Now don't take offense, Captain. . . . but really the best we could do under the circumstances would be. . . . give and take fifty one way or the other. . . . let us say. . . . or perhaps . . . . around about. . . . say three hundred dollars?

Bell almost choked, but he jammed his fists down in his pockets and managed to control his voice. —Don't you think that's a lot?

If the shipbreakers were surprised at his reaction they contrived to hide it. Instead they assumed a worried look and Bell hoped that it was genuine.

—Perhaps we have been reckless, but when we make an offer we stand by it.

—I wouldn't want to see you two gentlemen stuck in any way.

—We'll just have to take that chance.

—Tell you what you do then. You show up here tomorrow morning with all the papers made out because I know that will take you quite a bit of time. Bring the three hundred in cash and show up early. About six o'clock, because I'll have a lot to do tomorrow. Soon as we sign and take my personal gear ashore, she's yours.

Bell held out his hand, and as each of the shipbreakers took it, he thought it was like grasping an eel. He took them by the elbows and escorted them past the stevedores to the boarding ladder.

—You've been a very sensible man, Captain.

—You might lay here for months before you could make half as good a deal.

—So long, gentlemen. Don't forget. Six o'clock.

Now, in the evening, he slowly paced the *Cannibal*'s withered decks. He traveled her full length from the taffrail aft to the bow, wandering rather than following any purposeful course, stopping for long periods to stare at a pinrail, or sometimes just leaning against one of the masts while he gazed at the sea. When he moved he would touch certain things which were familiar to him and he was strangely content. When the sun disappeared, he watched the short afterglow and saw the sea turn to bronze and then a deep black. When Venus appeared in the twilight, he seated himself comfortably on the forehatch and lit his pipe, and it occurred to him that perhaps it was the defeated who had the deepest appreciation of peace.

As night closed down on the *Cannibal* he glanced at the forestay and smiled. Marine regulations called for an anchor light to be hanging there, but on this night it would not be needed. No. When the time came, and it would be soon now, he would light her running lamps, both port and starboard. The thing must be done just right.

He was planning exactly how he would manage alone when

he heard someone singing across the water. After a moment, he recognized the voice as Old Brown's. He turned to look toward the shore and saw him rowing for the *Cannibal*. He was singing "Miss Bailey's Ghost," and he appeared to have the greatest difficulty coordinating his oars.

Bell watched him splash along until he came to the *Cannibal*'s side, and when he saw that he was drunk, he stretched out a hand to assist him over the bulwark.

—Ahoy, Davey! I'm drunk! Positively scuppers awash!

—Good.

—I seen Ramsay ashore. He just come from the doctor and he was celebratin' drunk, too.

—Better yet.

—Now I got to tell you before I forget it. Ramsay said to give you a message. Says to tell you he was going out first thing in he morning and buy a pair of suspenders. I dunno what the hell he meant by that, but then he was awful drunk.

Old Brown waved a bottle in the air and amost dropped it as he thrust it toward Bell.

—Have a drink, Davey!

—No thanks.

—G'wan!. . . . Yer might as well. It's all over the water front er sold the *Cannibal* to the wreckers. We'll both git drunk!

Old Brown attempted a formal bow and Bell caught him just efore he fell on his face.

—Not now, Brown. But I'm sure glad to see you.

—Now ain't that a nice thing for you to say. . . . or was yer ast lonesome?

—If the *Cannibal* was still mine would you sign on for nother voyage?

—Sure! When do we sail?

—Now.

—Yer the one's drunk! Yer ain't got a crew!

—Yeah. You and me. Put down that bottle and bend a hand.

Confused and unhappy about parting with his bottle, Old rown stumbled aft behind Bell. He was astonished and some the dizziness left him when Bell deliberately took his hands d placed them on the spanker sail halyard.

—Together, we heave.

—You gone crazy, Cap? Go back to yer mints!

—I was never so sober. Heave!

Together they threw their weight on the halyard and the spanker rose slowly past the stars. Bell made the halyard fast with a quick turn and then placed one arm affectionately around Old Brown's shoulders. He led him forward and said, —Now, for the jib. Then we have time for a drink.

When the outer jib was full up, Old Brown collapsed against the forward bulwark and fought for his breath. He smacked his lips and watched Bell heave in on the jib sheet. Then he saw Bell vanish momentarily down the forepeak hatch.

There were several small fish playing about the *Cannibal's* bow and their movements caused little curlicues of phosphorescence beneath the surface of the water. Old Brown was politely asking the fish if they remembered where he had put his bottle when he heard the heavy anchor chain slither through the hawsepipe. The fish scattered. Old Brown turned around just in time to see the bitter end of the chain tumble across the deck as if drawn into the sea by a gigantic magnet. When he heard the last link plop into the water he rubbed his eyes and resolved that for the rest of his life he would leave the bottle alone.

Then he saw that Bell was standing beside him. He was looking up at the stars, which had begun to move slowly past the inner jib, and he was smiling. He said quietly, —She'll come around all right.

And Old Brown said, —I've been shanghaied, by God!

Watching the shore lights begin to move when they should be still caused Old Brown to close his eyes tightly. He immediately lost all equilibrium and slumped over the bulwark.

It was several minutes before Old Brown regained his sense and realized that there was a light breeze off the land. It was fragrant with the smell of earth and greens and flowers. But Old Brown ignored it, for now he could only smell his own breath, which reeked of whiskey, and he wished he could not. He told himself that he was sober, but then how had he managed to leap from the foredeck where he last remembered being, and now stand propped against the wheel? And he was steering the *Cannibal* through the jaws of the breakwater! She was moving very slowly, barely ghosting along without the slightest sound. So this was them delirium tremens!

And though he wanted to shout with terror, he clung instinctively to the wheel. He looked frantically about him an saw a figure moving near the lamp locker. On the port side the figure suddenly turned a bright red and Old Brown was certain of his fate. That could only be the Devil. The figure turned dark again. That must be the Devil and he was on a direct course to Hell!

The figure was moving aft and he was dragging a body beside him! In one hand he held a long spear. It was a moment before Old Brown finally recognized it as an ordinary pry bar. He sighed with relief when he saw that the man was Bell. His arm encircled the neck of the *Cannibal*'s figurehead.

Bell laid the savage woman gently on the deck and stood thoughtfully fingering the pry bar.

—I split her a bit. Couldn't help it.

—Davey. . . . how'd I git here?

—You required a little assistance.

—Where's everybody?

—Ashore.

—But we're sailing!

—That's right.

—Tell me I'm still drunk, Davey. Please! Where we goin'?

—To a funeral.

Old Brown shook his head mournfully when he heard Bell chuckle. He believed that he was sober now and he reasoned that David Bell had finally broken under the strain. The man was mad. And there was so little he could do to help him.

Bell said, —With this breeze we should be well enough off shore in about an hour. Then we'll put a match to her. She'll go down like a lady. . . . with some dignity.

—Oh God. . . . where's my bottle? I need a drink!

When the lights of Honolulu were just even with the horizon, they brought the *Cannibal* up into the wind. And as she lay slack, rolling slowly in the sea, Bell descended to his cabin and brought up his journal. When they lowered the figurehead into the skiff, he placed his journal carefully beside it; then they returned to the deck.

They stuffed a pork barrel with rags and saturated it with kerosene, and then they lowered the barrel into the cargo hold and pushed it against the foremast where it was stepped into he keelson.

Now as calmly as if he were lighting his pipe, Bell held a

match to the rags. When the blaze was full, he nodded to Old Brown and they climbed out of the hold. On deck they stood looking down into the hatch and their weathered faces were amber and then yellow in the firelight. They had not exchanged a word since they first lowered the barrel, and now they kept their silence as they turned away and walked to the bulwark.

Bell freed the skiff's painter and they lowered themselves into it. They took up the oars, and fell into a slow rhythm of stroking. They continued to row until they were well away from the *Cannibal*.

When the flickering light from the hold suddenly increased in brilliance and began to illuminate the night so that the whole length of the *Cannibal* was clearly apparent, and even her rigging could be easily defined, Bell paused in his rowing and laid on his oar. He did not consider it especially remarkable that Old Brown chose to rest at the same time.

The sea was nearly flat and they could hear each other's breathing as they watched the growing fire. They saw long tongues of flame dart upward beyond the level of the *Cannibal*'s bulwarks and they began to hear the snapping and popping of burning timbers. It was not long before she began to settle in the water and miniature explosions of sparks shot toward the stars. Then the jib caught fire and finally the spanker, and their faces were again bright yellow. At last the stars were hidden in smoke and there was only one thing in the sea and the night, and that was the flaming *Cannibal*. When the foremast crunched and toppled into the sea, they gripped their oars a little tighter and looked at each other. It was easier somehow than looking at the flames.

Bell turned to the figurehead which he had propped up in the skiff as if she were a passenger. She was now a savage silhouette against the flames. He said quietly, —Going to be some awful disappointed shipbreakers.

—What'll you do now, Davey? Yer right back where ye started.

—No, I'm not. I got eighteen dollars. . . . and maybe something else. I'll go to sea for two years. Then I'm coming back to Honolulu.

They bent their heads a little to shade their eyes from the glare of the fire and they gradually began to move their oars

They dipped the oars gently at first, but in time, the tempo of their rowing quickened as if by a display of energy they would show their indifference to the flames. And anyway, who wanted to hang around when a friend was gone forever.

About the Author

ERNEST K. GANN spent 19 years as a commercial airlines pilot, flying a million and a half miles. In his twenties he was a barnstorming stunt flier and became an airline flier in the early years of commercial aviation. During World War II he attained the rank of captain, flying missions for the Air Transport Command and was decorated with the Distinguished Flying Award. After helping to chart aerial trails around the world, he left flying to devote his full time to writing. Among his best selling books are *The High and the Mighty, Island in the Sky, Blaze of Noon, Benjamin Lawless, Soldier of Fortune, Trouble with Lazy Ethel,* and *In the Company of Eagles.*

Mr. Gann is also an experienced sailor, and in his magnificent SONG OF THE SIRENS, he writes of the sea and his sea-faring experiences with all the artistry that drew so many thousands of readers to FATE IS THE HUNTER, his famous bestselling book on flying.

MOVIE TIE-INS FOR FASCINATING READING

_____ 81138 ORCA, Arthur Herzog $1.95

_____ 81200 MACARTHUR, Clay Blair Jr. $1.95

_____ 80767 NETWORK, Sam Hedrin $1.75

_____ 80796 THE CREATION OF DINO DE LAURENTIIS'
KING KONG, Bruce Bahrenburg $1.75

_____ 81881 LOOKING FOR MR. GOODBAR,
Judith Rossner $2.50

_____ 80850 NEW YORK, NEW YORK,
Earl Mac Rauch $1.75

_____ 80739 THE FRONT, Robert Alley $1.50

_____ 80868 PAPILLON, Henri Charriere $2.25

_____ 81394 VALENTINO, Irving Schulman $1.95

Available at bookstores everywhere, or order direct from the publisher.
MTI 10-77

POCKET BOOKS
Department RK
1230 Avenue of the Americas
New York, N.Y. 10020

Please send me the books I have checked above. I am
enclosing $_____ (please add 50¢ to cover postage and
handling). Send check or money order—no cash or C.O.D.'s
please.

NAME_____

ADDRESS_____

CITY_____STATE/ZIP_____

MTI 10-77